A Perfect FIT

Bridge City Beats Book One

STEPHANIE LOUISE

Contents

For Jason—I couldn't have written a love story without first living in ours.

Content Warning

This book contains: profanity, explicit sex, sexual assault (brief and not graphic), discussions of parent death, stalking, substance abuse, drug overdose, physical and emotional spousal abuse, infidelity (NOT by main characters), violence, brief mention of suicide, and needles.

1

Tyler

MAY 1995

The chartered plane trembled and dipped as it plowed through a dense layer of storm clouds, darkening the inside of the cabin as if someone had flipped a switch. Tyler's stomach lurched behind the twelve-string guitar in his lap. Watching *La Bamba* in his hotel room the night before had been a huge mistake.

He pulled in a deep breath, slowly letting it out while struggling to kick images of twisted steel and broken glass from his mind. Even before the movie, he'd despised flying, but until buses could travel over oceans, they were a necessary evil when the band toured overseas.

The pilot mumbled something over the loudspeaker, but Tyler was too keyed up to catch more than *final descent* and *early*.

"What'd he say?" he asked no one in particular, his white knuckles strangling the neck of the guitar.

The band's manager, Sophia Cruz, was seated a few seats up and across the aisle. She set down the paperwork she'd been sifting through and turned her head, sympathy warming her gaze when she saw his face. "We're two hours ahead of schedule, Ty. Almost home. You okay?"

He nodded, forcing a tight smile until she turned back around. After nearly twenty hours of confinement and turbulence, he ached for wide open spaces, solid ground, and a warm, welcome home embrace from his wife, Amy. He could almost smell her signature scent of jasmine lotion, red wine, and cigarettes—an unconventional yet dead sexy combination that hooked him the moment they met. It hinted at rebellion, an unapologetic reliance on comforting vices, and an underlying sweetness not everyone could see. That was Amy in a nutshell.

As thoughts of his wife calmed him, the clouds shifted from gray to nearly black, and Tyler was convinced the incessant rattling in the rear of the cabin meant they'd freefall any second.

Sophia shot a concerned look that he acknowledged with a weak thumbs-up. Hoping to distract himself from impending death, Tyler's attention shifted to the world outside his window. He stared, waiting for something, anything to break through the blurry gray fuzz. After a few more deep breaths, the clouds dissipated, and downtown Portland's tangle of rain-darkened bridges and murky waterways came into view a few thousand feet below. A smile curved his lips.

Home.

The sight always soothed his nerves at the end of a long, grueling tour, and this time was no different. His jaw and shoulders went slack, releasing the pent-up tension they held throughout the flight. The familiar urban-rural clash of skyscrapers and evergreens meant the long stretch of shuffling between venues, being pawed at by strangers, and laying his head on a different pillow every night was officially over.

While the nonstop chaos of Tomorrow Mourning's month-long stint in Australia had been exhilarating, it came with its share of stress and headaches. The end was a welcome relief.

A woman's low moan in the back of the plane shook him from his thoughts.

"Zip up, Zacky," Tyler shouted while gently strumming his guitar. "We're home."

Their drummer, Adam, crunched potato chips and swigged Australian lager across the aisle while their bassist, Zack, finished up with his latest conquest—a striking blonde Kiwi who caught his eye backstage in Sydney.

Adam unbuckled his seatbelt, plopping down beside Tyler. "Fifty bucks says he pays the pilot to fly her ass back home as soon as he nuts." Their manager's head spun around, revulsion scrunching her face. "Sorry, Soph." Adam shrugged as she slipped headphones over her ears and cranked the volume on her Walkman. He leaned over the shared armrest and held out the bag of chips, the dark, earthy scent of hops thick on his breath.

Tyler laughed, sliding his hand into the greasy bag and grabbing a few. "Wouldn't surprise me. It also wouldn't surprise me if Sophia took a separate plane next time."

His eyes drifted back to the window, the city growing larger by the second.

"What are you gonna do when you get back?" Adam jabbed his elbow into Tyler's ribs, spilling a brown, bubbling drop of beer on the armrest. "You can hang with me and Zack at our pad if you aren't sick of us yet."

Tyler's fingers stilled over the strings. "Thanks, but Amy and I need time alone to figure some stuff out."

"No doubt. I know that tabloid bullshit's been screwing with your head."

Just the mention of that article set Tyler's stomach churning again. The day before he left for Australia, a tabloid rag claimed Amy was unfaithful. He'd stared at the blurry photo until his eyes crossed. It was impossible to tell if it was his wife, but he couldn't imagine Amy cheating. Especially with a guy who'd wear a fedora and wallet chain.

"You gonna do all that figuring out before or after you rip each other's clothes off?" They laughed at Adam's transparent attempt to reverse the frown setting in on Tyler's face. "It's been a month, dude. *A month.* That's so unfair to your balls."

Tyler huffed out a tense breath. He'd watched his bandmates enjoy all the groupie action they could handle, but for him, it'd been a long month with only his right hand to keep him company. "After. Definitely after."

While Sophia chatted with Adam about some drumstick endorsement deal, Tyler's mind buzzed like a microphone on the fritz, his thoughts returning to the tabloid. To that fuzzy fucking photograph.

It wasn't the first time they'd dealt with unfounded rumors, and it wouldn't be the last. Since his second date with Amy, unscrupulous reporters had picked apart their private lives, tossing the juiciest bits to the gossip-hungry wolves.

Considering who he married, he should've seen it coming. As the uncontested queen of Portland's underground music scene since the late eighties, Amy already had a rabid following. Her antics were legendary around town, inspiring more than a few scathing articles over the years, so she was well accustomed to the scrutiny of the masses. In fact, she seemed to revel in it. Court it, even.

Tyler, on the other hand, was repulsed by it. He couldn't believe people made a living by inventing drama and sniffing out sordid details of a stranger's relationships. And it seemed like nothing was off limits or too intrusive: Was Amy pregnant? Did Tyler screw the groupie that smashed her lips against his cheek in Austin? And most recently, did Amy make out with some fedora-wearing douchebag outside a record store in Seattle?

Adam finished his conversation with Sophia, turning back to Tyler. "So, after a month of stewing about that article..." The volume of his voice lowered. "Do you think it's possible?"

Tyler scratched the dark stubble on his chin, staring blankly at the seat in front of him. The nagging thought he couldn't shake was once Amy's career troubles began, the relationship that once seemed untouchable had started to feel vulnerable and fragile. His long hours in the studio and her long nights out partying hadn't helped. A distance was growing between them, and the fear that the month apart would make things worse wouldn't let him go either.

"No." He felt a twinge of guilt for taking so long to say it. "There's no way she'd do that to me. And I'd love to get my hands on the asshole that wrote it."

"Just ride it out." Adam waved a dismissive hand. "It'll be yesterday's news when some spoiled starlet throws a tantrum in a Starbucks or some shit." His left eyebrow twitched, the telltale sign he was watching his words. "But I gotta say, it's not cool that she only called you twice in Australia. Even my psycho mom called more than that."

Tyler squared his shoulders, the relief of being home tainted by the sudden prodding. "Seriously, Adam? She's trying to pull what's left of her band together. Her manager told her she's a heartbeat away from being a fucking has-been. How do you think that feels?"

Tyler would never admit it to Amy, but her manager was probably right. When her lead guitarist was arrested for possession of heroin and her drummer was shipped off to rehab, their label dropped them, and her career took a major nosedive. So did her ego. He hated watching his once self-assured, intensely driven wife struggle to find footing but secretly hoped she'd shed the toxic dead weight of her junkie bandmates and get back on top without them.

Adam touched his wrist. "Not trying to start a fight. I know how lonely you get on the road. That's all."

"I get it, man." Tyler's knee bounced as he picked at loose threads poking out of a rip in his jeans. "Everything will be better once her career's back on track. Now that our tour's over, I can focus on helping her out of the hole she's in. Hard to be a decent husband when I'm working nonstop."

Downtime was rare, but he'd spent most of it brainstorming ways to help her get back to the passionate, creative firecracker he fell in love with. They could take a vacation away from all the noise and pressure. Maybe write a few songs together. Maybe even record them, pass them around town, and get her fans hungry again for what she had to offer. And maybe bridge the distance in their marriage in the process. Hopefully then, they could start a family.

"Good luck, dude." Adam squinted. "Just don't forget about our band while you're trying to fix hers."

"After all we've been through together, that's fucking impossible." They bumped fists, squashing any lingering tension. If only every relationship hitch were solved so easily. "I had a blast with you guys but can't wait to get home to her."

Zack's female companion shrieked before belting out a chorus of his name.

"Speaking of blast…" The corners of Adam's mouth tipped up in a smirk. "I'm impressed he can get her off while they're buckled in." He dug into the Styrofoam cooler at their feet and cracked a fresh beer, passing it to Tyler. "Damn, I need a chick."

"That's easy." Tyler nodded in gratitude, taking a long swig. "Try finding something real for a change instead of settling for a quick, empty bang like Casanova back there. Takes more effort, but it's worth it. Trust me."

He hoped his bandmates would someday find partners who made them want to be better, do better. Like Amy had done for him. She was his first and only love. Despite their struggles, he wouldn't trade it for all the one-night stands and meaningless groupie encounters in the world.

"I'm not settling down when I'm only twenty fucking six." Adam ran his fingers through the freshly dyed burgundy spikes on his head. "Although, your brother called yesterday and said Charlotte broke up with that dickbag bartender. I'd settle down with a quality piece like that in a second." Adam crushed his empty can, and Tyler's head turned. "Maybe I'll ask her out."

Tyler punched him in the shoulder. "The hell you will. And if you call her a 'piece' again, I'll break your fucking nose."

"Ouch, asshole!" Adam's laughter echoed in the cabin as he punched him back. "I fucking knew it. You have a hard-on for the sexy punk girl."

"I'm married, idiot." He let his balled-up fingers unfurl. "But Charlotte's a good friend and way out of your league. No offense."

Tyler laughed when Adam hit him again. That second one stung, but he refused to react and give Adam the satisfaction. Their dynamic hadn't evolved much since meeting as freshmen in high school, teasing and pummeling each other like siblings.

"Fuck off." Adam belched, popping open a fresh can. "I'm a damn good catch."

"Sure, if you want a guy who won't call you back, might forget your name, and refers to women with terms like *piece*."

Adam slapped a hand to his heart. "Harsh. You make me sound like a dick."

"There's a good reason for that, man. Zack isn't any better. I love you guys, and you're talented as hell, but you need to grow up." He jabbed a pointed finger at Adam. "And I'm serious about Charlotte. She's on the rebound. Pull your one-and-done bullshit with someone else."

A flip of Adam's middle finger and a heavy pull of his beer put the subject to rest. Tyler downed the rest of his lager and began playing the hard-driving opening riff of a new song he was working on. Strands of dark hair hung over his eyes, blocking out the world while he hummed along with the music. As he became lost in the notes and the feel of the strings vibrating beneath his fingertips, he barely registered the wheels touching the runway. Zack's groans and stuttered expletives broke his concentration.

"Zack, Jesus Christ! You couldn't wait 'til we were home?"

"Sorry, brother." Zack's laughter was muffled, probably by his companion's bare skin, but Tyler had zero interest in turning around to find out. "Take it as payback for all the times we had to listen to you and Amy go at it on our planes."

"And tour buses," Adam chimed in.

"And behind thin hotel walls," Zack added before the moans resumed.

Tyler shrugged, his cock shifting as he thought about finally getting to touch his wife after a month apart. If he had his way, they'd have a weeklong celebration without leaving their bedroom.

The petite, blonde flight attendant left her seat behind the pilot's door as the plane stopped, her cheeks flushed red. He guessed it was her first time being confined with a rock star who was getting his rocks off. "It's safe to leave your seats, gentlemen. Anything else I can help you with before you depart?"

Tyler shook his head. "We're good, thanks. Sorry about the animal noises."

"Thank god for headphones," Sophia muttered as she gathered her things and moved to the exit. "See you later, savages." She sounded gruff, but the smile gave her away. Even though the guys could be disgusting and crude, it was clear she also found them amusing as hell.

"Take it easy, Soph." Tyler waved before grabbing the bouquet of roses he'd set on a vacant seat. They were already wilting, and a few loose petals drifted to the floor. He knew he should've waited to buy flowers closer to home, but when the flash of red caught his eye in the Sydney airport, it was impossible to resist. Amy was going to love them.

After saying goodbye to his bandmates, he slipped into the backseat of the sleek black Town Car parked on the tarmac and lit a cigarette. A pang of disappointment hit when he saw Amy wasn't inside, but he quickly shrugged it off. Maybe an even better surprise awaited him at home. The anticipation of seeing her, plus the rush of nicotine, made his head swim.

He met the driver's eyes in the rearview mirror. "Thanks for picking me up, Louis. If you blow through a few red lights to get me home faster, I'll pay you double."

2

Charlotte

I'm never dating again.

Charlotte plucked the photo of the cute but slimy bartender from her fridge and tore it in half. A few days before, she caught the bastard she'd been seeing for a month with his hand up another woman's shirt. It turns out he'd been spending his lunch breaks in the bar's parking lot with the busty redheaded waitress before cruising over to Charlotte's after last call for a booty call. Well, she wouldn't be calling him or stepping inside that bar again. With its impressive live music lineup and generous pours, she was more heartbroken about losing the bar than that cheating dickhead.

She should've known better than to trust a guy who made a living selling Blow Jobs and Slippery Nipples to giggling college girls.

She mostly hoped he wouldn't show up at her gig that night to try to weasel his way back into her life, but a wicked, vindictive part of her rooted for it. Her good friend, Matthew, knew about the car groping incident and would, without a doubt, kick his ass for hurting her. Not that she couldn't handle herself, but as an only child, it was nice having a big brother type who always had her back. Come to think of it, if his actual brother, Tyler, showed up, he'd get in on the action, too. He was sweet and laid-back but looked like the kind of guy who could throw a punch, with his tall, solid frame, powerful arms, big hands...

In the three years she'd known Tyler, she'd never thought of him as a big brother, though her life would be considerably easier if she did.

A knock at the side door startled her. She moved the lacy curtain aside to find the grinning, pink-cheeked face of her best friend and bandmate, Sandra, peeking through the wrought iron security bars. Charlotte punched the code into her alarm system's keypad and yanked her in by the wrist.

"Get in here, bitch. I can't decide which corset to wear tonight."

"I have cramps so bad I just want to eat chocolate and cry. Can we trade problems?"

Charlotte cupped her friend's cheeks. "Oh, babe. I'm sorry. But after being cheated on by yet another asshole, I'd be more than happy to swap." She headed into the bathroom, returning with two white pills. "Take these."

Sandra hummed "White Rabbit" as she grabbed a water bottle from the fridge and tossed back the Midols. "My angry uterus thanks you. And fuck that guy. His chin dimple looked like a tiny butthole. Even if he didn't have a butthole chin, he thinks Prince is overrated, so double fuck him."

Charlotte laughed, nodding at the dead-on assessment. "If he'd wanted to keep it casual so we could both feel up other people, I would've been cool with it. He's the one who wanted to make it exclusive, for fuck's sake."

"Jackass." Sandra chugged the rest of her water, tossing the empty bottle into the trash can beside the fridge. "Andy from Polyps asked for your number. Interested?"

Charlotte scoffed. "Even if his band weren't named after rectal lumps, it'd still be a big hell no. No musicians, remember?"

"Right." Sandra's eyes rolled at one of Charlotte's few unbreakable dating rules. "Too much travel…"

"And too much temptation." If she couldn't trust a bartender at a dive bar not to maul his coworkers, how could she trust someone who touches people with their music not to touch people backstage? Especially when they're miles from home and lonely. Of course, there were other, heavier reasons for the rule, but she'd save that nonsense for her therapist.

"The next one will be better," Sandra said. "I can feel it."

"We'll see." After a long string of losers who all seemed great at first, she had no reason to believe the next one would be different.

"You're the only one with the power to control that, you know?"

Charlotte sighed. *Here it comes.* Sandra was never shy about her opinions and had plenty when it came to Charlotte's relationships. She meant well (and she was usually right), so Charlotte let her continue.

"You keep going out with worthless fuckwits because you know you won't get too attached. Then when they forget your birthday or hit on your friends or feel up a waitress, it won't hurt so badly."

Charlotte nodded at the blunt, annoyingly accurate critique. "Wow. Okay then." She had no interest in lingering on the topic one second longer, opting for the easiest, most reliable way out. "Wanna hear what I think about you always falling for chicks who can't commit?"

Sandra glared.

Charlotte grinned, pleased with her friend's reaction to the taste of her own hard-to-swallow medicine. "So, on to more important things…" She headed for her bedroom, Sandra trailing behind. Two corsets hung on the knobs of her dresser. "Black or green?"

Sandra's lips twisted in contemplation. "Green. It'll make your dark hair and pretty brown eyes pop for the audience."

Charlotte grabbed the black one, hanging it back in her closet. There was nothing they couldn't rely on each other for—from a ride to the airport to a shoulder to drench with tears to a blunt but loving opinion on absolutely anything. It'd been that way since fourth grade. An older boy threw dirt in Charlotte's hair at recess, and Sandra kicked his shin so hard he ran crying to the teacher. They were inseparable when Sandra returned after a day's suspension. They shared a love of music, eventually joining the high school band to learn as many instruments as possible. Sandra's powerful, pitch-perfect voice blew Charlotte away whenever they sang along to their favorite albums, and she constantly encouraged her to find an outlet for her talent. It wasn't until Charlotte had played in a handful of local bands and then found herself without one that Sandra gave performing a shot. Together, they formed Killing Daisies with their good friend, Amber, on drums and a revolving door of bass players that never quite fit.

"Can I borrow that black and teal skirt you wore to the Crystal Ballroom show?" Sandra began digging through Charlotte's closet and froze. She pulled out a red T-shirt with the words Scarlet Love Letter emblazoned across the chest. "Whoa. Why in the hell do you still have this?"

Charlotte snatched the shirt from her hand. Years old and faded from a thousand washings, it still caused a rush of adrenaline to flood her veins, sending her back in time. Cheering crowds, lights, angry love songs, red wine and mayhem. Him. "Yes, you can borrow my skirt, and I still have this because it's part of my history. You can only appreciate how far you've come by occasionally reflecting on where you've been."

Sandra crooked an eyebrow. "Did you read that in a self-help book, Wise One?"

"No, smartass." Charlotte gave her shoulder a playful shove. "My therapist said it, and it's true." She glanced at the image of her old band on the shirt before crumpling it and tossing it on the bed. "Don't you sometimes read middle school diary entries or look at old yearbook photos and appreciate who you've become? How much you've changed?"

"I guess. But if I were you, I'd burn that thing along with every other reminder of Amy Cuntface Carey." Sandra scowled at Amy's face peeking out from a wrinkle on the cast-off shirt. "But I get it. And if looking at the past helps you fully grasp the badassness of our band, more power to you."

"Hey, speaking of Amy, did you hear about her latest DUI?" Charlotte asked. Sandra's casual eye roll said she hadn't heard but wasn't surprised. "Crashed her fancy car into the fountain at the Belltown Suites in Seattle. I appreciate having a frontwoman who doesn't drive into fucking fountains."

"You're welcome. She's gonna kill someone one day, mark my words." Sandra found the skirt she wanted to borrow, draping it over her forearm. "You know I love tossing back the booze, but you'd have to be a massive piece of shit to drive afterward."

Charlotte gave her a quick hug. "And I'm glad you're not even a microscopic speck of shit, let alone a massive piece." She nodded at the T-shirt on the bed. "But that's Amy in a nutshell."

"With an emphasis on the nut." Sandra sat on the bed and crossed her long, purple-denim-clad legs. "Was she arrested?"

Charlotte huffed. "What do you think? Her rich-ass parents shielding her from consequences is the main reason she's so fucked-up."

"If it were anyone else, I'd say it was a shame to see all that talent wasted. But since it's Amy, I'll just marvel at the glorious karma."

Despite a lingering desire to claw Amy's eyes out, Charlotte was grateful to have been in her inner circle at her peak. No performer she'd seen before or since could captivate a crowd like Amy Carey. When her husky, melodic roar of a voice rang out, and the club lights danced across her pale skin, you knew you were witnessing something rare and brilliant, like a dazzling comet that only comes around once in a lifetime. Unfortunately, all that talent came with a ruthless, take-no-prisoners ambition and cold, callous heart.

Charlotte's eyes drifted back to the shirt. "Imagine where she'd be if she focused on writing songs instead of getting trashed and chasing a movie career that'll never happen." It was no surprise to Charlotte that when Amy's star faded in the music world, she sought another possible route to the attention she desperately craved. So far, that was also a bust.

"Finding a guitarist who can stand her for more than a week and a drummer who isn't a cokehead jerkoff would help too. And the fountain crashing isn't doing her image any favors." Sandra checked her nails, frowning at a chip in the black polish on her thumb. "Tyler's the only thing she's got going for her, but the spell she's got him under can't last forever."

Charlotte was surprised it'd lasted three years. As smart as he was, he still hadn't figured out who Amy was at her core. Loyal and trusting to a fault, it was as if he only saw and believed things that wouldn't disrupt the blissful life he thought he was living. They were his best and worst qualities wrapped up in one sexy, dysfunctional package.

"Enough about her," Sandra said, yanking Charlotte back to reality. "Other than giving you nifty nuggets of wisdom, how's therapy going?"

"Great, actually." She sat beside her friend on the black bedspread. "Last week was my final session. It was weird pouring my heart out to a stranger at first, but I'm having fewer nightmares, and it's easier to shut down my panic attacks before they get out of control."

"Glad to hear that, sweetie."

"I'm glad to say it." Charlotte exhaled a long, slow breath. "Of course, if that twisted fucker ever comes back, things could go south again."

"Don't think that way." Sandra nudged her knee. "After therapy and self-defense classes, you're stronger now. Nothing can take that away. And you have a security system, bars on your windows, and an army of people who adore you that'll run his balls through a shredder if he tries anything. No one can touch you."

As much as she wanted it to be true, Charlotte knew no one could predict what triumphs or tragedies were heading her way. She didn't need a therapist or anyone else to tell her that. Life had already imparted that lesson the hard way.

3

Tyler

Tyler popped a mint to freshen his breath as the Town Car pulled through the gates of their sprawling home overlooking the Willamette River. *Mansion* was more accurate, but god, did he hate that word. As he tucked the pack of mints back into his pocket, something caught his eye at the end of the driveway.

A fucking Mercedes. Cherry red and pristine, as if it had just come off the lot.

"Jesus. What happened to the other one?" he mumbled.

"What was that, Mr. Hall?"

"Nothing." Tyler slipped on his backpack, grabbing the flowers and guitar as the car stopped. "Thanks again for picking me up, Louis. I know PDX is a jungle."

"Of course, sir."

Tyler glanced at his watch as the driver popped the trunk. "We landed so early, I thought I'd have time to kill waiting for you."

"My mother taught me if you're not early, you're late."

"Smart lady." After the driver set down the suitcase, Tyler shook his hand. "Enjoy your night off, my man." With the flowers tucked under his arm, he picked up the luggage and headed for the house.

When he walked through his front door, Pink Floyd played at low volume, and the lights were dimmed. A lacy red bra lying near his boot made him grin—a sexy breadcrumb. Amy loved playing naughty games, and his pulse kicked up, imagining what delicious surprise she had in store for his homecoming. He set his guitar on the cushioned bench beside the door.

As his eyes roamed further, he spied matching panties on the bottom step of the staircase. He imagined his wife stripping off her clothes, piece by piece, leaving a tempting trail for him to follow to the ultimate prize. His cock stiffened at the sight of the black silk lingerie draped over the back of the couch. He couldn't wait to discover where in the house her beautiful bare curves waited for his touch.

A moan in the living room, too low to be female, abruptly shook him from the fantasy, halting his approach.

Tyler's eyes squeezed shut.

No. Please, no.

When they opened again, his vision blurred as tears of pain and rage gathered, threatening to spill. His mind raced, desperate for an explanation that didn't mean his life was seconds from crumbling. When that failed and the sounds continued, a fiery knot formed in his gut, pulling and twisting like an ulcer. His grip on the flowers tightened, stems snapping between his fingers.

As he prepared to take the steps that would make it impossible to deny the truth, the beer from the plane threatened to come back up.

He swallowed hard and rounded the corner. When he reached the edge of the rug behind the couch, the sight of his wife's blood-red hair in another man's fists made him freeze, the broken roses slipping from his hands. The hard plastic suitcase followed, landing on the buds with a thump. Amy gasped, her shocked face popping over the back of the couch. Her wild hair shot in all directions, the bulk of it cascading over her bare breasts.

"Tyler!"

Even in the soft light, he saw the color drain from Amy's face as her hand clapped over her gaping mouth. In their three years together, it was only the second time he'd seen her speechless. The two instances were bookends—marking the first and last days of their relationship.

She sat up further, her lower half still concealed by the back of the sofa. "You're early."

When her crimson-tipped fingers fell, he caught the matching lipstick smeared to her chin. Amy's wide, panicked eyes darted between him and whatever soon-to-be-dead man she was straddling. She scrambled to her feet, snatching the black slip draped over the back of the couch and pulling it on. The burning, acidic lump climbed higher in Tyler's throat when the blond crewcut of her bodyguard, Rafael, came into view. The bastard's lips twitched as if holding back a smile, earning him a swift fist to the jaw as Tyler charged forward.

"You backstabbing motherfucker!" The words roared from his throat as pain exploded and throbbed in his knuckles. The adrenaline heating his blood made it easy to shove aside. "I trust you to keep her safe, and this is what you do?"

Amy shrieked, her nails digging into his shoulders. "Tyler, stop!"

His head snapped to her. "I'm early? That's what you say when I find you screwing this brainless meat brick on our goddamn couch?" He glared at Rafael, a quaking fist poised to strike again. "Get the fuck out of my house!"

Rafael grabbed his boxers and slipped them on, all six and a half feet of him rising to stand as he rubbed his reddening jaw. "I'll give you that one, asshole. But come at me again, and I'll drop you to the fucking floor."

Tyler shoved his shoulders hard, the obnoxious smirk instantly dropping off Rafael's face. "I'm not afraid of you, you steroid-sucking maggot. By the way, I sign your paychecks, and you're fucking fired." He snatched Rafael's clothes off the floor, throwing them in his face. "Go!"

When Rafael stepped forward, Amy touched his chest, shooting a look that made him dress quickly and head for the door.

After it slammed shut, she stared at Tyler, gnawing her bottom lip. "Calm down, and we'll talk about this."

She wrapped her arms around herself, his gaze falling to the soft ivory skin he could recognize blindfolded, with nothing but his other senses to guide him. All he'd wanted was to come home and melt in those arms. The thought that they'd never wrap around him again made a sob catch in his throat.

"Calm down?" He kicked his suitcase, petals scattering across the floor from the ruined roses underneath. "You just threw a grenade at our life, Amy! When I was buying you flowers, you took your clothes off for someone else. Do you have any idea how humiliating that is? How much it hurts to know I'll never be enough for you, no matter how hard I've fucking tried?"

His voice broke, the truth in his words and the deeply entrenched hurt they triggered overwhelming him. His mind cycled through all the gestures, large and small, he'd done to make her happy. The surprise gifts, romantic getaways, and countless love notes left on her pillow. When she didn't appreciate them, he just tried harder. Until then, he'd never questioned the impulse or where it came from. Had he always felt inadequate in her eyes, or was that insecurity planted later, festering over time?

"You are enough, Ty." She gestured at the coffee table, where a nearly empty vodka bottle sat beside two glasses. "I was upset about the shit with my band and drank too much."

His attention shifted to the powdery white residue beside the glasses. His eyes clamped shut. *Fuck*. It was worse than he thought.

"You promised me." His voice quivered. "No pills, no powders. Did you just wait for me to leave so you could have a goddamn free-for-all?"

"I'm hurting, Tyler." She set a hand over her heart. "I just wanted it to stop. Don't pretend you don't know what that's like."

His fists clenched, anger blazing in his chest at her attempted redirection. "Don't you dare throw that in my face! You know damn well I haven't touched that shit in years, and you're supposed to be done too. And you're not supposed to fuck someone else while I'm working my ass off and sleeping alone."

"I don't know what else to say." She threw up her arms. "I made a mistake."

His foot shifted, making a rustling sound. He bent to pick up the ripped-open condom wrapper beside his shoe, waving it between them. "How many mistakes is it now? You going to tell me I was gone all month, and you waited until less than two hours before I'm supposed to be home to fuck him for the first time?" He tossed the wrapper to the floor.

"I'll never do it again. I swear on my life." She grabbed for his arm, and he yanked it back. He didn't miss the absence of a denial in her response. "Have a drink to settle your nerves, and we'll talk it out."

Amy grabbed the vodka bottle, filling one of the glasses halfway before offering it to Tyler. As he stared at her lipstick print on the glass, the certainty he could never forgive her thoroughly took hold. Regardless of what drove her to sink so low, she'd made a choice there was no coming back from.

Life as he knew it was over.

He dragged in a stuttered breath. "I have nothing left to say to you." He swiped a tear as he took the glass, the liquor helping to shove down the burning lump threatening to choke him. "And I'll calm down after I sign divorce papers to get you the hell out of my life."

"No!" Panic dilated her pupils. She reached for him again, but after scrutinizing his expression, she pulled back. "I'm sorry, Ty. I was lonely because you were gone so long and—"

"Don't you dare blame me for what you did!" Tyler gripped his hair, tugging the roots until it hurt. "I begged you to come with me, but you refused."

She stepped close enough for him to smell the stale smoke in her hair, vodka on her breath, and another man's sweat on her skin. "Did you really expect me to tag along on your big tour with your packed crowds to remind me what I've lost?"

"No, Amy." A knot squeezed in the center of his chest. Suddenly, their divide felt greater than when he was on the other side of the world. "I was hoping you'd want to come because you'd miss me if you didn't. We could've used every free moment to figure out how to fix things. Instead, I slept alone for thirty nights while you're here stabbing me in the back."

"It meant nothing!" The whites of her eyes were tinged with pink as she stared up at him, pleading. "I'm so sorry—"

"Stop saying that!" His death grip on the glass tightened, pain spiking in his swollen knuckles. "Sorry means shit when I can still smell him on you!" He slammed the glass on the table, barely resisting the urge to throw it at the wall.

Tyler roughly wiped at the hot, stinging tears trailing his cheeks, willing them to stop. It'd been years since he cried. The last time was over a friend's death that pinned him to the floor with grief. This time, he grieved what he and Amy would never be again. They'd never again share those slow, hungry kisses that left them breathless. No more late nights lying in bed, chain-smoking, and listening to old records. Her beautiful face would never again rest against his chest as they fell asleep in each other's arms.

"I love you." Her bottom lip shook, and he looked away. Despite his anger, it killed him to see her in pain. "Remember how hard we fell for each other? We can get that feeling back. I know we can. Remember that feeling and fight for it."

Just then, a flood of memories he'd long since pushed aside rushed in, though they were far from the shining ones she hoped for. Amy stumbling through the door, three hours late to his twenty-fifth birthday party, with no underwear or explanation. Backstage after her Viper Room gig, when he could've sworn a smear of her signature lipstick shade was on her drummer's neck. Amy taking money from his bank accounts after draining her own to fill her closets with shit she never wore twice.

Then, he thought about the warnings from friends and family. His brother, Matthew, was instantly put off by her brash attitude and shady reputation, urging him to ditch her. Adam and Zack worried that her unreasonable demands on Tyler's time and attention affected the band. Charlotte and Sandra, who knew Amy better than most, said she'd break his heart one day. At the time, he was too blinded by lust and then love to listen to any of it. Now, a chorus of *I told you* so echoed in his head. As if all those well-meaning loved ones got together to stick the point.

They had told him so.

Perhaps his greatest fear was true, and they were right.

"I'll go to that marriage counselor if that's what you want," she said, yanking him back to the present. "You know I'm not the groveling type, but I'll do anything, Tyler. Name it."

Staring into the eyes he'd been yearning to connect with since long before he left on tour, he saw desperation. Maybe even fear.

But not love.

That hurt worse than anything else she'd done.

Tyler shook his head as her words fell to the floor, empty and powerless. "Too late for that. And if you really love me, you have a fucked-up way of showing it." He huffed out an exhausted breath, the adrenaline buzz receding. "Do you know how many groupies I've turned away? How many girls have slipped me their number or their goddamn underwear over the years? I never laid a finger on any of them. You're the only one I've wanted since the day we met. That's what love is."

He turned to leave, and she grabbed his arm, the contact searing his skin. And pissing him the hell off. "Don't fucking touch me." He tore away, grabbed his luggage, and headed for the stairs.

"You can't divorce me, Tyler. I won't let you."

He laughed darkly as he ascended the tall, winding staircase. "Let me? Try to stop me." He froze on a middle step as something occurred to him. "I guess I owe you gratitude for one thing, Amy." He turned his head, their eyes connecting. "Making me sign that prenup. You always thought you'd be the bigger star, didn't you?"

"Fuck you." Her apologetic mask dropped, and she glared like she wanted to punch him. The shift in her demeanor said he'd scored a direct hit on the nerve he aimed for.

Good.

"Shame that didn't work out." He took another step. "Guess you should've saved some of those royalties instead of snorting them up your nose and buying a bunch of superficial crap."

She ranted at his back as he made his way to their bedroom, but it was all background static to the ringing in his ears and pulse throbbing in his skull. After locking the door behind him, Tyler collapsed onto his back on the bed, trapped sobs making his shoulders quake. If only he'd had the presence of mind to swipe the whiskey bottle off the fridge to dampen the pain with a few burning gulps. Just enough to shove it back while he gathered his things and took the first shaky steps away from the life they'd built together.

Starting over.

Alone.

The cold of the bedspread seeped through his clothes, making him shiver. Their bedroom always felt like winter. Amy couldn't sleep unless the a/c was cranked, and she piled the blankets a foot thick. Tyler hated it. He'd have to slip the stacked covers to his waist to avoid feeling suffocated or waking up drenched in sweat.

In his anger, he felt the seemingly minor marital concession darkening in his heart, morphing into resentment. How many other things had gone in her favor by default, forcing him to adjust or suffer?

But then, he thought of how good it felt when she pressed her chilled body to his, absorbing his heat. The peace he felt having her so close as she drifted off to sleep. The kind of peace he'd been chasing since the night his childhood was fractured by tragedy. He turned his head, Amy's pink silk pillow inches from his face. His fingertips skated over the fabric, every breath he pulled in tainted by the scent of her perfume. Of her.

A tear slipped down his cheek.

What if giving up was a mistake? It hurt now, but what if time made it easier to bear? Could he, somehow, forgive what she'd done?

His gaze drifted to a wedding photo on the wall beside the bed. Tyler grinned like a love-drunk fool at his bride, their hands joined beneath the floral arch. Amy looked impossibly beautiful, her skin golden and glowing in the beams of the high Hawaiian sun. As if the island itself knew she belonged in a spotlight. They were barefoot, toes buried in the sand as gentle waves lapped at their ankles.

That day was perfect.

It felt like the start of the life he'd always wanted—one with love, security, and family.

Something crashed downstairs.

He imagined Amy throwing a vase or plate against the wall, not an uncommon end to one of her tantrums. He understood the catharsis of breaking shit, but shouldn't he be the one throwing things and screaming?

The warm, fuzzy wedding memories stuttered to a halt.

If she'd wanted that life too, would she have risked throwing it away?

There was a lot he could forgive and accept, but cheating wasn't on that list. Trust and loyalty were essential in his world, and she'd just proven herself incapable of both. He chucked her pillow at the photo, knocking it from its nail and sending it clattering to the floor.

Fuck this.

He rolled to sit up, reaching for the bedside phone and hitting the speed dial button for a cab company. An urgent need to run far and fast took hold, and he knew exactly where to go. He sputtered out the address for his brother's apartment building and hung up before falling backward again.

When they were kids, Matthew's room was the first place Tyler ran when the world beat him down. They'd read comics, watch corny old sitcoms, and listen to loud, angsty music, distracting themselves from the struggle of growing into men without a father to show them how.

He could always tell Matty anything. Or they'd sit silently, reveling in the comfort of being truly understood. None of their friends knew there was often nothing in their cupboards but mushy canned peas from the food bank and stale cracker crumbs. Or how their mom left for days because it was easier to give up and run away than to be a grieving single parent to two broken kids who despised rules.

In the end, both women taught him that no matter how hard you try to earn the love and respect you desperately need, you end up with stale crumbs and burning starvation that never goes away.

The cab would arrive in fifteen minutes. As the initial wave of shock wore off, days of broken sleep combined with fading adrenaline and jet lag made Tyler's eyelids heavy. He sank further into the cool, smooth bedspread, a deep yawn taking hold. Knowing full well he'd fall into a mild coma if he succumbed to the pull of sleep, he slapped his cheeks and got to his feet. His skin itched with a craving for nicotine, so he slid a cigarette from his pack and lit it, his lungs burning from the deep inhale.

Thudding footsteps climbing the stairs were followed by pounding on his door.

"Fuck off, Amy! I'm packing my shit, and then I'm out of here."

When the pounding continued, he stormed to the door, swinging it wide.

She'd put on a fur coat since he'd been upstairs, concealing most of her skin. "Don't go, sweetheart. I made a mistake—"

"So did I," he gritted out. "And after three years of swallowing bullshit, I'm going to correct it."

She gasped at his harsh words, wiping away tears stained black from the mascara running down her face. "Don't say that. I love you! We can fix this."

"I'm going to Matthew's." He averted his gaze, dumping dirty clothes out of his backpack. "Tomorrow, I'll have our lawyers draw up divorce papers. Don't touch my studio or my guitars." Tyler dug through his suitcase, pulled out a small blue bag, and tucked it into his pocket. He shoved some clean boxers, socks, and jeans into his backpack and slid his arms into the straps before grabbing his favorite guitar off the wall. "Now, get the hell out of my way."

⚬

When the taxi arrived, Tyler tossed his backpack in the trunk and climbed into the backseat with his guitar. The driver turned, and his eyes bulged when he saw Tyler. He looked just shy of thirty and judging by the Soundgarden on his stereo, the guy was in Tomorrow Mourning's demographic.

"Oh, god." The driver gaped. "You're Tyler Hall."

Fuck. Not now. Tyler held his hand up in an awkward wave. "Hey, man. Thanks for the ride."

"Damn, I wish I had a camera. My girlfriend's never gonna believe this."

"I'd be happy to sign something if you don't get all fanboy on me." He'd hoped the ride would give him a chance to stare out the window in silence, pondering how he'd managed to screw up his life. Instead, he was trapped in a car with a gushing cabbie who wouldn't stop gawking. *Fucking perfect.*

The driver's face reddened before he faced forward, shifting the car into gear. "Sorry, Mr. Hall. I pick up celebrities sometimes, but no one as famous as you. I'm a huge fan. *Huge.*"

Tyler slipped on his dark glasses despite the sun setting behind the hills. "Thanks. What's your name?"

"Charles, but everyone calls me Chuck."

"Do you like being called Chuck?"

Charles/Chuck scrunched his forehead, glancing at Tyler through the rearview mirror. "Used to, I guess. When I was younger. Now, it doesn't seem to fit."

"I know just what you mean, Charles. Mind if I smoke?"

He held his hand over the no-smoking sign and laughed. "Go for it. My boss owns the car, and he's an asshole." He pulled his cigarettes from the glove box, sparking one up.

Tyler lit his own and held the pack in the air. "Here's to sticking it to the assholes."

Charles tapped his pack against Tyler's. "Hear, hear."

As they entered downtown, Tyler found himself smiling as they passed his favorite piece of street art—a concrete wall with Keep Portland Weird drawn ten feet high in bright green and pink spray paint. The welcome flash of a pleasant memory halted when a Harley zoomed past his window, weaving through traffic and earning a few honks from frustrated drivers. His muscles tensed, the knots in his stomach tightening until the rumble of the motorcycle was drowned out by the sounds of the city.

He leaned back in his seat and sighed, his eyes on the tacky beige ceiling. If thoughts of happier times couldn't distract him, maybe this guy could. "How late are you out driving this thing?"

"At least until two. I'd be happy to pick you up if you need a ride home."

"No, thanks." Tyler couldn't stomach the thought of returning to that place. Thanks to Amy, it would never feel like home again. "I was just curious about your job. Must be interesting driving around the city, meeting new people."

Charles' eyebrows pinched, his upper lip curling like he'd just heard the most ridiculous sentence of his life. "Mr. Hall. My job and the rest of my life are boring as fuck compared to yours. You don't want to hear about it."

That sinking feeling settled into Tyler's chest. It hit him whenever "regular people" shrugged him off as being too far above them for small talk. It made getting to know anyone outside his circle of friends nearly impossible.

"It's cool if you don't want to talk about it. And you can call me Tyler. I'm just another guy. We probably grew up on the same cartoons, listening to the same bands, and drinking the same beer."

"Are you kidding?" Charles turned around, his eyes popping wide. "The man who wrote 'Walk in the Shadows' isn't just another guy. The man who married Amy Carey, one of the hottest chicks on the planet, isn't just another guy."

Three smoke rings puffed from Tyler's lips, hovering for a moment before vanishing. Rebuttals rattled in his head—*At least you can go to the grocery store without being mobbed. At least you know your family loves you for who you are, not what you can do for them. All the fame, talent, and money in the world don't matter if you're too lonely and broken to be sober for more than a few hours.*

Instead, he changed the subject. "You said you have a girlfriend?" *I bet she's never fucked a bloated assclown on your sofa.*

"Yeah. Stacy. Even bigger fan than me. Flashed her tits from the front row last time you played the Rose Garden."

Tyler turned to watch the city lights go by, the conversation shut down for the rest of the blessedly short trip.

After signing a page in Charles' notebook, Tyler exited the cab, knocking hard on the dusty, peeling door of Matthew's apartment. His brother co-owned and operated High Notes, a thriving craft brewery in North Portland, with his college friend, Evan. He could easily afford a nicer place but hadn't bothered upgrading from his busted-up bachelor pad. It drove their mother crazy, but as long as he was happy and safe, Tyler didn't care where he lived.

After another knock, his kid brother greeted him in a faded Ramones shirt, a lit joint in his hand, and a mile-wide grin on his face. "Well, well. From Down Under to my doorstep."

Tyler slid his sunglasses to the top of his head.

As Matthew took in the sight of him, the joy on his face collapsed. "Jesus, dude. You look like shit. The jet lag can't be that bad."

Tyler's jaw clenched, a sharp spike of pain shooting through it. "I just caught Amy screwing Rafael in my living room." His gaze dropped. "And that's my shirt, you damn thief." He pushed past Matthew, grabbing two beers before ditching his guitar and backpack and sinking into the tattered couch that always smelled like pot and pepperoni.

"What the fucking fuck?" Matthew slammed the door, making Tyler jump. "Seriously?"

"Yup." He tossed one of the beers to his brother. "Can I crash here tonight? I'll go to a hotel if it's a problem."

Matthew sat beside him, slinging a long, bony arm around his shoulders. "I'm so sorry, man. Stay as long as you need. At least the rest of the week. No way in hell I'm letting you sit around some hotel room alone with that image in your head."

"I don't need a babysitter, Matty." Tyler pressed the cold bottle to his sore knuckles.

Matt's eyebrow raised. "Don't you?"

"I know what you're thinking, and you can stop." Tyler shot him an impatient look. "We've been over this a thousand times."

"What am I thinking?"

He looked his well-meaning but paranoid brother in the eye. "It's been over two years. I did a few fucking lines, and you'll never let me live it down."

"*A few fucking lines?*" Matthew's voice raised, something he did so rarely that Tyler flinched. "You could've died, asshole! You did it because you were hurting after losing your friend and wanted an easy fix. I bet this feels even worse. You might be tempted to instantly shut off what you're feeling, and I worry about you."

"Don't. It was a stupid mistake, and I swear, I'm good." A mistake was putting it lightly. Young people dying from a bad hit of heroin was practically an epidemic in their town. Remembering the desperation that brought the rolled-up hundred to his nose and the sheer recklessness of the act made him shudder. He popped the cap off his beer, chugging the whole thing before getting another. "We're gonna need to do a beer run, though."

"Actually, there's plenty of booze where we're going."

Tyler's forehead wrinkled as he sat back down. "Going? I'm not moving from this spot. My heart was just ripped from my goddamn chest, the image of my naked wife straddling that spray-tanned dickhead is burned on my retinas, and I'm gonna drink until I pass out on your smelly ass couch."

"No chance. You can sit around feeling sorry for yourself tomorrow." Matthew grabbed a piece of paper off his counter, balled it up, and tossed it at Tyler's head. "Tonight, we're going to this."

Tyler unfurled the crumpled edges, the corners of his mouth tipping up at the black-and-white image of Charlotte Ross and her trio of bandmates. Hovering above the women's heads were thickly scrawled black letters:

Killing Daisies

Saturday, May 6

Apocalypse 1222 NE Halsey

Doors Open at 8

To Charlotte's left was frontwoman Sandra, the enigmatic wiseass with wild curls pouring over her shoulders. Amber, their drummer, was on her right with darkly painted lips curled into her signature *Don't fuck with us* snarl. The name of their latest bassist escaped him, but she towered behind them in a shredded L7 T-shirt. His eyes landed on Charlotte's barely-there grin and arched eyebrow. It was an expression laced with the promise of mischief, or perhaps it presented a dare. Either way, he was taken aback by the sudden burst of anticipation sparking in his veins at the thought of going to her show. When his gaze slid to the corset molded to her curves, he granted himself a few seconds of ogling before crumpling the paper and shoving it into his pocket.

"Charlotte's band is headlining, and we're not missing it." Matthew returned to the couch. "At least this time, you won't have to sneak around to see your friends."

Tyler slipped the sunglasses off his head, tossing them onto the coffee table. "If you think I'm ready for silver linings, you read me wrong." Still, he had to admit it'd be nice to hang with his brother without Amy's usual, exhausting interrogation about who else might be there.

"Fine. Plenty of time to celebrate the upsides. Right now, hit the shower, and I'll give you something to wear that doesn't smell like beer and depression."

Tyler quirked an eyebrow. "Like my Ramones shirt, maybe?"

Matthew's stoned chuckle became a cough. "I think I have your Nirvana shirt in my closet, minus the reek of my sweat and weed smoke." He sniffed the shirt he was wearing, his nose wrinkling.

"Is it fucked-up that I'm kind of relieved?" Tyler hit his second beer almost as hard as the first, draining half in one gulp.

"That I have a clean shirt you can wear?"

"No, dumbass." He bumped Matthew's shoulder with his own. "Relieved Amy gave me a final straw we can't come back from." He rolled the bottle cap over in his fingers. "I'm ready for kids, and she's still getting blitzed all hours of the night, hanging with addicts and burning through our money on superficial junk. I kept hoping she'd change, but—"

"You're finally realizing she doesn't want to."

"Exactly." Tyler nodded, reality sinking in further. "I'd never bring a kid into that. And if I had to give up having a family because she couldn't get her shit together, I'd end up miserable, resenting her." He tossed the bottle cap on the table. "We had lots of great times, but when I think of everything I've forgiven and ignored over the years... It was always going to end with a crash."

"Just like it started."

Tyler let out a mirthless laugh. "You're not wrong." He tugged the joint from between Matthew's fingers, taking a drag.

"Can I tell you something without the risk of your boot nailing me in the shin?"

Tyler's lips tipped up in a wry smile. "No promises."

"I'll take my chances." Matthew set the joint in an ashtray, a thick ribbon of smoke curling its way to the ceiling. "You need to find a way to make yourself whole instead of waiting for someone to hand you the missing pieces. Especially someone so selfish, your needs would always come last or not at all. You did it with Mom until you finally realized she was incapable and gave up, and you did the same shit with Amy."

"Goddamn, Matty." Tyler picked up the joint, taking another puff. "Why don't you tell me how you really feel?"

"Oh, it's coming." Matthew was quiet until Tyler met his eyes. "You deserve a hell of a lot better than Amy Carey and always have. It was young lust that went too far. Sure, the first year or so was great, but then she took you for granted, doing whatever the hell she wanted while trying to dictate where you could go and who you could see. That weight on your shoulders was crushing you, man. Which is why it's fitting and fucking phenomenal that you're relieved that bullshit's behind you."

"I'm relieved, but I also feel sad and broken and so angry, it's hard to breathe." He touched his chest, swallowing thickly. "What do you mean I need to make myself whole? How fucked-up do you think I am?"

"Don't take it like that. It's just..." Matthew cracked his knuckles before taking back the joint. "You spent a lot of your childhood taking care of me, then put all your energy into your band, and then you had Amy's crazy demands. You've put yourself last for so long. Do you even know what you need? Take time figuring that out before someone else comes crashing in."

Tyler went quiet for a moment. All the nights spent away, staring at hotel room ceilings, had given him plenty of time to think about what he wanted his future to look like. Based on that, he had a vague idea of what he needed. He'd just never put it into words.

"The fame, the fans..." Tyler began, "I know it won't last forever. I want a full, happy life, so even if it all disappears tomorrow, I'll be okay." He sighed heavily, his shoulders sinking. "But what if the career I've built makes it impossible to have the home life I want? Clearly, I suck at balancing the two. What if I fail at every relationship like I did at this one? And how can I ever trust someone again?"

"Whoa." Matthew touched his shoulder. "Slow down, Ty. You didn't fail. I saw how hard you tried. You just fell for the wrong person. You were twenty-three and lonely. It happens. The fact that you were capable of such a major commitment is a good sign. Hell, I'm twenty-three now and can't even commit to getting a pet." Matthew swigged his beer, wiping his mouth with the back of his hand. "There's plenty of time to find someone who'll appreciate you. Someone you can trust. And I bet she'll jump at the chance to shit out a bunch of your kids."

Tyler laughed. "Wow, thanks."

Matthew gave his shoulder a reassuring squeeze. "It's gonna be okay, brother. I promise. You've been through worse and come out swinging, and I've got your back until you get there."

The comforting words from the man who knew him better than anyone released some pent-up tension in Tyler's aching jaw. "Thanks, Matty."

"Speaking of swinging…" He gently touched Tyler's swollen knuckles. "Did you punch Rafael or the wall?"

"Rafael." He flexed his fingers. "Playing guitar will hurt for a while, but it was worth it."

"Hell yeah." Matthew fist-bumped his unhurt hand and stood. "Now, let's get you cleaned up and ready to go, pretty boy. Maybe you can drown your sorrows with the hot-as-balls fans trying to climb you wherever you go. Nothing beats a good rebound lay."

Tyler scrubbed his face with rough, calloused fingertips. Just the thought of strangers touching him roiled his stomach. "I can't even think about other women yet. Especially ones who want the version of me they created from reading *Spin* and picking apart lyrics."

He got empty sex out of his system years ago, when a little dirty, no-strings-attached fun in between gigs was enough. Now, he wanted a real, lasting connection, not blowjobs from random women in rock clubs.

"You know…" Matthew kicked his shoe. "There's always Charlotte."

Tyler's head lifted. "What about her?"

Matthew's lips tipped up in a smirk. "Come on, bro. You know that girl's had it bad for you since the night you met. Are you gonna tell me it's all one-sided? Keep in mind, I've been able to sniff out your bullshit since I was five, and you tried to make me eat a pebble by saying it was chocolate." He took another slow drag before smoke blurred his face.

Tyler's eyes rolled as he got to his feet. It wasn't the first time Matthew had brought up Charlotte having a crush on him, but it was the last thing he needed to hear after the day he'd had. Besides, just because Matthew and Charlotte were close and confided in each other didn't mean there was any truth to it. His brother often talked out of his ass to annoy him, so it was easy to shrug off the comment as his typical nonsense.

"For fuck's sake, Matty. I've been separated for less than an hour, and you're throwing this at me? I'm not some dirtbag who's been drooling over other women while I had a wife at home."

"Whoa." He held his hands up. "You know damn well that's not what I meant."

Tyler knew his brother better than that. Of course, he wasn't accusing him of being unfaithful, even in his thoughts. He also knew Matthew needed to learn when to butt out and shut up.

"Listen up, Cheech." Tyler returned the joint to the ashtray. "Even if it were true ages ago, like I said, I'm not interested in anyone." He walked down the long hallway and into the bedroom, with Matthew following behind. After rifling through the drawers, he pulled out a black Joy Division shirt, holding it in the air. "This one's mine too, fucker. Stealing my shit, just like when we were kids. Do you have any clothes that are yours?"

"Hey, when you invite me to your house to get wasted, I borrow your shirts. Now, I get to reciprocate."

Tyler laughed despite the raw, hollow ache in his chest. "Doesn't count when they're still mine, but whatever."

4

Charlotte

Charlotte studied Sandra's face, trying to figure out why the lead singer of their band was nauseous thirty minutes before hitting the stage. "Are you just nervous?"

"I don't get nervous. I get excited." Sandra swigged her ginger ale. "That's not it."

Charlotte touched her forehead. "No fever. Have you eaten anything today?"

Sandra wiped a few beads of perspiration from her upper lip. "Three slices of pizza and a few Oreos. Then, half a bag of Cheetos."

Charlotte laughed. "Are you allergic to vegetables? No wonder you're feeling sick."

"Whatever, bitch. I'm healthy as a horse and have a bomb-ass metabolism. I'm gonna eat like a ten-year-old with their mama's credit card until that changes." Sandra's petite, toned five-foot-nothing frame made her claims impossible to refute. She sat at the white and gold vanity table and dug through her cosmetics bag.

"At least we know you're not pregnant." Charlotte sprayed a tiny burst of hairspray on her crown before smoothing a few flyaways. The sharp, chemical scent tickled her nose.

"Right?" Sandra leaned closer to the mirror as she applied mascara. "One of the many perks of being a lesbian. Carelessness during casual sex won't haunt us for eighteen years."

Charlotte plucked a tube of pink gloss from the bag, dabbing it onto her lips. "Is that chick you met at Dante's coming tonight?"

Sandra grumbled, running her fingers through her unruly mass of auburn curls. "Nope. She's moving to Eugene, so that's a bust. Any of your peeps coming?"

"Just Matthew." Charlotte tried not to smile as she felt Sandra's stare. "And maybe Tyler."

"And maybe Tyler." Sandra's reflection smirked at Charlotte's. "Mmhm."

She'd mentioned the show to him before he left on tour, but he didn't commit to going since it was the day he was getting home. Hell, he seemed so distracted by the tabloid mess she'd be surprised if he even remembered. That doubt didn't stop her from hoping he'd be in the audience on the biggest night of her career.

"Shut up, Sandra." Charlotte bumped her friend's shoulder with her hip. "We're just friends for the hundred thousandth time."

"Which one of us are you trying to convince, sweetie?" Sandra finished touching up her silver eyeshadow and looked at Charlotte through the mirror. "I see how you are around him."

"How am I?" Charlotte crossed her arms over her corseted chest. "Enlighten me."

Sandra set down her makeup brush, sitting up straighter. "You get fidgety. You stay close but not close enough to cross any lines. And your eyes get the same hungry look as when we saw *Legends of the Fall*."

Charlotte fanned herself. "I'll cop to having hungry eyes for Brad Pitt. The rest of it's in your crazy, curly head."

"I wish it were." Sandra exhaled a heavy sigh. "You're playing with fire, and I just want you to be careful."

Charlotte's eyes rolled to the ceiling. "I had a crush when we first met, but that's ancient history. He's married, and I'm not that stupid."

"No, but we both know you can be self-destructive and naïve." She smiled at Charlotte's raised middle finger. "Just don't forget for a second who wears his ring."

Sandra's words made memories flash through Charlotte's mind, starring her old friend and former bandmate, Amy Carey. Long coffee shop talks after practice. The shopping trips for clothes and jewelry as they crafted their stage personas. All the parties, drunken laughter in smoke-filled rooms, lovers that came and went, the countless hangovers eased with Bloody Marys. In the early days of Scarlet Love Letter, Charlotte idolized her. Amy was everything she wasn't but desperately wanted to be—outspoken, untamed, unapologetic. She'd witnessed how Amy's words could reduce people to dust if they dared to cross her. Charlotte envied that ability until, one day, it was aimed at her.

She snapped out of her daydream. "Do you honestly think I'd put myself in Amy's crosshairs again? I won't do anything stupid, but I'll be damned if I let that bitch tell me who I can be friends with."

The dressing room door opened, and Amber, their drummer, strolled in. Her pale blonde locks were slicked back, and her burgundy lipstick and heavy eyeliner looked perfectly applied. "Are your sexy asses almost ready? We're on in twenty."

Charlotte smoothed the front of her platinum miniskirt. "I'm good to go."

"Turn around." Amber made circles in the air with her finger, and Charlotte turned her back to her. "You missed a hook, hooker." She secured the final latch on the back of Charlotte's emerald green corset before fluffing up her dark chestnut waves. "Perfect." She grabbed her drumsticks off the makeup table, twirling them between her fingers.

Sandra snatched a grape from a snack tray the club staff set out. "I think my stomach's starting to feel better."

"Awesome." Charlotte turned, popping a blackberry into her mouth. "Now I won't have to worry about you hurling all over my fabulous new guitar."

"My stomach's a little wonky, too, after seeing the size of that crowd." Amber aimed a drumstick toward the rumble of the amped-up audience in the main hall. "Our biggest gig to date! How cool is that? Long gone are the days of playing our hearts out for a dozen drunk dudes heckling us to take our shirts off."

Charlotte had played plenty of sold-out shows with Scarlet Love Letter, but it almost felt like cheating. Amy had a built-in fanbase from earlier bands who'd follow her anywhere. Killing Daisies had a rough time paying their dues, so it felt like they'd earned every bit of their success.

"Thank god," Sandra said.

"No, thank Eliza," Charlotte chimed in. "Hiring her was our smartest move ever."

They'd played small, smoky dive bars and countless local festivals before Eliza Marsh slipped them her business card at a benefit show for Safe Start, a women's crisis center where Charlotte often volunteered. The band had been on an upward trajectory ever since, with a killer record deal, gigs at larger, more prolific clubs, and a steadily growing fanbase. Tickets for their upcoming Canadian gigs were selling fast, and it felt surreal every time she saw the tour posters with her band's name at the top in big, bold letters instead of buried beneath a list of more popular groups. She couldn't wait to get on the road to thank the fans who made it all possible.

As if summoned by their chatter, Eliza appeared in the doorway. "Hello, my Daisies. Are you the reason my ears are burning?"

"Guilty." Amber aimed a broad smile in her direction. "We're talking about how lucky we are to have you. Thanks for getting us this gig."

"You bring the talent to the table. I have a knack for connecting talent with opportunity." Eliza's heels clicked across the floor until she settled into a plush chair covered in purple velvet. "Sandra, honey, you look pale. You okay?"

"I'll survive. Any word on the benefit album for Safe Start?"

"Still waiting to hear from distribution, but it's looking good. Keep spreading the word so we can secure studio time with the artists when everything's set." She leaned forward, folding her hands over her knee. "Are you in agreement yet on the songs you're contributing?"

Charlotte nodded. "We're going with 'Fading' and 'Never Again,' the song I wrote for the project. They just need some polishing."

"Excellent," Eliza said. "Let me know when they're ready. Are you opening with 'Dark Wish' tonight? You stirred up the pit with that one at the Crystal Ballroom show."

"That's the plan." Sandra swiped a piece of notebook paper off the vanity table. "Wanna see the setlist?"

"Absolutely." Eliza took the handwritten sheet, skimming it. "Hmm. I'd swap 'Swept Up' with 'Hollow' and close with 'Cherish.' It'll balance out the vibe better, keeping them wanting more."

She picked a ball of purple lint off her otherwise pristine trousers, dropping it to the floor. Charlotte couldn't imagine such a prim-looking woman listening to their brand of raucous, melodic punk, but Eliza had seen the band's potential regardless of personal taste. She worked her ass off for all her clients but claimed to have a sweet spot for Killing Daisies.

"So," Eliza said, leaning back in her seat, "how does it feel to sell out a room holding two thousand fans?"

"It feels like..." Charlotte paused, searching for the right words. "It's only the beginning."

Eliza smiled. "I don't doubt it. I've watched your band evolve from a formidable yet rough around-the-edges opening act into the in-demand headliner you are today. I hope you're all as proud as I am of how far you've come."

"Hell, yeah, we're proud." Sandra hooked her arms across her bandmates' shoulders. "And we're ready to light that fucking room up."

"That's the spirit." Eliza stood from her chair, brushing invisible remnants of purple velvet off her trousers. "Since my mosh pitting days are far behind me, I'll be in my comfy VIP seat on the balcony if you need anything. Have fun." She waved, shutting the door behind her with a click.

"Goddamn, I love that woman." Sandra squeezed Charlotte and Amber in a group hug. "But not as much as I love you badass bitches."

"It's mutual." Amber squeezed back before pulling away. "Just don't smudge my eyeliner."

"Where the hell's Jackie?" Sandra glanced at her watch. "She should be here by now."

Amber groaned. "She was arguing with her boyfriend at the bar, crying and shit, saying she didn't want to play. Eliza talked to her before coming in here. I guess if we had to, Molly could fill in for Charlotte on guitar, and she can play bass."

"No. Fucking. Way." Charlotte couldn't keep the rough edge from her tone. "I play guitar on that stage or nothing."

Since Amber came along after Charlotte was booted from Scarlet Love Letter, she got a pass for suggesting that. Anyone else would've found a spot on Charlotte's shit list. Long gone were the days of letting someone dictate her role in a band or anything else in her life.

"Okay, princess." Amber smoothed Charlotte's hair. "Message received. Don't bite me."

Charlotte grabbed Amber's arm, lightly clamping on with her teeth while Amber squealed. There was a knock at the door, and Amber walked over, still laughing her head off.

"Hey, Matty. Everyone's decent. Come on in."

Matthew entered, towering above everyone in the room, holding a beer bottle. "You ladies look a hell of a lot better than decent. All three of you are smokin'." He adjusted his black-rimmed glasses before tucking his free hand into the pocket of his faded jeans.

Charlotte pecked his cheek, leaving behind a pale pink smear. "Thanks, Matty. Amber fluffs my hair, and you fluff my ego."

"I'll fluff more than that if you ask nicely," he said, weaving to the side to dodge Charlotte's swat. "Still driving us home, Sandarella?"

"Yup," Sandra said. "Feel free to get nice and wasted, kids. If we get separated after the show, meet me in the lot at the end of the block."

"Cool, thanks. Can Tyler ride with us?"

Charlotte tripped over her feet on the way to the mirror. "Is he coming?" The thought that he'd be in the audience for their biggest show made her the third band member with a stomach doing backflips.

"Yeah, we shared a cab here, but I lost him at the bar. He's had a hell of a day, and he's super jet-lagged, but he made it."

Sandra shook her head. "Sorry, dude. With two passengers and our gear, I'm at capacity. Unless you want him sitting on your lap."

Matthew laughed. "Cab it is, then."

Charlotte returned to the mirror for one last makeup check, noticing the blush rising on her cheeks. It'd been a long month, and she couldn't wait to see Tyler's charmingly crooked smile again. When she caught Sandra's reflection, Sandra cocked an eyebrow. Charlotte's eyes narrowed in a homicidal glare that disappeared before she turned back to Matthew.

"Wanna hit the drink table?" She suddenly craved some liquid courage.

He pointed at his almost full bottle. Charlotte snatched it from his hand, put it to her lips, and poured the rest of the contents down her throat.

"Now you need another drink." She let out a tiny burp and grabbed his elbow, dragging him through the doorway.

5

Tyler

While waiting for his Jack and Coke, Tyler avoided eye contact with the horde of excited concertgoers. He'd already told a few handsy women to fuck off in the politest terms he could muster in his sour mood. A few other barely dressed twenty-somethings circled, and he could feel their probing stares as they worked up the nerve to talk or slip a phone number into his pocket.

He'd dreamed of being a musician since he was five but might've thought twice if he'd known a complete lack of privacy was the price of admission.

"Hey, Tyler. I love your band." A brunette wearing too much makeup took the stool beside him, her knee brushing his hip. She leaned closer, breathing vodka fumes in his face. "If you're looking to party, my car's outside."

"Not interested." He moved further down the bar to wait for the drink that was taking too damn long. In his periphery, he saw her stomp off, disappearing into the crowd.

A quick hello or autograph was fine, but that wasn't enough for some. They had to gawk like he was an alien or try to fuck him for a story to tell their friends. He couldn't understand why people felt entitled to a piece of you simply because they connected with your art. He'd never in a million years think of pestering Roger Daltrey at a grocery store to tell him *Quadrophenia* was the best album ever made.

Once he got his drink, he waded through the thinnest edge of the crowd, making his way to the front. The scents of cigarette smoke and beer near the bar merged with sweat and cheap perfume closer to the stage, making him feel claustrophobic and sick. He almost regretted coming but was genuinely excited to see Charlotte's band headline and determined to make the most of it.

He looked up for the first time, searching for a familiar face in the handful of crew members setting up equipment. Under the glare of club lights, he felt exposed. Vulnerable. Surrounded by reminders of why he rarely went out in public. He removed his sunglasses to avoid looking like a pretentious douche, making the feeling worse.

He kicked himself for not wearing a hooded sweatshirt beneath his jacket. When he had to be in public, he was most at ease behind wide-rimmed sunglasses and hoods. And Halloween masks—they were his favorite. He could go anywhere in one of those things. The previous Halloween, he donned a Jason Voorhees mask and went to Powell's, browsing for books before grabbing a chocolate milkshake at Denny's. The straw fit perfectly through the mask's mouth hole. He'd practically lived at those spots back when he was a scrawny music nerd in high school, and he reveled in the warm familiarity. It was exhilarating to be anonymous, even for a few hours. If only it were socially acceptable to dress like a slasher film character more than once a year.

"Molly!" When she didn't react, Tyler cupped his free hand around the side of his mouth and shouted again. "Molly!"

The tiny blonde head of Killing Daisies' guitar tech turned, her eyes lighting up.

"Hey, Ty! Good to see your scruffy face." Molly pinched his chin and shook it. "Looking for the girls?"

"Yeah, can you get me backstage? Wasn't sure I'd make it, so I didn't get a pass."

"Pssh." Molly waved her hands dismissively. "No worries, my dude. Your face is your pass, but some of the newbies might not be cool enough to recognize you yet. Follow me."

As Tyler walked behind her, a sad wave of nostalgia rolled in. He missed the electricity of club shows. People scrambling to swap out instruments and equipment, boxes of merch hustled from the back of a van to tables out front.

While he was grateful for his band's hard-won success, there was much to love in those wild early days when they were still paying their dues while struggling to pay rent.

Molly glanced back. "Totally different than what Mr. World Tour's probably used to."

"No, it's cool. It's great. You don't know how good you have it 'til it's gone, you know?"

"Yeah, I love it too." She put a hand over her heart. "Nothing beats a sweaty, smoky rock club."

Molly opened one of the beat-up yellow doors in the hallway, grabbing something off a table. She slipped a black lanyard over Tyler's head, a laminated card settling in the center of his chest.

She glanced at her watch. "Shit! Sorry to ditch you, but I gotta grab Sandra's guitar."

"It's cool. I think I know my way around."

"No doubt." She turned, heading down the hallway on quick feet. "Enjoy the show!"

Tyler was still waving when he was startled by a pair of soft, cool hands covering his eyes from behind.

"Guess who."

The voice beside his left ear was distinctly feminine with a touch of gravelly edge.

If the sound of her voice hadn't been a dead giveaway, Tyler would've recognized her by the perfume she always wore—like what he imagined wild, exotic orchids would smell like. Maybe someday, he'd sniff an orchid to see if he was right.

"Hmm... let me think." He smiled, playing along. "David Bowie?"

"I can play all his songs but wouldn't look nearly as hot with a bright red mullet. Try again."

He laughed, imagining her on stage sporting the iconic Ziggy Stardust look. "Betty White?" His smile grew as she giggled in his ear.

"Wow. You suck at this, but you're getting warmer. Betty and I both have big tits and a sassy attitude."

He laughed again, suddenly forgetting how miserable he was. "Could it be… Charlotte? I hope so because I'm out of guesses, and my eyelid itches."

The hands fell away, and Charlotte moved to face him, crushing Tyler in a tight bear hug. His eyes closed as he melted into the warm embrace. It'd been weeks since he'd experienced anything more than an affectionate back slap from his bandmates, and a dizzying rush of comfort caught him off guard.

He didn't want to let go.

"I missed you!" She pulled back but remained close enough for him to see specks of silver glitter in her eyeshadow.

While he often caught guys shooting pervy looks at her body, the sweetness and warmth in her eyes snagged his attention the night they met. Like you could see what a rare, genuinely good person she was just by looking at them.

"I missed you too, headliner." He tapped her boot with the tip of his shoe. "Congrats on selling out the house tonight."

She bounced twice and shrieked with excitement, making a few people in the hallway turn their heads before resuming their duties. "I still can't fucking believe it. Speaking of sold-out gigs, how was Australia?"

"Hot, dry, kangarooey." Tyler lit a fresh cigarette, needing to do something with his restless hand.

She laughed, the unfiltered joy of it trailing down to his toes. Though they usually only got to hang out a few times a month, he'd missed her too. He hadn't realized how much until that moment, feeling the electric buzz of anticipation and pride coming off her.

"Did you just turn an animal into an adjective? No wonder Zack and Adam let you write all the lyrics."

He took a long pull off his nearly empty drink, ice cubes clinking against the glass. "The tour was fun, but I'm glad to be home." Aside from the crash and burn homecoming, it did feel good seeing familiar faces and places again.

"And home's glad to have you." Her smile slipped. "Where's Amy tonight?"

The misery came rushing back. With it, vivid images of Amy and Rafael doing the nasty on his couch. He tapped his ash into an empty beer bottle someone had set on a speaker.

"Different subject, please." Leaning on avoidance, distraction, and alcohol was the only way he'd get through the night without a meltdown. Besides, this was a big night for her band. She didn't need his drama in her head right before she hit the stage. "What's been going on with you?"

"Well, I dumped the bartender for feeling up a waitress."

"Heard about that." He swirled the ice in his glass. "Fucking loser. His chin dimple was ridiculous. By the way, Adam wants to be next in line."

She barked out a laugh. "He's cute, but I think I can do better than the guy who fingered his sister's best friend in a gas station bathroom."

Tyler's head tipped back, laughter roaring from his chest. "Holy shit, I forgot about that! Fucking Adam."

A man carrying an amplifier in each hand came up behind Charlotte, gruffly clearing his throat. They pressed themselves against the wall, letting him pass. Two more men followed, one carrying a pile of looped cords and the other, a microphone stand.

"Let's get out of the way." She aimed a thumb down the hallway. "Wanna see my shiny new guitar?"

"Abso-fucking-lutely."

Charlotte clapped, dragging him by the wrist to her dressing room. She walked to the closet, pulling out a black guitar case covered in stickers. Her ecstatic grin made Tyler forget everything weighing him down, the beginnings of a smile making his lips twitch. She set the case on the velvety loveseat beside the door and opened it. Carefully, she pulled out the black Fender Stratocaster with a tortoiseshell pickguard, gazing lovingly at the instrument as if it were a beloved child.

Tyler wolf-whistled. "Beautiful, Charlotte. May I?"

She held out the guitar. "By all means."

He set his drink on the makeup table. His hand was wet from condensation, so he wiped it on his jeans before taking the guitar. Charlotte pulled the cigarette from between his fingers, taking a puff.

"Breaking it in tonight?" He played the theme song to *The Munsters* before shifting into "All Along the Watchtower."

Charlotte clutched invisible pearls, a look of mock horror on her face. "It? You're one cold son of a bitch, Tyler. *She* is making her debut tonight, but there won't be breaking of any kind. I already told Sandra if she pulls crap like she did in Dallas, I'll gouge her green eyes right out of her head."

He remembered the story well. Over the summer, Killing Daisies played a punk festival in Dallas, and Sandra smashed her guitar to pieces before making a run at Charlotte's prized mint green Telecaster.

"I've busted up a guitar or two in my day." Tyler scratched the stubble on his chin. "But they were always mine. Sometimes, the music just grabs you by the balls and inspires a few moments of sheer madness."

"Well, our Sandra's plenty mad without the balls." She took another hit, the grayish smoke hovering between them.

Molly's head popped into the room. "Char, I need your Strat. Promise I'll be good to her."

Charlotte handed her the guitar, arching an eyebrow at Tyler. "See? She knows a lady when she sees one."

He laughed, raking his fingers through his hair to push it out of his eyes. "Have you seen my brother around?"

Charlotte nodded at the doorway. "Went to smoke a bowl with one of the lighting guys about fifteen minutes ago."

Another female head popped in that Tyler didn't recognize. "Charlotte, your bandmates are asking for you. Almost go time."

Charlotte inhaled deeply and let it out, her hands fluttering at her sides. He knew exactly how she felt. Even after hundreds of live performances, he still got pre-show jitters, too. But as soon as the colored lights roam the space, illuminating the sea of faces in the crowd, that feeling disappears, and you're flying high on adrenaline for hours.

But until then?

"Want a hit off my Jack and Coke?" he asked.

"Gross. I'll be fine." Charlotte came in close, tucking a loose strand of hair behind his ear. "Don't disappear after the show. I want to hear all about Australia."

"Sure." Tyler's mouth went dry, his pulse thumping in his neck. "Now go be a badass rock star."

When she headed for the stage, Tyler downed the rest of his drink. For the first time since coming home, he wasn't craving something harder.

As a close friend to half the members, he was biased, but Tyler was convinced Killing Daisies was one of the best bands to come out of Portland. And one of his favorite bands of all time. Their performances were an explosive mix of boot-stomping drumbeats, basslines that rumbled the rafters, and complex, angsty rhythms from Sandra and Charlotte's dueling guitars that absolutely blew him away. They were like a glittery, punk rock hurricane. Everyone in the room was directly in its eye, enjoying every second of the ride.

Aside from the Daisies' killer sound, they were also a hell of a lot of fun to watch. While Sandra pranced around the stage, bouncing in front of the microphone on the balls of her tiny feet, Amber sweated her heart out on the drums with the tip of her tongue sticking out the side of a massive grin that never slipped. He still couldn't remember their current bassist's name, but from what he'd heard from Charlotte and Sandra, it didn't matter because she wouldn't last much longer than the last one. The first time he saw Charlotte onstage with Scarlet Love Letter, she was on bass, and the way she played compared to this chick, it might as well have been a different instrument. Then again, no one on earth played like Charlotte. Like that first time, he couldn't keep his eyes off her. She was even more mesmerizing on guitar and grew better with time. And more beautiful. That was also impossible to miss.

"You're drooling, bro."

Tyler turned his head, shoving Matthew's chest while his brother laughed his stoned ass off. "I already told you—"

"Yeah, yeah. You're not interested in anyone." Matthew sipped whatever iced brown liquid was in his plastic cup. "Maybe she's too sane for you. You obviously prefer chicks who might burn all your clothes or boil your bunny."

He shoved Matthew again, his attention returning to the stage. To Charlotte. Before she came along, he didn't even think he could have a platonic relationship with a woman, let alone one who currently had every hetero guy in the room staring like she was their next meal. He was surprised Matthew never pursued her, but it was also a relief. Given his record of terrible breakups, she probably would've come to avoid Matthew like a rabid rat and, by extension, Tyler.

After the second encore, the audience was still screaming and chanting the band's name, but they'd gotten their money's worth and then some. When the women left the stage, they were drenched in sweat, grinning like they'd just experienced the most incredible high of their lives. He knew from experience they had.

Tyler and Matthew descended the stairs, giving them room.

"Anyone else get hit with a tampon?" Sandra handed her guitar to Molly before pulling a wrapped Tampax from between her breasts and waving it in the air. "Bet you only get cool things thrown at you, like panties and cigarettes." She tossed it to Tyler, and he caught it.

"Got hit with a bottle once." He threw the tampon over his shoulder. "That wasn't so cool."

Charlotte handed off her guitar before stomping down the stairs in her signature big black boots. "Gave you a gnarly scar, though." She ran her finger along the two-inch line of raised skin on his left temple.

Tyler scrubbed his hands over his face, concealing the embarrassing blush he felt heating his cheeks. Even though they were just friends, he was still a guy. If he had no reaction to being touched by a gorgeous woman who could wail on guitar like she just did, it was time to check his pulse.

"I have some band shit to go over with the girls." She touched her glistening chest, rapidly rising and falling as if she'd jogged a mile. "And I need to catch my damn breath! Meet you guys in my room?"

Matthew saluted, hooking his elbow through Tyler's as they walked back down the hallway toward her dressing room. Tyler touched his scar, certain he could still feel the pressure of her finger sliding along his skin. Either he'd already had too much to drink or not nearly enough.

After a few minutes of chatting with Matthew about the show, the door burst open, and Charlotte bounded into the room.

"Whew! Please tell me you missed that bad note I hit during 'Savior'." She flopped onto the purple loveseat beside Tyler, sweaty strands of dark hair glued to her forehead and cheeks.

Tyler tossed her a hand towel. "Nope," he lied. "The entire set sounded phenomenal." That was the truth.

He looked around, taking in the various posters and playbills tacked to the walls from performances the theater had housed over the years—everything from Black Flag to Phantom of the Opera.

"You're goddamn right it did!" Matthew chimed in from the nearest corner of the tight space, where he sat perched on the edge of a guitar amp. "That new song's a banger."

Charlotte bolted upright in her seat. "It is, right? I wrote it about the fucker who stole the hubcaps off my car. Who does that?"

"Crackheads and stalkers, I'd imagine." Tyler cringed, wishing he hadn't let the s-word slip. The glare he got from his brother made the guilt worse. While Tyler was busy with Amy and his band, Matthew had been there for Charlotte when some psycho started leaving threatening messages outside her house, on her car, and even inside the studio where her band was recording.

Her shoulders lifted. "My stalker was more interested in scaring the shit out of me than ripping parts off my car, but you never know."

"Sorry I brought it up," Tyler said. "I wasn't thinking."

"No worries. Hopefully, it's all in the past. And thanks to my kick-ass therapist, I can talk about it without losing my shit." She sniffed the bouquet of fragrant purple and white flowers arranged in a vase on the coffee table. "It's been almost a year since the last note, so I like to think the asshole croaked or moved far, far away." She tugged the card from between the blossoms, smiling as she read it. "Aww... They're from Eliza."

"Your manager?" Matthew asked.

She nodded, her hand flying to her mouth. "Oh, my god."

"What is it?" Tyler sat straighter.

Charlotte fell against the back of the loveseat, letting out a shriek of joy while her fists pumped in the air.

Tyler and Matthew looked at each other and laughed.

"I think she's cracked, dude." Matthew shook his head.

She sat up, clearing her throat. "Four of our Canadian shows have already sold out, and this is Eliza's way of saying congrats."

"Charlotte!" Tyler grabbed her shoulders, shaking them as she laughed. "That's incredible!"

"Congratulations," Matthew said. "When you're as big as Tyler, I can tell people I saw Killing Daisies back when they opened for karaoke at the Lamplighter."

She stuck her tongue out in his direction. "We have come a long way. Not bad for a few twenty-five-year-old chicks from the Eastside." She swept her hair off her neck, draping it over one shoulder.

"Not bad at all." Tyler leaned back, threading his fingers behind his head as his attention strayed to the exposed skin between her shoulder blades. "Oh, shit. Charlotte, your, uh, thing came undone."

"My what?"

He cleared his throat, shifting in his seat. "Your corset. The hooks at the top."

She turned, a coy smile tilting her lips. "Can you fix it? I don't want to bounce out of this thing on the walk to the car."

Matthew got to his feet. "Or I can do it."

Tyler glared as Matthew held back a grin, sitting back down.

"I've got it." Tyler struggled to get the tiny latch in place, his knuckles grazing her skin.

She was even softer than he remembered.

"Can you imagine if Sandra walked in?" Matthew chuckled. "I'd ask if she wanted to make it a foursome just to see the look on her face."

Charlotte tossed a bottle cap at him. "How's it going back there, Ty?"

Finally, he got the hook in place and sank back against the cushion. "All good."

The door swung wide, turning their heads.

Tyler's entire body tensed at the sight of Charlotte's leather jacket-clad ex-boyfriend. Her ex's bloodshot eyes dilated as they moved between the two men before landing on Charlotte. Tyler had only seen him in photos, but there was no mistaking the dickhead with the chin dimple and douchey flipped-up collar. A dickhead who'd picked the wrong day to try to make amends for being unfaithful to someone Tyler cared about.

"Look who it is, Matty." Tyler stood, planting himself within swinging distance of the guy's face. "Chimple the Cheating Fuckwad."

Matthew came up beside Tyler, shoulder to shoulder. "And he was just leaving unless he wants another ugly ass dent in his face."

"Okay, let's turn down the testosterone, boys." Charlotte wedged her way in front of her friends. "What the ever-loving fuck are you doing here?"

He tugged on the lanyard around his neck. "You invited me, remember?" You looked hot up there, babe. Sorry about—"

Charlotte laughed in his face, startling him.

"I looked hot? I'm glad the noises from my guitar didn't distract you from my tits." She waved slowly before her hand turned around, flipping him off. "No one gets second chances in my world. You made your choice, and it wasn't me. Bye-bye, asshole."

"Come on, Charlotte." He tried to approach, but Tyler blocked his path. Before Chimple could protest, a wave of recognition swept over his features. "Oh, shit. I can't believe I didn't notice before. She said she knew you, but I didn't believe her." He covered his mouth, his fingers decorated with ugly silver rings of various sizes and shapes. "You're Tyler Hall."

Tyler nodded toward the exit. "And you're a worthless shithead who's about to turn the fuck around and never bother her again."

"Hey, I'm a fan of yours, man." He leaned in, his voice lowering. "You know how it is when a ripe hottie's on your jock. I made one little mistake, and Charlotte's being a total rag about it. Can you help me out?"

Tyler suddenly wanted to add a few more bruises to his knuckles. "Yeah, man. I'll help you out." His hand clapped on the asshole's shoulder.

"The hell you will." Charlotte shoved past them, sticking her head out the door before belting an eardrum-piercing whistle.

Tyler gripped the front of Chimple's shirt to yank him into the hallway when two beefy security guards stepped in, muscling him out of the club.

Deflated, Tyler sank back into the couch. "Way to ruin my fun, Charlotte."

"I'll admit, I may have fantasized about you guys clocking that fucker, but he would've sued the shit out of you." She slid a hair tie off her wrist, twisting her hair into a loose pile on top of her head before returning to her seat. "Now, let's forget the last five minutes ever happened, okay?"

Tyler gave a nod. "Consider it done. As long as you go back to basking in the afterglow of the best show of your career."

At that, her smile returned, cooling the remains of his temper. "Consider it done."

"Hey, who sent those?" Matthew pointed to a bouquet of daisies on the makeup table, tied with a black ribbon.

"Oh. No idea. Maybe Chimple left them during the show. Hilarious nickname, by the way." Charlotte walked to the flowers, fishing out the card. "Big things are coming your way." She turned, her brows drawn together. "What the fuck's that about? It isn't even signed."

Tyler shrugged. "Kind of weird, but it sounds like someone knows tonight's just the beginning of your band's success. Selling out shows isn't easy."

"Which is why we should be celebrating." Matthew left his perch, grabbing a beer from the mini-fridge. "Why are we sitting in here with our thumbs up our butts when all the action's in the other room?"

"I'm not in the mood for that sort of action." Charlotte's gaze fell to the carpet. "Some dickheads from the club staff brought coke, so everyone will be unbearably obnoxious all night, talking garbled nonsense a mile a minute and sniffling like it's cold season. Then, Sandra and Molly will probably make out while all the guys hold their beers in their laps to hide their stiffies. Hard pass."

Tyler watched her for a moment before grabbing two beers from the scratched-up mini fridge. He handed one to Charlotte. "I'm with her. That sounds lame. I'd rather talk Charlotte into letting me play with her Strat again."

Matthew wiggled his eyebrows as he sipped his beer. "Ooh, sounds dirty. Can I watch?"

"Gross, Matt." She set her boots on the coffee table, her legs crossing at the ankles. "You can finger my strings anytime, Ty. Maybe you can infuse her with some of your mojo, magic, whatever, so we can rock arenas someday, too."

"Careful what you wish for, my friend. It isn't always the epic experience they promise in the brochure." Tyler returned to the loveseat, cracking his beer.

"So," she said, nudging Tyler's elbow, "what were your favorite things about Australia?"

"Hmm... I pet a koala. Byron Bay was incredible. Zack and I went scuba diving in the Great Barrier Reef while Adam puked on the boat. He was seasick for hours."

Her lower lip jutted out. "Poor Adam. Hope it wasn't before a gig."

"We had the night off. Probably would've blown chunks all over his drum kit if we didn't."

Amber bounded in, her bleach-blonde hair falling over her forehead and an oversized green hoodie pulled over her stage clothes. She pointed at Matthew. "Molly has some homegrown, and we're about to smoke. Join us?"

"Hells yeah. You guys in?"

Tyler and Charlotte shook their heads.

"I'm so jet-lagged, I'd just crash."

"And I've been drinking, so I'd get the spins." Charlotte held up her beer.

"Whatever, party animals." Amber pulled Matthew out the door by his arm.

A few beats of silence passed. Tyler couldn't remember the last time he'd been alone in a closed room with Charlotte, but even though it was rare, it wasn't awkward. They'd known each other too long and too well for that.

She turned, a smile tugging her lips. "Do you know how much that boy misses you when you're gone? I think he'll hide in your luggage next time."

"He knows he has an open invitation. I missed him too." He bumped her shoulder with his. "And I missed you. I thought about you on the cab ride over. Guess what we passed?"

"What?"

He looked forward to the reaction the next few words would bring. "The Keep Portland Weird graffiti."

An ear-to-ear grin bloomed on her face, just as he'd hoped. "Oh, my god! I think about you every time I pass it, too. What a night that was."

He imagined the same memories of the night they met playing in her head.

Walking hand-in-hand to the painted wall. Roaming the city in the dark, the cold wind whipping their faces.

"I can't believe no one's washed it off or covered it up in the last three years," she said.

"My fucking heart will shatter if that day comes." He clutched his chest.

"Do you ever wonder," she began, her smile falling, "what might've happened if I hadn't left that night?"

He averted his gaze, pouring the rest of his beer down his throat. It took him a few beats to convince himself she'd said the words.

"Charlotte..."

She waved it off, faking a smile that didn't reach her eyes. "Forget it. I don't know why I said that. Fucking beer, I guess."

"Of course, I have." He waited until she looked at him. "Our friendship's important to me, and I wouldn't trade it for anything, but... yeah. I've thought about it."

They were quiet again, sipping their drinks, letting the conversation they'd managed to avoid for three years hang heavy in the air. The truth was, Tyler had gone over that night about a hundred times in his head, imagining what would've happened if he'd ended up with Charlotte instead of Amy. He concluded he wasn't good enough for Charlotte back then. He was too young, reckless, and impulsive to be who she deserved. Instead, he ended up with the woman who, it turns out, wasn't good enough for him.

"So, how's the writing coming?" he asked, desperate for a subject change to guide them back to safer territory.

She let out a breath, the warmth of it grazing his face. Just like the night they met. There was clearly no escaping those memories, but even though they were complicated, he'd never want to.

"Great. I'm working on a few songs the girls are hyped about. And one I love that they aren't into yet. You know how it goes." She flicked a speck of glitter off her skirt. "Remember that Safe Start fundraiser we performed at last year?"

He nodded, remembering how tight their set was as he and Matthew watched from the front row, cheering their heads off.

"They've started a shelter program to help women kick drugs and get back on their feet, but they're low on funding. They'll have to turn people away. So, I tossed ideas to Amber and Sandra about how we could pitch in, and Eliza's helping us put together a compilation album of local artists to raise money."

It never failed to impress him how kindhearted she was. Especially when it came to helping others avoid the trauma she'd experienced as a child. He imagined all the mothers the program could help before their addictions stole them away from people who loved them.

"That's awesome, Charlotte. Let me know if we can do anything. Writing a check, a song, whatever you need."

Her eyebrows raised. "Sure, a song would be great. We could use a few big names to grab as much attention as possible. Thanks, Ty." She brushed ashes off the sleeve of his green army jacket. "You seem distracted tonight. Everything okay?"

He let out a humorless laugh. "Nope. Not at all. And I should take my dark cloud out of here and sleep it off before I ruin your night."

"Fuck that." She nudged his elbow. "Spill your guts, my friend. What's up?"

Tyler grabbed another beer and took a long drink, steeling himself. "I'll spare you the revolting details, but I caught Amy cheating." He took another sip to help swallow the lump rising in his throat. "I'm crashing at Matty's and divorcing her ass."

Charlotte's jaw dropped, shock rounding her eyes. "Seriously?"

"You know we've had problems for a while, but I hoped we'd get back on track when I got home." A puff of air escaped his lips as images of Rafael and Amy on the couch invaded his mind. "Not even close. I've been such a fucking fool to hang on this long."

"Oh, Ty." Charlotte frowned, her warm, guitar-calloused fingertips settling on his wrist. "I'm so sorry."

He sighed, taking in her expression. "Fuck, I'm the one who's sorry. I told you if I busted out my dark cloud, I'd ruin your night."

"Stop." She gave his arm a playful shove. "I'm a native Oregonian. I can handle dark clouds."

The corners of his mouth turned up in a halfhearted smile. Emotionally and physically drained, he rested his cheek against the back of the loveseat. Charlotte looked at him with a sad smile on her lips and pity in her eyes. He reflexively slid his arm behind her, the contact helping to soothe his raw nerves.

"You're lucky you knew her when she was still on top," he said. "Ever since her tour was canceled and her last album flopped, she's been... different. There's a darkness that wasn't there before. It's like she gets off on making people miserable, and I'm her favorite target."

He'd never told anyone that, not even Matthew. Whether he'd been protecting Amy or shielding himself from judgment, he didn't know. Now that there was no reason to hold back the truth, it felt good to get it out.

"She was getting off on people's misery long before you came along, trust me." Charlotte grabbed a lock of his hair and tugged. "Maybe you'll hate me for saying this, but I've always thought you could do better. And that getting married at twenty-three was insane."

He chuckled at that. "I appreciate your honesty. And you deserve better than a fuckwad bartender who can't keep his hands to himself." He touched the tip of her nose. "And I could never hate you, Charlotte. You're one of my all-time favorite humans."

"Ditto."

He was glad to see her smile return. A genuine, pity-free Charlotte smile this time. It had popped into his mind whenever he felt homesick and low during the tour, but nothing beat the real thing.

———◆◇◆———

Tyler, Matthew, and Charlotte trailed behind the throng of loud, drunken revelers shuffling out of Apocalypse. When they made it into the crisp predawn air, Tyler tossed his cigarette to the concrete, smashing it under his shoe.

"No rain?" He squinted at the cloudless sky, a million points of light suspended above their heads. "I'm still in Portland, right? I know I'm not that wasted."

"I guess Mother Nature missed the memo." Charlotte wrapped her arm around his waist, steadying him. "And yes, you are pretty wasted, my dear."

The warmth of her skin and the sweet scent of her hair made him pull her closer. As he held her against his side, she looked up through long, dark lashes and grinned. Maybe it was the alcohol or the lonely month away, but he couldn't tear his eyes from her. She was so beautiful, that radiant smile warming every vacant, lonely space in his heart. He thought again about the night they met, his hand itching to touch her face.

Matthew glanced over, his head swaying. "If you stand any closer, you'll get her pregnant." He belched so loudly it echoed in the street.

Tyler glared at his brother. "Shut up, shithead. And let me bum a smoke. I'm craving a menthol." He didn't know if it was the booze or the cold, but Charlotte's cheeks suddenly looked pinker.

"Don't say that too loudly, Matthew," she said. "If one of Amy's spies overhears, she'll have us all whacked."

He belched again, tossing Tyler a menthol. "Amy's the one who's whack."

Charlotte let out a drunken giggle, slugging Matthew's shoulder. "How's that for a whack, you goofy butthead?"

He rubbed the spot. "Dammit, Charlotte! Why don't you hit like a girl?"

"I do. You just need to stop hanging around ones that are weak as shit." She punched the air in front of his face, and he flinched. She and Tyler burst out laughing and almost walked into a tree.

"Who put that there?" Tyler mumbled.

"Mother Nature strikes again!" Charlotte patted the bark before steering him toward the sidewalk. "Your cab will be here soon."

"I hope it's not Chuck."

"Chuck?" she asked. "Who the fuck's Chuck?"

"That sounds like the beginning of a chorus, you guys." Matthew broke out in song loudly enough for every living thing on the block to hear. "Who the fuck's Chuck? He stole my truck. It's just my luck—"

Charlotte clapped a hand over his mouth. "In the name of all that's holy and awesome, shut the hell up, Matt."

A yellow cab pulled up to the curb.

"Here's your chariot, Ty." She opened her arms for a hug, and Tyler squeezed her against his chest, inhaling the wild orchids. "Thanks for coming to my show."

"Thanks for giving a shit that I'm back in North America." He let her go, stumbling back a step. "I almost forgot!" He dug into his pocket and pulled out a small blue bag, handing it to her.

"What's this?" She stared at the bag in her palm.

"Something I got in Sydney." Tyler shrugged. "Saw it and thought of you."

She opened it, pulling out a silver eucalyptus leaf necklace.

"You lost that fern pendant you wore all the time, so I thought you might like this."

"It's beautiful." She wrapped her arms around his neck, her warm, fluttering breaths tickling his ear. "I love it, Ty. Thank you."

"You're welcome." His heart rate kicked up, and he inhaled deeply before she let go too soon.

"Are you fucking *kidding me*, Tyler?"

The screeching voice made a shudder creep up his spine. He turned to find Amy running toward him at full speed from halfway down the block, murder in her eyes. Before he could react, she shoved his shoulders, knocking him back a few steps. He trapped her wrists in his hands as she struggled to get at Charlotte.

"Keep your hands off him!" Amy screamed, still trying to break free.

"Long time no see, you crazy bitch." Charlotte shook her head, a rueful smile playing on her lips. "Where's your overgrown fuckboy? He get fed up with your shit too?"

"Backstabbing little skank! You've been drooling over my husband for years, playing all innocent, but I know who you really are." Amy stopped struggling, shifting her attention back to Tyler. "How long, Tyler? How long have you been screwing this no-talent cunt behind my back?"

Charlotte scoffed. "No talent, huh? Tell that to the two thousand people who paid to see my band tonight. When was the last time you sold out a venue, sweetie?"

Tyler tightened his grip on Amy's wrists as she seethed, lunging at Charlotte.

Intermittent flashes lit up the street as someone snapped photos of the confrontation. He scanned the sidewalk where dozens of mumbling people gathered to watch the spectacle play out. After shooting an apologetic glance at Charlotte, Tyler dragged Amy inside the club.

"Where the hell are you taking me?" She still fought, but it was halfhearted since she was no longer playing it up for the crowd.

He released one of her wrists, and she landed a sharp slap across his cheek.

"Goddammit, Amy!"

His face stung as he turned the knob on the first door in the hallway. It opened to a small coat closet where they'd had a few naughty encounters in their wild, early days, but this was to be a far different experience. He pushed her inside, pressing his back against the door.

"Don't fucking hit me again," he warned, releasing her other wrist.

She took in the space, her perfectly manicured eyebrow raising. "Are we about to have angry make-up sex in this closet?" Her hand slipped beneath his shirt, and the second she touched his skin, he jumped away as if she'd burned him.

"No chance in hell. I just got you off the street before you did something that got us arrested."

Her lips, heavily glossed in their usual shade of crimson, pressed into a tight, angry line. "You gave me that bullshit speech about not even thinking about other women, and I find you with Charlotte Fucking Ross, of all people? How long have you been screwing her behind my back, you goddamn hypocrite?"

He huffed out a hot, exasperated breath. "Unlike you, I've never cheated. Charlotte's a friend, and I hugged her goodbye. End of story." He threw up his hands. "Not that it matters since we're separated. What I do now's none of your damn business."

Her hazel eyes rolled. "You know as well as I do that we're in this for life." She stepped closer, the scent of jasmine sweeping over his chest. "Remember when you said that at our wedding? You looked so handsome with the sun on your face, the ocean wind blowing through your hair."

As a hand lifted to touch him, he captured her wrist. Her throat moved as she swallowed, returning it to her side.

"Those people don't exist anymore." His chest burned, a surge of painful memories he'd tried to bury striking all at once. "But I remember a lot of things, Amy. Like when I saw you grab Zack's crotch when you thought I was in the bathroom. Or when you shoved your tongue down my sound engineer's throat. You just played it all off like it was a goddamn joke! And what about the rumors you've been screwing Issac for years? Have they been true this entire goddamn time?" The coats hanging all around them absorbed his shouted words. "Issac's bedded groupies all over the world. His dick probably has the fucking Ebola virus at this point. Now I have to get an STD test tomorrow for fucking my wife!"

Amy's hands knotted in her hair. "Don't be disgusting. I'd never touch him. I got close last year when you were all mopey, constantly accusing me of shady shit I never did, but—"

"I'm sure you did all of it, Amy!" The rush of his breath ruffled the hair around her face. "All of it! And I've been a weak, pathetic fool for trusting you when the truth was staring me in the face. I'm done with that. Done with you."

She stepped closer, her intense gaze trained on his face. "I can't let you go, Ty. You're the best thing in my life. My career's careening off a cliff, my family isn't speaking to me, and my band's in shambles." She grabbed his hand before he could react, clinging with a death grip. "Please, I need you."

"You need me for the wrong reasons." Tyler wrenched his hand free.

Her gaze skittered across his face, clearly searching for a way through the wall he'd put between them. "We'll have a baby. I know it's what you want. A few stretch marks and saggy tits aren't the end of the world."

"Amy..." His eyes slid closed, his heart stuttering in his chest. An image of the future he'd ached for only hours before burned brightly in his mind. For a fleeting moment, he let it chase away the fear of living alone, dying alone. When his eyes reopened, she'd moved closer. The warm alcohol haze made it easy to forget why he should resist the temptation to taste her. To skim her plump bottom lip with his teeth until she moaned his name.

"I'm taping that indie film in L.A. this weekend. Come with me, and we'll start trying. Or we can go to that little cabin you love and just be together." With a tear sparkling in her eye, she stepped closer. "We'll be even stronger than we were. Please don't give up on me." The damp heat of her breath on his lips and the scent of her skin drew him closer. "I promise I'll never hurt you like that again."

With her words, the memory of her buck naked and riding Rafael broke through the fog. "Fuck this. You won't hurt me again because I won't let you." He grabbed for the doorknob.

She fisted the front of his shirt, pulling him away from the only exit. "We can start over! We can—"

"Stop!" Tyler pried her fingers loose, stepping back. "There's no 'we' anymore, Amy. If you're really sorry for what you did, show me the respect of leaving me alone. Let me build a new life. Get clean, get into therapy, and do the same." His finger stabbed the air inches from her face, making her flinch. "And stay the hell away from Charlotte."

"Don't let it get to the media," she said once he turned around. "Please. My tie to you is the only thing keeping the press interested, and I can't lose the exposure. Don't say we're separated. At least give me that."

Her priorities didn't surprise him. They just reinforced that he was doing the right thing.

"Fine. When it gets out, it won't be because of me."

Tyler walked out of Apocalypse, drawing a deep breath of cold air. His cab still waited at the curb, but he needed a moment outside to regroup before being confined in another tight space. He was grateful the crowd had dispersed, drifting further down the street in pairs and small, huddled groups. Their drunken laughter echoed off the darkened storefronts.

"You okay, man?"

He turned to find Matthew and Charlotte leaning against the club's brick wall, aiming concerned looks in his direction.

"Figured you guys had taken off." Tyler lit a cigarette, watching the smoke curl around his fingers. "I'm beat. Meet you back at your pad." He pounded Matthew's fist.

"Cool. Key's under the mat."

Charlotte's eyes found Tyler's before she gave him another quick hug good-bye. "Hell of a way to end the night, huh?" When she pulled back, he saw genuine concern on her face. "Take care of yourself, Ty. Call me if you need someone to talk to besides this knucklehead." She aimed a thumb at Matthew. "See you at movie night at Sandra's?"

"You got it." He crawled into the backseat, waving as the cab pulled away.

"Have a good night, Mr. Hall?"

Tyler made out Charles' blurry face behind the wheel and sighed.

"Hey, Chuck. Gotta light?"

6

Charlotte

After Tyler's taxi made a right on 122nd and disappeared, Charlotte and Matthew headed toward the parking lot to meet Sandra. Charlotte looked at the necklace still clutched in her hand, marveling at how the intricate veins in the leaf shimmered under the electric glow of the streetlights. While she tried not to look too much into the gesture, the gift was proof Tyler had thought about her when he was on the other side of the world. When she slipped the chain over her head, the silver leaf settled in the center of her chest—directly over her thudding heart.

"You like him." Matthew said it like a statement, not a question, and anxiety prickled her throat.

"Who, Tyler? Of course, I do." Charlotte kept her boots moving forward. "So do you. So does Sandra. He's one of our best friends. What's your point?"

Matthew's knees wobbled, his palm smacking the nearest wall to steady himself. "You don't fool me, Charlotte."

She turned to him. "Did you and Sandra get together and decide to gang up on me or something? Give me a smoke before I hit you again." The scent of curry wafted over from a nearby restaurant, making her stomach growl.

He lit a menthol, holding it out.

"Do you really think I'm dumb enough to have feelings for a married man?" She took the cigarette. "He's fun to go to shows with and stuff, but completely off limits. And I'm fine with that."

"So, now that he and Amy broke up, you won't try to hit that?"

Charlotte stopped again, hands on her hips. "'Hit that'? Really? Are we in high school?"

Matthew's feet slowed. "You know why I never made a move on you when we first started hanging out?"

Smoke streamed from her lips as she laughed. She was grateful he'd never pursued her that way. Matthew was good-looking but a bit young and immature for her taste. As a friend, it made him a hell of a lot of fun. As a boyfriend, she would've strangled him the first week. She preferred having a sweet, protective brother from another mother who enjoyed many of the same simple joys she did. Like getting stoned and eating pizza while wearing sweatpants.

"Because you prefer uncomplicated blondes to hella complicated brunettes?" She walked faster.

"True." He jogged to catch up. "But also, because you've been crushing on Ty since you met."

When Charlotte thought about that day, her chest squeezed. Walking away from Tyler was one of her biggest regrets. She'd had way too many post-show beers to keep heading down this particular stretch of memory lane for the second time that night.

"I'll admit, I had a crush back then, but me and Tyler are meant to be friends." If only she could believe that. She took another deep hit of minty nicotine and passed the cigarette to Matthew. "And so are we. You know as well as I do that if we hooked up, one of us would royally fuck it up, and our friendship would end. I'd never risk that."

"Agreed. Plus, you're into brooding artist types, and I'm holding out for Debbie Harry. Or Lisa Kudrow."

She burst out laughing. "Talk about diverse tastes. They're both blonde though, so I was right about that." Her voice slurred—way too many beers.

A chilly breeze kicked up, rustling the leaves on the trees and making her shiver. The adrenaline and alcohol had kept her nice and toasty until that point, making it easy to forget her black peacoat in the closet at the club. She rubbed her goosebumped arms, picking up the pace to get her blood pumping faster.

"Want my flannel?" Matthew started to slip off his gray and black plaid overshirt.

"No, we're almost to the car. Thanks, though."

"If you do have a thing for Ty, you know I'm not judging you, right?"

"Back to this?" She sighed impatiently, opting to dodge the question. "I just hope for his sake he's finally figured out he can do better than Amy. I guess we both learned that lesson the hard way."

She thought about their conversation in her dressing room, how sad Tyler sounded when he said it was over. The way each syllable hung heavy with resignation hadn't left her. It wasn't the first time she'd heard him on the brink of calling it quits, but maybe this time was different. Maybe he'd actually follow through.

"You know why he's stayed so long, don't you?"

Charlotte shrugged. "Because she's exciting, gorgeous, and he loves her? Or at least, he loves the fake ass version he saw before her true colors bled through."

"It's more than that. Tyler wants what our parents had. When we were kids, we'd avoid whatever room they were in because they were always pawing at each other." Matthew grinned, his hazy blue eyes lifting to the night sky. "Back then, we thought it was gross, but looking back... Who doesn't want that? To be so crazy about someone you can't even look at them without wanting to touch them."

"Sounds pretty amazing to me."

"Right? Almost two decades later, he still talks about how Mom and Dad looked at each other. When I first saw Amy and Tyler together, all I saw was lust."

She could've done without that reminder. She dragged a hand through her hair, the roots still damp with sweat, and tried to shrug off the memories of that time. Losing her shot with Tyler was bad enough. Having to witness Amy all over the man she didn't deserve was pure torture.

"I'll admit," Matthew said, "it grew to be more. I think he found what he was looking for their first year or so, and he's been chasing that ghost ever since. Hoping things will get better so they can have kids and a happily ever after.

Getting supremely fucked over in the process." He smacked a lamppost, the metallic clang echoing through the empty street. "It kills me that even with all the people in his corner, he's still so goddamn lonely he thought being on his own was worse than living like that."

Charlotte touched her chest, her fingertips brushing the silver leaf. That loneliness was written all over Tyler's face the moment they met. No matter how massive his crowds were or how fiercely his friends loved him, it was always there.

"You think it's really over?"

"After what she pulled today, probably." Matthew sighed, his head shaking. "But who fucking knows with Tyler? That fool doesn't know when to quit sometimes."

She went quiet, digesting his words. She wished she could help somehow. To get Tyler to open his eyes and build a better life before enduring more pain at the hands of someone who'd never been worthy of all he had to offer.

"Can I tell you a secret?" Matthew asked.

"Yes, please."

"He has feelings for you, too."

She stopped, her wide eyes stinging with the cold. "What are you talking about?"

He chuckled at her expression. "Are you really that surprised? He won't even admit it to himself, but the way he was holding you outside that club tonight's Exhibit A."

"That's a bit of a stretch." She shivered, rubbing her arms as she turned his words over in her head. "I was keeping his drunk ass from kissing the sidewalk."

"The way he looked at you..." Matthew grinned. "It wasn't the sidewalk he wanted to kiss." He slipped out of his flannel, wrapping it around her shoulders. "Why do you think Amy flipped out like that? She sure as hell saw it, too."

"Oh, please. She would've flipped out if I'd handed him a toothpick."

"Exhibit B," he continued, undeterred, "was how he smiled when he opened the flyer for your show. He was wrecked and exhausted and ready to give up, but he fucking *smiled*, Charlotte. All he wanted to do was get shitfaced on my couch, but he made it tonight. To see you play."

Sandra ran up behind them and jumped on Matthew's back, her legs wrapping around his waist and spindly arms circling his neck. "Giddyup, motherfucker! How amazing was I tonight?"

Matthew returned the cigarette to Charlotte, tucking his hands under Sandra's knees. "You were a guitar-wielding goddess, Sandarella. And as payback for letting me watch, I'll do my best not to puke in your car."

She slid off his back, pointing to a row of shrubs in front of a darkened restaurant. "You'd better bend over those bushes and get it out before you even look at my ride."

He ruffled Sandra's hair. "You just want to check out my finely sculpted ass. Admit it."

"Gross, dude." She slapped the back pocket of his jeans and laughed. "Just the thought of a hairy male ass does nothing except make me gayer."

Once Matthew had convinced Sandra he wouldn't throw up, they all climbed into her ocean-blue hatchback.

He leaned forward, sticking his head between Charlotte and Sandra in the front seats. "If you drive us to Burger Hut, I'll be your best friend."

Sandra pushed a tape into the cassette player. "Only if you buy me curly fries."

"Deal." He gave a thumbs-up. "Hey, we just came out with a few new seasonals at High Notes. You guys wanna come for a tasting tomorrow?"

Matt's brewery specialized in Northwest Pale Ale and lagers—varieties that had become Charlotte's favorites after years of sampling his latest concoctions. One of her favorite perks of their friendship was drinking for free.

"Ick." Sandra's tongue jutted out. "I'm sure what you make is fabulous, but I'm so not a beer girl."

He looked at Charlotte, an eyebrow cocked above the rim of his glasses.

"If you go for a run with me in the morning, you're on."

"Running?" His face scrunched in disgust. "Ugh. I guess. But you'll quickly discover why I played Dungeons and Dragons in high school instead of soccer."

As Matthew and Sandra sang along to the music, Charlotte's thoughts drifted back to Tyler. Matthew's words from moments before felt tattooed on her brain.

He has feelings for you, too.

Hearing that from his brother almost made it worse because it didn't change anything. Tyler was still off-limits. He was still married and could end up back with Amy if she convinced him to forgive her. When her thoughts circled back to the day they met, she cranked up the stereo to help drown them out.

The backs of his fingers brushing her cheek. Her hand in his. The unmistakable trust in his eyes as he shared his secrets.

She turned up the volume, Joan Jett's thunderous voice flooding the car. The musical chaos quieted her brain, but one nagging fact was inescapable—she had intense, definitely romantic feelings for a married man. Despite her best efforts to squash those feelings over the years, they were real, growing stronger every time she saw him.

And she feared a lot more than a bad reputation.

7

Tyler

January 1992

The Marquis was one of Tyler's favorite venues long before he set foot on its massive stage. The vibe was great, the diverse crowd had plenty of room to breathe on the floor, and it showcased local up-and-coming bands every night of the week. Its high, muraled ceilings created stellar acoustics, and the club's well-stocked bar offered an array of liquors and mixers from around the world. The decor was very "Old Portland" and made him feel like he was sipping his bottle of Widmer in another era. Or a Gus Van Sant film.

"Tyler! What's up, man?" Scott gave him a friendly back slap, spilling some beer on his green army jacket. They'd worked together in the kitchen at Glisan Pizza Company in high school and lost touch after graduation. "I hear your band on the radio all the time now. You're blowing up fast."

"Yeah, it feels good to get decent airplay after five years of busting our asses. It hasn't felt fast to us." Tyler assessed the beer stain on his sleeve. Nothing a good spot cleaning wouldn't fix. "What band you here to see?"

"Scarlet Love Letter," Scott said with a smile. "I'm going out with Sarah."

"Lead guitar, right?" .

"Yeah, she's incredible. I'm deeply in like, my friend. Deeply."

Tyler laughed. "Cool. Never seen them, but I've heard good things." He'd also heard the lead singer, Amy Carey, was a stunning, incredibly talented train wreck.

Scott held up the backstage laminate strung around his neck. "Hey, we're twins!"

Tyler looked down at his pass. "Yeah, our manager hooked me up. We're trying to find a killer local band to open for us this summer. I came to scope out Crestfall, and they were great, so mission accomplished. I'll probably bail after my beer."

"Seriously?" Scott glanced at his watch. "Scarlet will be on soon. If you stick around, we can hang backstage afterward. I've never known you to pass up hot girls and free booze."

That clinched it for Tyler. He shrugged. "Might as well."

The overhead lights dimmed, and the crowd quieted as three brilliant green beams illuminated the stage. The portly owner of the Marquis appeared, approaching the microphone at its center. "Ladies, gentlemen, and everyone in between, welcome to the stage, Scarlet Love Letter!"

The crowd exploded as a striking woman with dark, waist-length waves strutted onstage and picked up the black and white bass guitar. She wore a silver corset, black miniskirt, and black combat boots, looking like the punk rock version of a Victoria's Secret model. Tattooed black and gray ferns and flowers covered her left shoulder. She hit a low E, and Tyler felt the tone vibrate through his chest.

"That's Charlotte Ross." Scott elbowed Tyler's ribs. "Scorcher, right?"

"Yeah, she's gorgeous."

He was captivated, watching her warm up with her eyes shut and a delicate smile on her lips until movement on the left side of the stage snagged his attention. A guy with bleached, spiky hair and a black leather vest sat behind the drums, spinning his sticks between his fingers. Tyler laughed at the young, poseur version of Billy Idol.

"That's Isaac. Total dick," Scott shouted, louder than necessary, directly into Tyler's right ear.

Scott erupted in screams and whistles when a tanned, curvy beauty walked out, swaying her hips for the audience. She took her place in one of the beams, holding a gold guitar. Judging by Scott's reaction, this was his girlfriend, Sarah. Tyler was grateful Scott was too busy cheering to shout in his ear again.

A red beam of light illuminated the spot behind the center microphone. The crowd began shouting, clapping, and stomping the wooden floor, making it tremble beneath their feet.

Curtains parted on the left side of the stage, and a tall, long-legged goddess with flowing crimson hair emerged, grabbing her guitar like a battle axe. Her tight black dress brushed the middle of her thighs, and her bra's red lace peeked out through the plunging neckline.

The infamous Amy Carey stood front and center, bathed in red light. "Howdy, Portland! Did you miss me, fuckers?"

The crowd went wilder than before. Tyler plugged his ears because the shrieking, vodka-scented woman next to him was going to make him deaf on the side Scott had spared. Her pink Scarlet Love Letter T-shirt was stretched so tightly across her chest that it surprised him she could expand her lungs enough to shout like that.

Amy growled, roared, and screamed through the bulk of their set, with a few pretty ballads mixed in for balance. She had a powerful, slightly raspy voice that demanded attention and serious skills on guitar. But her dynamic stage presence grabbed him and didn't let go. Tyler wouldn't have called it love at first sight, but he definitely wanted to fuck Amy Carey when she strutted into that spotlight. Judging by the hungry looks on the men's faces—and some of the women's—he wasn't alone.

Charlotte Ross was the only thing successfully competing for his attention amid the musical chaos and furious crush of the crowd. The beauty of her blissed-out face and those skilled fingers flying across her strings was unlike anything he'd seen. She seemed content on the sidelines while Amy worked the crowd, but after being around musicians most of his life, he could see who their most talented member was.

After the show, Tyler, who hadn't even wanted to stay, didn't want to leave. He followed Scott backstage and waited, nursing a Scotch while nodding to the beat of the Bikini Kill album playing on a stereo in the corner.

And then he saw her.

When Charlotte Ross walked in, their eyes briefly met as she approached the drink table, grabbed a bottle of red wine, and poured herself half a glass. She took a long sip, slowly scoping out the room before walking back toward the exit.

Tyler pushed off the wall to catch up. Her eyes widened when she saw him, and he slowed his movements.

"Hi. Sorry. Um, I'm Tyler. Didn't mean to startle you. I just—"

"Not interested."

He blinked. "What?"

"In whatever you're going to try to sell me. I'm not interested."

"No, I just wanted to say that was an impressive set."

"Thanks." She crossed her arm over her chest. The uncertainty in her expression was clear. "You friends with Isaac?"

Tyler fought to keep a straight face at the thought of being friends with the moron in the corner choking on a bong rip.

"Nope. Never met him. I'm here to see Crestfall. My band's looking for an opener, so our manager sent me to check them out."

"What band are you in?" Charlotte sipped her wine, her posture still stiff and unsure.

"Tomorrow Mourning."

Her face brightened. "I've heard of you guys! My friend, Sandra, keeps raving about your show at La Luna, and I've heard your album at least a dozen times in her car. Great stuff."

"Thanks." He was relieved she was beginning to relax. "If you're free, you guys should see us at Satyricon next Saturday. I can leave passes at the door."

"Sure, thanks." Her smile grew. "Sandra will flip her shit when I tell her. You the frontman?"

"Is it that obvious?"

She chuckled softly. "You give off that vibe, I guess."

His forehead creased with equal parts confusion and curiosity. "What vibe is that?"

"Confident, bold, and good-looking with a healthy dash of cocky. Crowds eat that shit up, so cheers." She raised her cup.

Tyler laughed, swirling the liquor in his glass. "Pretty accurate assessment less than five minutes in."

"I'm a woman of many talents." She lifted her cup to her grinning, incredibly kissable lips. He wanted to know what they tasted like before the night was over.

"I don't doubt that. Your skills on that stage were impressive. Ever fronted a band?"

"Nah, too much pressure." A handful of loud drunks stumbled in. Charlotte moved closer to Tyler, raising her voice as the room's volume increased. "I'd rather focus on my instrument than hyping the audience."

"I get that." As the alcohol warmed him from the inside, Tyler struggled to keep his eyes from drifting into inappropriate territory. The woman was wearing the hell out of that corset. "So, how long have you been playing bass?"

"Six years." She wiped sweat from her forehead with her wrist. "Guitar's my first love, though. Been playing that since I was twelve. I'm hoping I can ditch the bass for it someday."

His brows pinched. "Why didn't you get a guitar spot?"

Charlotte tossed back the rest of her wine. "It's a seniority thing. Sarah's known Amy longer, so she got lead." She shrugged as if it didn't matter, but a subtle dip in her tone gave her away. "I'm just glad to be in a band that's progressing. My last two were full of flakes with zero ambition."

"Been there. You can only rock out in your mom's garage so long before it gets sad."

"Exactly!" Charlotte touched the back of his hand, his skin tingling from the unexpected but welcome contact. "I wanted to do my thing in front of an audience, and here I am."

"Here you are. With an empty glass. Can I get you another drink?" Tyler pointed at the table.

"I'm good, thanks. So, what'd you think of Crestfall?" Something was off about her expression.

"Unique sound, great lyrics. I could see our fans being into them."

Charlotte looked around and took a step closer to Tyler. "Can I tell you a secret?"

He half-smiled, enjoying the conspiratorial air between them.

She moved to his ear, lowering her voice—finally, a person who respected his desire to preserve his hearing. "The lead singer, Chad, is a pompous, misogynistic sack of crap. He keeps calling us 'honey' and 'accidentally' walking in on us when we're changing. He even had the balls to tell me my butt's too big for the fucking skirt I'm wearing!"

From what he'd seen, there was absolutely nothing wrong with Charlotte's butt, or any other part of her, for that matter. Tyler wanted to find the guy and punch his face in for being such an asshole.

"Is that the secret you want me to keep?"

She shook her head. "I smeared salmon mousse all over the closet in his tour bus. And under his mattress." She laughed, mischief sparkling in her eyes. "Good luck getting backstage booty when your bus reeks like rotting fish, Chad."

"Nice one." Tyler laughed at the mental image, high-fiving her. "You shouldn't have to put up with that shit."

"I'd boot him out on his ass if I could, but Amy has our manager convinced he's a misunderstood genius or whatever." Charlotte's eyes rolled. "I just thought you might want a heads-up about what kind of guy you're thinking about being around for however many weeks on tour."

"Thinking's over. He's out."

"Really? Sweet." Charlotte rubbed her hands together. "I'm one step closer to blacklisting the motherfucker."

Their eyes remained connected as they laughed. Tyler was thrilled that this beautiful woman seemed to be flirting with him but was also surprised by how comfortable he felt. From her eyelashes to her take-me-as-I-am attitude, there was nothing fake about her. He felt no pressure to be anything but himself. It was a rare experience, and he was eager to see where things went.

Charlotte's eyes drifted across the room, and her smile fell.

He followed her line of sight to a guy with a green mohawk rubbing his nose while passing a small mirror to the girl beside him. She picked a straw off the mirror and inhaled a thin line of white powder.

"I have to go." Charlotte's feet were already moving toward the exit. "Great meeting you, Tyler."

"Wait. What?"

She bolted from the room on quick, heavy steps before he could blink.

In his experience, seeing drug use out in the open was as much a part of backstage life as hard liquor and handsy groupies. Why had it bothered Charlotte so much? He headed for the exit, hoping to find out if she was okay.

He searched the faces in the crowded hallway and spotted a splash of dark hair rounding a corner. He followed to find her tossing back a shot of clear liquid at the bar.

"Hey, what happened back there? Did I say something wrong?"

"It's not you. I... Hard drugs freak me out." Her jaw tightened, and she leaned closer, her voice lowering so only he could hear. "My mom died of an overdose when I was a kid."

"Jesus." He didn't know what he'd expected her to say, but it wasn't that. "That's awful."

Sadness settled into her features, removing all traces of the warm, carefree smile from earlier. If they hadn't just met, Tyler would've pulled her into his arms. Instead, he signaled to the bartender to give her a refill and serve him a shot of whatever she was having.

"Sorry," she said. "I shouldn't blurt out something so heavy, especially to a stranger. Feel free to run far and fast." As soon as it was poured, she tossed back her shot. "Sometimes performing shuts off my filter."

He caught the slump of her shoulders, the slight tremble of her fingers as they clutched the empty glass. The demons she wrestled with were ones he knew well—grief, resentment, the nagging compulsion to shove the hurt deep inside yourself so you can face the world.

"Don't apologize. I lost my dad when I was ten." Her chin lifted, and she sucked in a sharp breath. "Motorcycle accident. The road was slick, and he didn't wear a helmet because he wasn't going far. If he had, he probably would've made it."

The flash of recognition in her expression made the urge to hold her even stronger. In their brief exchanges, he'd learned they shared a passion for music, but above that, they shared a pain most people never know. One with no bottom that cut so deeply, on some level, you were always bleeding out.

"I tense up and get a stomachache every time I hear a motorcycle, so I get it." He swallowed the emotion rising in his throat. "And for the record, I smoke weed, but I think hard drugs are disgusting. I'd never touch them."

Her mouth tilted in an adorable half-smile. "Good to know."

"Hey, I have an idea." He tossed back his shot, slamming the glass on the bar. "I've had a riff stuck in my head all week. I hear it before I sleep, when I wake up. It's haunting me, and I want the city to tell me what comes next. Wanna get out of here?"

Her eyebrows drew together as she studied his face. Being scrutinized after such a rare, raw moment of vulnerability felt strange. It was even stranger that he didn't want to run from it. His gaze fell to her lips as they twisted and puckered in contemplation, his own itching to find out if they felt as soft as they looked.

The corner of her tempting mouth tipped up again, and she held out her hand. "Lead the way."

Her skin felt like warm silk, and the way her smile bloomed at the contact made him tighten his grip. They headed into the cold night air, a light breeze dragging orange and gold leaves along the abandoned sidewalks.

"So, where are we going at one in the morning?"

"This is Portland, Charlotte. The city's at her best when all the drones are safe in their beds, and the misfits roam the streets looking for trouble."

Her eyebrow lifted. "Are we looking for trouble?"

"No, we're looking for inspiration."

They made it to the end of the block, past the front of a boarded-up restaurant. He led her to the side wall where someone had spray-painted Keep Portland Weird ten feet high in bright green and pink between an orange graffiti penis and a Sasquatch bumper sticker.

Charlotte's unrestrained laughter made him grin. "If massive orange dicks inspire you, we've hit the jackpot."

"The important part is what's under the dick." He joined in when she laughed again. "Keep Portland Weird. It's like someone had witnessed enough mundane bullshit that day to compel them to do something about it."

Her head tilted as she stared up at the words.

"It's a declaration," he continued. "A plea to everyone who passes to let the city hold on to its weird, freaky nature. You can take your million Starbucks franchises and mini-malls and shove them up your ass. We own this city. The weirdos who want to savor our smoky whiskey bars and overcrowded rock clubs before some asshole bulldozes them to build condos or another Nike factory."

"Wow." She nodded slowly. "I feel like a fool for getting distracted by that penis."

They laughed, her voice rough from the cold and pouring everything into singing backup at her show. "Wanna see something even cooler?"

"I'm a native. There isn't much in this city I haven't seen."

His grin widened at the glint of a dare in her eye. "Trust me."

Tyler tugged her by the hand another three blocks, past homeless people huddled under blue tarps and loud partiers drifting out of bars and strip joints with glowing neon signs.

He stopped to listen. Giddy anticipation bubbled through him when he caught the distant sounds of a guitar. It grew louder as they picked up their pace, and he led Charlotte up a flight of creaky steps to a second-floor apartment.

"Wait." Her feet stopped, and she tugged his hand. "Who lives here?"

A broad smile stretched his face. "You'll see."

He opened the door without knocking, and they entered the cramped room with tan walls and ratty brown carpet. Eight people sat on cushions around the source of the guitar music—a man with a shock of shoulder-length white hair and a gray beard nearly reaching his belly. The sounds coming from his strings were hypnotizing—calming and stimulating all at once. As Tyler lowered himself onto an empty cushion, he felt like a restless snake being charmed back into its basket. Charlotte took the spot beside him, her eyes round and glued to the strings being plucked and strummed with a skill that only comes from decades of dedicating your soul and sweat to your craft. As the music swelled, he saw her quickly swipe a tear from the corner of her eye.

Five songs later, the spell was broken. The guitar was returned to its rack, everyone thanked the player for sharing his gift, and the small, fortunate audience drifted out the door. Tyler took Charlotte's hand again as they headed back toward the club.

"So, what did you think?"

She took a breath and held it. "Who was that?"

"Everyone calls him Master Jim. He used to play clubs around the city but turned his nose up at fame every time it came knocking. Now, he plays in his living room every night from eleven to whenever he's finished."

In high school, Tyler sat in that living room for hours every weekend, soaking in brilliance the cold, brutal music industry never had a chance to tarnish. There wasn't a music class in the world that could compare to what he learned sitting on that apartment floor.

"I've never heard anything like it," she said. "His chord progressions, his speed…"

"I know." The look of awe on her face warmed his chest. He took note of how her skin glowed when something moved her, and he hoped to have the chance to see it again sometime. "I've never brought anyone else to Jim's. He's been like a special secret I've never wanted to share, but after seeing how you play, I knew you'd appreciate him."

A crease formed between her brows. "How do I play?"

He breathed in the night air, pulling in the scent of evergreens and wet earth from the previous morning's storm. "When you came out, you acknowledged the crowd, but it was obvious they weren't what brought you there. The second you touched the strings, your head tipped back, and your eyes closed like nothing mattered but what you've created with your band. You were sweating two songs in because you poured everything into those notes. Like you needed them to breathe."

The fluorescent glow of the Marquis Club lit up the sidewalk ahead, and she stopped before the light touched them. They stood in the shadow of an oak tree that dwarfed every manmade structure on the block. When he turned to face her, all he saw were the edges of her chocolate-brown eyes and the shape of her mouth. He inched closer, her warmth and the scent of red wine and wild flowers radiating from her skin.

"I do." At the quiver in her voice, he gently stroked her knuckles with his thumb. "I need music to breathe. When my mom would come home trashed, the voices on my records talked me down from the ledge. Janis, Iggy, Bowie, Patti. They lulled me to sleep when I'd find her passed out on the floor, and I was afraid she wouldn't wake up. They knew where it hurt because they hurt too." She exhaled, the warmth of it rising to his face. "When I learned how to make my own music, it was like ripping open those wounds so they could get the oxygen they needed to scab over and heal."

Every word reached into his chest, touching the wounds he'd been just as desperate to close. Wounds only music had the power to heal. This woman, a stranger just an hour before, was tormented by the same demons that drove him. She spoke truths he'd struggled to articulate since he lost his father, truths he was sure no one would ever understand. He didn't play music to become famous; he played to be that voice for other broken people. One that makes them feel seen and safe. The voice that talks them down from the ledge, drowning out the one in the back of their mind that whispers *jump* in their most desperate moments.

"Did you find the inspiration you were looking for?" she asked.

"No." His hand lifted, the backs of his fingers grazing the soft skin of her cheek. "I found something better."

The door of the club slammed against the brick wall behind it. A flood of people clad in black leather, torn blue jeans, and babydoll dresses poured onto the sidewalk and into the street.

She cleared her throat and dragged him into the light. "One more drink before last call?"

A corner of his mouth hitched up, a rush of warmth heating his face when her smile returned. "Lead the way."

When they returned to the backroom, the crowd had thinned, but Scott was still beside Sarah on the couch, murmuring something in her ear. About a dozen other people were drinking, smoking, and laughing with half-closed eyes and drunken smiles. Janis Joplin's soulful voice crooned about freedom beneath it all.

Tyler poured a glass of the wine he saw Charlotte drinking earlier and handed it to her before pouring himself another two fingers of Scotch. They leaned against the wall as it hummed with vibrations from the music.

When she lifted the wine to her lips, a gruff female voice shouted in a nearby room before erupting into laughter. The click of high heels grew louder, and Tyler's head turned toward the sound.

"Boring." Amy Carey stood in the doorway with a hand on her hip. "No wonder so many dead rock stars come from the Pacific Northwest. No one here knows how to party properly, so they off themselves or OD on a bathroom floor."

Charlotte took a deep drink, her mouth pinching into a tight line as she set down her glass. "Really fucking funny, Amy."

Amy covered her cherry-colored lips with two fingers, hiding a smile. "Oops. Didn't see you there, doll." She strutted to the drink table and poured herself a glass of red wine.

A man who looked like he ate steroids for breakfast approached her, and Amy pulled something small from the pocket of her fur coat, slipping it into his hand.

Charlotte muttered a curse, and when Tyler looked at her, she was clutching her stomach, her face pale.

"You all right?"

Her gaze skittered over his face, a struggle playing out behind her eyes. "Look, I have to go. Thanks for an amazing night, Tyler. See you at your show on Saturday, okay?"

"But—" He reached for her arm, grazing the fabric of her sleeve as she bolted out the door before he could say another word.

Tyler stared into the amber liquid in his glass, a familiar wave of loneliness rolling in. The room suddenly felt cold and empty without her, and he decided to leave after that drink. He tossed back half and found Amy scanning the faces in the room, stopping at his.

"Well, hello. Don't I know you from somewhere?" As she approached, the overhead lights created a soft halo effect around her red hair, waking up the flecks of gold in her hazel eyes. She looked even more beautiful a few feet away than on the stage.

Before he could respond, Scott jumped in. "Tyler's pretty famous around here. He's in a band too."

"Do you always let this little ass-kisser speak for you?" Amy's face twisted in a challenging smirk Tyler found sexy and bitchy in equal measure.

"The only thing he kisses in this room is her." Tyler pointed at Sarah, tucked under Scott's arm on the stained couch.

Scott turned to Sarah. "Not that you're a 'thing', honey."

Tyler sipped his drink. "Yeah, sorry, Sarah. Bad choice of words. I blame the Scotch." He took another sip.

"Such a gentleman." Amy laughed the same laugh he heard from the other room—unrestrained with a touch of maniacal. "So, what do you do in your band... Tyler, was it?"

"Singer, guitarist, songwriter, devil worshipper. Same as you."

"I doubt very much you're the same as me." She snatched a pack of Virginia Slims from Sarah's hand. Tyler grabbed his lighter and sparked it. Their eye contact held, and Amy's eyebrow cocked as she inhaled, the paper at the tip glowing red before crackling into ash. "Thank you, Tyler. Or do you prefer Mr. Hall?"

His forehead wrinkled. "So you do know who I am."

Amy sat on a folding chair, gingerly crossing her long, bare legs. "Of course. You're in Tomorrow Mourning. I know the Northwest music scene like Stephen Hawking knows black fucking holes." She laughed once. "Sometimes the scene here feels like a black fucking hole."

"Are you kidding?" His eyes bulged. "Nirvana, 7 Year Bitch, Soundgarden, Alice in Chains, Mudhoney, Pearl Jam—"

"Blah, blah, blah." She tapped her cigarette over a potted plant. "Most of that's MTV-ready commercial horseshit. Give me The Wipers or Dead Moon over those sellouts any day."

Amy reached out and dragged a folding chair across the wood plank flooring until it was alongside hers. She grinned at Tyler as she patted the plastic cushion.

He rubbed the back of his neck and exhaled, taking the seat. "We'll have to agree to disagree on that one. Just because a band gets big enough to sell a few million records or play arenas doesn't mean their art isn't as pure or valid as an indie hustling to sell merch to keep a roof over their heads."

Conversations continued around them, but Amy's focus didn't shift from Tyler.

"Do you think you'll pack arenas someday?" she asked. "Are you defending that to convince yourself you won't be a sellout when that day comes? *If* that day comes."

He leaned forward, their faces a foot apart. "Hell yes, I'm going to pack arenas. My band is that good. And when we become that successful, I'll be sure to save you a seat right up front so you can yammer on about what sellouts we are while we're busy blowing the minds of twenty thousand screaming fans."

Amy's plump lips pressed together, and she nodded as if she'd decided something. "Well, okay then. While we're on the subject of blowing minds..." Her hand settled on Tyler's thigh and squeezed. "Wanna see my dressing room?" Her long nails dragged along the inside of his leg, pausing at the crook of his knee.

He'd never been so publicly, shamelessly propositioned before. He was no virgin but was used to being the pursuer. Even when a woman approached him first, they were never so bold. Clearly, Amy Carey was a different creature altogether—an alpha female who took whatever she wanted and didn't make apologies. The shift in his crotch made it evident to him—and probably to her, given her proximity—that he liked it.

Tyler stood, tugging Amy's hand to get her onto her feet. He slid his fingers into her hair, pulling her face to his. His tongue parted her lips, and he heard her low hum of pleasure over the background music and chatter. As he gently pressed his palm to her throat, he felt the sound vibrate through her skin.

He broke the kiss, his hands falling to his sides. "I love strong women, but if you're looking for a pussy to lick your boots while you're stepping on his face, you've got the wrong guy."

Amy's mouth opened and shut again. He got the feeling this wasn't a woman who often found herself at a loss for words.

While waiting for a response, he played with the little gold pendant between her breasts. An angel. So, she was a fan of irony. "Still want to go to your dressing room?"

She moved close enough to whisper. "Say 'pussy' again, but slower this time."

Tyler blew out a puff of air and began to turn around. Amy grabbed his shoulders, jumped, and wrapped her legs around his waist. Their eyes locked as she spoke against his lips. "My room. Now."

8

Charlotte

When Charlotte entered Satyricon with Sandra, all access lanyards swinging around their necks, her eyes roamed the space, searching for Tyler. Half an hour before showtime, the floor was a sea of bodies. Low, excited chatter echoed off the walls and ceiling like they were in a cathedral awaiting midnight mass. She grabbed Sandra's hand, weaving them through the crowd toward the bar.

On the way, she hoped to glimpse his jet-black hair drifting over his forehead or the disarming, slightly cocky grin she hadn't been able to chase from her mind all week. That close to showtime, she figured he was backstage doing jumping jacks, shots of Jack, or whatever pre-show rituals he favored, but she couldn't help herself. Or was he the type of frontman who was above jitters? Maybe he felt uneasy everywhere else, as if nowhere was home except the stage. After their night of roaming the city and sharing secrets, she looked forward to learning more about the sexy guitarist with a past not so different from her own.

"I can't believe you scored these passes, Char." Sandra's words interrupted her thoughts. "Half the damn city's crammed inside this building."

"It's all who you know, sweetheart."

Then, she saw him.

At the left edge of the stage, just behind a gap in the curtain, Tyler stood with a beer bottle in his hand, laughing at something. As she changed course to head in that direction, she saw who he was with and stopped. A head of long, scarlet hair blocked her view of his face like an eclipse. When the head shifted, Charlotte got an unobstructed view of Amy's lips locking with Tyler's, her hands buried in his hair.

"What's wrong?" Sandra asked.

Charlotte's stomach dropped to the floor. When her eyes burned, she felt like a fool. One hour. That's all they had. And yet, as crazy and illogical as it was, she felt she'd lost something she was meant to have.

"Another missed opportunity, that's all." She stabbed a finger at the stage, and Sandra's eyes shut when she spotted them.

"Well, fuck. He is cute if you like that sort of thing." She pulled Charlotte in for a hug. "Sorry, hon. Maybe Amy will get bored and ditch him in a week like the last guy."

"Maybe."

Charlotte knew this was her fault. She'd run away that night like her hair was on fire, and of course, Amy moved in. He was the hottest guy backstage, and his band was on an upward trajectory with no ceiling—just Amy's type.

And he was lonely. Vulnerable. It was written all over his face.

Charlotte was no stranger to loneliness, though hers was self-imposed. After losing her mom, she'd built walls around her heart topped with barbed wire and sprinkled with hair-trigger hand grenades. It was safer to date sexy, often stupid, assholes who were only interested because she looked good in a skirt. Truly liking someone leads to love, love leads to loss, and loss leads to heartbreak. Who the hell wants that twice in a lifetime?

But for whatever reason, it was different with Tyler. She couldn't remember ever feeling at ease so quickly. Or when someone had felt comfortable enough with her to share their own painful truths so freely. And the way he understood what music meant to her was the clincher. It made her feel seen and connected to someone in a way she'd never experienced.

That feeling was why she vowed, at that very moment, to never date a musician.

"Hey." Sandra hooked a finger under Charlotte's chin to avert her eyes. "Drinks. Music. We're here to have a good time. And if you're really hankering for a spankering, there are at least fifty other dudes here who need a shave and a haircut as badly as the one you're drooling over."

Charlotte laughed despite the disappointment burning in her gut. "Hankering for a spankering? How do you come up with this shit?"

"It's a gift."

Sandra ordered two bright red shots at the bar and handed one to Charlotte. They tossed them back, fiery cinnamon burning a trail to her stomach. When the lights went down, they moved through the crowd to get as close to the stage as possible without risking bruised ribs when the pit inevitably began churning and bubbling front and center.

The crowd erupted when Tyler broke through the curtain and claimed his spot behind the microphone. Charlotte's face heated as he picked up his guitar and adjusted the tuning pegs. His faded jeans hung low on his hips, and the swirls and lines of tattoos peeked out from the sleeves of his black T-shirt. She wanted to trace them with her finger and ask what they meant.

Bright lights flashed above their heads, and a crooked smile played on Tyler's lips as his gaze wandered through the crowd. Tomorrow Mourning's drummer and bassist took their places, but Charlotte's eyes never left Tyler. He stepped to the microphone.

"Hey, Portland! Looking good tonight."

Again, the crowd whooped and roared, a few wolf whistles sounding behind her.

Amen, sisters.

"When I was backstage, I—"

As Tyler scanned the crowd in Charlotte's direction, their eyes locked. His words died mid-sentence. A fluttering rush of butterflies invaded her stomach as their smiles of recognition grew together.

"Shit. Train of thought derailed, I guess." He brushed the hair out of his eyes without breaking their contact, her stupid heart thudding in her chest.

God, she wanted *more*.

She just couldn't believe that was the end for them.

Then, he winked at her. Fucking winked. A move that would look cheesy and lame from anyone else suddenly made her wet, frustratingly hungry for that mouth she'd come so close to kissing.

"This first song goes out to all the beautiful misfits who want to keep Portland weird."

Charlotte laughed as the drummer kicked it off, Tyler's grin gradually fading as the music swept him away. Her body's ridiculous reaction to him was all the confirmation she needed.

She'd been right along.

Relief softened the sharp edges of regret and disappointment. As she stood there, tingling with the electric sparks of lust that could too easily become like and then love, she knew she was better off.

She had no interest in the kind of heartbreak Tyler Hall could dish out.

She laughed harder, feeling like the target of some absurd cosmic joke sent to remind her that real love wasn't in the cards for her.

"What's so funny?"

Charlotte shook her head, slinging an arm around her best friend's shoulders.

"Life, Sandra. Fucking life."

───────◆◇◆───────

After the show, Charlotte and Sandra headed backstage to mingle with the bands. The sting of disappointment over losing her shot with Tyler lingered, but she knew Sandra was right. There were plenty of other sexy, tortured artist types to choose from. She shouldn't allow herself to be so hung up on a guy after one night. One *hour*. It was ridiculous. Still, part of her couldn't shake the nagging regret of walking away.

They strolled down a narrow hallway plastered with multicolored fliers advertising past and future shows, and she slowed at the sound of Amy's distinctive, throaty laugh.

"We'd know that cackle anywhere," Sandra mumbled.

Charlotte put a hand up. "Play nice."

She took a deep breath, and Sandra trailed behind as they followed the sound into a dressing room twice the size of the ones she was used to.

"Hey!" Amy spotted them first, rushing over to kiss them both on the cheek. She reeked of red wine, and her signature blood-red lipstick was smudged. Charlotte refused to think about the reason for that. "Look who it is. Charlotte and her little buddy. What are you doing here?"

Charlotte plastered on a smile, trying not to gawk at how hot Tyler looked with his back pressed against a wall. Sweat glued his shirt to his toned chest, and his hair fell over his forehead in a way that made her want to smooth it back. "Tyler invited us after our last show."

Sandra pushed past them to shake his hand. "I'm Sandra. Huge fan. You guys blew the motherfucking roof off tonight."

"Thanks." Tyler grinned. "Glad you ladies could come out. This is my brother, Matthew." He aimed a thumb at the slender blonde guy with glasses straddling a chair by the mini-fridge. Matthew waved and swigged his beer, giving Charlotte a quick head-to-toe scan. "My bandmates are around here somewhere, probably breaking hearts and decency laws. Want something to drink?"

Sandra's eyes flitted around the room. "Got tequila? Feels like a tequila night."

Tyler shook his head. "Nope. I can get you some at the bar, though."

Sandra looped her arm through Amy's, earning a look of surprise with a dash of disgust. "We'll grab it. Back in a jiff."

Too wasted to protest, Amy went along as Sandra dragged her out the door.

Charlotte didn't know whether to pinch her or hug her for that later. "The show was great. I loved the Fugazi cover."

Tyler grabbed a towel off the back of a chair, wiping sweat from his forehead. "Thanks. This bozo and I bumped '13 Songs' on repeat back in the day."

Matthew scoffed. "That came after your Paula Abdul phase, right?"

Tyler kicked his chair.

Charlotte's eyes shot to the doorway and back to Tyler. She knew she didn't have long before Amy came barreling back in. "So... You and Amy, huh?"

Tyler shrugged, something in his expression making her chest tight. "Yeah, it just sort of happened. I can't even explain it myself."

"That makes two of us," Matthew mumbled.

Tyler shot him a look.

Charlotte moved further into the room, sitting on a folding chair. "She's hard to resist, I get it. I've been basically worshipping her since I joined the band. I wish I were half as brave and talented as she is."

"Charlotte..." Tyler glanced at the doorway, his voice lowering. "I've seen you both play. If you're worried about being less talented than she is... don't be." The corner of his mouth hitched up.

Fuck, that mouth.

"That's totally off the record, though."

She smiled. "Of course."

Matthew set down his empty beer bottle. "He's not bullshitting either. When he lies, his upper lip twitches like he's doing an Elvis impression."

Tyler laughed, slugging him in the arm. "Fuck off, Matty."

She scoped out the room, a shiny black and blue guitar in the corner snagging her attention. "Holy shit. Is that a Superhawk?"

Tyler nodded, his eyebrows raising. "Yeah. Wanna play it?"

"Are you kidding? Of fucking course I do." She stood, carefully lifting the guitar from its rack. After tuning it, she played the first song that came to mind—Led Zeppelin's "Thank You." It was off a record her mother played while doing normal things around the house, like mopping or making spaghetti. Those were the times from her childhood she clung to tightest.

When she finished, Matthew applauded, and Charlotte bowed.

"Damn, Charlotte," Tyler said. "You're a madwoman on bass, but the guitar's definitely your instrument."

"Tell that to your new girlfriend," she murmured.

He smiled, but it didn't touch his eyes. "Line-ups change. Hell, you might even be in a different band someday. I'm sure you'll find a way to make it happen."

Matthew left his chair. "I've gotta hit the head."

The door shut behind him, and as Charlotte gently strummed, there was a palpable twinge of awkwardness in the air. She searched her brain for something to say, but nothing she thought up seemed to fit the situation.

Tyler cleared his throat. "So, the other night—"

"I hope we can be friends." Her gaze lifted, settling on his face. His stubbled, achingly handsome face that was too damn far from hers and destined to stay that way. But if he was going to be around Amy, around their band, Charlotte needed to tell her hormones to calm down and accept that friendship was all they'd have. "I had a great time with you. And I have a hard time talking about my mom because no one gets it, but you understand."

"I had a great time with you, too, Charlotte. I never open up to new people, but you made me feel comfortable immediately." Their eye contact held, igniting the same pull she felt the other night before he touched her face. He cleared his throat, looking away. "And hell, I spend most of my time with guys who can burp the alphabet and think debating Dorito flavors qualifies as deep conversation, so you're a breath of fresh air. In every sense."

"Thanks, I think. I'll admit, I was hoping..." She shook her head, dismissing the thought. He'd made his choice, and she wouldn't make him feel guilty about it. Besides, she was safer this way. "It doesn't matter. You know where to find the best graffiti and cool old guitar wizards, and I'd like to be friends."

Two guys rushed in, shoving each other's shoulders before plopping on the leather sofa.

Tyler nodded slowly, a grin widening on his face.

"Adam and Zack, meet my new friend, Charlotte."

9

Charlotte

Charlotte adjusted her sweaty headband while Matthew huffed and puffed beside her. The early morning jog was her idea, and given the miserable grimace on his beet-red face, she'd never hear the end of it. The air was crisp, birds were singing, and there wasn't a cloud in the sky—perfect conditions to sweat out the weekend's liquor and stress with a good, shockingly out-of-shape friend.

"Almost there, dude. One more block."

"Remind me," he wheezed, struggling to catch his breath, "why we're torturing ourselves."

"We smoke, drink, and eat like crap." She tightened her ponytail as it whipped against her neck. "Without balance, you fall."

He choked out a rattling cough. "Let me guess. Therapist wisdom."

"Bingo." She focused on the refreshing burn of chilly morning air rushing in and out of her lungs and her heart pounding in her chest. Running always made her feel vibrant and alive, as if she were lit up from the inside. She'd stopped during the year her stalker was harassing her. Hell, some days, she couldn't even leave the house. But with her therapist's help, she'd fallen back in love with running, savoring the exhilarating freedom of being out in the fresh Oregon air.

"Well, it's my turn to bring the pizza to movie night," Matthew said. "You bet your ass I'm balancing this madness with triple sausage and extra cheese."

He coughed again, swiping a hand across his forehead. "Unless I die on this sidewalk."

"Such a drama queen." She laughed, poking his arm.

"Eat a butt." He poked her back. "Speaking of movie night, is Amber going?"

Charlotte slowed to match his pace. "Amber? No, she's got plans with her sisters. Why?"

He groaned. "I know that tone. Don't make a thing out of it. She's fun to toke with."

"Mmhm. Sure she is. Nothing to do with her being blonde and awesome." They rounded the corner, and she jogged backward to taunt him. "Race you to the door."

Matthew stopped, bending forward with his palms on his knees. "You win. I'm the rotten egg. Whatever." He stayed hunched over, dragging his feet. "I'll catch up."

Charlotte reached her driveway and turned to face forward, fantasizing about the glass of ice water she'd chug when they got inside. When she saw what waited on her doorstep, she gasped, her sneakers cementing in place.

"Fuck, I'm wiped. I—" Matthew got to the porch, his eyes locking in the same spot. "What. The. Fuck."

At least two dozen smashed daisies were scattered across her porch. Their delicate white petals were ground into the concrete, stems flattened. A tied black ribbon lay beneath it all, and red paint was splattered over the mess.

"Charlotte, get inside and lock the door."

"It's happening again, isn't it?"

Matthew pushed her toward the door. "Get inside. Now. Set the alarm and call the police."

She checked the empty street and sidewalks before returning to the destroyed flowers. A scrap of folded paper caught her eye beneath the stems. She plucked it out.

As she unfolded the note, Matthew read over her shoulder.

You shouldn't jog in dark clothes, sweet Charlotte. Too hard for drivers to see you. It'd be a shame if a car broke all your pretty bones.

"Fucking hell." Matthew pulled the keys from her sweatshirt pocket, unlocked the door, and shoved her inside before punching in the alarm codes. "Lock it behind me and reset the alarm, okay?" He took her hand, setting the kitchen phone into her palm. "Call the police. I'm going to look around."

"No! Don't go out there!" She swallowed the scream lodged in her throat as she clung to his sleeve. "This is worse, Matthew. Worse than just notes."

He sighed impatiently, pushing his glasses further up his nose. "I'll be fine. Call the cop that helped you last time. Barstow, right?"

"Barlowe." Charlotte's shoulders tensed at the name she'd hoped never to need again. It conjured memories of panic attacks stealing her air, cops invading her spaces to collect evidence that went nowhere and going over reports that blurred from her tears.

"Call him. We'll figure it out."

When Matthew was out the door, she thought of the daisies in her dressing room with the unsigned card. *Big things are coming your way.* At the time, what sounded congratulatory now sounded ominous—a threat.

Charlotte locked the door and reset the alarm with trembling hands.

It's happening again.

The walls of her kitchen began to spin. Her hands felt like they'd been buried in ice as they clutched the hard plastic of the cordless phone. She sank into a chair, bending forward to rest her head between her knees while focusing on her breath.

The messages from nearly two years before flickered through her mind.

Your pale skin looks so pretty against that silky black bedspread.

That alarm won't save you when I'm ready to begin.

I need to know what your blood tastes like.

The numbers on the phone grew hazy as she pressed the speed dial button for the police.

"My name is Charlotte Ross." She fought to keep the quiver from her voice. "Look up my file and tell Officer Barlowe my stalker's back."

⸻ ◆ ⸻

After filling out the police report, an officer questioned Charlotte's neighbors, but no one had seen anything unusual. She blamed the overgrown boxwood hedges concealing the porch.

When the officer left, Matthew helped scrub paint off the concrete, his eyes darting around the neighborhood every few minutes. She knew he was trying to keep his cool, but the pulse ticking in his neck and the way he chewed his bottom lip gave him away. The shock of seeing those paint-splattered flowers still burned in her veins, and she was grateful not to have to handle it alone.

"Why now?" She scrubbed harder, tiny yellow pieces of sponge breaking off in her hand. "It's been almost a year! Why is this happening now?"

Matthew poured a bucket of water over the mess, rinsing off the paint they'd loosened. "I don't know." He touched her wrist, stilling her movement. "I won't let anything happen to you."

Charlotte appreciated his reassurance. But she knew the person watching would probably strike when she was alone. She'd have to be ready for that. "Will you help me pick out a gun?"

He dropped the bucket, and it clattered to the bottom step. "What? No! Way too dangerous."

"This is dangerous!" She gestured at the diluted red paint trickling off her porch. "He was in my fucking dressing room, Matty. I'm buying a gun whether you help me or not. I took those classes when this first started. When it stopped, I didn't see the point, but now…"

He picked up the bucket, setting it on the top step. "This could be all that happens. Maybe someone you pissed off's just messing with your head." With his hand, he pushed red water off the concrete and into the garden bed beside the porch. "Like Chimple. Being tossed out on his ass at the club must've been humiliating."

"He's not this gutsy or creative, and he's probably moved on to his next conquest by now. Besides, I never told him about the first notes. It'd be a hell of a coincidence."

"Maybe it was a certain whacko ex-bandmate. I still say she wrote them."

"She left for L.A. this morning. And I know she didn't write them." The possibility Amy was her stalker had crossed her mind. How could it not?

But when Charlotte reflected on how tight they once were, it seemed impossible. The last few notes hinted at rape and torture. Even with the bad blood between them, she couldn't imagine Amy ever tormenting her like that.

"Amy can be vindictive and cruel," she said, "but a woman wouldn't threaten the things this maniac did. Besides, she's about to be single and broke. Too much of her own shit to deal with to bother with me." Charlotte scraped at a stubborn streak of paint with her thumbnail. "It's a man, and I'm gonna nail his balls above my fireplace once I figure out who he is."

Matthew tossed the sponges into the empty bucket. "I'll go." He sighed. "To help pick out the gun. When do you want to go?"

A sound behind them made her jump. They turned to find the neighbor's tabby cat scratching at her wooden siding. Charlotte took a slow breath, counting to five as she let it out. She suddenly wished her therapist made house calls.

"Yesterday."

10

Charlotte

Movie night at Sandra's always offered a sorely needed, laid-back break from the backstage parties and chaotic energy of club shows. It also helped Charlotte block out the images of smashed flowers and threatening notes.

When she first arrived, she'd told Sandra and Tyler about what happened. She let them freak out before asking them not to mention it again. They all needed a fun, normal night with their friends, and she wasn't about to let some twisted asshole's antics spoil it.

"The scene where the dude's arm got ripped off was nauseating." Charlotte unwrapped a mini-Snickers and popped it in her mouth. "Matthew's officially chosen his last movie."

On her left, Tyler's knee kept pressing against hers, and the faraway look in his eyes told her he didn't even realize he was doing it. It was a welcome distraction from the disturbing violence on the screen. On her other side, Matthew chomped fistfuls of popcorn so loudly she missed half of the god-awful dialogue.

"It was cool how the tendons hung on until the killer whipped out the garden shears." Sandra mimed the chopping motions of the shears. "Impressive improvising for a guy brain-damaged from a medical experiment."

Matthew reached for the popcorn on the coffee table and took an overflowing handful, several kernels falling beside the bowl. "Thanks, Sandra. At least someone appreciates art when she sees it."

"I'm with Charlotte." Tyler touched his stomach. "That shit was gross. If you think that's art, I'm worried about you, man."

"I did like how the farmer was concerned about the welfare of his cattle," Charlotte said. "And it was sweet how he shed a tear imagining his wife's face as he was disemboweled. On a side note, I'm never eating red meat again."

Tyler chuckled. "Maybe the movie's vegetarian propaganda."

"Mission accomplished, Mr. Director." Charlotte grinned. "Pass the broccoli."

Sandra tossed a piece of popcorn at Charlotte, landing on her shoulder. Tyler leaned over, angling his chin to pick it up in his mouth without using his hands like a bird pecking at a seed. She smiled, appreciating that he seemed to be back to his usual, fun-loving self so soon after his breakup.

"Char, only you'd spot sentimentality in a slasher flick." Sandra hopped off the couch, clutching her empty glass. "Who needs another Sandrarita?"

While Sandra took Matthew's held-out glass, Charlotte and Tyler shared a knowing look. The fruity, blended concoction was so cloyingly sweet she'd brush her teeth at least twice when she got home.

Charlotte picked up her cup, swirling the remaining bright green liquid. "No thanks, babe. Still working on this one." After a tiny sip, she set it on the coffee table beside the blue and gold Blockbuster Video case.

"I'm good, too," Tyler said. "I got stuck as the designated driver, so one's my limit."

Sandra left for the kitchen.

"We're grateful for your sacrifice, Ty." Matthew snatched a handful of peanut M&M's from a bowl on the table. The dude was perpetually stoned with a chronic case of the munchies. When he caught Charlotte's eye, he shot her a goofy, red-eyed grin. She wished she hadn't turned down the joint he offered after dinner because she'd give anything to feel that relaxed. "Now we won't end up bashed and bloody in a ditch like the poor babysitter."

Charlotte groaned, covering her face. "Don't remind me of that. I liked her because she rescued the kids while staying spunky as hell. I had to look away when the killer grabbed that rusted machete."

She'd glanced at Tyler when it happened to find him cringing at the screen. When he noticed her looking, he comically puffed out his cheeks like he might vomit. They laughed and turned back to the television.

Matthew bent forward, grabbing Tyler's attention. "How long's Amy in L.A.? We should grab your stuff while the house is empty."

"Until Tuesday night." Tyler's jaw clenched.

Charlotte wanted to elbow Matthew in the ribs for killing the upbeat vibe by bringing *her* up.

"What's she doing in L.A.?" Sandra popped her head around the corner. "Making friends with the Manson Family?"

"Fair guess," Tyler said. "She's in some stupid straight-to-video movie about a volcano."

Charlotte nodded slowly. "Will she be playing the volcano?"

Sandra chuckled as she returned with two glasses filled to the brim with bright green slush. "An uncontrollable force of nature spews fiery destruction over everyone in its path." She lowered her voice, adding the dramatic flair of a movie trailer announcer. "Sorry, Ty. Tequila makes me catty." She sipped her Sandrarita, crunching ice in her teeth.

Matthew laughed, his lips and tongue stained green. "Let's go Monday when I'm off work. I'll borrow Evan's truck."

"Thanks, but I'm not ready to go back there yet. I'll take a rain check." Tyler stood, pulling a pack of cigarettes from his pocket. "Anyone wanna join me for a smoke?"

Charlotte got to her feet. "Can I bum one?"

He held his pack open, and she slid one out.

"Be careful," Sandra said, her voice stern.

"Yes, Dad." Charlotte pecked her cheek as she passed.

Sandra tapped Matthew's ankle with her toe. "While they're outside getting lung cancer, will you help me with these dishes?"

Matthew gathered cups and bowls as Charlotte followed Tyler onto Sandra's front porch. She caught his visual sweep of the front yard and empty street before nodding to himself when he was satisfied.

The night air was brisk, but her thin, black cardigan was enough to keep her comfortable. She was glad she'd chosen the jeans and wool socks that ensured her lower half would remain toasty and goosebump-free.

White string lights wrapped around the porch's brick columns offered just enough illumination to make out Tyler's hand as he lit their cigarettes. He appeared in better spirits than the last time she'd seen him. Probably because he'd been laughing and joking with his friends all night instead of having his heart stomped on like a ratty welcome mat.

"I know we all agreed not to talk about it," he said, "but are you okay?"

Smoke drifted from Charlotte's lips in a sigh, a fresh surge of anxiety tingling in her chest. "I'm fine. When we talk about it, I'm not. Hopefully, the cops are figuring shit out, and there's nothing else to be done about it. He wins when we worry, and that fucker's *not* going to win." Her tone was harsher than intended, but his expression reflected nothing but sympathy.

"Hey, come here." He pulled her to his chest, her eyes shutting at the rush of suddenly having him so close. Tyler's hugs were always the sweetest torture, especially after such an emotionally exhausting day. She gave herself a pass to savor the feeling of melting into his fresh, woodsy scent and warmth. "I'm sorry. I won't bring it up again, but if you ever need anything..."

His heated breath puffed against her neck as he spoke, ruffling her hair. She couldn't resist pulling him closer, tighter.

"I know." Her life was full of uncertainties, but wondering if he had her back wasn't one of them. She slipped from the embrace before she did something stupid, like kiss his neck or slide her fingers up his shirt. "How're you doing, Ty?" She took a few steps back, leaning her hip on the porch railing. "You were dealing with some heavy stuff after my show."

He took a drag, blowing smoke out the side of his mouth. "Actually, other than stressing about... the shit we agreed not to talk about, I'm good."

"Really? Not just trying to spare me from your dark cloud?"

"I'm serious." He grinned in a natural, easy way that made her believe it. "All things considered, it's been a fun, chill night. I'm good. Really."

"Happy to hear it." Charlotte shivered as an icy wind rustled the leaves in the front yard and whipped across the porch. "Speaking of chill."

Tyler held his cigarette between his lips as he shrugged out of his green army jacket and held it in front of her. She slid her arms through the sleeves. The cloth was warm from his skin, and when he turned his head, she put her nose to the collar and breathed in. It was like taking a small, teasing hit of a drug that was always in painfully short supply.

"Thanks, Ty." She wrapped an arm around herself.

He winced. "I trust you, but please watch your hot ashes."

"Shit. Sorry, did I burn it?" She checked the sleeve and didn't see any damage.

"No, you didn't." His eyes stayed locked on the jacket, frown lines framing the sides of his mouth. "It just... It means a lot to me, so I get nervous."

"I see you wearing it a lot, but I don't think I've ever asked where you got it." Charlotte tilted her head, a few strands of hair falling against her cheek. She tucked them behind her ear. "What's the story there?"

"It was my dad's."

"Oh. Maybe I shouldn't—" She moved to take it off, but his hand on her arm stopped her.

"It's fine. He wouldn't have wanted me to let you stand out here shivering."

Tears sprang to Charlotte's eyes, her own grief stirring. "Sounds like a good guy to me."

"The best." His voice sounded small, his eyes distant. "I slept with that jacket on my pillow every night after the funeral because it smelled like him. It became like a second skin when I was big enough to wear it."

"I wish I'd saved more of my mom's things." Charlotte flicked the ash off her cigarette. "I remember my dad shoving all her stuff into boxes, like, a week after she died. I think it hurt him too much to see her everywhere. It felt like he was erasing her, and I hated him for it." Her shoulders lifted weakly before dropping with a sigh. "Then, he was so paranoid something terrible would happen to me I practically couldn't sneeze in that house without giving him a panic attack."

It almost felt disloyal to judge her dad's reaction to grief so harshly, but she was being honest. With Tyler, she could only be real.

"Anyway," she said, "it kind of stifled me."

"That sounds awful." The genuine compassion in his gaze felt nearly as comforting as his hug. "My mom didn't try to erase my dad, but she gave me plenty of other reasons to resent her. When she was around, she was yelling or crying or both. She'd changed so much that it was like I'd lost two parents instead of one." He rubbed his stubbled jaw. "It was easier just to avoid her. That feeling was mutual until my band took off, and she saw dollar signs."

Charlotte had never met Tyler's mother, which was probably for the best. After all the stories she'd heard from him and Matthew, it'd be hard not to give her hell for how she treated her sons.

Tyler sat on the porch swing, stilling it with the tips of his boots. He patted the space beside him, and she joined him on the swing.

"You were twelve, right?"

She nodded mutely.

"Damn. It's fucked-up how much it changes you to lose a parent so young. When I think of everything I lost after that day..."

When he trailed off, she gave him time to finish the thought, but the tortured look in his eyes told her whatever it was would remain locked in his mind. For now, at least. She hoped someday he'd feel comfortable enough to let it out.

"I think about that too," she said. "My mom missed my graduation, my first gig. She won't be there to help with my veil at my wedding. And she'll never meet the grandkids I might've given her someday." Charlotte's gaze moved to a falling oak leaf, brown and brittle at the edges. It landed near her foot. "Whatever I become, she'll miss it all."

Tyler slid his arm behind her, his fingertips grazing her neck. "She'd be proud of you, Charlotte."

When she turned, their faces were inches apart. The warmth rising in her cheeks and the embarrassing blush that came with it made her want to turn away, but she couldn't. An overwhelming urge to run her fingers through his hair made them twitch. The desire to kiss him was even stronger, and finally, she had to look away when it became too much to bear.

"Thanks, Ty. Your dad would be proud, too." Charlotte rested her head on his shoulder, the weight of her grief lifting, but the usual burn in her belly remained. Of all the feelings he stirred in her, the relentless longing for *more* made the deepest cut. Thankfully, his friendship was sweet enough to temper the ache. "For a couple of broken kids, I think we did okay."

"We're not broken, Charlotte." He rested his head against hers. "Just a little bent."

She chuckled softly at that. It would hurt if friendship were all they'd ever have, but at least they could share moments like this. The porch went quiet except for the faint rustling of leaves in the trees and the croaking of frogs in the hedges behind them.

"With the divorce stuff," Charlotte said, "you know we're all here for you, right?"

"I do. And I'm grateful." Tyler squeezed her shoulder, the weight of his hand lingering. "There may be a lot of liquor and tears in my future, but I've lived through worse. I'll be okay."

"Of course, you will. If you ever need a drinking and crying partner, I'm your gal." Charlotte's knee nudged his. "I'm glad you came tonight."

"Yeah." He pushed his foot against the ground, making the swing gently sway. "Me too."

The front door opened, and Charlotte lifted her head off Tyler's shoulder. He sat straighter, smashing his cigarette into an ashtray on the railing behind them. She did the same before tucking her hands into the pockets of the borrowed jacket. Matthew and Sandra walked onto the porch.

"Ready to go, guys?" Matthew's gaze shifted between them and settled on the jacket Charlotte wore. His lips crushed together to suppress a smile. "Some of us have real jobs in the morning."

"Sure, man." Tyler tucked his cigarette pack into his pocket. "Although you make beer for a living, which doesn't sound like a real job so much as an excuse to drink for free."

Matthew scoffed. "Says the guy who gets paid to sing songs and get hit on by supermodels."

Tyler shrugged a shoulder. "Touché."

"It's fucking freezing out here." Sandra rubbed her arms. "You guys need to go so I can crawl inside my nice, warm bed."

They took turns saying goodbye to Sandra before she locked the door behind them. Tyler led the way to his car and opened the passenger door for Charlotte before taking the driver's seat.

"That was fun." Matthew slid into the back. "Glad you could make it this time, Ty."

"Me too." Tyler smiled at Charlotte as she pulled his jacket closed over her chest. He turned the heater on.

The warm air blowing through the vents made her eyelids heavy as they drove.

Matthew tapped the back of Tyler's seat. "Hey, could you drop me at home before you take Charlotte? I have some, uh, urgent business to conduct in the bathroom that couldn't be done at Sandra's."

Tyler laughed, tossing an empty plastic soda bottle at his brother. "Goddamn, you're disgusting."

"I applaud your respect for Sandra's nose, but I second that." She touched Tyler's elbow. "What do you have going on tomorrow?"

"The band has a radio interview in the morning, and since Amy's gone, we're recording the new tracks in my home studio."

"Really?" She knew how excited he must be to get cracking on the next record. "When do we get to hear the new stuff?"

He cocked an eyebrow. "You know how it is. Let no one taste a cake until it's fully baked."

"I hope I have some weed left so I can get fully baked," Matthew mumbled.

"You should've asked the queen of green back there," Charlotte said. "Sandra's always happy to share." She yawned and looked back at Tyler, her cheek settling against the cool vinyl headrest. "As soon as the tracks are ready for outside ears, I want to listen."

"You got it." He smiled, obviously pleased with her interest in his music.

They dropped Matthew off first, and once he shut the door, the car went quiet except for the rhythmic tapping of Tyler's thumb against the steering wheel. He hit his turn signal and pulled away from the curb.

"Charlotte?"

"Yeah?" She yawned again. Still drained from her show the night before and the stressful morning, she couldn't wait to slip into pajamas and crash.

"Have you ever been in love?"

The question caught her off guard. It wasn't a subject Tyler usually brought up with her. He rarely even asked about the guys she was dating aside from whether or not they treated her right. She wondered where he was going with this.

"Why are you asking me that?"

"I realize how ridiculous it sounds coming from a married man, but I guess I just wondered... how'd you know? Love, lust, and infatuation all shoot the same chemicals through our systems, so how are we supposed to tell them apart?" He clicked the wipers on as fat droplets of rain pelted the windshield.

"I was in love once." Charlotte sighed, bittersweet old memories charging in. "Senior year, Darren Rogers. He looked like a young Gavin Rossdale and smelled like pine trees and cherry Jolly Ranchers." They laughed. "But it didn't last long."

"How did you know that's what it was?"

She focused on the thin streams of rain sliding down her window. "Because I wanted to be with him every second, and it hurt when I wasn't. When we were together, nothing and no one else mattered. But he got into NYU, and I'm an Oregon girl to my core, so we knew it was doomed."

Charlotte rubbed her hands together in front of the vent as a chill ran through her. She hadn't thought about Darren in years, and considering how self-centered he was, she was sure it was mutual.

"Sorry it didn't work out." He glanced away from the road for a moment, and their eyes connected, that familiar empathy in his gaze that always made her feel warm and fuzzy inside.

"I'm not. Looking back, he was pretty shitty to me, but I was so young and naïve I accepted it. I try to be more careful about who I let into my life, but the last few losers have proven I'm still not careful enough. Not knowing who my stalker is makes it worse. I never know who to trust."

"It's so unfair that someone's messing with your head like that." His finger stopped tapping. "What keeps you putting yourself out there, knowing you could end up hurt?"

She sat quietly, gathering her thoughts as the car turned down her narrow, tree-lined street. "I was a lot more closed-off before taking therapy seriously. But now..." Her gaze settled on the side of Tyler's face. "I know the right person's out there. At least, I hope they are. If I give up, I eliminate the chance I'll ever connect with them. Even though a few wrong ones might slip in before they get here, it's worth the risk."

Charlotte averted her eyes, fidgeting with a button on the jacket, feeling guilty for the half-truths. She could've said so much more, but it didn't feel like the right time or situation to go further.

The truth was, the right person was sitting beside her. But no matter how certain she was, it didn't change the facts. He was married to Amy. Even though he seemed more ready to change that than ever, he could still go back to her. Charlotte wasn't about to set herself up for a rejection from Tyler that would hurt even worse than the first.

Their friendship was strong but not invincible. It wouldn't survive that.

She'd let Darren Rogers get closer than intended, but with his determination to go to college out of state, their relationship had an expiration date. So, it was safe and mostly fun while it lasted. She loved him as much as she could love anyone with the walls she'd carefully constructed around her heart.

Despite the progress made in therapy, she knew she'd never let herself fall for someone completely. Because there were no guarantees they'd be strong enough to catch her when she did. Or strong enough to stick around when things got ugly, complicated, and hard.

And what if something tragic happened?

She knew the pain of being left with nothing but photographs and fading memories. Of having to exist with a vital piece of yourself gone forever.

Could she live through that again?

Being alone was safe and comfortable—two feelings she'd happily choose over the risk of a broken heart. One-night stands, guys cute and fun enough to date for a while, and impossible fantasies about longtime crushes had to be enough.

Charlotte stopped fiddling with the button and looked at Tyler, needing to witness his reaction. "Can I ask you a question?"

"Of course." The finger tapping resumed. "Anything."

It dawned on her why he'd led the conversation in this direction. He'd just been blindsided, betrayed by the person he'd committed to most in his life. He was probably questioning every decision that brought him to that place. Perhaps he was even considering the possibility his friends had been aware of from day one—that lust and manipulation, not love, had led him to make the biggest mistake of his life.

Like Charlotte, he probably didn't know what the real thing felt like.

A question burned on the tip of her tongue, and she took a deep breath before letting it fly. "Are you still in love with Amy?"

His shoulders sagged like the weight of his mistakes had dropped on them all at once. Perhaps it was an unfair question to pose while the wound was so fresh, but it was too late to take it back. "Well, anything but that."

The car went quiet again as they pulled into Charlotte's driveway. Her body remained angled toward his as the soft white light of the full moon swept over the windshield, illuminating his face when the car stopped. The corners of his mouth were downturned and the shadows beneath his eyes said he hadn't had a decent night's sleep in a while. His bottom lip twitched as if he were holding back words he wasn't ready to let out. A sudden glimmer in his eyes made her wonder if it was tears he held back.

A pang in her chest made her want to wrap her arms around him until every trace of sadness lifted. Until she was certain he knew how loved and appreciated he was by the ones who truly knew him.

Instead, she slipped out of his jacket and set it on the backseat. When she unbuckled her seatbelt, his attention snapped back to her.

"Shit." He cleared his throat and blinked hard. "Sorry, my mind wandered, I guess."

She touched his hand to stop him when he reached to unbuckle his seatbelt. He looked up, and the moment their eyes met, the ache in her chest deepened. The urge to hold him became so intense she had to pull her hands back to safety, folding them in her lap. "You don't have to walk me up. But you're welcome to come inside if you need to talk more."

His eyes darted lower, skimming across her lips before returning to meet her gaze. It was so fast and unexpected that she wondered if she'd imagined it. When the sadness in his features faded and a crease formed between his eyebrows as if he were working out a puzzle in his head, he did it again, erasing all doubt. For the second time that night, he was so close she could feel the heat from his skin and hear his gentle breaths as they shared the same air. Her logical brain knew he was only looking at her that way because he was lonely and vulnerable, but still, her pulse kicked up like a bomb seconds from exploding.

"Look, Ty, I—"

A loud crash hit the window beside Charlotte's head. "What the—"

She covered her face as Tyler threw his body over hers, folding her forward.

Shards of glass clattered against the inside of the door, sliding down the back of her arm before falling to the mat at her feet.

"Don't move!" His arms wrapped around her, squeezing so tightly it was hard to draw air. Neither was breathing much anyway, too petrified and focused on sounds outside the car as they waited for whatever came next.

"What the fuck," she whispered.

She felt the furious pounding of his heart against her back, and his fluttering exhales against her neck. Stinging tears filled her eyes.

"You're okay," Tyler said. "We're gonna be fine." They remained huddled for a handful of minutes that felt infinite, but his actions said everything.

When she felt his weight slowly lifting, she rose, her limbs shaking from the shock.

"Charlotte, are you hurt?" He took her face in his trembling hands, frantically searching for injuries.

"I-I don't think so." She checked her arms. No blood or scratches. When she looked at the window, there was a fist-sized hole in the center. The glass around it fractured into a tangled cobweb of hundreds of tiny cracks. Whatever hit it was solid, thrown hard enough to break through the thick pane.

And it was aimed at her.

As the realization sunk in, her lungs seized.

It could have killed me.

Quick, panicked inhales made her head swim, black spots invading her vision.

"Charlotte, look at me. Long, slow breaths, okay?" He took a few himself, his eyes darting from her to the darkness outside the car and back again. "I've got you."

Nodding, she followed his lead. Soon, the dizziness subsided, but the terror of another assault gripped tighter every second. She stared through the hole in the window, paralyzed, waiting for a figure to emerge from the shadows.

She was sure this was *the moment*. It was the term she used with her therapist for the first (and probably last) confrontation with her stalker in the flesh. The moment she'd have to fight or die. The one she'd been dreading since that first note.

She wasn't ready. "Tyler, we have to go." She couldn't bear the thought of that monster hurting him, too. Running was the only option. "*Now.*"

He pressed a hand to her head to keep her below the dashboard. "Stay down."

Tyler scanned the yard and empty sidewalks through the unbroken windows, and she did the same. The area was full of hiding places and shadows the streetlights couldn't touch. Anyone could be taking cover in one of those ominous patches of darkness, waiting for the chance to strike again.

He turned off the car and grabbed the door handle.

"What the hell are you doing?" She gripped his sleeve.

"I want to find the fucker who did that and kick his ass!"

"No!" The thought of Tyler rushing out in the dark to hunt down someone capable of such a violent act made a fresh surge of panic flood her body. "Take me to Matt's or a hotel. We have to go!"

He popped open his glove box, pulled out a small black and green taser, and set it in her lap. She shuddered at the thought of being close enough to some dangerous psycho to use it.

"I have a knife in my pocket," he said. "I'll be okay."

"I won't!" She tugged his sleeve harder. "Please don't leave me alone." Her shallow, panting breaths and heart thundering against her ribcage made her lightheaded, and she grabbed the dashboard for support. "Let's just go. I can't be here right now, and I'll never be able to sleep after that. Take me back to Sandra's. Anywhere but here."

Tyler took one last look at the yard before turning the engine back on. "You'll be safer at Matt's." He put the car in reverse, his jaw working. As they pulled away, she spotted something at the edge of the driveway—a rock or maybe a brick. "I'll take the floor, and you can take the couch."

She wiped at the first hot tear trailing down her cheek. "His couch smells like pepperoni."

Nervous laughter filled the car, her fear lessening with every block they moved away from whatever the hell just happened. She looked back at the shattered window and shivered.

She'd have a dent in her skull if that glass hadn't held. They'd be covered in her blood. She might've died right in front of him, causing a ripple effect of trauma in the lives of everyone who loved her.

Leaving them with nothing but photographs and fading memories.

At a red light, the gentle touch of his hand on her shoulder made her jump, but she was grateful he didn't pull back. Instead, the pad of his thumb swept across her collarbone in slow strokes until her muscles relaxed.

"Why would someone want to hurt me?" she asked. "What did I do?"

The hand on her shoulder squeezed. "Nothing. You did nothing to deserve that. Maybe it wasn't even meant for you, and we were just in the wrong place at the wrong time. We'll figure out who it was and make damn sure they pay."

It was impossible to believe something so violent wasn't personal. The sound of the shatter, deafening in the small space, still echoed in her mind. The object—whatever the hell it was—had been inches from taking her life.

Who hated her enough to want her dead?

"What if they try again?" Her voice sounded as weak and small as she felt.

"I won't let that happen." The blue in his eyes darkened, the conviction in his tone leaving no room for doubt. "You're safe with me, Charlotte."

She could still feel his weight on her back, shielding her from whatever came next. The terror was still there, but that memory tempered it.

Because after years of feeling on edge, waiting for the worst, his actions had done more to make her feel safe than any words ever could.

11

Tyler

When Tyler and Charlotte walked into Matthew's apartment, he was on the couch playing Nintendo in his boxers. One lamp was on, and the dim light focused on the center of the room, giving everything it touched an eerie yellowish glow. The game on the television cast flickering shadows on the walls, stoking Tyler's anxiety. Matthew turned, his expression flat before morphing into obvious confusion. His eyes were half-closed, and the place reeked of pot.

"Get some clothes on, dude." Tyler covered Charlotte's eyes, and she laughed, swatting his hands away. "Lady present."

Charlotte scoffed. "I haven't been called that in a while. Sorry to barge in on you, Matty. Is it cool if I crash here tonight?"

Her tone sounded casual, but the way she hugged herself gave away the nervousness beneath the surface.

"What? Why?" He grabbed a shirt and sweatpants from the back of a chair and pulled them on before returning to his game. "I thought Ty was taking you home."

"I did." A spike of pain shot through his clenched jaw. When he rubbed the spot, he realized his hands were still shaking. "Some asshole smashed my window beside her head, so we booked it out of there." He studied Charlotte's reaction. A barely-there quiver in her lower lip was the first crack in her composure. She hugged herself tighter.

The plastic controller fell from Matthew's hands, smacking the edge of the coffee table before tumbling onto the carpet. "What the fuck?!" He rushed to Charlotte, holding her shoulders as he checked her over, just like Tyler had. "Are you okay?"

She shrugged, another transparent attempt to appear unfazed. "Just shaken up." The tremble in her lip worsened, and she clamped onto it with her teeth.

Tyler knew she was likely replaying the crash in her head, too. That terrible sound reverberated through his skull. The high-pitched shatter had eclipsed everything but the primal instincts to survive and protect. Even though he could see Charlotte was unharmed, the trauma they'd experienced was too fresh for relief to sink in.

"Who the hell would..." Matthew's face pinched into an angry scowl, and he turned to Tyler. "It was fucking Amy, wasn't it? She probably had her meathead bodyguard do it."

Tyler didn't know what to say. If someone had suggested even days before that Amy had done something so vicious, he would've defended her without hesitation. She had no qualms about spreading nasty rumors about someone who wronged her or planting an unflattering story about a rival in the press, but mostly, her methods of revenge were harmless. He'd never imagined she could be capable of causing physical harm.

But he wasn't so sure after witnessing her rage toward Charlotte outside the club and feeling the sting of her slap across his cheek. The timing of the smashed, paint-splattered daisies didn't help her case either.

"I honestly don't know." Tyler wished he could erase the worry from their faces. "She can be irrational and lash out when she's angry, but I've never seen her do anything like that. Besides, Rafael's probably in L.A. with her. She never travels without him."

"Now we know why," Matthew muttered, earning a shoulder smack from his brother.

"Not now, asshat." Tyler grabbed the cordless phone off the wall and passed it to Charlotte. "You should call the cops. File a report so they can check things out at your place."

She returned the phone to its cradle. "Stand outside in the cold while police-men poke around my yard with flashlights? Sounds as appealing as a drunken blind man waxing my bikini line." She pulled an elastic band from her pocket, sweeping her hair into a ponytail. "I'll call first thing tomorrow. Whoever it was is long gone, and I'm dead on my feet. Can I have a pillow and blanket so I can pass out and put this day behind me?"

Arguing was tempting, but she was probably right and clearly exhausted.

Matthew went to the linen closet and dug out a tie-dyed blanket, pillow, and clean pillowcase.

"Thanks, Matt." Charlotte took them and started slipping the case onto the pillow.

As Tyler watched her, the memory of glass shattering beside her head made his heart race, sweat beading on his forehead. He grabbed Matthew's sleeve, tugging him toward the hallway.

"Let's find a spare toothbrush and some clothes she can wear." Tyler silently shut the door behind them when they reached the bedroom. He huddled close to Matthew, his panic boiling over. "She could've been seriously fucking hurt! Even killed!" he hissed in a whisper, his heart pounding as furiously as in the seconds after the crash. "Why would someone do that?"

"I don't know. But they aren't getting away with it." Matt's hands coiled into tight fists at his sides. Obviously, they both wanted to smash the bastard's face in. "Chimple seemed upset about their breakup but not that upset. If it wasn't Amy, it's the stalker, right? Or do we have another asshole to worry about?"

Tyler swallowed the lump in his throat. He was still processing the gravity of the attack and how much worse it could've been. There wasn't enough headspace to try and identify the culprit yet, but whoever it was had to be stopped. Fast. This was a major step up from notes and flowers because this wasn't just about scaring her.

They wanted her dead.

"Everyone outside our circle's a suspect until proven otherwise," Tyler said. "We trust no one until it's figured out."

"Agreed. And we watch Charlotte before she leaves for Canada next week. After this, maybe they'll increase security for the tour."

There was a knock at the door, and Charlotte peeked in. "You guys done making out in here? I'd love to brush my teeth and change."

Matthew laughed weakly and headed for his bathroom. "Yeah, Ty's stubble was starting to burn my chin anyway."

Tyler took the fact that she was telling incest jokes as a good sign. He dug through his backpack and handed her a pair of plaid boxers and a T-shirt. "They'll be big on you, but they're clean, I promise."

She held the clothes to her chest. Her fingers were still shaking a little, as were the corners of her mouth as it tipped up in a tight, forced smile. "Thanks."

Matthew returned with a toothbrush, and she took it. "Bathroom's all yours. It's been a long time since a female's been in there, so... Sorry."

Her nose wrinkled, a genuine smile replacing the one worn for show. Even when unintentional, Matthew had a gift for obliterating intense moods. It worked best on his favorite people, and Charlotte was high on that list. "I'll hold my breath. As long as nothing's living in your shower or crawling on your toilet seat, we're good."

"No guarantees." When she left, Matthew nudged Tyler's arm. "Hey, it's not all bad. Bet you didn't think you'd end the day sleeping with Charlotte."

Tyler punched him in the shoulder. "Shut up, dick."

Matthew howled with laughter, and Tyler shoved him into the wall. Matthew probably wouldn't outgrow the urge to taunt his brother about women, and Tyler wouldn't outgrow putting him in his place when he did. The normalcy of it was comforting, the tightness in his throat easing.

"You let her wear Dad's jacket," Matthew said, rubbing his shoulder.

Tyler blinked. "What?"

"You don't even let me wear Dad's jacket. And I sure as shit never saw Amy wearing it."

Tyler didn't know what to say, so he said nothing.

When Charlotte exited the bathroom in his clothes, he froze. His pulse kicked up. Even without makeup and her hair in a messy ponytail, she was one of the most beautiful women he'd ever seen. His awareness of her curves pressed against his Bad Religion shirt only added to the effect.

Her eyes landed where Matthew rubbed his shoulder. "Did you get hit? What did you say?"

"Nothing." He gave her a quick hug and shuffled down the hallway toward his bedroom. "Good night. See you two rock stars in the morning."

When Tyler and Charlotte were alone, their eyes connected, the corner of her mouth tipping up before she looked away. There it was—the same sweetness and warmth in her big brown eyes that drove him crazy the night they met. After the stress of the crash, he let himself hold onto those feelings like a safety line.

"Thanks for getting me here, Ty. Sandra's overprotective ass would've flipped out if I'd gone there."

"Yeah, calm and cool aren't her strong suits."

He walked to the couch, moving his pillow and blanket to the floor beside it. She turned off the light before stretching out on the sofa under the fuzzy tie-dyed blanket. The sounds of cars driving by and an occasional siren announced the endless activity of the city. When his eyes adjusted to the darkness, all he could see were the outlines of objects and the soft glow of the VCR display.

The sudden stillness in the room made his mind ramble, nebulous thoughts easily pushed away by daytime distractions and terrifying events finally taking shape.

A few nights before, he was in a penthouse suite in Sydney, dreaming of coming home to his beautiful wife and their beautiful life. But it was a fantasy. A story he told himself to avoid the painful reality that ended up clubbing him over the head. He'd gladly take crashing on the floor of Matthew's shabby apartment over living that sort of fiction one more goddamn second.

Once Tyler broke every tie to Amy, the new life he built for himself would be real. Even with the inevitable challenges and risks, he vowed to always choose reality over comforting, hollow delusions from then on.

"Ty?"

"Yeah?"

He was surprised when Charlotte's soft, warm skin touched his hand. The guitar string callouses of her fingertips curled against his palm. Their joined hands rested on his chest, and when his heart started racing, he knew she could feel it.

"Thanks for making me feel safe."

He squeezed her hand, the slight tremble of emotion in her voice making his eyes water. "I'd do anything for you, Charlotte."

He felt the truth of that in his bones. He'd do anything for this girl who'd never hurt him or made him question her intentions. Who was honest, genuine, and kind. Just knowing people like her existed in such a cruel world was a comfort.

And while the place inside his heart Amy had occupied for three years was still raw and tattered, it suddenly didn't feel beyond repair.

Before Tyler could talk himself out of it, he brought Charlotte's hand to his lips and kissed it. The sharp catch in her breath made his heart thump even faster. He returned their hands to his chest, where they stayed until her breathing grew slow and even. She pulled the hand back in her sleep, and its absence made him think of the night they met. How empty that room felt when she left it. When she left him.

But this was different. Charlotte was so close he could smell the orchids that followed her wherever she went. He wondered if there was any truth to what Matthew said about her having feelings for Tyler. If it was true, was it only one-sided? Or did the spark from that night still flicker inside him, too, waiting to ignite?

When she shifted, and her hand returned, he found himself wishing for the impossible. Wishing he was good enough for someone as sweet and loyal as Charlotte. Wishing his baggage wasn't piled into an Everest-sized mountain, making it impossible for anything but friendship between them. His life was too messy to make her the priority she should be. He was living out of a backpack and crashing on his brother's couch, for fuck's sake.

And with the separation so fresh, Tyler wasn't sure he could trust himself not to backslide in a weak moment. He'd been close in that closet at the club. What if he got wasted one night and woke up in Amy's bed? Charlotte wouldn't forgive that, and he'd never forgive himself if he ruined their friendship because he was too stupid to resist old habits.

Besides, he had his shot that magical night downtown and blew it.

Nothing but a time machine could change that.

Charlotte Ross should be with someone who instantly recognized her worth. Someone wise enough to hold onto her regardless of shiny, tempting distractions that came along, making promises they couldn't keep.

And like she told her cheating ex backstage, she didn't give second chances.

She belonged with someone who got it right the first time.

Although the truth stung, Tyler knew she deserved someone better than he could ever be.

12
Charlotte

Charlotte splashed cold water on her face before throwing on the jeans and black cardigan she'd worn to Sandra's the night before. She had to admit that wearing Tyler's clothes gave her a little thrill, but wearing boxers wasn't an option with all she had planned. She needed to file a police report and see if anything happened at home while she was away. Then, she'd meet with Sandra and Amber to finalize set lists for the Canadian shows and polish the songs for the benefit album.

The thought of telling the girls about the shattered window made her queasy. When she found the first creepy note on her doorstep, they'd raced over, arriving long before the police. They insisted on staying for a few nights in case of trouble, but it quickly became clear their main goal was distraction. And helping her through the anxiety that tightened her chest and had her flinching at every unexpected sound. While the extended slumber party—complete with mud masks, cheesy junk food, and even cheesier rom-coms—helped, panic rumbled beneath the surface.

As she splashed more water on her face, the words scrawled on a pink scrap of paper were as clear in her mind as if the note were in her hands instead of an evidence locker.

The songs from that pretty throat can never sound as beautiful as your screams.

Since things had never progressed beyond notes, she'd figured someone was just trying to rattle her. But last night...

The violence was an escalation Charlotte never saw coming. When that glass broke, she was sure she was about to face the moment that felt inevitable until the notes stopped. She'd hoped the self-defense classes and years of therapy had prepared her, but she'd been paralyzed by fear, desperate to run, knowing full well she wasn't strong enough to fight.

The looming threat of danger remained, but something kept her panic at bay—or rather, someone.

As she patted her face dry, she remembered holding Tyler's hand the night before. The room's quiet had sent her mind reeling, and it was a reflex, an impulse triggered by an overwhelming need for a comforting connection. He was probably as surprised as she'd been.

Before reaching down, she'd had a flash of the glass exploding. Touching his hand instantly shifted her thoughts to how he'd protected her. Before she could blink or react, he'd thrown himself in front of whatever danger might be next.

After years of putting up her defenses, he'd shown her how freeing it could feel just to let go and trust.

I'd do anything for you, Charlotte.

His words weren't nearly as surprising as the kiss that followed. It was only on her hand, but still, it further disrupted the ugly thoughts and sent a rush of need through her. She turned her hand over, looking at the spot his lips had touched.

A soft rapping at the bathroom door startled her. She opened it to find Tyler holding two steaming mugs of coffee.

"Uh, I figured you were doing girly shit in there, and I know you need caffeine before you can function, so... here." He thrust a mug in front of her, and she took it.

Is he nervous?

"Girly shit, huh?"

He rubbed the back of his neck. "Yeah, you know. Lining your eyes, painting your lips, washing your face. Obviously, not in that order."

"Obviously." She took a sip of coffee, holding back a smile. "Thanks for the clothes."

She held them out, and he took them, their fingers brushing in the exchange.

"Is Matty up?" she asked. "I want to get home to file the report and check on things."

"Not yet. I can wake him if you want."

"Let him sleep." While she wanted the report behind her, she was in no hurry to set the worst parts of the day in motion. "Sure you can't join us?"

The struggle in his eyes made her feel guilty for asking. He had his own shit to deal with and couldn't drop everything to be the security blanket for a nervous friend.

"I wish I could. I'm meeting Zack and Adam in an hour for those interviews. They'd kill me if I ditched them."

"I forgot about that. We'll be fine." Charlotte pushed past him, sitting on a stool at the kitchen counter. "Fight or flight muddled my brain last night, but I kind of wish I'd stayed home instead of letting that asshole drive me away. I've learned in therapy that I can't let fear keep me from living my life." She spooned sugar into her coffee and stirred it in. "Anyway, the cops will meet us there to file the report, so we'll be safe."

"Sure, and Matty's tougher than he looks. A guy twice his size fucked with his girlfriend in eighth grade, and Matty beat the shitbag into hamburger meat. Took three football players to pull him off."

Charlotte's jaw dropped. "Sweet Matty?"

"He'll protect you if someone tries anything."

She knew that was true, though it'd never been tested like it had with Tyler. Matthew popped by almost daily when the notes started, scanning her neighborhood for strange cars, double-checking locks, and eventually helping her dad install the ugly but comforting metal bars on her windows. Instead of mud masks and rom-coms, Matt's approach was bringing over his Sega Genesis console with coffee and lemon muffins from her favorite cafe. Though she wasn't a huge fan of video games, she had to admit whipping his butt at Mortal Kombat was cathartic as hell.

Tyler pulled something from his pocket, placing it in her palm. She looked at the taser in her hand and blinked. "This might help too. Hopefully, no one gets close enough for you to need it, but keep it just in case."

The thought of zapping some creep trying to attack her sent an icy shiver up her spine. "Thanks. I guess."

Matthew emerged from the hallway, yawning and scratching his belly. "Morning, party people. Did I miss any more scary shit?"

"Nope." Tyler poured him coffee and set it on the counter.

"Good. You guys have a nice slumber party in my living room?"

Tyler and Charlotte found each other's eyes, sharing a brief smile. She wondered how he felt about the night before and whether he'd tell Matthew about kissing her hand. She also hoped to god she didn't drool or snore throughout the night.

"Totally." She twirled a lock of hair like a ditzy teenager. "Ty let me braid his hair before the pillow fight, then we talked shit about the popular girls before we ate cookie dough and fell asleep."

Matthew grinned, his half-closed eyes making it clear he'd decided to wake and bake. "Man, chick sleepovers sound awesome."

The kitchen phone rang, and Matthew answered it. "Hello?"

"I've gotta jet." Tyler grabbed his keys and sighed, turning to Charlotte. He was obviously still conflicted, but it wasn't his nature to back out of band commitments. "I'll call later for an update on what the cops say."

"Cool. Tell Zack and Adam I said 'hey'."

As she raised her mug to her lips, he touched the back of her hand—the exact spot he'd kissed. "Be careful."

She swallowed the warm, rich sip and nodded, his deep blue eyes never leaving hers. The contact and sincere concern helped soothe her frazzled nerves, but something else in his expression worried her. In the moments before the window broke, he'd looked so sad and tortured it hurt to look at him. A shadow of that remained, darkening his eyes and clenching his jaw.

Her friend was hurting, and he needed help.

It dawned on her that the chaos in Tyler's life had been overshadowed by hers. After handling their responsibilities, they should take a break from their stresses. And no matter how much she hated hearing about Amy, Charlotte would let him vent about his broken heart. Maybe then, the healing could begin.

"Hello?" Matthew said again, louder. "Well, fuck you very much." He hung up. "Stupid pranksters."

"They didn't say anything?" Charlotte asked.

"Nope. Just breathing, but not in a pervy way."

"Weird." Tyler's eyes darted to her and back to his brother. "Watch out for her today. Last night was..."

"Don't stress. I've got her back." Matthew slung his arm around Charlotte's shoulders like Tyler did when someone needed comfort. With all their differences, the brothers were alike in all the ways that made them incredible friends. They were loyal, fiercely protective, and would give anything for the people they loved, whether it was a kidney, a safe place to crash, or midnight bail money. The last few days had reminded her how lucky she was to have the Hall brothers on her side. "When I leave for work, she'll have Sandra and Amber and the kickass home security features I hooked her up with."

"And we'll be listening to your interview," she said, "so don't fuck up."

The smile he returned was so weak at the edges it was barely there.

Yeah, the guy needed a break.

When Tyler was out the door, Charlotte called the Portland Police. While recounting the previous night's events, the one thing keeping her grounded was the memory of Tyler's body over hers, shielding her without hesitation.

But, like all the feelings she wished could last forever, that sense of security was gone too soon. In its place was the fear that her attacker would burst through the door to finish what they started.

13

Tyler

"**G**ood morning, Bridge City! You're listening to Maniac Mornings on KPQD, Portland's home of rock-n-roll."

While the bald, goateed deejay spewed his usual obnoxious schtick to morning commuters, Tyler gave his bandmates a warning look to be on their best behavior. He wasn't optimistic after watching Zack chug two double-shot lattes and Adam shamelessly hit on Tara, Baldy's baby-voiced, bleach-blonde cohost.

"Don't crash your cars, ladies," Tara said with a saucy wink. "We're here with Tyler Hall, Adam Hyatt, and Zack Maine of Tomorrow Mourning. How are you doing, guys?"

Adam leaned into the closest microphone. "Happy to be home, Tara. That Aussie tour was a blast, but it kicked our asses."

"Welcome back! The Rose City loves you maniacs." Baldy's over-the-top enthusiasm and faux laughter were already grating Tyler's nerves. "And watch that cursing. Don't wanna corrupt those kiddos out there." He pressed a button that made the sound of laughing children fill the room. Tyler and Adam shared a knowing glance. These ridiculous interviews were easily one of the worst parts of the job. "Any local shows to put on our calendars?"

Zack sat forward. "U.S. dates will be announced soon, and there's no way we'd ever leave you out, Portland."

"Lookin' forward to that." Tara pressed a button on her soundboard that triggered a burst of recorded applause. "There are rumors your next album's veering toward a different sound. That maybe you guys are jumping on the grunge bandwagon going on up in Seattle. Any truth to that?"

Zack laughed. "That's a big hell no, Tara. We don't do bandwagons. A lot of what's coming out of Seattle's incredible, but we've got our own thing, and we think we do it well. Our last album sold more copies than a downtown Kinko's at rush hour, so our fans must agree."

"Fair enough. Glad to hear you're staying true to your signature sound." She turned to Tyler, grinning like a kid who'd gotten away with stealing a candy bar. "Pretty quiet over there, Tyler. Hoping we won't toss any tough questions at you? I know one that's on our listeners' minds this morning."

Tyler exchanged a baffled look with his bandmates. "What are you talking about?"

"Oh, come on." Tara's disbelief rang false, raising Tyler's hackles and making him sit straighter. "You must've seen the paper this morning."

Adam gripped the microphone in front of him, his knuckles white. Obviously, he didn't like this turn either. "Do we look like we get up at the asscrack of dawn to read the goddamn newspaper? Just tell us what the hell you're talking about."

"Whoa! Watch the cursing, dudes." Baldy belted out an obnoxious guffaw, earning peeved looks from everyone.

"Settle down, Adam." Tara raised her hands in mock surrender. "Maybe it's news to you too. Saturday night, your buddy Tyler was getting awfully friendly with a member of Portland's very own girl group, Killing Daisies." She looked at Tyler. "Care to explain?"

Stunned speechless, Tyler's eyes locked on the woman who seemed inexplicably determined to rattle him. He sensed an agenda beyond ratings but didn't care what it was. There were more important things to worry about than imaginary drama and people who got off on amplifying it. He raised his hands at his bandmates before they jumped in.

"What is this?" Tyler asked. "We're here to talk about music, not schoolyard gossip invented by bottom feeders."

"Hmm... Was there a denial in there somewhere? Maybe I missed it." Tara cocked an eyebrow. "Funny how some of the juiciest gossip turns out to be true."

Tyler laughed, more out of disbelief than humor, because this wasn't funny at all.

"Are you for real, lady?" Zack shot a death glare at Tara. "Either we move on from this bullshit, or you'll be talking to three empty chairs for the next half hour."

Baldy's eyes darted to Tara, widening in a warning. "No need to bail, boys. We can play nice. Right, Tara?"

"Sure, we can." Tara nodded, but the look on her face made it clear she wasn't interested in backing down. "It just seems like Tyler can't because that's not even the worst of it. He was also caught getting rough with his wife, the legendary Amy Carey. Shame on you twice, Tyler Hall."

His stomach lurched, bile stinging the back of his throat. Thousands of people in his hometown had heard the accusation. Then he remembered Charlotte was one of them. The realization that this might embarrass her quickly turned his shock into rage. One look at his bandmates said he wasn't the only one—their faces were red, their muscles tensed.

"Fuck this." Zack shot up from his chair. "Interview's over. How dare you come at him like this, you fake ass, chuckling dickheads."

He stormed out as Adam stood, flipping the deejays the bird. "Your station sucks anyway. Home of rock-n-roll, my ass! You played Hootie and the goddamn Blowfish before we got here. Bunch of poseurs. Let's go, Ty."

Tyler swallowed the angry lump clogging his throat. As much as he wanted to run from this disaster, he knew he had to defend himself. For his band's sake as well as Charlotte's. They didn't deserve to be dragged down by his mistakes.

He took a deep breath, doing his damndest to keep his voice steady. "No one who knows me would ever think I'd be unfaithful to my wife or harm her in any way. I was supporting a friend, and there was a... misunderstanding. That's all I have to say about it." It had to be enough. If he stayed one more second, he might put his fist through the Plexiglass divider. He stood, turning toward the exit.

"Misunderstanding, huh?" Tara's eyes narrowed. "Was that the first time you grabbed your wife and yanked her around, or do you usually wait until no one's watching?"

Tyler's hands coiled into fists, his eyes locked on her self-satisfied grin. Even silent, she was goading him. He suspected she was trying to push him into lashing out, helping to prove her accusations. That he had a temper he had no problem unleashing on women. He couldn't let that stand.

As Tara opened her mouth, Tyler went to his microphone.

"I want to assure our fans that I respect women. Always have. Well, maybe not Tara so much, but I respect every woman who hasn't ambushed me with ridiculous lies and accusations after inviting me somewhere. And unlike Tara, I respect hard-working female musicians enough not to refer to their band as a 'girl group'." Tyler earned an eye roll from Tara, and he continued before she could interrupt. "Don't believe anyone who says otherwise. I'm going through personal stuff like anyone else, and I have the right to keep it private."

Baldy's eyes nervously darted between them before landing on Tyler. "I'm sure it's tough being in the public eye. Can I get a few easy questions in before you leave?"

"Nope." Tyler stared at the smug woman who was clearly pleased to have provoked a ratings-boosting response. "I hope you're fired for this baseless, unprofessional attack. Good luck booking musicians who aren't squeaky clean and boring because no one worth a damn would risk having to put up with this crap." He looked at Baldy and smiled. "Hey, I didn't even swear. You're welcome, asshole."

When Tyler stormed out, their manager, Sophia, hurried over with a look as incensed as his must've been. "Tyler, I'm so sorry this happened."

He touched her arm. "Take a breath, Soph. It's fine."

"I don't need a breath. I need a lawyer to sue these fools for slander. It's far from fucking fine." Her strong words surprised him. Tyler couldn't recall ever hearing Sophia swear, and even amidst the ugly feelings he was dealing with, her display of protectiveness for his band touched him. "She's friends with Amy, Ty. That's what this is. An intern at my office worked in the mailroom here and said Amy was here all the time, chumming it up with that snake in there."

Tyler's eyes shut. He should've guessed. Amy had as many friends in the industry as enemies. She'd always understood the value of publicity from various avenues, whether through fans' word of mouth, producers singing her praises to other influential players in the industry, or a morning deejay talking up her latest single to thousands of rock fans.

"Let's just go." He nodded at the exit. "Adam and Zack are probably in the parking lot trying to figure out which car is hers so they can piss on the windshield."

Sophia sputtered out a laugh. "I hate how easy that is to imagine. I am sorry, Tyler. I shouldn't have let that happen. And I should've warned you about those damn photos."

He stopped.

"Photos? What photos?" Then he remembered the flashbulbs going off during the confrontation with Amy, imagining the images the paparazzi caught, entirely out of context, in their ruthless quest for blood.

"I'm on your side. You know I am. But it's not hard to see why Amy was upset enough to confront you and set up this sucker punch interview." Sophia dug through her handbag, pulling out a newspaper folded open to the front page of the entertainment section. She sighed as she handed it over, two large color photos staring him in the face.

"Fuck." The word stretched out into at least five syllables.

In the largest image, Charlotte's arm around him wasn't the worst of it. Her cheeks were flushed, and her brown eyes sparkled from the marquee lights above their heads. As she looked up at him with a slight smile curving her lips, she looked like a girl waiting to be kissed.

At the time, he didn't see it that way. Maybe all the beers he'd tossed back were to blame, or maybe it was something else. He knew he hadn't crossed any lines, so his conscience was clear. Regardless, there was no denying how it appeared.

For once, Amy's jealous reaction was understandable. At least, it would've been if she hadn't fucked her bodyguard a few hours before that photo was snapped.

In the second image, he held Amy's wrists, anger twisting his features as he led her into the club and away from Charlotte. The caption made him want to vomit.

Hometown Rock Hero is Wife Abuser?

Sophia tugged the paper from his hands, shoving it into a trashcan. "So, I did some digging, and guess who's friendly with the author of this hit piece."

It felt like he'd been punched square in the chest. "Fucking Amy."

"Exactly." She continued toward the exit, and Tyler followed, dazed by the dueling images burned into his brain and the information overload. "Apparently, after the writer published a few glowing reviews for Scarlet Love Letter as a freelancer early in his career, Amy pulled some strings and got him a steady gig at the *Portland Mirror*. And here we are."

They burst through the double doors leading out of the building and headed for the parking lot. Adam and Zack were smoking, their arms gesturing wildly as they hollered out of earshot, undoubtedly about what they'd just endured. Adam kicked a dumpster, the clang echoing.

When Tyler thought back to the broken window, the possibility Amy was behind it seemed more likely than ever. Considering her shameless, unwarranted assault on his character and reputation, he realized he couldn't put anything past her.

Adam and Zack turned, their angry words halting as Tyler and Sophia approached.

She cleared her throat, her eyes moving between the three men. "Time for damage control, gentlemen. Our P.R. team will attack this nonsense head-on. If Amy thinks she can hurt the career you've worked so hard for, she's sorely mistaken." She turned to Tyler. "Your fans know who you are, Ty. It'll take more than a couple of unflattering photos to change that. And remember, she's not the only one with powerful friends in this town." With those reassuring words and a single wave, Sophia slipped inside her black BMW and drove off.

"Soph showed us the photos when we ran into her in the lobby." Adam smashed his cigarette under his boot. "This is bad, bro."

"You guys know I wouldn't—"

Adam waved him off. "Give us some fucking credit. I've known you since we were kids, and I've never seen you kill a damn spider, let alone get rough with a chick. But I've seen that crazy bitch scream in your face and disrespect you more times and ways than I can count. You never touched her. Hell, you never even yelled back. You'd just walk away. Wife beaters or whatever the fuck they're trying to call you, don't walk away."

"It's over, right?" Zack asked. "For real? She's not gonna bat her snake eyes and get you to forgive her?"

"Yeah, man." Tyler nodded as he lit a cigarette and took a deep drag. "It's over."

"Halle-fucking-lujah!" Zack punched the sky. "We can finally rant about how much we hate her without getting our asses kicked."

"Dude." Tyler shook his head, the events of the ridiculous morning fully sinking in. "Let the ranting begin."

14

Charlotte

"Why don't we have a song about bridges? We drive over them daily, they make excellent metaphors, and they're even part of song structure." Sandra's babbling was getting on Charlotte's already frayed nerves. The cops poking around her yard had her reliving a nightmare she'd thought was over, and the sound of breaking glass kept replaying in her head. Listening to some hack morning deejay attack Tyler was the cherry on top of the shit sundae. "Bridges, man! Fucking bridges."

Sandra, Charlotte, and Amber were having their weekly band meeting at Charlotte's house. It was built in 1912, and Sandra said it was her favorite place to work because the "old school" vibe got her creative juices flowing. The spare bedroom/music room floor was a mess of cords, amps, and instruments, in case they flowed in a direction everyone liked.

"So, write a song about bridges," Charlotte said, hoping to settle the matter so they could get some actual work done. And if there was one thing capable of quieting her nerves, it was music. She needed to get out of her head and get lost in the notes, focusing on nothing but the weight of her guitar and the words she was singing. "I'll stick to writing about what I know. Like living with the crippling fear of being murdered or eating microwave dinners by my damn self while watching Seinfeld."

"Not sure if you guys have talked to Eliza today," Sandra said, "but she booked Zoe from Sentient to fill in on bass for the Canadian shows. Now that we have set lists, I'll pass them on. She's taken, so it's temporary, but at least we'll be whole for the upcoming dates."

"Sweet!" Amber clapped. "One less thing to stress over."

"Fucking Jackie," Sandra said. "She could've at least ditched us for a decent band. Not wasting her talent playing god-awful Led Zep covers with her dumbass boyfriend."

"She's been flaky since they hooked up." Amber shrugged. "Barely made it to our last gig. Good riddance."

"Agreed," Charlotte said. "I'll keep playing bass when we record, but let's put feelers out for a permanent replacement. I'm going to Center of the Road later, so I'll check their board." Unless they were touring, she never missed hitting her favorite record store for a weekly fix of new music and feminist and punk zines. The band found their two previous bassists with an ad on the "Musicians Wanted" board in the shop, so maybe the third time would be a charm.

Sandra looked at Charlotte. "Hey, where were you last night? I called half an hour after you left my place, and you didn't answer."

Charlotte adjusted her perfectly tuned strings, weighing whether to tell her band about the window or avoid the topic altogether.

"Why'd you call?"

Sandra put her hands on her hips. "Why are you dodging the question?"

Amber jumped in. "Ooh, please say you were too busy making out with Tyler to answer the phone."

Sandra's head whipped in her direction. "What the motherfuck are you talking about?"

Amber laughed, clearly pleased with Sandra's reaction. "You said she was wearing his jacket! That's one step above holding hands in my book. And that photo of them in the *Mirror*—"

"For fuck's sake, you guys." Charlotte set her guitar on its stand.

When she was grabbing coffee on her way to practice, some teenage girls had a newspaper open on their table. Charlotte did a double-take when she saw her face. Without a word, she snatched the paper, skimming the article as the girls' shrieks of surprise turned into low whispers when recognition hit. At the words *wife abuser*, she slammed the paper down and left, too angry to stand in line for caffeine that would only worsen her already tattered nerves.

"Love triangle, my ass," Sandra said. "Charlotte's way too smart to hook up with a guy tangled in Amy's bullshit. Even one that looks like Winona Ryder and Keanu's love child."

"Enough!" Charlotte shouted. "We're *not* talking about that disgusting fucking article. Understood?" Her bandmates nodded, exchanging concerned looks.

The claim that Tyler and Charlotte were having an affair was the least offensive part. The idea that Tyler would hurt anyone, let alone a woman, was ludicrous. At her show, he was eager to throw her cheating ex out on his ass, but she knew he'd never get violent unless he were defending someone he cared about. Besides, she was there. She witnessed the entire encounter in front of the club. He pulled Amy away so she couldn't get at Charlotte, not because he was some abusive Neanderthal.

"All the *Mirror* is good for these days is covering the bottom of a birdcage. No one with half a brain believes the shit they write." Sandra mimed zipping her lips shut. "That's all I'll say about it."

"Thanks. Umm... I have to tell you guys something." Since practice was derailed anyway, Charlotte might as well rip off the Band-Aid and get all her recent drama on the table. "When Tyler was dropping me off last night, someone threw a piece of brick at the window by my head. I'm perfectly fine. See?" She gestured to her face. "Still gorgeous. It was scary, but nothing happened."

"Oh, my god!" Sandra set down her guitar and rushed to Charlotte, hugging her painfully tight. "Why didn't you come back to my house?"

"Or mine?" Amber asked.

She looked at Sandra. "You know I love you, but your overprotective ass would've made me freak out more than I already was. I had enough of that when I lived with my dad. Also, you're scrappy but tiny. I needed level-headed people who could throw down if whoever's fucking with me is a three-hundred-pound wrestler or some shit." She turned to Amber. "And you live with four sisters. You don't need me leading some whacko to your house."

"That makes sense." Amber joined in on the hug. "Who'd want to hurt you? You're like the nicest person ever."

Sandra stepped back. "Did you call the cop that helped you last time? Barlowe, right?"

"Yeah, I called him." Charlotte pulled away, picking up her guitar. "He's looking into it but thinks it was neighborhood kids. There've been a lot of broken mailboxes and egged houses on my block, so he figures they just got carried away. Regardless, I'll try not to go out alone. My house is like Fort Knox, so I'm safe here."

Sandra rubbed her chin. She did that whenever her brain was working overtime and when she was nervous. As she processed Charlotte's bombshell, both had to be true. "I'll tell Eliza to get extra security for the tour. And call Barlowe back. The fucked-up flowers on your porch, the ones in the dressing room, and now this? There has to be more he can do. Like driving your street every day, watching for anything weird."

Charlotte sighed, flashbacks of a childhood spent with a paranoid, overbearing father shuffling in. "I'll be okay. I promise. Now, can we please get back to work? The tracks for the benefit album still sound too green."

"Fine. Let's ripen that shit." Sandra squeezed Charlotte's shoulder until their eyes reconnected. "But later..."

"I'll call Barlowe again, you wonderful, bossy broken record."

Amber grabbed a Coke from the mini-fridge. "Was he the cute one with the mustache and tight butt?"

Charlotte laughed, grateful for the lightened mood in the room. "Yep. Want his number? If you've got a damsel in distress fantasy, you can't go wrong with a cop."

Worry lines remained etched on Sandra's face. She picked up her guitar, playing while humming a tune Charlotte didn't recognize.

"Ooh, interesting. New ballad?" Charlotte asked.

Sandra nodded and continued until closing it with a delicate finish.

Amber perked. "Hey, I kinda loved that. Play it again."

Sandra's hand dropped to her side, the worry lines deepening. "Has anything else happened you haven't told us about?"

Charlotte grumbled. "No. Just play, Sandra."

As Sandra started over, Charlotte played a few chords behind it. Amber hit "record" on the boombox at her feet, tapping out a beat with her hands and toes.

When they finished, Amber ended the recording and groaned. "I need my drums, dammit! Either the next practice is at my house, or you get a kit in here, Char."

"My neighbor's a grouchy old dude who told me to shut up because I sang while watering my plants. He'd put the cops on speed dial over drums."

They've been here enough.

After running through the songs for the benefit album until they were happy and tweaking a few for their upcoming LP, Amber took the tape from the boombox and slipped it into her purse. "I'll play with this when I get home. Loved where you guys went with 'Sated'."

"I get all my best ideas in the shower." Sandra bowed, her mass of auburn curls brushing the floor before settling on her back when she flipped upright. "Our benefit tracks are ready to rock, and the new album's off to a killer start, bitches! I can't wait to show Eliza our progress." She unplugged her guitar, setting it inside its felt-lined case. "If anyone gets a lead on a bassist, call me."

Amber collected her notebook and water bottle. "You guys think Tyler knows someone?"

"Ooh, yeah," Sandra said. "He knows all kinds of talented motherfuckers."

Charlotte twisted her hair into a loose bun, fastening it with the elastic band from her wrist. "I can ask, I guess." She ignored the obnoxious smirk on Sandra's face and picked up the candy wrappers they'd tossed on the floor. "I was gonna see if he wanted to hang later anyway. I feel bad that my problems overshadowed his, and I bet he could use someone to talk to. Besides Matty, of course." She dropped the wrappers into the wastebasket behind the door.

"What were you two talking about on my porch after the movie last night?" Sandra wrapped her cords and gathered her gear. "The air out there felt intense."

Charlotte sighed, recalling the sensation of slipping her arms into his jacket, still warm from his skin. "Nothing much. I can't believe I didn't know that jacket he always wears was his dad's." She thought of how his face fell when he told her. The way the edges of his mouth tipped back up when he said what a good guy his dad was. Charlotte wished she could've met the man who helped bring two of her favorite people into the world. "And I said we have his back with the divorce shit."

"Hold up." Sandra froze. "I thought he said separated. Is a divorce definitely happening?"

"Yep." A smile stretched Charlotte's face. "I think he's done. For real this time."

"Wow." Amber's eyebrows shot up. "That's huge. Good for him."

Sandra set down her gear. "Remember how confident and tough Ty was when we first met him? That woman's ground him down so much, I don't know if he'll ever get back there."

"Of course he will," Charlotte snapped, her smile evaporating. "Once he's out and has space to hear his own thoughts, he'll find himself again. And we'll be there to support him while he does."

Sandra touched her arm. "Goes without saying, Char. And we'll support him by throwing the biggest divorce party in history."

"Sounds like a plan." Charlotte's smile returned.

"Keg's on me," Amber chimed in.

"Thanks, guys. And I'll let you know what he says about potential bassists."

"Too bad Amy's so impossible," Amber said. "She knows more musicians than all of us put together. Maybe it's time to offer an olive branch?"

Sandra's eyes burned a hole through Amber's skull. "Only if I can hit that bitch over the head with it for what she did to Charlotte. And Tyler. Hell no. End of discussion."

"I second that 'hell no'." Charlotte rubbed her arms. She wondered if there'd ever come a time when the mention of Amy didn't make her feel like screaming, crying, and punching things simultaneously.

"Oops. Terrible joke. Just trying to diffuse the bummer vibes." Amber's shoulders caved forward before she shot an apologetic glance at Charlotte. "Sorry."

"Don't sweat it, babe." Charlotte waved it off. Fortunately for Amber, she only had secondhand accounts of Amy's insanity to go by. It was easier for her to make jokes without poking old scars with a sharp stick. "Need help getting this stuff to your cars?"

Sandra took her guitar case in one hand and amp in the other. "To that, I offer the third 'hell no' of the day. Thanks for letting us invade your space, sweetie." She pecked Charlotte's cheek and headed for the door.

"Anytime."

Amber walked to Charlotte and paused. "Sorry I brought up Amy. I guess I just—"

"Again, don't sweat it." She hugged Amber. "See you Saturday?"

"Yep. Stay safe, Char."

When her bandmates left, she armed her security system and stared at the numbers on the panel, lost in thought. Fear of the brick thrower's intentions remained, but right then, something else was even more distressing. The tender edges of old wounds had been scraped, and tears pricked her eyes. Her mind drifted to her final night in Scarlet Love Letter.

There'd be no olive branch extended to Amy, now or ever. It wasn't in Charlotte's nature to offer forgiveness for things she could never forget.

And it wasn't in Amy's nature to ask for it.

15

Charlotte

Amy gently brushed Charlotte's damp hair off her forehead as they sat on a bench on the rooftop of Hideaways. They were coming down from the rush of playing a sold-out show downstairs, and Amy said she needed fresh air to bring her back to earth. As usual, Charlotte happily followed.

"You were amazing tonight, Charlotte. I've never seen you let loose like that, and the crowd ate it up."

Charlotte was flying extra high after filling in for Scarlet Love Letter's lead guitarist, Sarah Slate. Sarah quit an hour before showtime when a positive pregnancy test made her rethink her life. Charlotte jumped at the opportunity. She knew every note by heart. And bored with playing bass, she desperately wanted to trade it for the instrument she'd been obsessed with since she was twelve. She also loved having more to sing, her voice melding with Amy's as they filled the space with Amy's beautiful words.

"I learned from the best," Charlotte said.

The corner of Amy's cherry-red mouth lifted. "Flattery will get you everywhere."

She'd learned a lot from watching Amy work her magic on audiences for almost a year. Charlotte went from clumsy and unsure onstage to a commanding presence who knew exactly how to entice a crowd to fall under her spell. She wasn't as brash and in-your-face as Amy, instead using the power of her playing to draw them in. That night, as she nailed the most challenging riff in their catalog, she caught the eye of a spiky-haired punk boy in the front row. He held his fingers up in a 'V' and licked the letter with such shameless vulgarity Charlotte had to laugh. Countless other faces seemed locked into an ecstatic trance, and she felt drunk with the power of turning people on with music.

Amy got to her feet. "I need a drink."

"Are you coming back up?" Charlotte cringed at the desperation in her voice. She wasn't ready for the rare one-on-one time to end. After marrying Tyler three months before, Amy gave him all her free time while her band got the crumbs. Charlotte had been getting the smallest piece for too damn long.

"Only if things are even duller down there." Amy grinned.

"I'm serious. Now that you're married, I hardly see you."

"Sorry, doll." Amy patted the top of Charlotte's head. "Things have been crazy because Ty was on tour, we're trying to find a house, and—"

"Don't apologize for having a life."

The last thing Charlotte wanted to hear about was their domestic bliss. Despite her best efforts to smother her feelings for Tyler under a pile of one-night stands, she couldn't shake the frustrating, totally fucking inconvenient certainty that they belonged together. But, like wearing blue eyeliner or using too much hair gel, she hoped it was a phase she'd eventually grow out of.

"Want a glass of Cab?"

Charlotte nodded.

As Amy disappeared down the stairwell, Charlotte pulled in deep, stinging lungfuls of midnight air. Despite the dissatisfaction about her band position, her life had turned out better than she'd imagined when she was an awkward, late-blooming band geek at Franklin High. Scarlet Love Letter steadily gained momentum after releasing an album they were incredibly proud of. Every show since the release had sold out in minutes. With her cut, she'd moved into a beautiful downtown loft overlooking Waterfront Park and bought her first car that wasn't over five years old. She had Amy to thank for a lot of it. Amy even got her the bartending job at Calamity, keeping the bills paid while she waited for the next wave of band money to roll in.

Charlotte was living her dream, but most of all, she had the opportunity to help struggling people find hope. At her darkest times, music saved her. Sharing that gift with others gave her purpose and fueled her fire. At every gig, she searched the audience, seeking out the most miserable soul, locking onto them as she pushed herself harder, waiting. Sometimes it took a few songs, sometimes only a few bars, but it always happened—that split second when their pain morphed into joy. When they went from feeling desperately alone to realizing they're surrounded by people who share a love that never rejects or disappoints. A love that's only a concert ticket or "play" button away.

Once that truth sinks in, you never forget it.

High-heeled boots clicked up the stairs, turning her head. Amy held out a glass, and Charlotte's fingers wrapped around the thin stem.

"Cheers, gorgeous." Amy returned to the bench, clinking their glasses together.

As they took their first sips, the question bouncing around Charlotte's brain all night refused to wait a second longer. She looked out at the sea of city lights below them and raised her eyes to the blanket of stars above. Other than the soft light of the half moon, their spot on the roof was bathed in darkness, a somber limbo between the two sparkling worlds.

"Cassie was great filling in on bass tonight." She tapped Amy's knee, covered in black fishnet stockings. "Maybe we can get her on permanently so I can take over for Sarah." She held her breath.

Amy crossed one long, slender leg over the other. "Actually, Lara Massie's taking over for Sarah. She's begged me for months to give her a shot."

Heat flooded Charlotte's chest. "But you just said how amazing I was tonight, and you know how badly I've wanted to play guitar. I've earned it, Amy."

Sarah had known Amy longer when they formed the band, so she snagged that coveted spot. Charlotte was sure she was next in line, and now that she knew exactly what she'd been missing, she couldn't stand the thought of going back.

"Earned it? Honey, I've known Lara since middle school. You know damn well the only way to earn favors from me is through time and loyalty. She has you beat on both counts." Amy lifted the wine to her lips.

"That's ridiculous!" Charlotte choked on the anger burning in her throat. "How have I not been loyal?"

"Let's see." Amy held up her manicured fingers, counting off the supposed grievances. "You let Starcrosser's manager talk to you about auditioning for them, you keep being friendly with my husband after I've repeatedly told you to back off, and right fucking now, you're questioning my ability to make decisions for the band I created."

"That's bullshit! You might've started Scarlet, but what it is now, we built together. All four of us. You just took it upon yourself to run things because you're obsessed with control."

Amy scoffed. "I'm in charge because I have more experience, wrote the songs, bought most of our equipment, and have the connections that got us this far. I was paying my dues in this town when you were still playing saxophone at high school football games, for fuck's sake. I've earned the right to call the shots."

Charlotte's eyes rolled. Sure, Amy was massively talented, but she also had a fat trust fund to buy equipment and favors with. Thinking her parents' money gave her license to make all the decisions was absurd. Something else was even more offensive, Charlotte's anger flaring. "So, because I caught the eye of another band's manager and was polite enough to hear him out, I'm disloyal?"

"Yes. It should've been a flat-out rejection. Instead, people thought you were searching for a new band behind my back. You made me look like a fool."

Charlotte knew that was an unforgivable crime in Amy's book, no matter how off-base it was. "And you know Tyler and I just talk about books and music and shit. We're friends. You have no reason to be jealous of that."

Amy laughed, but it sounded forced and phony. "I'm not jealous, Charlotte. I'm just terrible at sharing my toys. If he has time and attention to dole out, it should go to me."

"You're unbelievable. You won't even give me a chance to take over for Sarah? Seriously?"

"It isn't your time to be in the spotlight." Amy's arm fell behind Charlotte, settling on the back of the bench. A finger lazily stroked the bare skin of her shoulder blade. "You're only twenty-two, doll. There's plenty of time to inch closer to the front."

Charlotte tried to let the dream of playing lead die, but it hurt too much. She brushed Amy's hand off her shoulder. "Fuck this. That's *my* spot. You know damn well I'm better than Lara. What matters is what's best for the band, not who you think's earned it through your ridiculous criteria."

Amy's nostrils flared and her eyes narrowed, their faces a breath apart. "Who the *fuck* do you think you're talking to? You'd still be slumming it in shitty garage bands without me, and you're trying to talk like my goddamn *equal*?"

Amy got to her feet. Refusing to be intimidated, Charlotte did the same before tossing her glass of wine onto the concrete. A wry smile tugged at her lips when the shatter made Amy flinch.

"No, Amy. I'm not your equal. Because I'm a better guitarist than you are."

Amy barked out a mirthless laugh. "You delusional little bitch. Nothing original ever came from that amateur poseur head of yours. That's why you didn't get Sarah's spot. You aren't good enough to play guitar for me. You're too average and weak to make it as a real musician." She twirled the ends of Charlotte's hair before her hand was slapped away. "You're just a pretty prop."

"If you really believe that, you're the one who's delusional." Charlotte swallowed the tears clogging her throat. The insults reeked of bullshit but hearing them from someone she'd looked up to still stung.

Amy's hazel eyes widened, their gold flecks catching the moonlight. "Well, guess what, sweetie? You just earned the chance to prove it because you're out of my band." She tossed her waves of wild red hair over her shoulder. "Let's see how you do without my coattails to ride on, you ungrateful little cunt. I'll make sure no one in this town will have anything to do with you. You'll be homeless before the end of the year."

Charlotte shook her head, disbelief transforming into disgust. "You know... I've heard the stories about you turning on people dumb enough to get close to you and never believed them. You sure put on a good show, don't you?" She stepped closer despite Amy looking poised to slap her. "But you're nothing but a big fake with a gaping black hole where your heart should be. That's why no one will ever really love you. You deserve those leeches like Rafael and Issac who use you for drugs, money, or fame. That's all you have to offer."

Amy's lips curled into a devilish smirk as she stepped forward, their toes nearly touching. "I think my husband would disagree. Clearly, you're too boring and average for him too. That's why his ring is on *my* finger."

Charlotte refused to let that get to her, searching for a retort that would cut through Amy's cruel veneer. Once she had it, it was hard to keep a poker face.

"I bet it stings that you were his second choice." Charlotte smiled as the fire in Amy's glare intensified. "You saw us talking, the way he looked at me. You couldn't stand that someone wanted me instead of you."

"Didn't take long to change his mind." Amy waggled her ring finger.

"Sure. But the only way you could get a man like him was by swooping in when he was vulnerable, putting on an act to keep him hooked. Hell, I'm only now getting to see the real you, and I can't wait to leave you behind. He'll figure you out someday and do the same."

A shadow in Charlotte's periphery spooked her, her head whipping around. Rafael, Amy's human tank of a bodyguard, stood a few feet away, his eyes landing on the broken glasses before slowly raking over Charlotte's bare arms. She shivered. The adrenaline from the show and the fiery exchange with Amy kept the nighttime chill at bay, but something in his eyes made her blood run cold. He'd always given her the creeps, though she could never put her finger on why. Now, being alone with two people she didn't trust made her want to run until her lungs gave out.

"I heard shouting." His attention slid to Amy and held, like a dog waiting for orders from his master. "You good?"

"Charlotte was just leaving. Make sure she doesn't try to swipe any of the shit I paid for on the way out."

Charlotte laughed bitterly as she inched around Rafael and toward the stairs, her heart pounding. When he stepped forward and touched her lower back to guide her, she spun around to face him, backing up to put distance between them.

"Don't fucking touch me. I'm going."

His gaze shamelessly dropped to her chest, his pupils expanding before his attention returned to Amy. She waved her hand, Rafael obediently backing away so Charlotte could pass.

She walked away numb, the shock of the encounter settling into her bones. In a matter of minutes, her entire future had shifted.

She no longer had a band.

She'd lost one of her best friends.

Knowing Amy, she'd probably make a call that took away the bartending job, too. Hell, she might even find a way to turn Tyler against her.

Everything that mattered most in her life was yanked away all at once.

Charlotte made her way downstairs and through the building, fighting back tears. Sadness fell like a heavy curtain behind her eyes. She thought of going to Sandra's but couldn't bear the *I told you so* lecture that was inevitable. And completely warranted.

But on the long walk home through familiar, winding streets, something unexpected happened. As she turned over the past year's events, she saw all the ways Amy had held her back. The countless rejected songs Charlotte had written. Amy's refusal to even listen to guitar riffs she came up with to elevate the band's sound. Amy even told her what to wear on their album cover so she wouldn't stand out too much. Charlotte had been so grateful for the opportunities and new experiences that she'd ignored all the ways her role had stifled her.

What initially felt like a curse came to feel like a gift.

When her head hit the pillow that night, the determination surging in her belly made it impossible to sleep. Instead, she started planning.

She would form her own band.

She'd get to live out the fleeting dream she tasted earlier that night and play guitar in front of thousands of screaming fans on her terms. All the songs that Amy rejected would get to be recorded and performed. The heartbreak was in there too, but she refused to let it diminish the excitement of the possibilities ahead.

And while she plotted out her future, she vowed to make Amy Carey regret ever thinking Charlotte belonged in the background.

16

Tyler

"**G**oddamn, we sound terrible." Zack gripped fistfuls of his short black hair as his bass hung loose across his chest. "What the fuck, guys?"

Tyler nodded in agreement. Their producer, Bruce Roman, sat behind the soundproof glass, rubbing the back of his neck and scowling. Obviously, he felt the same. Maybe a morning session wasn't the best idea, but they'd hoped to get a full day of recording in. They couldn't have anticipated the disastrous interview and tabloid fallout that left them all too stressed and exhausted to bring their A games.

"Maybe your heinous chili dog breath's slowly killing us," Adam chimed in from his seat behind the drums. "I can smell your reek from here, dude."

"Your mom seems to like me just fine." Zack tossed a pick at Adam's forehead. Adam raised his arm, threatening to hurl a drumstick in retaliation.

"You sound like a couple of twelve-year-olds," Tyler said. Adam and Zack hadn't changed much in the maturity department since high school, but their talent and passion for their music were undeniable. When they weren't in piss-poor moods, that is. "I know we're all burnt out. Bruce said we can cut out early, but can we get this track recorded first?"

Adam wiped the sweat from his upper lip. "I'd love to, but it's hard to focus when Zack's backing vocals are flat."

"Your sister's flat." Zack chucked another pick at Adam.

Tyler rubbed his temples. He'd take a bullet for his bandmates, but sometimes, he wanted to knock their obnoxious skulls together until they cracked.

"First, my mom, now my sister," Adam said. "You gonna insult my damn dog next?"

"Guys!" Tyler's shout startled them. "Pretty fucking please with brown sugar on top. Let's record the damn song."

Zack played the opening bass line of The Rolling Stones' "Brown Sugar".

Tyler kicked the nearest wall. He could really use a drink. He practically drooled thinking about the Macallan in the kitchen cupboard. One of the many benefits of having a studio on your property is that your vices—and the instant relief they offer—are always close at hand.

He looked up to find Bruce's eyes and goateed mouth scrunched in an impatient grimace. Time was money, and Bruce didn't appreciate either being wasted. His eyes narrowed on Tyler, and he gave a quick nod. Whenever Adam and Zack got on Bruce's nerves, he counted on Tyler to get them in line.

"Adam, quit screwing around," Tyler said. "Zack, sorry buddy, but you were a little flat on the chorus. Let's stay focused and nail it this time."

As they usually did when Tyler pulled out his "dad voice," his bandmates put on their serious faces. The next take was flawless.

Bruce left two songs later, but Adam and Zack stuck around to decompress, as they always did after a session.

"Are we banned from the house or what?" Zack took a long drag from his freshly rolled joint. "I've got cottonmouth like a motherfucker."

"It's still mine, so we're not banned from anything." Tyler hadn't planned on going in until Matthew helped move his stuff. The studio had a bathroom and plenty of snacks, but the fridge was empty except for a moldy lime and a nearly empty bottle of Jäegermeister. "There are water bottles under Adam's kit."

"Water's for fish, man." Zack ashed the joint over a potted ficus with more brown leaves than green. "I need beer."

Adam took the joint, blowing a thick white ring into the air. "Same here. We deserve some celebrating after locking down those tracks."

Tyler hit his cigarette, sinking back into the cushy black office chair behind the soundboard. Celebrating was the last thing he wanted to do. He was worried about Charlotte and couldn't shake the tabloid image of his angry, twisted face. The photo had branded the bold, black print of *abuser* on his brain.

What toll might it take on his career? Would it hurt the sales of the next album? Would there be more and more empty seats in the venues, or would it become harder to get booked in the first place? It wasn't fair to Adam, Zack, and everyone who counted on them for a paycheck to have that stain on what they'd worked so hard for. And he wouldn't put it past Amy to have more tricks up her sleeve if the public shaming didn't satisfy her thirst for revenge.

Tyler rubbed his forehead, his planted feet twisting him side to side in the swiveling chair. All the unknowns hanging over him made him feel caged and restless, like a pacing tiger in the zoo. Too many things were out of his control, and he wanted to take some power back.

Zack waved in front of Tyler's face. "Earth to Tyler. House? Drinks?"

He nodded once, getting to his feet. Without music to focus on, his brain kept kicking into overdrive. A beer wouldn't change that, but a few glasses of Macallan might do the trick.

"Fine." Tyler smashed his cigarette into the nearest ashtray. "Please resist the urge to break Amy's shit."

Zack laughed. "You know us too well, my dude. I'd never hit a woman, but putting my fist through one of her pictures would make my fucking day."

Adam stood, stretching his arms above his head. "Behave yourself, Zacky. We're not making any more trouble for Ty than he's already got."

They crossed the thin strip of lawn separating the studio from the main house, anxiety prickling Tyler's throat with every step. When he opened the door, the eerie silence made it worse. After all the shocks and chaos of the previous forty-eight hours, the quiet was such a contrast, it was disturbing.

Still, he'd gladly take that over what greeted him the last time he'd stood in that spot—the moans of his wife and her fuckboy during their revolting bang-fest on his couch.

"Damn. Hella creepy in here, right?" Zack pushed past them on his way to the kitchen.

"Seriously." Adam followed, flipping off every photo of Amy he passed. "Feels like that cheating twatwaffle's watching us through the walls or some shit."

Tyler trailed behind, tossing his army jacket onto the bougie antique chair no one ever sat in. It was one of many pretty things in the house that dented his bank account and served no actual purpose.

His eyes wandered, landing on the weird clown sculpture from Paris, the hideous orange tapestry from Venice, the custom leather couch that cost more than most people make in a year—all useless crap Amy *had* to have. His guitars, notebooks, band T-shirts, and his dad's jacket were the only physical things that mattered to him. She could keep everything else or burn it for all he cared.

On the walk to the kitchen to grab drinks, memories of their life together were everywhere—a vase of dried wedding flowers on the bookshelf, the crystal snow globe from their Fiji honeymoon, the silver jukebox she bought for his twenty-fourth birthday. It was like an eight-bedroom, four-bath shrine to a dead relationship.

"You know what sounds good after that brutal session?" Adam grabbed two beers and handed one to Zack. "Your hot tub."

"Oh, hells yeah." Zack popped the cap, and his head tipped back, guzzling his beer before belching and grabbing another. "We had some epic times in that tub. Seems right to take one last soak."

Tyler's house was the scene of countless wild parties, some lasting for days. In particular, the hot tub had seen its share of dirty action, including an orgy Zack and Adam pulled together with six female guests while Tyler and Amy were inside making out on the couch.

That fucking couch.

He suddenly wanted to demand it in the divorce just to torch it.

"Yeah, sure." After swiping the bottle of whiskey from the cabinet, he poured several shots into a crystal glass.

Adam tapped Tyler's arm with his bottle. "You're way too fucking quiet today, bro. Don't let the divorce bullshit eat you up when you should be looking forward to the awesome single life you've been missing out on."

"Yeah, I can't wait to start dodging starfuckers and gold diggers." Tyler opened the sliding glass door, entering the expansive backyard while Adam and Zack followed. He stripped to his boxers, and they did the same. He'd had eight-foot privacy fencing installed around the yard's perimeter when they first bought the place so they could fully relax, which was exactly what he needed.

"Not gonna lie, there's some of that." Adam kicked his tattered jeans to the edge of the cedar deck. "But most dudes would kill to be in your big black Docs. You're young, rich, talented as hell, and that face of yours is a pussy magnet. Think about all the model-hot women, wet and ready, throwing themselves at you backstage. Now you get to say yes."

"Nothing beats having different lips wrapped around your cock every night," Zack added, grabbing his crotch for emphasis.

"Grow up, man." Tyler's upper lip curled in disgust. "You sound like a skeevy hair band dickhead." He ignored his bandmates as they fist-bumped, yammering about the club they'd hit that night to pick up girls.

The brisk breeze swept over Tyler's bare skin, making him shiver, but the cold felt more reviving than uncomfortable. He looked out at the fruit trees lining the rear of the property and flowering bulbs poking up between evergreen shrubs and ferns. Nature always calmed his nerves, even when it was as carefully plotted-out and manicured as the nature outside his backdoor.

Tyler turned on the jets and slid off the cover, dipping his fingers in to test the temperature. *Perfect.* He set his whiskey on the deck before sliding inside the hot, bubbling water. Sitting back with his head on the waterproof cushion, he let out a full-body sigh. As his muscles relaxed, he picked up the glass, taking a sip that made heat trail down his throat.

"I gotta ask, man." Adam wet his hair and shook it like a Labrador. "What's up with that pic of you and Charlotte outside Apocalypse?" He must've seen the anger rising in Tyler's expression because he held up a dripping hand as if to say *hold on.* "I know you didn't cheat on Amy Scary. But now that ding, dong, the bitch is dead, is something starting there?"

Tyler had been asking himself the same thing, and no simple answer existed. Getting a fresh perspective from two people who knew him better than most might help. Since Matthew and Charlotte were close, it was hard to talk about her without worrying he might let something slip after too many beers. Laying out his cards to Zack and Adam was worth a shot.

"I keep thinking about the night I met her. The connection we had, the spark." He set down his glass, his eyes moving from one friend to the other. As expected, their faces were judgment-free. "When you're drawn to someone and things go a different way, where does that spark go?"

Zack slicked back his wet hair. "I think we all agree me and Adam are no experts on relationships."

They all laughed at the absurd degree of truth in that statement.

"But I know all about sparks." Zack's expression turned serious. "When you lock eyes with a chick who's different somehow. Fucking special with a capital 'S,' you know? It's like the universe smacked you upside the head, saying *that's* the one you belong with. Maybe not forever. Maybe just a weekend you'll think about the rest of your life." He jabbed a dripping finger at Tyler. "But you listen to it. If the spark between you and Charlotte never fully went out, I say you throw kerosene on that bitch and let it rip."

"Damn, Zack," Adam said. "You gonna start reciting poetry now or what?"

Zack splashed Adam's face before flipping him the bird.

"Don't be a dick." Tyler splashed him, too. When Zack met his eyes, Tyler saw the immature jokester leave the building, a wounded man taking his place. "You ever hear from her?"

Adam groaned, his eyes rolling. "Is this about fucking Mandy? Don't start that shit right now. We're having a nice soak."

Mandy was a thirty-year-old club promoter Zack had a fling with in Denver the year before. Tyler had never seen his hit-it-and-quit-it friend so hung up on someone. Zack took her out to dinner, sent flowers, and called her for weeks after their tour moved on. Ultimately, the distance didn't work for her, and she broke it off. Zack dove back into the endless supply of backstage booty while pretending nothing was wrong, but Tyler and Adam knew the truth. Zack had finally opened his heart to the possibility of real love, and it was crushed.

"Old news." Zack swigged his beer. "We're still talking about Charlotte and what Tyler's gonna do with her now that his shackles are off."

They laughed, the heaviness in Zack's expression fading.

"I kissed her hand." Tyler laughed again as Adam choked on his beer.

"You fucking *what*?" Adam coughed, wiping his mouth with his wrist.

"We slept at Matty's, me on the floor, her on the couch. We'd just been through something intense, and... I don't know. It made sense." He shrugged, the memory of her soft skin against his lips making him shift in his seat. "The night we met, I'd never wanted to kiss a girl so fucking badly. Those gorgeous brown eyes of hers looked up at me and her mouth was inches from mine." As he described it, he felt the magnetic pull as if he were back in the moment.

All he had to do was lean in, and everything would've been different. He'd know what it felt like to kiss Charlotte. To stoke that spark and give in to that delicious pull.

"But she doesn't give second chances, so how I feel doesn't matter." Tyler reached for his glass, the electric tingle in his chest fizzling out. "I hurt her. We both felt something, and I chose someone else. Someone who became her enemy. I don't know if I could've stayed friends with someone who did that, but she's a better person than any of us."

Adam and Zack nodded in agreement, their sympathetic eyes set on Tyler.

"I blew my only shot, and I'm never leaving the friend zone." He swallowed the last of his whiskey. "But it's still a hell of a lot better than not knowing her at all."

"Ty—" Adam began, but Tyler waved him off.

Admitting out loud the situation was hopeless made him wish he hadn't brought it up. The pity in their eyes only made it worse. "Let it drop, okay?"

"Fuck that noise." Zack leaned forward, the tips of his hair dripping. "Since when do you quit so easily? You're the guy who flew to L.A. to camp out in front of Bruce Fucking Roman's office because you refused to take no for an answer. Now, a goddamn rock legend's on our team. Because you fought for it."

"Fuckin' A." Adam raised his beer. "The shit holding you back from chasing Charlotte is all in your mind, brother. What if she's waiting for you to get your head outta your ass to make the first move?"

"Nailed it." Zack tapped the neck of his bottle against Adam's. "And Charlotte's a solid ten. Don't wait until some other asshole figures that out and hooks her."

"Like this asshole." Adam pointed at himself. "She's not just hot. She's a kickass guitarist and feisty as hell. I love that shit."

"Watch it." Tyler glared at his laughing, about-to-be-drowned bandmates.

"Go after her, Ty," Zack said. "Throw kerosene on that shit now or regret it later."

They'd given Tyler a lot to think about when he'd already had more than he could handle. He climbed out of the tub before grabbing three towels from the storage box on the deck. The breeze made the hair on his arms and legs stand up, but the whiskey kept his insides warm, and his nerves mostly settled.

The guys got out, drying off on their way inside the house.

Tyler lit a smoke, turning to grab a water bottle from the fridge when he noticed Zack's attention locked on the refrigerator door. He moved beside him, following his line of sight.

"Maybe I'm trippin'..." Zack's finger slammed on a photo attached to the door by a small black magnet. "But isn't that the same fedora the dude wore in that tabloid pic?"

It wasn't on the fridge when Tyler left for Australia and didn't look familiar. It looked like a Scarlet Love Letter promo shot taken under the Burnside Bridge. Amy's red dress barely covered her underwear as she posed with her arms splayed and her back against a concrete wall. Her drummer, Issac, stood beside her, looking as ridiculous as always with his lips pursed and chin raised, the usual pompous glint in his eye. Tyler confirmed Zack's suspicion about the hat before narrowing in on a single detail—the silver wallet chain spilling from Issac's left pocket.

Tyler walked to the fancy leather couch, stubbing his cigarette on the headrest, leaving a dozen charred circles behind.

"That. Fucking. *Bitch*!"

He raced upstairs and into their bathroom, digging through the trash until he found it—the blurry tabloid photo of a woman who looked like Amy making out with some fedora-wearing asshole. He stomped back to the kitchen, his bandmates stunned silent, probably waiting to see if he'd actually lost his mind. He yanked the photo off the fridge, sending the magnet flying.

He set both photos on the kitchen table to be sure she'd see them.

Tyler promised himself it was the last time he'd allow himself to be fooled.

The last time he'd accept less than he deserved to avoid being alone.

"You okay, man?"

Tyler barely registered Adam's hand on his back as he grabbed a Sharpie from the junk drawer, drawing a thick black circle around the man's head in the tabloid shot. He did the same on the promo—circling the head of her drummer, Issac, whose signature blond spikes were hidden underneath the same fucking hat.

In his gut, Tyler had known the truth all along.

Believing Amy's endless denials meant his life could stay as it was.

Now, he didn't know if he'd been more afraid everything would change or nothing at all.

With the marker in his fist, he imagined Amy coming home and seeing the photos. It didn't feel like enough. That betrayal wasn't worse than the other things she'd done, so what would it accomplish? He didn't need another empty apology.

Hell, she'd probably put the photo up for him to find just to shove the knife in deeper.

Tyler had never been vindictive, but the rage firing in his chest made him want to lash out.

She'd humiliated him.

Spread vicious lies about him in the media.

Threatened his career.

Why should she get the last word? After making everyone think she's the victim, no less.

"What's going on in your head?" Zack asked.

Tyler snatched the kitchen phone, dialing the band's publicist before he could talk himself out of it. "Hey, Tracy. It's Tyler Hall. I'm gonna fax you something I want splashed all over the goddamn gossip rags tomorrow morning. And I want it made public that Amy and I were separated *before* the fucking photos were snapped outside Apocalypse. And that I'm divorcing her ass." He hung up, taking in the worried looks of his friends. "Any objections?"

Adam and Zack glanced at each other, shrugging before they looked back at Tyler.

"Okay then." Tyler took the photos to the fax machine beside the kitchen table, feeding them into the machine.

"You sure, Ty?" Adam watched over his shoulder as he dialed. "Once it's done, there's no taking it back."

"Yeah, man." Zack grabbed the Macallan, refilling Tyler's empty glass. "Have another drink before you do something you regret."

As Tyler imagined the look on Amy's face when she realized what he'd done, he started laughing. If they hadn't thought he'd cracked before, they were definitely thinking it now.

But he felt the opposite. Reclaiming some control over the situation made him feel saner than he had in days.

"You know what, my friends?" He picked up his glass and raised it in the air before tossing back a heavy gulp. "I'm done with regrets. Done taking her bullshit lying down." A smile tugged at a corner of his mouth. "From now on, I'm fighting fire with fire."

❧

When his bandmates left, Tyler sat on the living room floor, the ends of his hair still damp from the hot tub. He poured another shot of whiskey. The kitchen phone rang as he took a long sip, but he let the machine answer. For once, he was enjoying quiet and solitude.

After a beep, a female voice filled the kitchen:

"Tyler, I haven't heard from you in a while," his mother said, "so I thought I'd check in. I hope you had a nice trip."

The uncharacteristic sweetness in her tone made him set down the glass and pay closer attention.

She continued, "My car payment's late. You gotta wire me some money."

There it is. He stood, shuffling over to the machine.

"Call when you get this—" Tyler hit the delete button and returned to the living room.

He tossed back the rest of his shot, pouring more as the phone rang again.

Knowing his mother wouldn't relent until he paid her bill, he crawled from the coffee table, using the arm of the cigarette-burned sofa to get to his feet. Lack of sleep, combined with the alcohol, made his limbs slow and heavy. As if he were trudging through a heap of wet sand.

"Hello?"

"Tyler? You sound like shit. Were you asleep?"

"Charlotte?"

"Yeah, it's Charlotte. Everything okay?"

He rubbed his eyes, the room blurring at the edges. "Yeah, why?"

"I don't know. You sound... off."

"Had a few drinks with the guys. And a few more after they left." He snickered, glancing at the half-empty bottle. "We laid down some new tracks, wanted to celebrate." He also wanted to celebrate going public with proof Amy's infidelity came before the photo of him and Charlotte, but he'd share that in person. "You okay? I was gonna call in a few to ask how the police report went."

"Yeah, I'm good. I'll fill you in on details later, but the police did their thing, and practice was decent. No more attempted murders." She let out an awkward laugh. "You're drinking alone in that big, empty house? That's no fun."

Tyler patted his pockets, coming up empty. He really needed a smoke. He walked the cordless phone into the kitchen, grabbing a carton of cigarettes from the cupboard above the sink.

"To be honest, being here's fucking weird." He ripped open the carton, removing a pack. "Like my stuff's here, but I don't belong. Hell, maybe I never did. I'm calling a cab as soon as I hang up."

He pulled out a cigarette, lighting it with the flame of the gas stove. As he drew the smoke deep into his lungs, the relief was so intense his eyes shut in bliss.

"Busy later?" she asked.

"Nope." He exhaled, the thick cloud of smoke hovering in front of his face. "Rest of my day's wide open. Something going on?"

"I'm heading to Sauvie Island to hit the Farmers' Market. Wanna join me?" She paused. "God, it sounds so stupid when I say it out loud. Forget it."

"No, I like fresh peaches as much as the next guy. Clean air and a change of scenery sound good, too. I just don't wanna get hassled." That was true, but he also didn't want to risk another unfortunate paparazzi shot ending up in the papers.

"Wear a hoodie and sunglasses. It's spring in Portland—you'll blend in. And peaches aren't ready until summer, so it's mostly asparagus and greens. Plus, this amazing candlemaker will be there, and I plan to shove way too much money at her. Pick you up in an hour?"

He caught himself before asking if it was safe for her to be in public, remembering what she said about not letting her stalker keep her from living her life. At least if Tyler was with her, he knew she'd be okay.

"Cool. You can tell me about your morning on the drive." He set up the coffeemaker for a sorely needed, sobering caffeine boost. "Is it just the two of us?"

Charlotte went quiet. "Yeah, I uh, I know when we usually go out, Matthew or Sandra's there, but I thought it'd be a good chance to talk without distractions. Is that okay?"

"Of course." Tyler's brows pinched. Something in her tone made him curious about what she wanted to discuss. "See you soon."

17

Tyler

"You did *what*?"

Tyler laughed at Charlotte's shocked face. "Maybe it's a dick move, but I wanted to give her a taste of her own medicine for once." She stared as he buckled his seatbelt.

"Balancing the scales a bit isn't a dick move." Her expression changed, a broad smile lighting up her face as she turned the key in the ignition and shifted into drive. "I'm impressed."

He knew faxing those photos and making the divorce public would poke the bear, but it would also send a message. Tyler was done with Amy's games, and there'd be consequences for her actions from then on. Soon, they'd be out of each other's lives for good.

"After that, I called my lawyer and business manager to ensure my accounts were secure. They're drawing up divorce papers as we speak." Knowing everything was in motion to set him free made him grin, the final threads of tension loosening in his chest. "She can't touch me or my money ever again. Guess which one might make her cry."

"It still has to hurt." Her smile fell. "It's okay to take time to grieve what you lost."

"I'll be fine." It wasn't just the whiskey lingering in his system that made it feel true. Every step away from his old life felt like a leap toward the one that he really wanted. And learning from past mistakes instead of making new ones might help the rest of his dreams fall into place. "I already knew she was a cheater and a liar. It just sucks getting hit over the head with how deep it went."

"I worry that my drama's been such a distraction you haven't had time to process yours. You've been through a lot this week." She squeezed his wrist, the pad of her thumb sliding along the exposed skin below his sleeve. "It's cool if you're not up for the farm. We could get wasted instead. Or go to a strip club or whatever guys do to feel better. Girls just eat ice cream and cry."

"I like ice cream." Tyler chuckled, sipping his coffee. Eager to talk about absolutely anything besides Amy, he opted for a subject change. "I cannot picture you in a titty bar."

Her lips quirked. "There's a lot you don't know about me, mister. I've stuffed my share of singles under sequined bra straps over the years."

"Okay then." He grinned at the naughty mental image. "I appreciate your concern, but I don't need to get shitfaced or stare at oiled boobs to feel better. I'm all in for the Farmer's Market, which isn't a sentence I ever thought I'd say."

Charlotte laughed. "It did sound super weird coming from you." She glanced over her shoulder and merged onto the highway. "I hope it'll help us get our minds off things for a few hours at least."

Tyler turned to her, a rush of gratitude sweeping in. She was taking time out of her life to help him feel better despite her own problems and a major tour to prepare for. He was grateful to have a friend who recognized what he needed. One who cared enough to bring him some joy as he picked up the pieces of his fractured life. The fact that she was beautiful and smelled like flowers and vanilla shampoo was a nice bonus.

"Do you think they'll have funnel cakes or elephant ears?" He sipped from his travel mug of black coffee, the scent thick in the closed space. "I'd kill for some sugary carbs."

"Ah, comfort food. I bet they will." She opened her window a few inches, letting in a rush of fresh spring air. The wind ruffled the top of her grass-green sweater, the fabric slipping to expose the pale skin of her right shoulder. A tiny freckle sat just beside the black strap of her bra, and he turned to face the windshield before she caught him staring. "It's crazy we've been friends for over three years and hardly went out, just the two of us."

"Add it to my list of regrets. Speaking of which, sorry you got yanked into that radio interview bullshit. You didn't deserve that."

"You have nothing to apologize for. That bitch was way out of line, and you didn't deserve it either." She looked at him, her gaze steady. "You didn't do anything wrong, Ty."

If that were true, why couldn't he shake the nagging guilt? He felt like he'd brought it all on himself, the stress compounded by his mistakes affecting people he cared about.

"So, what did the cops say?" He figured they might as well get all the uncomfortable topics out at once.

Charlotte tucked her hair behind her ear, her throat moving as she swallowed. "They found a chunk of brick in the driveway, and someone trampled the flowers under my bedroom window." Her eyes left the road to connect with his, her pupils wide and glossy. "Could've done without that image in my head."

"Jesus!" His heart hammered at the thought of some creep peering inside her window. Or worse, trying to find a way through it. "There has to be more we can do while that fucker's still out there." He pushed the hair from his face, thinking. "I can hire a bodyguard."

She scoffed, checking her rearview before changing lanes. "Hell no. I live alone because I'd go insane without my personal space. I'm not having some hired goon follow me around." Her eyes flickered back to his. "Eliza beefed up security for our tour, so I'm covered there. And my house is locked up tight."

He struggled to think of a way to ease her worries while making a mental note to drive by her house often to check on things. "I'll be your bodyguard if you'd like." He rolled up his sleeve, flexing and unflexing his bicep, making it dance. "These guns pack quite a punch."

She smacked his arm. Her smile was back, but it trembled at the corners. It was a start.

"I'm sure they do. But I don't need you or Kevin Costner or some juiced-up Rafael clone to take care of me. I'm tougher than I look."

"If you change your mind—"

"You'll be the first to know."

Tyler slid a zippered black case from between the seats. If anything had the power to shift things in a more positive direction, it was music. "Mind if I flip through your CDs?"

"Be my guest." She touched his hand. "As long as you don't mock me for anything you find."

"Oh, now I have to look."

She laughed as he unzipped the case. He was glad to see her grip on the steering wheel loosen and her shoulders relax.

"Well, now. Here's the first surprise." Tyler held up the disc. "ABBA, Charlotte? Explain yourself."

She grinned, pulling the fallen sleeve back over her shoulder. "I put it on when I'm feeling blue. It's impossible to be sad while singing along to 'Dancing Queen.'"

"I'll have to test your theory sometime." He slid it back inside and kept flipping.

"Any dark clouds on the horizon that need obliterating?" She tilted an eyebrow.

"None I can't handle. No ABBA required." Despite his awful morning and afternoon, Tyler felt lighter in her presence. Somehow, Charlotte made it easy to set aside his burdens and enjoy whatever the day had in store. His stomach dropped when he reached the last disc. "You have got to be kidding me."

"What?" Her forehead wrinkled. "What is it?"

He slipped the CD inside the player and pressed his lips together, stifling a grin. When the music started, they broke into hysterics.

"I told you not to mock my taste, asshole." She swatted his shoulder.

"Shh... here it comes." He put a hand over his heart and sang along with "I Think I Love You" by the Partridge Family.

He almost lost it when she joined on the second verse. Together, they belted the lyrics as they drove across the Sauvie Island Bridge. When the song ended, they laughed so hard his side ached.

Charlotte wiped beneath her eyes and turned off the stereo. "How in the hell do you, Tyler Fucking Hall, know the lyrics to the cheesiest, most wholesome song ever written?"

"Guess I'm just as lame as you." He grabbed her raised middle finger and shook it. "Actually, my mom let the TV babysit us a lot, and I liked watching reruns of those goofy old sitcoms with perfect families. *The Brady Bunch, Happy Days. The Partridge Family* was the coolest because they played music together."

She glanced over. "I bet you totally wanted to be Keith."

"Oh, Charlotte. You have no idea." He took another long sip of his coffee as she laughed. "I tried to dress like him, studied how he held his guitar. His hair was stupid, though."

"I thought it was cool." She swept her long, dark hair over her shoulder and shrugged.

"If you tell anyone, I'll never forgive you. You know that, right?"

She mimed zipping her lips shut and tossed the invisible key out the window.

They turned off the road and onto the dirt driveway of Daybreak Farm, the host site of the Sauvie Island Farmers' Market. After exiting the car, Tyler spun around while Charlotte assessed his disguise. He wore a gray hooded sweatshirt, dark glasses, and faded jeans with well-worn Doc Martens peeking below the cuffs.

"Honestly," she said, "I wouldn't recognize you if I saw you on the street."

"Cool. Last thing I need is a photo of me eating roasted corn in some tabloid. It would really hurt my street cred."

Charlotte laughed in the way that always made him laugh, too. Her brown eyes twinkled, her nose scrunched up, and her hands flew to her chest. As if every inch of her was involved in the party and your inches couldn't help but join in.

"That and the Keith Partridge thing would end your career altogether," she said.

Tyler glared as he pulled his hood over his head and followed her to the entrance.

"What is that?" He pointed to a furry beige animal not much bigger than a Chihuahua.

She laughed that laugh again. "You've never seen a pygmy goat before? Oh, my god. You have no idea what you're in for, my friend." When they reached the pen, she whispered something to the farmer. Tyler hated secrets, but he trusted Charlotte.

The farmer—a short woman in overalls with a gray braid down her back—opened the gate to the pen, ushering them inside. "Now, get on all fours and wait."

"*Excuse me*?" Tyler gaped at the farmer, then at Charlotte, who went beet-red from laughing so hard.

"Trust me," she said, catching her breath. "You'll love this."

"Why do I get the feeling something will be put on or in my ass?"

Charlotte doubled over, clutching her middle. "You're gonna make me pee my pants! Your butt will be safe and untouched, I promise."

She took his hand and knelt in a patch of grass that appeared free of goat poop. He still wasn't convinced.

"Come on, Ty. Just do it. Or you can join the other chickens in that coop over there."

He shook his head, getting on his hands and knees beside her. "Now what?"

The farmer made a clicking noise with her mouth. Four goats rushed over, and a little black one with white spots jumped onto Tyler's back.

"Charlotte! Oh, my god!" He laughed so hard tears spilled from his eyes. Tiny hooves tapped along his shoulder blades before the goat let out a high-pitched bleat. Another jumped on his back. "I'm covered in goats!"

A gray one jumped on Charlotte, settling on her head, and they cry-laughed so hard they were gasping for air.

After petting and feeding the goats, Tyler and Charlotte washed their hands and walked toward the brightly colored flags and banners of the Farmers' Market.

He hooked his arm through hers. "I've seen Paris from the top of the Eiffel Tower, watched morons almost get gutted at the Running of the Bulls, and hiked a volcano in Hawaii. But until today, I'd never been covered in adorable farm animals."

Charlotte smiled. "You're welcome." She pointed at a booth.

"Your candles?"

"My candles."

At the end of the day, Tyler was lugging three bags of produce, candles, and handmade goat's milk soap while Charlotte held a massive bouquet of pink, yellow, and purple tulips in the crook of her arm. She opened her trunk, and he set the bags inside.

Charlotte plucked a gray candle from one of the bags, handing it to Tyler. "My gift to you. For being a good sport and keeping me company."

He lifted it to his nose, breathing in the sweet, herby scent. "What is that?"

"Lavender, rosemary, all kinds of stuff. It's a clarity candle."

"A what?"

"I dated a girl who was into Wicca, and she'd make these for people needing clarity in their lives. It's probably wishful thinking mumbo jumbo, but who knows?" She rested her hip against the car, her eyes set on his. "Sometimes, people get used to accepting awful shit and don't know how to move past it. They need some help."

"You dated a girl?"

"That's what you got out of what I just said? Yes, newsflash, I'm bi. Now, actually listen to what I'm saying." She touched his arm. "I know you're upset about the photos of Issac and Amy. I also know you've seen and heard about other terrible things she's done and stayed anyway."

Charlotte looked to the sky, streaked with brilliant shades of orange and gold. She shook her head before meeting his eyes again. "It's like you've had a massive blind spot for her bullshit. Or maybe you're just a masochist. Either way, you deserve better, Ty. Maybe this candle will erase that blind spot once and for all so you can move on." Her shoulders lifted. "Even if you don't believe in this stuff, it couldn't hurt. Worst-case scenario, your room will smell pretty."

He was quiet, touched by her thoughtfulness. "Thanks, Charlotte."

A light wind blew a few strands of hair over her eyes, and she brushed them away. She studied his face for a moment, a welcome echo of the night they met. When she smiled, he leaned in, pressing his lips to her cheek in a gentle, lingering kiss. The feel of her soft skin, the hitch of her breath, made him want so much more than either of them was ready for.

Obviously, she feared he could backslide with Amy. Could he guarantee he wouldn't? And what could he offer Charlotte besides more complications she didn't need? He was knee-deep in a messy and public break-up, emotionally battered, and crashing on his brother's couch.

Plus, she was leaving for three weeks. A lot could change. If they'd ever have a second chance, that wasn't the time.

"I'll miss you, Ty." She touched his chest as he pulled back. The gentle contact and the softness in her gaze made him want to kiss her again. Not on her hand or cheek but on those lips curving up in a small, sweet smile that made him feel appreciated for the first time in a long time. "Don't forget about me when I'm in Canada, okay?"

His arms opened wide. "Impossible."

She lifted on tiptoes to hug him, her cheek brushing his before her chin rested on his shoulder. He wrapped his arms around her, pulling her closer as he replayed all the best memories of their day in his head—singing together as they drove over the bridge, those ridiculous goats, and hearing her carefree, contagious laughter after so many hard days. He was rewarded with that very sound as he tipped back to lift her off her feet.

He couldn't remember the last time he'd felt so happy and free.

Tyler set Charlotte back on her feet, and the scent of her hair lingered for a few moments after they parted. It was intoxicating and beautiful. Nothing in the bags in the trunk could come close. In fact, they couldn't hold a candle to it.

18

Charlotte

"**I**'m completely and totally fucked."

Charlotte curled under a blanket on her couch, the phone wedged between her ear and shoulder. While talking to Sandra, she clutched a half-full glass of Southern Comfort, hoping to tame the feral butterflies that invaded her stomach during her farm outing with Tyler.

"Did something happen?" Sandra's panicked tone made Charlotte regret her word choice.

"No, nothing like that."

"Well, that's an interesting way to begin a conversation. Why are you completely and totally fucked?"

"I have feelings for Tyler." Charlotte took a quick sip, chasing it with a longer one.

She held the phone away from her ear while Sandra laughed and whooped like a maniac.

"Well, hallelujah! You finally admit it. What brought this on?"

"I took him to the Farmers' Market today, and he was adorable and funny and sweet, and I've never wanted to kiss another human being more in my entire life." She drained her glass, coughing as the liquor burned a fiery path down her throat.

"You didn't tell him, did you?"

"Of course not! I'm no perfect princess, but I'm not shitty enough to tell a still-technically-married man I want him." Charlotte refilled her glass with the bottle on the floor. "He's so strong and tall and sexy, I wanted to take a bite out of his bicep."

Sandra laughed. "You're so fucking weird."

"I'm definitely fucking weird. And stressed the hell out. What am I supposed to do, Sandra?" She swung her arm, liquor sloshing out of the glass and onto the carpet. "Pretend my feelings aren't there? Every time I see him, it's harder." She tossed back another hefty swig, and the room spun a little when she lowered her head. "Oh, and he kissed my goddamn cheek. So, there's that."

"Hmm. Not to take anything from your experience, but I kiss your cheek all the time and I'm not trying to get in your pants."

Charlotte's eyes rolled. "It wasn't the same, weirdo. He looked at me like he wanted more. Fuck, *I want more*."

"Calm your hormones for a sec. Your words are starting to slur, but hopefully, you're sober enough to hear this."

"Go on."

"Maybe Tyler's finally wising up and dumping Amy. Maybe he'll fall in love with you after that. And maybe he won't. It isn't healthy or fair for you to sit around waiting for a *maybe* when there are so many great people who are actually single. Any of them would be lucky to have you. Still with me?"

"Mostly."

"Good. Because this one might sting." Sandra sighed. "I'm sorry, but if the person you end up with isn't Tyler, it's probably not possible for you to continue being his friend."

The words brought a lump to Charlotte's throat. Imagining Tyler out of her life didn't sting. It scorched. Especially after the day's glimpse into what they could be once Amy was out of the picture.

Then again, what if that possibility of more was just a silly, one-sided fantasy? He seemed to feel something too, but what if she was wrong? Was she setting herself up for another gut punch of disappointment? If so, being nothing but friends would hurt too much. She set down her glass, blinking back tears.

"I gotta go."

"No, don't." Sandra sighed again. "Sorry, Char, but what kind of best friend would I be if I told you what you want to hear instead of what you need to hear? I love the shit out of you and don't want to see you get hurt."

Charlotte sniffed. "I'm already hurt. Do you honestly think telling me to stop being his friend will make me feel better?"

"I'm not saying that, exactly. I'm saying imagine how hard it'd be to date someone available while still having feelings for Tyler. And how much more it'll hurt if you're full-on in love with him a year from now, and he's back to lying next to the bitch who screwed you over. Can you honestly say you'll have fun hanging out with the guy who breaks your heart every time he walks away?"

Charlotte pulled a tissue from the box on the side table and blew her nose. "All this is my fault because I'm the one who walked away. He met *me* first. He was so cool and charming, and I bailed, leaving him vulnerable to that predatory cuntrag."

Sandra groaned. "You need to stop replaying this version of the story in your head, sweetie. You've been beating yourself up for years for taking care of yourself. You saw Bitchface pass those drugs to Rafael and got the hell out of there. It totally sucks that Amy swooped in, but maybe it wasn't meant to be."

Wasn't meant to be. God, Charlotte hated that phrase. It made it seem like people were powerless over their lives. That disappointment over missing out on what you want was inevitable. Coming from logical, grounded Sandra made it as surprising as it was infuriating. "Where'd that come from? You believe in fate all of a sudden?"

"Hell no. But I believe in people making stupid mistakes that make them unworthy of someone as amazing as you. You know I love Ty, but he was an idiot for not choosing you when he had the chance."

Charlotte took another drink, drowning what remained of the butterflies. It was the first time talking to Sandra had made her feel worse.

"Why do I keep doing this, Sandra?"

"Doing what, hon?"

Charlotte dabbed her nose, tossing the tissue into the wastebasket beside the couch. "Wanting the wrong people. Getting into relationships with nowhere to go but down. Why can't I find something easy and uncomplicated?"

"Where's the fun in that?" Sandra's soft laughter crackled in her earpiece. "You have a big heart. It's so wide open that now and then, it's bound to let in a few people that don't belong there."

Charlotte scoffed. "You know as well as I do that's bullshit. I don't let anyone in."

"That's the real bullshit. Sure, you used to push people away. You were protecting yourself from pain, and who doesn't have unhealthy ways of doing that? But you and your therapist worked some serious voodoo. You changed. You let Matty in, Amber, Tyler. And Amy, before you knew better. Even though you still tend to go for chumps who can't break your heart, you need to recognize how far you've come."

She hated when Sandra made so much damn sense that arguing was impossible. "I'm beat. I'm going to bed."

"Okay. Sleep it off, and I'll see you in the morning. Canada, baby! Woohoo!" Sandra let out an ecstatic screech. "We'll talk more on the plane. Love you."

"Thanks for listening." Charlotte slid down the couch to lie on her side. "Love you too."

She hung up, hugging her knees to her chest. Part of her wished Sandra had just said what she wanted to hear—comforting but hollow assurances happiness was around the corner. But she was grateful to have a best friend who loved her enough not to.

Opening her heart to undeserving people had burned Charlotte in the past, but Tyler wasn't undeserving. Not at all. In fact, she couldn't think of anyone more worthy and in need of a considerate, trustworthy partner. She could've sworn she caught flickers of interest when they sat on Sandra's porch swing and again as they walked arm-in-arm through the market. He made her feel at ease, and perhaps she did the same for him. After all, even with the stress of Amy's infidelity hanging over his head, he'd laughed and joked with Charlotte as if his cares had vanished.

Maybe it was wishful thinking, but maybe it was something else. Something real.

Still, as she stood on unsteady feet, shuffling past the stacked suitcases toward her bed, the fear of being hurt by someone she cared about was impossible to ignore. She hoped Tyler really would leave Amy this time. Maybe she'd return from her Canadian tour to find him happily single.

Then, maybe she could get the second chance she'd waited more than three years for.

19

Tyler

When Charlotte dropped him off after their trip to Sauvie Island, Tyler sat on the curb outside Matthew's apartment, smoking and thinking. The clarity candle sat beside him, the scent hanging faintly in the air as he turned the day over in his mind.

Considering it began with the crash-and-burn interview, that disgusting abuser article, and the evidence that Amy's infidelity had gone on longer than he knew, it was a miracle he was smiling. The time with Charlotte made all that garbage disappear for a while.

He knew his smile and upbeat mood would trigger a hundred questions from his brother, but Tyler wasn't sure how much he was ready to say. There were conflicting feelings as the day wound down, and it seemed wise to process them a bit before Matthew tossed in his two cents. Then again, maybe Matthew could help him sort through the fears, uncertainties, and memories swirling through his head like a damn hurricane.

When Tyler finished his cigarette, he tucked the candle under his arm before grabbing his produce bags and heading for the lit-up apartment. On the way in, he spotted a rusty old Camry parked in Matt's space. Sometimes, neighbors stole his spot, forcing him to park on a sketchy side street, which made Tyler uneasy.

"Hey, Matt!" Tyler pushed through the door. "You know whose beat-up Camry's in your spot?"

"Your brother just left. And that car is mine."

Tyler dropped the bags onto the counter, his smile disappearing. He took a deep breath before turning around.

"My last one was repossessed this afternoon because your check was late."

He gave an awkward wave, making a mental note to kick Matthew's ass later for not giving him a heads-up about her visit. "Hi to you too, Mom."

She sat at the kitchen table, an unlit cigarette in her hand and familiar scowl on her face. His mother always managed to look disappointed in him before he'd even had the chance to disappoint her.

Tyler pulled a lighter from his pocket, sparking up a cigarette. "Need a light?"

Her last birthday had nudged her closer to fifty than forty, but the only evidence was the smoker's lines around her mouth and a few silver streaks above her forehead, usually drowned in toxic dye.

She shook her head, the golden pile of hair on top not moving an inch. "I'm trying to quit. I find if I hold one and go through the motions, I can resist actually smoking it."

He stifled a laugh. Jenna Hall was well-practiced at pretending. Though, the resisting harmful temptations part was a first. He wondered how far that recently acquired skill extended.

"Seeing anyone new?" he asked.

She tapped the cigarette tip against the table, a few dark brown shreds of tobacco falling out. "I could ask you the same question, young man. But no, I'm done with men for a while. The last one, Andy, maxed out my credit card before ditching me for a former Vegas showgirl. That's where they live now. I hope they blow all their money on poker, get fat on buffets, and rot in the stinking desert."

"You always could paint a charming image, Mom." He pulled a paper bag of mushrooms from one of the grocery bags and set them on a shelf in the fridge.

"Hey, maybe that's where you get your way with words." Her thin shoulders shrugged beneath the cream-colored blouse that was stain, crease, and wrinkle-free. He wondered how someone so damaged on the inside could always manage to look pristine on the outside. "No need to thank me."

Tyler smiled, shaking his head. He'd gotten his smartass sense of humor from her too, but he'd never give her credit. He'd learned a long time ago that getting too friendly left him vulnerable, and that's when she'd pull the rug out from under him.

"What brings you to Portland?" He put the lettuce in the crisper drawer. It was probably the first time in years that the apartment contained actual vegetables.

She touched her hair with her free hand and lowered it when she seemed satisfied it was still frozen in place by her usual gallon of Aqua Net. "Well, I heard you and Amy are divorcing. It's shitty I had to find out from an online news site instead of my son, but we both know you're not the king of communication."

Tyler bit his tongue, knowing he communicated fine with people who didn't treat him like a burden his whole life. People who didn't only come around to demand money or favors.

"That was fast. The story wasn't supposed to go out until tomorrow."

"Huh. You need to get a computer, son. Things spread like wildfire on the internet, much faster and wider than any newspaper."

He had no interest in wasting time staring at a screen. Besides, from what he'd heard, the internet was mostly used to swap recipes and talk shit to random strangers in something called chatrooms. So fucking pointless.

"So, is it true?" she asked.

"Yeah, we broke up. You never liked her anyway."

His mother scoffed. "Understatement of the year. I sniffed out her greedy ass on day one. Could've made ten times your money with all her talent, but why bother working hard when she married the golden goose?"

He'd taste blood any second with how hard he had to bite down to keep from saying something mean. Like how ironic it was for her to judge Amy for spending his money instead of earning her own when his mother did the same damn thing. Her son was the golden goose and felt like little else to her.

"Anyway," she said, "I'm here because I wanted to make sure you're going through with a divorce and being careful about the division of assets."

There it is.

He set the box of cherry tomatoes on the counter harder than intended, the bottom corner of the box caving in. "Just so I'm clear, you're concerned about my money and not how I might feel after my heart was ripped from my chest and stomped on by her high fucking heels? Do I have that right?"

She rolled her eyes, flicking her unlit cigarette with her thumb. "Oh, give it a rest, Tyler. All you think I care about is your damn money."

"What reason have you given me to think otherwise? You never call for anything else, you never came for holidays when Amy invited you, and you haven't held down a job to support yourself without my help in years."

She rubbed her temples. "I know you think I'm the worst mother on earth. I'll admit, I made a lot of mistakes with you boys. Although Matthew never talks to me like this."

He crumpled the empty grocery bag, tossing it in the garbage. "He was too young to remember the worst of it. And I protected him from a lot because that's what you do for people you love. People who count on you to take care of them."

She slow-clapped, the scowl deepening the lines on her face. "Good for you, son. You were the parent I couldn't be. And do you know why?"

"Don't you dare bring Dad into this," he gritted out. She loved blaming a dead man for her shortcomings, and he wasn't about to let her go there this time.

"You're not playing fair, so why should I?" She squared her shoulders. "Your father made a stupid mistake that took him from us. I can't tell you how many times I told him to wear a damn helmet. He had little boys at home and a wife who adored him. That's how reckless he was, yet you've never been mad at *him*. Instead, he got painted as some perfect hero and never had the chance to prove otherwise. Don't get me wrong, he was an incredibly kind, loving man, but he had flaws too, Tyler."

She was right. he'd never felt anger towards his dad for not protecting himself that night. In fact, he'd been angry at himself. If Tyler hadn't been relentlessly begging for sour gummy worms all day, his dad wouldn't have left and would still be alive. That's the story he'd told himself for years, hating himself for being selfish. There was plenty of anger toward his mother for her reactions to the loss, but he never examined any other feelings about the accident because it hurt too much. It was easier to blame himself and the deeply flawed woman stuck trying to survive the crater-sized hole in their family.

Tyler had buried the horrible truth beneath layers of comforting denial and delusion—an old, ugly habit he was determined to break. Wouldn't confronting the roots of that tendency be an essential part of the process?

"All your rage and hurt was aimed at me like a goddamn bullet." She thumped her chest. "I never call because all I hear in your voice is judgment. Who needs that? I never came to your big, fancy holiday parties because Amy's faux friendliness and backhanded remarks made me want to smack her smug face. And you buying into her bullshit made me sick. I was just so disappointed in you, Tyler."

He winced. Everything she said was true. Of all the voices urging him to kick Amy to the curb, his mother's had been the easiest to discount. He'd been too stubborn to listen, convinced she was a selfish, greedy mess who hadn't given Amy a fair chance. In reality, his mother had seen Amy's true colors, and he'd been a damn fool. And kind of an asshole.

"You saw the men I let into my life," she said. "*Our* lives. I always hoped you'd be smarter than me. Amy's abuse wasn't always so obvious, but it was there from the start, and you just took it. I thought I'd raised you better than that, even if my choices were to be used as cautionary tales." She closed her eyes, massaging her temples again with tight circles. "And for your information, I can't keep a job because I have panic attacks so severe, I can't breathe. What employer would be okay with me bolting out the door to gasp for air and throw up in the parking lot? And I've been getting these migraines that make it hard to leave the house."

"Jesus, Mom."

He left the rest of the groceries on the counter and sat beside her. The usual resentment that sat thick in his chest when she was around disappeared as he took in the obvious pain on her face. He felt sorry for her. More than that, he realized how futile it was to continue feeling angry at her shortcomings when she was doing her best to get by, just as he was.

Maybe it was finally time to forgive. Or at least to try.

To accept her for who she was instead of holding onto who he wished she could be.

"I'm sorry that's happening to you," he said. "Have you seen a doctor?"

She waved a dismissive hand. "I only ask for money because I feel like that's all you're willing to give me. I'm not sure I have the right to ask for more. But now that the snake's out of your life…" Her eyes found his, and her tight, raised shoulders relaxed. "Maybe things can be different."

For years, Matthew had encouraged him to make amends with their mother. To forge a relationship not marred by resentment and old wounds. After hearing her explain herself and seeing the hopefulness and vulnerability in her eyes, it felt like that might finally be possible. Then, a thought popped in that surprised him. He wondered what she'd think of Charlotte.

"Why are you smiling like that?" The tense lines around her eyes smoothed.

"Just thinking about the friend I was with today. Charlotte. I think you'd like her."

She leaned back, her eyes wide. "I was kidding earlier. You don't waste any time, do you, son? Another thing we have in common." Her free hand touched the pockets of her dark denim jeans. "Ah, screw it. Pass me that lighter."

Tyler laughed, the tightness in his chest unfurling. "She's just a friend." He lit his mother's cigarette and slid a glass ashtray between them.

"Mmhm. Same girl I've heard Matty talk about?"

He nodded, tapping his ash over the tray.

"Friends don't make you smile like that. Is she pretty?"

His smile grew as warmth rushed to his face. "Pretty doesn't cover it."

"Uh-oh. I know that look. You're a goner." They laughed together for the first time in ages. "Can I give you some advice?"

He nodded, listening. It'd been a while for that, too.

"Before getting swept up in a new relationship, build a life for yourself that doesn't revolve around anyone else." Smoke curled between them as their eye contact held. "Sorry I never showed you how."

"Mom…"

"Just listen." She touched his hand. "You deserve the kind of love I had with your father." Tears gathered in the corners of her eyes. "But I was so wrapped up in him that I crumbled when he was gone. Then, I moved from one relationship to the next, looking for someone to make it all better again." A tear escaped, slipping to her chin. "Don't make the same mistake. You'll never find real, lasting love until you're strong enough on your own first. And you need an equal partner who's just as strong."

He knew she was right about that, too. If he jumped into a new relationship with Charlotte or anyone else, she'd become his crutch, not his partner. His broken pieces would still be there, just shoved aside to deal with later. He needed to learn to be happy alone before he could be truly happy with someone else.

"I think first…" He went quiet, the puzzle pieces connecting in his mind. "I need a safe place to land. Besides Matty's couch." They laughed. "My career's chaotic and loud and demanding, so it'd be nice to have a home that's the opposite of that." He'd never put that feeling into words, probably because he knew it'd be impossible to achieve with Amy. It felt good to say it, to let himself imagine a place that was calm and recharging instead of wild and unpredictable. He smiled, but it was muted, bittersweet. "Until kids come along. I can't wait for that kind of chaos."

She patted his hand. "That's sweet, son. Start building that beautiful life. One thing your success has proven is that you're capable of anything. And I'd love to be here for you if you let me." Her gaze slid to the candle beside him. "What's that?"

He picked it up, holding the smooth gray wax to his nose, and inhaled.

"A clarity candle. And you know what?" The scent made him think of Charlotte and their perfect day at the farm, his smile growing. He'd miss her while she was on tour, but it gave him time to tie loose ends. Time he'd spend making himself stronger, wiser, and ready for whatever came next. "I think it worked."

20

Tyler

Three Weeks Later

Tyler dipped a French fry into a mixture of ketchup and hot sauce and took a bite. Over lunch at The River Maiden, a cozy cafe overlooking the Columbia River, Charlotte shared details of her Canadian tour and the band's adventures between gigs. They'd explored Stanley Park, went snowboarding in Edmonton, and ate their weight in poutine. Fortunately, there were no creepy incidents, and she seemed refreshed and happy after the break from the stresses back home.

"Enough about me," she said. "What's been going on in your world?"

"Moved out of Matt's. I'm at the Sturgess Suites until I find a more permanent place."

"Really?" Charlotte's eyebrows raised. "That's awesome."

"Signed the divorce papers too." So far, Amy hadn't signed, but he hadn't expected her to make it easy. "Unless she wants to fight it, I'll be free in just over two months."

"Wow!" She smiled. "You were busy while I was gone. What made you finally decide to take such major leaps?"

"All the credit belongs to the candle."

Charlotte shoved his shoulder. "C'mon. Be serious."

Tyler leaned back in his Adirondack chair. It was a beautiful, cloudless day, and brightly colored sailboats dotted the water upstream. He tucked his hands behind his head as the sun warmed his skin.

"I realized I had to burn down the old to make way for the new." He sipped his iced tea. "And my mom actually gave me advice that helped change my perspective."

In particular, he'd taken her advice about gaining independence and inner strength. Living by himself was lonely at first, but he was learning to appreciate having his own space and the freedom to do as he pleased. When he lived with Amy, people came and went all hours of the day and night, and he was enjoying the peaceful, reliable recharge at the end of the day. When he felt restless, he focused that energy on writing songs. When he felt low, he started journaling instead of leaning on other people, alcohol, or his usual distractions.

"You helped me move on too, Charlotte."

"Me?" She set down her burger and wiped a blob of mustard off her lip. "What did I do?"

"You got me thinking. Why did I have that blind spot for Amy's bullshit? Why did I accept being taken for granted and lied to for so long?"

She set her napkin in her lap, giving him her full attention. "Go on."

Tyler lit a cigarette to steady his nerves. "It'd be easy to say it was loneliness or weakness, but it was more than that. After Dad died, my needs didn't matter. I felt like *I* didn't matter. When I met Amy, I wanted love so badly that I was willing to accept abuse as the price I had to pay for it."

Using that word—abuse—to describe Amy's mistreatment still felt strange. He'd never been bruised or battered. At least not on the outside. Since his mother said it, the word had scratched at the back of his mind. It fit when he reflected on the constant manipulation, declarations of love followed by actions that were anything but, and the tantrums that ended with broken glass on the floor. And it made her pulling strings to brand him as abusive in the media even more ludicrous and offensive.

Charlotte frowned. "That's awful, Ty. I'm so sorry." She fidgeted with her necklace—the silver eucalyptus leaf he bought in Australia.

He shrugged a shoulder. "At least it's behind me. It feels good knowing the person I am now would never live like that again. And I realize how lucky I've been to have people who didn't give up on me, like you and Matty. And my band. You guys have given me the breaks and reality checks that kept me out of a padded cell all these years."

Charlotte tugged the cigarette from his fingers and took a drag. "I had a blast with you at the farm, and you can call me anytime you need a break. A straitjacket would be a terrible look for you."

"Yeah, that was a great day." A lopsided smile lifted the corner of his mouth. "I can't remember the last time I laughed that hard. And it felt good going to a normal place, doing normal things again." He squeezed a lemon wedge over his glass. "Being with you reminded me that not everything has to be a struggle. You're kind, Charlotte. You don't hurt people on purpose. And you're easy to talk to."

"Wow." Her eyes were downcast as she moved a straw around her marion-berry milkshake. "It's nice to be thought of like that."

His real motive for inviting her out made his stomach twist with nerves. Adam and Zack's encouraging words ran through his head, one word, in particular, standing out and becoming his mantra.

Kerosene.

"You helped me see I deserve better," he said. "That I should be with someone who actually listens when I talk and looks me in the eye when I need connection."

When Charlotte met his gaze, feelings rushed in that Tyler hadn't let himself acknowledge in years. In many ways, she'd sparked his interest when they met—she was this sexy, talented woman who was up for anything. And his darkness recognized hers. In that brief exchange, he knew she was someone he wanted in his life. And then she was gone. Amy got her hooks into him, and despite the friendship that blossomed, their paths diverged in many ways.

Now, it felt as if their paths could finally meet again.

"That's great, Ty." Charlotte held out the cigarette. "You deserve someone who'll give you all of that."

"Charlotte..." He leaned forward to take it, his fingers touching hers, holding the contact for a few beats. "I deserve someone like you."

He studied her expression, catching surprise along with something that made his palms sweat.

"Damn, Tyler." Charlotte blinked hard, clearing her throat. "I don't know what to say."

"Then just eat your burger." He smiled, another mega dose of clarity rushing in. "And share some of those tots."

She tossed a handful at his face, holding back a grin.

"At least wait for me to open my mouth, crazy woman."

Charlotte watched as he picked them off his lap one by one and tossed them in the air, catching them in his mouth. Some of them, at least.

Tyler walked Charlotte to her car and leaned against his ancient but reliable Land Cruiser, parked a space over.

"Good luck with that legal stuff," she said. "Amy will hire a shark, so watch your back."

"Amy is a shark." He imagined her sniffing his blood in the water before flying into a frenzy. "I'm ready for a fight."

Charlotte took a step closer. "I'm proud of you, Ty."

"Thanks." He pushed off the hood to stand up straight. "I'm proud of me too."

That pride was different from what came after nailing a complex riff or writing a new song. It ran deeper. After shedding parts of his life that no longer fit, a new strength had taken hold. One that would allow him to stand up for himself and demand respect. To go after what he wanted without regret or apologies.

"So," she said, "what comes next for you?"

"Matt's helping me get the rest of my stuff from the house tomorrow." Just saying the words made him feel lighter, and he smiled, thinking of all the freedom he was gaining. "It's exciting to think of the possibilities opening up. I can get a place in the woods outside the city like I've always wanted. I can travel anywhere and do anything she's held me back from. I can see Matty more." He tapped the tip of her boot with his. "And you."

Charlotte smiled. "I'd like that."

After a few beats of silence, her gaze fell to his lips. Her throat moved as she swallowed. The look in her eyes reminded him of the photo taken of them outside the club.

She looks like she's waiting to be kissed.

Anticipation charged the air between them, electricity sparking in his chest. A million thoughts raced through his mind—those rooted in insecurity and fear were the loudest—but nothing stopped him from reaching out and taking her hand. He felt the pulse in her wrist quicken, his heart thumping just as fast.

"Charlotte?"

"Yeah?" Her fingers fiddled with her necklace, and he noticed they were trembling.

"Remember the night of your show, when your arm was around my waist to keep me steady?" As he spoke, fuzzy details from that night sharpened. The way her warmth and her scent compelled him to pull her closer. How beautiful she looked up close. How hard it was to let her go.

"Of course." Her eyebrows pulled together. "Why?"

"In that photo of us, the way you looked at me..." Tyler paused, catching the unmistakable flare of desire in her eyes, her lips gently parting. He tucked a lock of hair behind her ear, his hand lingering against the blush of her cheek. "How have I never noticed it before?"

She dropped the necklace, her hand falling to her side. "Because you couldn't. Someone would've been hurt. And you'd never hurt people you care about."

It stirred something in him to be seen that way. To have someone recognize the good things that had gone unnoticed and unappreciated for so long. Tyler stepped closer, his fingertips caressing the petal-soft skin of her face. "I was blind and stupid about a lot of things. I'm sorry, Charlotte."

She took his other hand, lacing their fingers together. "You see me now, don't you? You see how I feel?"

He gave a small nod. "I do."

"Better late than never," she said with a wry smile.

He took another step. The pad of his thumb slid along her lower lip, and she drew in a sharp breath. "Is it okay if I…"

"Hey, Tyler!"

They startled, their heads turning toward the loud female voice. He sighed impatiently at the intrusion, his hand dropping from Charlotte's face as a woman with bright green hair and a pierced eyebrow ran over. She held a Tomorrow Mourning CD insert in one hand and a black marker in the other. "I saw you eating and grabbed these from my car. Can I get your autograph?"

He held back the grumble of frustration as he released Charlotte's hand to take the items. "Sure. What's your name?"

"Gigi. I saw you play the Rose Garden last year, and you were on fucking fire."

"Thanks." He scrawled a brief personalized note on the insert before signing it. "That was the night Adam broke a drumhead, right?"

"Yep. And Zack told god-awful knock-knock jokes to keep the crowd happy while they fixed it." She snickered. "Classic."

"Gigi, where'd you go?" A confused-looking guy in a leather biker jacket stepped from behind a minivan, waving her over.

"Damn," she said. "Gotta jet. Sorry to hear about Amy and Issac. Those photos were fucked-up. You deserve better."

He glanced at Charlotte, and she blushed, her gaze rising to the cloudless blue sky.

"It was cool to meet you, Tyler. Can't wait for the new album." The girl touched his arm before leaving with the biker.

"Sorry about that," Tyler said.

"It's fine. I'm even getting them sometimes." Charlotte's smile slipped. "So… what were you going to ask me?"

Tyler opened his mouth to speak, but the words wouldn't come. The reminder that his personal drama was still on public display had stolen them. It suddenly felt selfish and unfair to start something with Charlotte before the baggage of his old life was completely behind him. His impulsive nature made it easy to lose sight of that and all the potential consequences of rushing into this, no matter how right it felt.

She deserved better.

"It's too fast, I'm sorry. We should—" He fished his keys from his pocket, turning toward his car.

"No, don't." Her hand on his shoulder made him turn back. "I've been waiting so long that it doesn't feel fast at all."

They smiled, sparks of anticipation once again zinging across his skin.

"Really?"

"I'm all in, Ty. Maybe for most people, this would be too fast, but we're not most people. We make our own fucking rules." Her quirked lips and arched eyebrow reminded him of the Killing Daisies flyer he couldn't seem to throw away. "Unless you aren't ready. I'd understand if you weren't."

Voices of people entering the parking lot turned their heads. After quickly scanning the area, he slipped his keys back into his pocket before taking her hand.

"Come on." He tugged her around the ivy-covered wall of an abandoned boat rental office. A broken, rusted rowboat sat wedged between two bushes, weeds growing through a ragged gash in the hull.

They settled beneath a weathered awning on the building's small porch, out of view of the diners and walkers enjoying the sunshine.

He released her, and they stood face-to-face, the tips of their shoes touching.

"Charlotte..." Tyler let out a long, heavy breath. It felt like he'd been holding it for years, releasing the stagnant air of his old life to make room for a fresh, cleansing breath that held the promise of something new. "Do you have any idea how badly I've wanted to kiss you?" He reached up, tracing her jawline with the backs of his fingers. "Not just now or at the farm, but if I could go back to the night we met, I'd grab hold of your face, and everything would be different."

She blinked hard, her brown eyes shining when they opened and found him again. "We can't go back." Her fingers settled on the hand stroking her face, and she leaned into the touch. "But things can be different starting now."

Tyler erased the space between them, cradling her face in his hands, moving closer inch by inch. "Is this what you want?" he whispered.

Her grin widened. "You're getting warmer."

He pressed his lips to hers and kissed her slowly, savoring every single thing that made Charlotte, Charlotte—her full lips, the sun-kissed glow of her skin, the heat of her breath, and those intoxicating wild orchids. All his senses soaked her in at once, desperately craving *more*.

He knew he'd made the right choice this time because nothing wrong could ever feel so completely fucking perfect.

As Charlotte's fingers raked through his hair, her lips parted, deepening the kiss. Her hunger made him ache to touch her, taste her, show her how much he wanted this too. How much he wanted her. The grip on his hair tightened, her desire crashing into his, igniting a heat so sudden and intense that a moan broke in his chest.

Like tossing kerosene onto a spark.

He pulled back an inch to catch his breath. "Holy fuck." Their eyes locked.

"One hell of a first kiss," she whispered against his lips before going back for more.

The force of his mouth on hers pressed her back against the ivy-covered brick, and he set his hands on the wall beside her head, caging her in. If they were caught, it would appear she was at his mercy when the opposite was true—Tyler had surrendered himself to Charlotte and the pull between them the second their lips touched.

Her hands slipped down the back of his neck and over his shoulders, pulling him closer. His skin tingled everywhere she touched, and he cursed the fact that they were in a parking lot instead of a bedroom. When her thigh pressed against his cock as it strained against his zipper, a sexy little sound rumbled in her throat.

"I can't wait to touch you," she said.

Obviously, he wasn't the only one wishing they were somewhere more private.

He kissed her again, drawing her lower lip into his mouth. She hummed with pleasure as his fingertips glided up her ribcage with a featherlight touch.

"Tyler?"

"Yeah?" He spoke against her lips, not wanting to part from them even to speak.

She set a hand on his chest, gently pushing him back. He felt a sting of rejection until he noticed she was breathing heavily. Her soft brown eyes were hooded, hungry, and locked on his mouth. It was too soon to tell what this was, but it wasn't a rejection.

Charlotte's pink, kiss-swollen lips and tousled hair made him want to toss her into his backseat, but again, she deserved better.

She pulled her keys from her pocket and smiled. "Follow me back to my house."

21

Tyler

Tyler was restless on the drive to Charlotte's. Now that he'd touched her and tasted her lips, being alone in his car with her scent on his clothes was torture. When she blew him a kiss at a red light, he thought his hard-on would tear right through his jeans.

While she parked, he waited at her side door. He figured it was the wisest entrance since trees concealed it from the view of the street or sidewalk. Amy had eyes all over the city. He knew damn well her infidelity, nor their impending divorce would compel her to behave rationally if they were caught together.

Charlotte's keys swung around her index finger as she walked up her driveway. Her saucy grin instantly shut down all thoughts of Amy and the possible consequences of what they were about to do.

"Tyler..." She pushed the key into the lock and turned, her fingers stilling on the knob. "Are you sure?"

"Right now," he said, covering her hand and turning it, "it's the only thing I'm sure of." He kissed her hard, pushing the door open and kicking it closed behind them.

High-pitched beeps sounded in the kitchen.

She grumbled, stepping from his grasp. "Gimme a sec."

Charlotte locked the door before punching a few codes into the security keypad. A final beep sounded, and with two long strides, she was back in his arms. He kissed every inch of her face as her fingertips slid underneath his shirt, digging into his bare skin.

"Bedroom," she mumbled against his mouth.

"You got it." He tossed her over his shoulder, earning a shriek of surprise and a healthy dose of Charlotte's full-body laughter.

"I had no idea you were such a caveman."

Tyler made a few primal, cavemanly grunting noises and smacked her ass with his palm. "I think we're about to learn a lot of new things about each other, Charlotte."

He turned on the light before bending forward at the foot of the bed, setting her onto the puffy black comforter.

She tumbled back, her hands coming to rest above her head. "Well, that was fun."

Tyler's fingers trailed up her legs, slowly pushing the hem of her knee-length skirt to her waist. He planted a lingering kiss on her inner thigh and whispered against her skin, "We haven't even started yet."

He grabbed her hips, dragging her to the edge of the bed, his erection pressed against the delicious heat at the center of her black lace panties. It'd been a long time since he'd touched another woman like this, and he'd forgotten what it felt like to start from scratch. Sprawled on the bed with lips swollen from his kisses, Charlotte was a tantalizing puzzle waiting to be solved.

And it was going to be a hell of a lot of fun figuring out where the pieces fit.

He pulled a condom from his wallet, setting it beside her.

She shook her head. "I'm on the pill and just got tested. If you know you're clean, I don't want anything between us."

"I just got tested too." His finger toyed with the tiny black bow at the waistline of her panties. "I'm clean."

Charlotte tossed the condom, making them laugh. Though he had zero thoughts about backing out, he was a little nervous about the major, permanent step they were taking. It was reassuring to see familiar shades of his sweet, funny friend moments before everything changed.

Tyler tugged off his shirt, dropping it to the floor.

Her lusty hum of approval made the front of his pants tighten. The flush of her cheeks and rapid rise and fall of her chest assured him she was just as excited. He slid alongside her, propping himself up on his elbow.

With one hand, he unbuttoned the top of her blouse, brushing his lips against the newly exposed flesh. Another button was undone, and his tongue darted out to taste the salt of her skin. After button number three, he pressed his lips to the bare center of her chest, her pounding heartbeat a faint, steady rhythm in the otherwise silent room.

"Change your mind at any point, and I'll stop," he said. "Just say the word."

Her throaty laugh made him grin. "I can assure you, that won't happen."

The black lace of her bra peeked through the opening in her blouse, the dark fabric an alluring contrast to her smooth, pale skin. After loosening the next button, he lightly brushed the inside of her thigh, starting at her knee and stopping just below the matching black lace between her legs. She trembled beneath his fingertips as they swept over the silky fabric. With the final button undone, his tongue circled her belly button and dipped inside, hinting at what he had in mind for a few inches south.

Tyler ran his knuckles along the skin of her taut belly and up to her neck. He slipped his hands underneath her back to unhook her bra, sliding the straps down her shoulders along with her blouse.

His breath caught in his throat as he took in the view. "You're so beautiful, Charlotte."

She brought his hand to her lips, kissing his palm. "That's sweet, but if you don't fuck me soon, I'm gonna lose my damn mind."

"I'm not going to fuck you." He grinned at her homicidal glare. "Our first time will be slow and perfect."

"You had me worried for a second." She landed a playful swat on his arm. "Bastard."

He laughed softly, his thumbs hooking underneath the waistband of her panties. "Our first time should be gentle. But our second time..." All traces of humor drained from his expression. "I'll fuck you until you scream."

Charlotte pulled in a quick breath, her teeth sinking into her bottom lip. "Promises, promises."

With a devilish grin, he slid the panties down her legs before lying beside her. Setting a palm on her cheek, he guided her mouth to his, parting her lips with his tongue, savoring her taste as he explored with slow, sensual licks. His finger grazed a leisurely trail from her chin to her belly button before his flattened palm continued downward.

Tyler groaned when his fingers reached the slippery heat between her legs. "It's so fucking hot how wet you are for me." In an instant, the need to take it slowly warred with an overwhelming desire to unzip his pants and sink his cock inside her in one swift push. Instead of succumbing to the urge to rush, he stroked and explored her sensitive folds.

Their gentle kiss soon turned ravenous. Charlotte's hips lifted off the bed, and his fingertips breached her entrance, his palm pressing firmly against her clit.

"I need more," she begged between panting breaths. "*Please.*"

The husky edge to her voice and plea on her lips was like a phantom hand tugging at his cock. There was nothing he wouldn't do to give her what she craved. When Tyler slipped two fingers deep inside her, she moaned against his mouth.

"Like that?" He made slow circles with the heel of his palm, pressing against her clit as his fingers rubbed the textured sweet spot on the front wall of her pussy.

"Fuck yes." Her eyes squeezed shut. "Just like that."

The puzzle of what pleased Charlotte in the bedroom was taking shape. His head dipped to kiss the tops of her breasts, drawing a nipple into his mouth and releasing it with a soft pop. "I want to taste every inch of you," he breathed against her skin. A shiver ran through her. As the movements of his fingers quickened, they were coated with another rush of the warm, slippery arousal he couldn't wait to have on his tongue.

Her thighs clamped around his wrist, and when his chin lifted, their eyes locked. There was a tenderness, a vulnerability in her expression he'd never seen.

The look drew him in, tethering them beyond the physical in a way he couldn't understand or explain. A crease formed between her brows, her eyes searching his face, making him wonder if the same perplexing feeling had struck her. The crease smoothed when he pushed his fingers deeper for a few strokes before resuming the rhythm and pressure she'd responded to before that charged moment shifted the air between them.

A soft whimper escaped her lips, and her back arched off the bed. She grabbed his wrist, pushing his fingers deeper into her core.

"Mmm... That's it, beautiful." Tyler moved closer to trace her parted lips with the tip of his tongue. "Let it take you."

Charlotte's lashes fluttered, but their eye contact held as she bucked against his hand. Knowing she was close, he went to his knees, dipping his head between her parted thighs. He lapped at the sensitive flesh around his fingers before softly sucking her clit between his lips. She gasped, her nipples growing harder, another rush of wetness coating his fingers and tongue.

"Fuck, that's good," she panted. "So close."

Her sweet taste made his cock throb in his jeans, the head swollen and tight, aching to replace his thrusting fingers. His tongue circled her clit again before flicking in quick little pulses. With that, his name stuttered from her lips, followed by a low, desperate cry as her orgasm tore through her. She was beautiful as she let go, her skin flushed and her toes curling. Underneath his forearm, the muscles in her belly tightened and twitched before going slack. As the peak of her climax receded, her hips fell to the bed. She kissed him, their tongues tangling together.

Her trembling fingers fumbled with the button of his jeans until it gave. Anticipation made him grip the sheets, his pulse thumping out a fierce drumbeat in his neck. She tugged down the zipper in one swift motion and broke the kiss.

"I can't believe I finally get to touch you." She got to her knees, slipping his jeans and boxers below his hips. When the room's cool air hit his cock, her pupils flared. "Oh, thank god."

Tyler laughed at her appreciative expression. "That's officially the best compliment I've ever received."

She let his jeans fall to the carpet. When her soft hand wrapped around his cock, he sucked a sharp breath through his teeth. The intensity of that first touch caught him off guard, the rush of pleasure short-circuiting his brain.

"I need you inside me." She threw a leg over him, straddling his hips.

Her sexy plea, her naked body above his, and the feel of her hand gripping, sliding along his length made it nearly impossible to hold back. But he was determined to spend a few more moments savoring every detail of their first time. The unwelcome thought that it might be their only time threatened to trespass, but he shoved it aside, focusing on the sensation of their bodies touching, moving, merging.

His lips pressed firmly to hers, tongues sliding together with long, languid strokes. He'd imagined what kissing Charlotte would be like, but no fantasy came close to the real thing. She was an *incredible* kisser. Like mind-blowingly fucking incredible. He couldn't wait to be inside her, but even if they did nothing but kiss for hours, he'd be a happy man.

But she wanted more. And her fingernails digging into his shoulder said she wanted it now. Tyler rolled her onto her back, settling between her thighs, his heart thumping like a kick drum.

"You sure you're ready?" He raised an eyebrow, a coy smile playing on his lips.

"Oh, Tyler." Charlotte touched his chest. "You have no idea."

He laughed softly as he lowered himself, sealing his lips to hers as the tip of his cock slowly pressed between her slick, heated folds. She kissed him harder, her fingers threading through his hair, as he slipped the rest of his length inside her, inch by inch, earning a sexy, gravelly moan that made his insides melt.

Charlotte pulled back, her eyes trained on his face with the same intense look as before.

"You feel amazing, Ty."

She brushed dampened hair from his temples. The tenderness in her expression and delicate touch made tears sting his eyes. Everything between them had changed in an instant, leaving behind the safe and familiar for unexplored, uncertain territory.

Tyler's only regret was that it had taken him so damn long to get there.

He withdrew before sinking back into her glorious heat, groaning as her tight inner muscles gripped him. It'd been years since he'd been inside of a woman without a barrier between them, in more ways than one. The sensation was overwhelming, and he locked away the memory of that feeling to replay at will.

"I want to take it slow, but you feel so fucking good," he said. "It's hard to hold back."

Their eye contact held, her fingers threading through his hair. "You don't ever have to hold back with me. Not anymore."

He knew she was talking about more than sex. They'd been holding back for years, depriving themselves of the connection that was now impossible to deny.

Charlotte's hips lifted, an undeniable request he quickly accepted by moving to his knees, grasping her hips with a firm grip, and pushing even deeper. Her soft brown eyes went hazy as he repeated the motion. She rolled her pelvis with his thrusts, a hypnotic rhythm playing out where their bodies connected.

"Kiss me." Her arms wrapped around his neck, their lips crashing together with such intensity the world around them blurred.

Charlotte rolled them over, mounting him without breaking the kiss. Tyler thrust upward, her thighs squeezing as tightly as the arms around his neck.

She released her arms and sat upright, his hands massaging her breasts as her head fell back. When it tipped forward again, tiny beads of sweat glistened at her hairline.

"You close, Ty?"

"Watching you will definitely seal the deal."

Charlotte grinned, biting her lip. She set her hands on his chest and shifted her pelvis, allowing him to sink even deeper. He shuddered, gripping the flesh of her ass as a potent rush of pleasure overtook him.

"You're fucking incredible." Tyler looked to where their bodies joined, a growl rumbling in his chest.

She followed his line of sight. "Mmm... I like watching you disappear inside me, too."

That's exactly what he wanted—to disappear so far inside of Charlotte and that feeling of connection that the troubles outside that room couldn't find them again. He slid a hand behind her head, pulling her down for a long, slow kiss that he felt down to his toes.

When she sat back up, he slipped his fingers between them, rubbing her clit in delicate circles that gradually increased in speed and pressure.

She drew in a ragged breath. "That's it." The muscles inside her squeezed and pulsed around his cock as her fingernails sank into his chest. "Oh, fuck—"

He struggled to hold back until she hit her peak, sweat drenching the hair at his temples with the effort. Fortunately, he didn't have to wait long. She let out a low, broken cry, her inner thighs twitching against his hips as her orgasm gripped her. Her hands slid over her breasts, her luscious lips parting with quick little breaths.

The sight of her surrendering to the pleasure rocking through her tipped Tyler over the edge. He groaned from deep in his throat as a fierce, core-shattering climax took hold, making a few tears slide down his face. Their primal sounds filled the air between them, melding together in an intense, intimate harmony.

Charlotte collapsed on top of him, her labored breaths tickling his neck. She raised her head, wiping his tears with a furrowed brow. Her worry lines smoothed as a mile-wide grin stretched his face.

"Wow," he said. "That was…"

"Yes." She nodded, an equally ecstatic expression lighting her eyes. "It was."

"I'd offer you water or a towel," he said between breaths, "but I don't think I can move."

Her fingertips grazed the center of his chest, tracing the lines of a black dragon tattoo. "I can wait until after."

"After what?"

Her smile grew, a wicked curve raising the edge. "After you fuck me until I scream."

True to his word, their first time had been an unhurried, sensual dance. After he'd recovered, their second time more closely resembled the Lambada—sweaty, wild, and just the right amount of rough.

Tyler had Charlotte bent over the bed on her stomach, his cock slipping into her wetness while she bit down on a pillow to muffle her sounds. He tugged the pillow away, tossing it to the floor.

"If I wanted you to be quiet, Charlotte, I wouldn't do *this*." He withdrew all but the tip before slamming into her over and over until she filled the room with her uninhibited moans and soft, sensual whimpers.

She clawed at the bedspread like an animal. "Harder."

The command sent an electric jolt between his legs, a crooked grin curving his lips. He slapped the warm flesh of her perfect, heart-shaped ass, a crack ringing out and his palm stinging.

She gasped, pushing back against his cock. "Fuck yes. *More.*"

Tyler struck the opposite cheek, the two red handprints blooming bright red on her ivory skin. He dipped his head to breathe against the shell of her ear. "You like it rough and dirty, Charlotte?"

"Rough, gentle, fast, slow..." Her voice was hoarse, spiked with a lusty edge that made his balls clench. "I like it all."

"Good answer." His fingernails dug into her naked shoulders and dragged down her back, earning an appreciative groan in reply. In seconds, white and then red tracks appeared, marking her skin.

She glanced over her shoulder. "Flip me over."

He pulled out, grabbed her hips, and flipped her onto her back. As his cock slid back inside, his teeth sank into the skin of her left breast. The bite of pain made her gasp, and he could feel her getting wetter.

"Almost there." She slid a hand between her legs, rubbing her clit in time with his thrusts. "Please don't stop." Charlotte tugged at the hair at the back of his neck with her free hand while a string of mumbled curses fell from her lips. She bucked against him as she came, their eye contact holding until the wave receded and her body relaxed.

Tingling heat pooled between his legs as his climax approached. Watching her let go was so goddamn hot he couldn't hold back another second. He gripped her shoulders, their bodies sliding with ease over the thin sheen of sweat between them. When Tyler came, he buried his face in the soft, sweet-smelling curve of her neck, muffling the strangled cry breaking in his throat. Her inner muscles clenched around him, coaxing every last drop of his hot, jetting release.

He fell onto his back, pulling her into his arms. Their heaving breaths made speaking impossible, so they lay in silence, basking in afterglow as they gradually returned to earth.

"You're amazing." He pressed a kiss to her damp forehead. "In every conceivable way."

She pinched his nipple, and he winced, then laughed at the unexpected spike of pain. "Not so bad yourself, mister."

He tucked a hand behind his head, the other drawing lazy circles on her collarbone. "Please tell me you don't have anywhere to be for the next... three weeks."

She giggled against his chest. "Three weeks, huh?"

"Minimum."

"If we went at it for three weeks like we did today, my pussy would be raw and covered in welts, and your cock would be worn down to a nub."

Her head bounced when he laughed. "Please don't put an image that disturbing in my head ever again."

"I can be a pretty twisted bitch, so I won't make promises I can't keep." She tucked her hands under her chin. "And I don't expect you to either."

The hand stroking her skin stilled. "What does that mean?"

"It means if you change your mind and—"

He pressed a finger to her lips. "Stop right there. I'm exactly where I want to be for the first time in years. Maybe ever." He brushed a few errant strands of dark hair out of her eyes. "But if you decide this isn't what you want, just say so, okay?"

She gave a slight nod. "Okay."

Tyler planted a kiss on Charlotte's forehead. When he pulled back, their eyes reconnected, her gaze warm, sincere. He imagined what his life might look like with a woman like her by his side and kissed her again.

He could see it all—his eyes and mind open to thrilling possibilities he'd never let himself imagine. There was a word for what allowed him to find this exhilarating, limitless new place.

Clarity.

22

Charlotte

"Were you just singing one of my songs?" A very naked Tyler walked into Charlotte's bathroom and turned on the shower.

He'd left the door open, the rich, dark scent of coffee wafting in from the kitchen. It was just after nine in the morning, and they'd need the caffeine boost after maybe four hours of sleep. She was exhausted and sore but happier than she'd been in a long time.

"You caught me. I'm a secret Tomorrow Mourning fangirl." Charlotte turned, batting her eyelashes and pushing her ample breasts together. "Please sign my tits, Mr. Hall."

"I don't sign tits." He grabbed a towel from the rack and tossed it at her head while she laughed. "Signed a fair amount of thongs, though." He tested the water temperature and stepped into the glass-walled shower.

"I bet you have."

Charlotte admired his firm ass in the mirror while scrubbing her face with apricot face wash. She couldn't remember the last time a guy had slept over or even stuck around long enough to shower. Most bolted after the sex, which was usually how she preferred it. And none had ever made coffee, which scored Tyler major points.

She stepped into the shower and let out a satisfied hum when the warm water hit her back, the sound echoing off the tile walls. The scratch marks he'd made tingled at the contact, a welcome reminder of how intense and dirty their second time had been. She rinsed the scrub off her face, the sweet, fruity scent lingering on her skin.

"Goddamn, you make sexy noises, woman." He joined her under the water and kissed her, his tongue slipping past her lips. Steam surrounded them like a cloud and rose from their skin. His hands slid down the tender skin of her back to grip her hips, pulling her against his hardening cock. "Let's see if I can inspire more."

Tyler's skills in the bedroom reminded her of how he worked a stage—passionate, deliberate, with a confidence that was well deserved. The things he did with his mouth alone were worthy of roaring applause.

Even sore and exhausted, she couldn't get enough.

Unfortunately, her libido had to take a backseat to prior commitments.

She groaned, stepping from his hold to grab the shampoo. "You're killin' me here, but I can't. I'm meeting the girls in an hour." She squeezed a dollop onto her hand before scrubbing her scalp. "Trust me, my pussy's furious I can't cancel."

He squeezed body wash into his palm, rubbing his hands together to work up a lather before sliding his hands up her ribs, leaving behind a trail of white, bubbling suds. The tempo of his breathing changed, desire darkening his eyes.

Obviously, she wasn't the only one who couldn't get enough.

It was wild watching him react to her body like that. Nothing like the innocent, platonic looks she was used to. Although, she'd caught him checking her out a time or two, usually when she'd just performed, leaving the stage sweaty and sated.

Just like she was after their first time.

Fuck, it was good.

She loved how he'd taken his time undressing her, slowly discovering her naked curves with his fingers, mouth, and hungry eyes, one undone button at a time. The way he got off on giving her pleasure made her feel sexy and treasured. And he responded to her touch like she was giving him a gift that was so much more than he'd expected.

Tyler lathered her breasts, her nipples pebbling beneath his touch. She found his eyes, and their gaze held. Nothing made the shift from friends to *this* more apparent than when their eyes connected. The feeling was so intense, so raw, it frightened her.

But she wouldn't hold back.

Not this time.

Not with him.

As Charlotte said right before their first kiss, she was all in. She'd raised a middle finger to the old, familiar voice urging her to run from the risk of a broken heart. Otherwise, she'd regret it forever.

She pressed her slick, soapy breasts against his chest. "You're gonna get me in trouble." She smiled against his mouth. "My band will have me flayed if I ditch them for a guy."

As much as she wanted them to stay locked in her house all day, shirking band duties wasn't an option. But doing the right thing wasn't easy when his wet, naked body was touching hers. Streams of water ran down his chest, blurring the tattoos she couldn't wait to trace with her tongue. The suds her breasts left behind slid over his happy trail of dark hair, down to the most perfect cock she'd seen outside of *Playgirl* magazine.

"*A guy*?" He stepped back, plastering an offended expression onto his face. "I'm Tyler Fucking Hall. The most famous string-fingerer ever to come out of Portland, thank you very much."

Those talented fingers traveled along her spine, settling at the small of her back.

"Mmm... String-fingerer." Her eyes fluttered closed before meeting his again. "Has a much better ring to it than guitarist. You should coin that."

"You seriously have to go?" He mock pouted.

"Seriously. We have to finalize recording schedules for the benefit album, and you're getting your stuff with Matty anyway. But once you're done and my meeting's over, I'll be starving. For food and you. We can meet here, order takeout, and make both happen."

Her eyes skated up from his chest, and the lust behind his thick, dark lashes stoked the insatiable ache low in her belly.

"You're gonna get yourself in trouble if you keep looking at me like that." His voice was a low, sexy rumble that made trouble sound very tempting.

"Get used to it." She pointed at her eyes. "I've been wondering what's under your clothes for a long time, so these peepers plan to drink you in every chance they get."

"Peepers? Fuck, you're cute." He scrubbed his hair and put a dot of lather on her nose. "I don't even use the word 'cute.'"

"Because it'll damage your street cred?"

Tyler laughed. "I can't believe you actually pay attention to the stupid shit that comes out of my mouth."

"Of course I do." Her eyes raked over his body again before settling between his legs. And deciding that being a few minutes late for her meeting wouldn't be the worst thing in the world. "But right now, I'm more interested in putting something into mine."

23

Tyler

Charlotte was toweling off her hair in her underwear when the phone rang. She tossed the towel on the bed and answered.

"Hello?" She ran her fingers through her long, wet locks. "Oh, hey, girl. What's up?"

She looked at Tyler, mouthing *Sandra* before pressing a finger to her lips.

Why would she want to keep it a secret that he was over? It's not like he'd never been to her house before. Did she want to hide their relationship from their friends? Even worse, was she having second thoughts?

"Huh. Wonder what that's about." Her hair dripped onto the floor, and she picked up the towel, patting the ends dry. "Maybe it's our chronic bassist drama. She can't be thrilled about that hole in the band when we need to record."

Tyler stepped into his boots while Charlotte opened her dresser, fishing out clothes and tossing them on the bed.

"Calm your tits, Turbo." She glared when he laughed and quickly slapped his hand over his mouth. "Nothing. The TV. Anyway, whatever the problem is, we'll figure it out at the meeting. I'll finish getting ready and head over. Later."

She hung up and grabbed her jeans off the bed, sliding them over her legs and hips. The pale blue denim accentuated the perfect curves of her ass, almost making him forget the question he'd been holding in.

"Why didn't you want Sandra to know I was here?"

She stopped buttoning her jeans.

"I need to explain this," she said, gesturing between them, "in person. You know how critical she is of people I date. And she'll probably think we're nuts for jumping in so soon after..."

"Right." Obviously, neither of them wanted to say *her* name.

"I'll tell the girls today if we have time before Eliza gets there." She finished buttoning and zipping her pants. "I can make Sandra understand why we're not making a huge mistake. And if she wants to be an ass, I'll be within smacking distance of her stubborn but adorable face."

Knowing she intended to tell her closest friends about them was a relief.

"Just don't tell Matty, okay?" He couldn't wait to see his brother's face when he heard the news.

"That's all you. But I'll need details about how it looked when his head exploded." Charlotte grabbed a lacy black bra, clasping it in front of her chest before turning it around and slipping the straps over her shoulders. Watching women get dressed was fascinating. "Sandra said there's some problem with the benefit Eliza needs to tell us about. I hope no one pulled out."

"Easy fix, if that's it." He sat on her bed, ruffling his wet hair with a towel. "No shortage of talent in this town. You still want a track from us?"

"Definitely. You're the biggest act that said yes." She shook out her hair before running a wide comb through it. "After we lock down the schedule, you can tell Adam and Zack what time slot's yours at the studio."

He admired her ambition. Making an album wasn't easy, let alone one requiring collaboration with eccentric, often demanding musicians with packed schedules.

She slipped on a sleeveless gray top. "Take note of all the buttons." She gestured at the front. "That was unbelievably hot, by the way. I'll never wear a button-up shirt again without getting wet."

Tyler was still adjusting to the evolution of their relationship. As friends, they'd discuss brands of guitar strings and books and new bands they discovered. They'd quote ridiculous movies to make each other laugh. While that felt intimate in its own way, things were now on an entirely different level.

And he was loving every second.

"You're killing me here, Charlotte. If you keep saying dirty things, I'll tie you to the bed and tell your bandmates you have the flu."

"I'm so tempted to call your bluff." She began buttoning her blouse.

"Who's bluffing?"

She shook her head, smiling. "Speaking of bandmates, we're still short a bassist since Jackie bailed. Know anyone?"

Tyler scratched the rough stubble on his chin. "Roger Scanlon from Phoenix Rose. And I think Luke from Black River's still available."

Charlotte's fingers froze on the last button. "Luke! We like the all-girl thing, but he's incredible. Maybe Amber and Sandra will be open to it. Thanks."

"No sweat. I'll give you his number later."

Tyler dropped his damp towel on the floor before pulling his semi-clean shirt over his head. Charlotte was almost to her dresser when she picked up the towel and tossed it into a hamper.

"Shit. I'm so sorry." He swallowed hard, kicking himself for already making a stupid mistake.

Her head tilted. "It's just a towel, Ty. But now that you know where the hamper is, I'll be within my rights to cut you if you do it again." Her laughter died when he didn't join in. She moved to stand between his knees, a puzzled look on her face. "Hey, it's fine. Really." She stroked his forehead, scrutinizing his expression while nervousness knotted in his gut. "Let me guess. You'd catch hell for being human?"

While waiting for the anger that never came, he thought about how normal it'd become to walk on eggshells to please someone. Triple-checking toilet seats were down, and his laundry was put away. How often had he done simple, careless things like leave a dirty plate on the nightstand or forget to pick up Amy's dry cleaning only to be screamed at or made to feel like a worthless asshole?

"You know me, Ty." She earned his undivided attention with a gentle kiss. "Remember when you said I'm safe with you? Well, you're safe with me, too."

He smiled at that, and she kissed him again. His lips were raw from all the action, but he couldn't get enough of her kisses.

She snatched something off the dresser before settling back between his knees, a silver necklace in her hand. "Help me with this?"

A pendant hung from the chain—a silver claw clutching a cream-colored pea-sized stone with shimmering dashes of color blended in.

"What's that?" Tyler took the chain, clasping the ends at the base of her neck as she held up her hair.

"An opal. My birthstone."

"October twenty-fourth, right?" He brushed his lips against her nape, his eyes closing at the sound of her sexy little sigh.

"Correct. Good boy." She spun around, patting him on the head.

He panted like a dog before taking her in his arms, lifting her off her feet, and spinning her in circles. Her squeal of surprise turned into laughter, and he silenced her with another kiss.

"Put me down, brute." She threw a few fake punches at his shoulders. "My band's waiting."

As Tyler set her down, a feeling of dread washed over him. The outside world wouldn't be warm and fuzzy like the one he and Charlotte had lived in since their first kiss. He wasn't ready to face it.

He'd have to go home, pack his things, and take them back to his hotel. Closing one chapter and beginning the next. But it wouldn't be nearly as easy as that. He'd have to prepare himself for a fight. He knew damn well Amy was.

The phone rang again.

"Damn, I'm popular today." Charlotte grabbed her well-worn Converse sneakers. "I'll answer in the kitchen so we can chug coffee before we jet. Thanks for making it, by the way."

He followed as her bare feet padded across the linoleum.

"Hello?"

Tyler poured himself half a cup since it was probably all he had time for. He sat at her kitchen table while she listened to the caller.

"Seriously?" The shoes dropped from her hand. "What kid? Did he trample my flowers, too?"

His head snapped to her. Worry replaced the relaxed expression she'd worn all morning. An arm wrapped around herself, telling him fear was in there too.

"And the notes?"

Tyler stood, hugging her from the side to let her know he was there. She looked at him, a corner of her mouth lifting.

"Okay. Thanks, officer."

She hung up, exhaling a heavy breath while she stared at the phone.

"That was Officer Barlowe. Some fifteen-year-old kid confessed to throwing the brick. And he said he smashed the flowers under my window."

"*What?*"

"Had nothing to do with the notes, though. Or the other flowers." She ran a hand through her hair. "My fucking head's spinning. I don't know what to think."

Neither did Tyler. They were all convinced it was Charlotte's stalker or even Amy, not some dumb, reckless kid. When he and Matthew were teenagers, they'd done their share of ding-dong-ditch and toilet-papering houses. Maybe bored kids in the nineties were over that sort of innocent fun, preferring the thrill of misdemeanor vandalism.

"It's good news, right?" Tyler said. "Someone wasn't trying to hurt *you*. We were just in the wrong place at the wrong time. The kid might've walked around all night with that brick, looking for someone to scare."

"Sure. Maybe." She slipped into her shoes.

The concern hadn't left her face.

He pulled her close, a soothing hand gliding up and down her back. Questions rattled in his head, but her silence said she needed a moment to process. Her cheek settled over his heart, the taut muscles in her arms relaxing.

"Why don't I feel relieved?" she asked.

He pressed a kiss to her forehead. "Because it only answers one of the questions. We still don't know who wrote the notes, but they never tried to hurt you physically. I'm relieved it's still possible they're just screwing with your head and not lurking in your goddamn bushes."

She nodded, going quiet again.

"Did he say why the kid confessed?"

"One of his friends called the cops, ratted him out."

"Wow. I want to buy that kid a new bike." He placed a knuckle beneath her chin, raising it. "This is good news. My morning was spent naked with you in the shower, and now we have one less thing to worry about. I'd say the day's off to a great start."

"You're right." Her relaxed smile returned along with the light in her eyes that dimmed when she was stressed. "I've become so used to the fear of what might come next that I don't know when to let it go. That stops now." She took his hand. "Hell, in the past seventeen hours, I've had some of the best sex of my life. That's something to be psyched about."

His eyebrow quirked. "Some of the?"

"Gives us a goal to work toward."

They laughed, his hands sliding down her body to settle in the back pockets of her jeans. "Guess we'll just have to practice later. A lot."

After one more kiss, she set the alarm, and they were out the door.

He pulled an extra hotel key from his pocket while she locked up. "Room seven twelve. In case you ever want to stop by wearing nothing but a long jacket and a smile."

She laughed, slipping the key into her purse. "I do own a pretty sexy trench coat."

Although he wouldn't complain if she showed up like that, he wanted her to have a safe place to go if she ever needed it. Around-the-clock security was in the lobby, and a police station was right next door.

When Tyler reached his car, he turned for one last look. He was grateful she was still smiling as she waved and drove off. He looked at the spot in the driveway where they were parked during the attack. Despite what he'd said to reassure her, he couldn't accept that some dumb neighborhood kid threw the brick that could've killed her. Could it be a coincidence that it happened at the same time as his divorce and the return of Charlotte's stalker?

While Tyler hoped she found relief in what Barlowe said, he didn't want her to let her guard down. Someone was still out there, watching. He could only guess what they might do next.

24

Charlotte

Sandra, Charlotte, and Amber waited for their manager, Eliza, in a booth at Rose City Roasters, a bustling coffee shop in Portland's Pearl District. The bright, checkered décor and vinyl booths offered a fifties diner feel, but chandeliers and other modern touches made it uniquely Portland.

They needed to finalize recording schedules for bands contributing to the album, and Eliza had news about the project. Dirty memories of the marathon sex session with Tyler made it hard for Charlotte to focus, but she'd never put the band in second place to anyone. Not even a red-hot, tatted-up rock star who did magical things with his tongue.

The waitress arrived with an iced lavender latte and a plate of hash browns for Sandra, a cappuccino for Amber, and a black coffee and lemon muffin for Charlotte. After all that naughty cardio, she was famished, and the mingling scents of bacon and pancakes in the air made her mouth water. And made her wish she'd ordered a lot more food.

"So, ladies," Charlotte said, "before we get into band business, I have news that doesn't involve something terrifying."

Sandra plunged her straw into her latte, taking a sip. "Thank god. Please tell us Barlowe has a lead about the broken window and fucked-up porch flowers."

Amber sat straighter.

"Actually, yeah. Not the flowers, but some teenager confessed to throwing the brick."

Amber clapped her hands. "That's great! One mystery's solved."

"Interesting." Sandra rubbed her chin. The absence of relief on her face said she was skeptical. "They're sure?" She squirted ketchup on her hash browns, spreading it with a fork.

Charlotte shrugged. "As sure as they can be. He remembered the color of Tyler's car and knew my address but said he didn't know who lived there. Seems totally random."

"Barlowe's still looking into the notes and flowers?" Amber asked.

Charlotte could see Sandra's wheels turning, her tight expression making it clear she wasn't ready to accept Barlowe's news as truth.

"Yeah. And I have other, happier news to share." She touched Sandra's hand. "You have to promise not to flip out and get us banned from this place, drama queen. I can't live without their lemon muffins."

Amber snagged a chunk of Charlotte's muffin, popping it into her mouth. "Goddamn! You aren't kidding. I'm getting one." She went to slide out of the booth before Charlotte grabbed the sleeve of her white T-shirt.

"Let me say this first."

"While we're young, Char." Sandra stirred the ice in her glass. "What's up?"

She pressed her lips together to contain the grin threatening to swallow her face. "Tyler kissed me."

Amber shrieked and bounced in her seat, earning annoyed looks from the preteen skater boys in the next booth. At least someone was happy for Charlotte. Sandra looked like someone had kicked her puppy.

"Are you motherfucking kidding me?" Sandra slammed her palm on the tabletop. "He's single ten damn minutes, and he kissed you? That's crazy!"

After teasing Charlotte for years about secretly liking Tyler, Sandra's reaction pissed her off. Nothing would spoil this new relationship before it even had a chance to get off the ground.

"Stop it, Sandra." Charlotte resisted the urge to smack the grumpy scowl off her face. "Don't shit on this. You know how much I wanted it to happen. Hell, you taunted me about it all the damn time."

"I know you have feelings for him, but I didn't think you'd jump in while he's still tied to Amy. It could end badly." Sandra shook her head. "What if it's just a rebound fling?"

Charlotte's stomach dropped as her best friend's words sunk in. The possibility that after being tied down for three years, he'd want to sow some wild oats was already buzzing in her mind. Why would a young, hot rock star want to go from one relationship straight into another? What if she wasn't enough for him? Then again, what if being with him wasn't as wonderful as she'd imagined? What if *he* wasn't enough for *her*? It was easier to ignore the fears before hearing them spoken out loud.

Charlotte took a deep breath. Letting unfounded worries take root would only bust up the cloud she'd been floating on since that epic first kiss. No one was robbing her of that rare bliss, not even Sandra.

"This is Tyler we're talking about." Charlotte crossed her arms over her chest. "You know he wouldn't do that to me."

Amber tried to jump in. "Of course, he wouldn't—"

"Breakups are brutal." Sandra pushed the curls out of her face. "They make people do impulsive things they'll later regret."

"For fuck's sake." Charlotte's eyes shot to the ceiling fan spinning above their heads. "I'm not some stranger he picked up at a bar because he was lonely. We have history. I've waited years for that man to come to his damn senses and wasn't about to go another second without making my intentions clear."

"What if he goes back to her?" Sandra half-shouted. The skater boys tossed her a dirty look before returning to their colas and fries.

"He won't."

"What if he does?"

"He won't, Sandra!" Charlotte's cheeks burned. "He's done with her lying, cheating, and using him for his status and money. And yeah, this is fast, but life's short, and it's what I want. Please just be my friend and be happy for me."

Amber slid across the seat and hugged her. "We are happy for you, honey. Aren't we, Sandra?"

"Well, shit." Sandra clicked her tongue, her shoulders sagging in resignation. "It's fast, but he is a great guy." She tapped the table in front of Charlotte when her gaze fell. "I love Tyler. You know that. But I love you more. And I swear I'll castrate him if he breaks your heart."

"I love you too," Charlotte said. "Both of you. Now let's get these schedules figured out so I can have a whole lot more sex with that gorgeous man."

Sandra spit a mouthful of latte across the table, onto the front of Amber's white T-shirt, and all over Charlotte's bare arm. "Charlotte, you *fucked* him?"

"Seriously, Sandra?" Amber grabbed a handful of napkins and blotted at her shirt while Charlotte grabbed more to soak up the mess on the table.

She laughed, staring down Sandra's glare. "Yes, and it was the best goddamn sex I've ever had. Seriously earth-shattering. My panties might catch fire just thinking about it. And if you try to ruin this high for me, you're the one getting castrated. Metaphorically, of course."

Amber high-fived her. "Get it, girl! Good for you."

Sandra coughed. Amber and Charlotte sat back in their seats in case another spray of latte was imminent. "I hope you know what you're getting yourself into. You already have one target on your back, and now you're moving to the top of Amy's shit list. Are you prepared to deal with that kind of trouble?" She coughed once more before swiping her lips with a napkin.

Charlotte slid the remains of her muffin in front of Sandra. "Chew on this instead of talking. You wouldn't worry so much if you knew how happy we've been since that first kiss."

"That's lust, sweetheart." Sandra's head shook. "And pent-up sexual tension. The night you met, he was thinking with his dick instead of his brain, and look where it got him."

"Oh, fuck way the hell off with that." Charlotte threw up her arms, sinking back in her seat.

"Whoa, let's bring the temperature down here, ladies." Amber touched their hands. "We're all on the same team. Sandra, you love Charlotte and want the best for her. But you need to learn when to back off and let her make her own decisions. Charlotte, you want to revel in the memories of the deliciously naughty deeds swirling around your pretty head and see where things go. And we can all agree that sometimes, you don't make the healthiest choices when it comes to dudes, but we trust you will this time."

"Thanks, Amber." Charlotte turned to Sandra, waiting for her to look her in the eye. "He threw his body over mine when the brick hit that window. Have I ever been with a person who'd do something like that? Maybe I'm finally done dating losers I can't trust with my heart." She shoved her lukewarm coffee to the edge of the table. "You can think I'm making a huge mistake, but it doesn't change the fact that this feels right to me."

Eliza's shiny black heels clicked over to the booth, turning the heads of several diners as she approached. Like the rest of her outfit, the shoes were out of place in the casual atmosphere. She wore a charcoal gray pencil skirt, a flowy white blouse, and a tailored black blazer buttoned at the front. The suit and her expression said she meant business.

"Sorry I'm late, girls. It's been an eventful morning, to say the least."

"What's up?" Sandra scooted to give her space to sit.

"We have a problem," Eliza said as a waitress approached, pen and pad ready. She rattled off a coffee order so complicated the waitress's hand struggled to keep up. "Marion Cole, the CEO at Safe Start, was unhappy when I told her Tomorrow Mourning was contributing to the album. Considering the recent accusations against Tyler in the press, the organization can't be associated with an abuser."

Charlotte's head whipped toward Eliza so quickly a nerve pinched in her neck. "Tyler is *not* an abuser!"

The outburst earned whispers and laughter from the skater kids. Sandra flipped them off with both hands before returning to her hash browns.

Eliza touched Charlotte's wrist. The waitress placed a mug and saucer in front of her before moving to another table. "I believe you. But those photos don't cast you in the best light either, Charlotte." Eliza blew on her mug and sipped, leaving a mauve smear on the rim. "Fortunately, the photos proving Amy cheated first helped sway public opinion in a positive direction. And the public's reaction to Tyler's disastrous radio interview was mostly good. His fans appear to be on his side, at least. But that doesn't change things with Safe Start."

"I'll talk to Marion," Charlotte said, anxiety prickling in her chest. "She knows how dedicated we are to their cause. Maybe she'll change her mind if I explain the truth."

"It might've been an effective strategy if that were the only problem," Eliza said.

Amber clutched her stomach. "I don't like the sound of that. What else is there?"

Eliza dabbed her lips with a napkin, setting it on her lap. "The producer pulled out. He wouldn't say why, but it doesn't matter. I called around, and everyone decent's booked during our studio time. If we push the recording dates back, we lose the acts with tours coming up, so it'd still be a bust."

Sandra groaned. "So, now we need a producer that's cool with having zero notice, an act to grab as much attention as Tomorrow Mourning would've, and a bassist to replace Jackie." She noisily sucked up the last sips of her latte. "Fucking fantastic."

"What about doing a show instead?" Charlotte asked, the idea entering her mind only seconds before she said it.

"Huh?" Sandra's face scrunched. "Why would we pivot to a new approach after all the time and energy invested in this one?"

"Hear me out," Charlotte said, a flutter of excitement making it hard to sit still. "We could potentially raise even more this way. And it would come all at once instead of trickling in like album sales. Between merch, tickets, a paid meet-and-greet area for autographs, and a cut of drink sales, we could pull in a shitload of cash all in one night and cut them a check fat enough to save their shelter program."

"Ooh, like Empire Records!" Amber beamed, clearly into the idea. "They put that show together in just a few hours. I love that movie."

Sandra laughed, loading her fork with hash browns. "If we talk them into letting Ty participate, he'll be our Rex Manning."

Eliza's eyebrows raised. "How about we focus on real-life logistics?"

"Apocalypse would be perfect," Charlotte said. "They already have solid sound and lighting crews used to working with multiple bands in one night."

"And the owner owes us one for the security breach that let that creep leave flowers in our dressing room," Sandra pointed out, her mouth stuffed with potato.

"I usually don't like last-minute changes, but..." Eliza nodded slowly, like she was working things out. "This could work. If we're all on board, I'll call the club to see what dates are open. Then, I can check with the bands set to record to determine who's available. If we lose a few, the others will get longer sets."

Charlotte did a happy dance in her seat, grateful for the positive vibes. She started a mental list of what they'd need to do to pull it off.

"Sorry to bring it back up, but so I know the full story," Eliza said, "what really happened outside Apocalypse?"

Charlotte grumbled. So much for positive vibes.

"Tyler hugged me goodbye, Amy charged at us like a rabid bull, and he stopped her from strangling me or whatever. End of story." Charlotte picked at her muffin wrapper, needing somewhere to direct her nervous energy. "And before you ask, I'm not in the middle of some fucked-up love triangle."

"More of a straight line now," Amber mumbled. Charlotte kicked her under the table. Eliza didn't need a rundown of her love life.

Sandra scoffed. "It's no mystery who tipped off the photographer about where to find juicy drama that made Amy look like a victim."

"Wouldn't surprise me," Eliza said. "She's still pretty well-connected from her glory days, after all. And Amy was notorious for planting stories in the press. The possibility she inspired the producer to back out also crossed my mind."

Amber's hands curled into fists. "How bad would it be if I spent a few days in jail for kicking her bleached teeth in?"

Sandra stroked Amber's slick blonde hair. "Settle down, you beautiful badass. Violence isn't the answer. But if she keeps screwing with our career, you'll have to get in line behind me."

"What do you think, Eliza?" Charlotte rubbed her arms as a chill ran through her that had nothing to do with her shirt being damp from Sandra's latte. "Can this derail our progress?"

"Your personal lives are none of my business." Eliza exhaled a long, slow breath. "Just be careful what you do in public. If you can avoid it, don't give her or anyone else fuel that could tarnish your image. The sky's the limit for you ladies, but the cruel reality is the wrong story in the press can change that overnight."

"Wouldn't being viewed as a 'bad girl' work in Charlotte's favor?" Amber asked. "She's in a punk band, for fuck's sake."

"Sure." Eliza lifted her mug and took a sip. "It could. Or it could go the other way. For instance, your fans who like Scarlet Love Letter might turn on you. People upset that one of rock's favorite couples broke up might take it out on Charlotte."

"That's insane!" Charlotte said. "I had nothing to do with that."

Eliza set her mug on its saucer. "Unfortunately, perception often holds more power than truth. It's tough to predict how the public will react to the incomplete, often biased information they receive. Further complicating things, women in any industry are judged harshly when their private lives are no longer private."

"Fuck this." Sandra slammed her fist on the table. "We'll fight whatever horseshit Amy plants in the press, whoever's messing with Charlotte will be shanked in prison, the show will raise piles of money for Safe Start, and we'll all live happily ever after. Now, let's get the hell out of here before I start throwing ice at those obnoxious fucking skater kids."

25

Tyler

Matthew held up his pint glass of stout, clinking it against Tyler's. "Cheers to your future, brother."

The guys were having their weekly "Beer and Bitching" session at Rogue in Southeast Portland. When Tyler wasn't touring, they met at a different brewery every Thursday at four, unloading their stresses from the previous week over drinks. Matthew liked keeping an eye on the competition, and it was cheaper and more fun than therapy. Plus, crowds were lighter than on weekends, so Tyler could relax and feel normal for a while. The pickup truck Matthew borrowed to get the rest of Tyler's stuff was parked at the curb.

"You signing those divorce papers was the best news I've heard all year. I'm proud of you for not crawling back."

"No chance." Tyler's fingers drummed along to the Fleetwood Mac on the jukebox. "From now on, if I'm on my knees for a woman, it'll be for reasons a hell of a lot more fun."

Matthew laughed, raising his glass again. "Cheers to that, too." He set his beer on a coaster and folded his hands on the table. "It's good to see the light back in your eyes, man. And I'm glad the things I've missed most aren't gone forever."

"Such as?" Tyler put down his beer, listening.

"Before Amy, I'd see you a hell of a lot more than once a week for drinks. And you were pretty happy most of the time. But she'd give you shit if Charlotte, Molly, or any other female wanted to hang with us, and you'd usually let her get her way to keep the peace. Or we had to sneak behind her back to go out with them. That's not what a healthy relationship looks like. You were like a beaten-down version of yourself, and nothing I said got through to you."

Tyler ripped tiny pieces off the cardboard coaster beneath his glass. "Sorry I let her put space between us."

"Don't be sorry. Just make sure you're stronger and wiser before you meet the next one."

Tyler cracked a smile. "I already have." He couldn't wait to see Matthew's reaction to his big news.

"What?" Matthew shoved his shoulder. "You've been holding out on me, you bastard! You've been separated for a month and already have another chick lined up? I wanna be you when I grow up."

"This girl invited me to a Farmers' Market, and I said yes. You know damn well that isn't my scene. But I went and had a blast. At a fucking *Farmers' Market.*"

"Please tell me you sampled tiny jars of jam and sniffed flowers. I need an image to think about next time I need a good laugh."

"Bite me." Tyler tossed a chunk of coaster at his brother's head, nailing the bridge of his nose. "Actually, I did both of those things. And let tiny goats walk on my back."

Matthew almost choked on his beer.

"Her idea." He smiled at the memory. Charlotte was just so damn fun and up for anything. It thrilled him to imagine what adventures they could share if things worked out.

Matthew studied Tyler's face, nodding slowly. "Damn, bro. You really like this girl. Do I know her?"

"Yep." Tyler lit a cigarette, blowing the smoke toward the open window beside them. His smile grew, his pulse kicking up in anticipation of the big reveal. He set down his beer and took a deep breath. "It's Charlotte."

Matthew's hand jerked, spilling his beer across the table. "*Charlotte*? Tyler, I'm... I'm speechless. How? When? What the fuck?"

"You don't sound speechless to me." Tyler laughed. He drained his glass, raising two fingers at the bartender for another round. "She helped me see what I've been missing. Besides the fact that they're both drop-dead gorgeous musicians, Charlotte and Amy couldn't be more different."

Matthew grabbed a pile of napkins from the aluminum dispenser, soaking up the spilled beer. "You don't have to tell me. Charlotte's my sister from another mister. One of the best people I know."

The server brought fresh beers, shooting Matthew an irritated glance as she gathered the dripping wad of napkins. Tyler thanked her before taking a cold, delicious sip.

"You weren't afraid to do normal shit and risked public humiliation." Matthew paused like he was processing, his eyes narrowing. "This isn't just a rebound thing, is it?"

"No." Tyler stamped out his cigarette and blew a stream of smoke out the side of his mouth. "Definitely more than that."

"You've been tied down for three years. Don't you want to play the hot groupie field a bit before jumping into another serious relationship?"

Tyler felt like Charlotte's brother was grilling him, not his own. He appreciated how protective Matthew was, especially with some whacko throwing bricks and leaving her fucked-up notes.

"Got that out of my system years ago. I want something real with someone who wants me for who I am, not what I do."

Matthew leaned in as the music shifted from soft rock to heavy metal. "Did you kiss her? Or did you…"

Tyler grinned, his face heating to an embarrassing degree. "Don't ask me that."

"I think I got my answer, you dirty dog."

Tyler laughed, pushing hair out of his face and leaning back in his seat. "All I'm gonna say is she's incredible. Even in my early days with Amy, I don't remember feeling a connection that strong. When Charlotte looks into my eyes, it's like she *sees* me, you know? She always has. I think Amy just went through the motions to keep me from leaving until that got boring, and she quit. Getting her to connect with me was a struggle, and I kept wondering what I'd done to make her so distant."

"Again, not to sound like Oprah, but that's not what a healthy relationship looks like."

If it weren't for their parents, Tyler wouldn't even know what a healthy relationship looked like. But what if he didn't know how to be in one himself? In many ways, his marriage had been doomed from the start, but wasn't he partly to blame for it turning toxic? All the traveling and endless pressures to create and promote often left him stressed and moody, with nothing left to give. What if those same failings poisoned his relationship with Charlotte? What if he tried his best to make her happy, and it still wasn't enough because *he* wasn't enough?

"Hey, where'd you go?" Matthew asked.

"What if I fuck it up?" Tyler hoped saying his fear out loud would take away its power, but it only made it more real. "What if we start strong, then I start touring and getting stuck inside my head, and we drift apart?"

"Stop." Matthew knocked on the table when Tyler's gaze fell. "You have what it takes to make the right woman happy. You just have to shut down your damn insecurities before they sabotage it."

Tyler hoped his brother was right. All he could do was keep working on himself and try his best to build the healthy, lasting connection he wanted more than anything.

"From what you're saying," Matthew continued, "it seems like you and Charlotte are off to a great start. It's a fast switch, but it's not like you've just met. You already know she's a kind, honest person you can trust. Success hasn't inflated her ego or made her materialistic, and she doesn't step on people to get what she wants."

Tyler nodded, agreeing with every word. And knowing Charlotte so well as a friend didn't mean their relationship would lack mystery or excitement—quite the opposite. The excitement would come from knowing her on a deeper, more intimate level, inside and outside the bedroom. He looked forward to figuring out how she liked to be held and touched and what she needed from a partner on her best and worst days. Like Matthew pointed out, it was also comforting to know she was good to her core and there wouldn't be any deal-breaking surprises leading to another heartbreak.

"It'd be nice not to see her with another loser." Matthew bit his lip, his expression serious. "But be careful with her. It's good that she already trusts you, but she's used to keeping people she dates at a distance, protecting herself. She's terrified of falling hard for someone and losing them. Sound familiar?"

All three shared that trait, a tragic side effect of losing a parent. And like Matthew, Tyler hated watching Charlotte's dating disasters from the sidelines, fearing she'd fall for one of the ridiculous jerks she brought around. He was starting to think it'd been so hard because of the feelings he'd kept buried all those years.

"I'm not going anywhere," Tyler said. "Don't gloat, but you were right. On some level, I've liked her since we met. It just wasn't our time, I guess. But now…" He looked up at his brother, his lifelong best friend, an unexpected swell of emotion making his eyes water. "This could be something amazing, Matty."

Matthew reached across the table, squeezing Tyler's shoulder. The familiar gesture and warm smile on his brother's face made him feel loved and miles away from lonely. "I know it can, brother. You deserve each other."

Knowing what Charlotte meant to him, Tyler couldn't imagine a higher compliment. "Thanks, Matty."

"And in case you didn't already know," Matthew said, jabbing a finger across the table, "if you break that girl's heart, I'll break your fucking face."

Tyler laughed. He didn't doubt his sincerity for a second. "If I break her heart, I'll deserve it."

◆◇◆

When Tyler walked through his front door with Matthew, their arms loaded with flattened boxes, he took the house's silence as the second good sign. The empty driveway was the first. He'd worried about a confrontation with Amy over the divorce papers and headlines like *Cheating Amy's Dirty Dalliance with Drummer!* that were still splashed all over the media thanks to his publicist. Not wanting to stand around long enough to jinx it, he put together the first box, securing the bottom with packing tape.

"Box up my records." Tyler passed Matthew a roll of tape. "I'll start on my bedroom."

As Matthew got to work in the living room, Tyler headed upstairs. When he opened the bedroom door, the scene that greeted him shot a fiery rush of adrenaline through his veins.

"What the fuck?!"

The box slipped from his hands.

All his band shirts were cut in half and strewn across the bed. Some he'd had since high school, and they were all reduced to worthless rags. His notebooks, filled with years of lyrics and band notes, were shredded and spread around like confetti. All the ideas he'd jotted down in those precious, fleeting moments when inspiration struck were lost forever.

One thing was clear—Tyler had poked the bear.

And the bear poked back.

"What's wrong?" Matthew gasped behind him. "Holy. Shit." He approached the bed, picking up a ragged scrap of black sleeve before dropping it back in the pile. "She's lost her goddamn mind!"

Rage and grief warred in Tyler's chest as he struggled to accept the reality in front of him. A jolt of fear broke through, stiffening his spine.

"Fuck! My guitars!"

They raced downstairs and across the lawn to his studio. Tyler's hands shook as he fished keys from his pocket and unlocked the door.

He flung it open, relief flooding in at the sight of his guitars and other equipment just as he'd left them. Still, misery churned in his gut over everything he'd lost. He bent forward, hands splayed on his knees, as he caught his breath, his lungs burning from the panicked sprint from the house.

"Maybe the shit in your room's all she did," Matthew said. "It royally sucks, but you'll have new ideas. Better ones. You can replace those shirts. Hell, I have plenty of your shirts at my place and won't even expect a thank you for keeping them safe."

Tyler shot an irritated glance at his brother. "Too soon, Matty."

"Sorry, buddy."

Tyler sucked in a sharp breath, his spine bolting upright.

"Fuck!" Another rush of terror struck, more potent than the last. "Oh, fuck!"

"What's wrong?"

Tyler flew from the studio and back to the house, Matthew on his heels. He ran straight for the ugly antique chair—the last place he remembered seeing his father's army jacket.

It wasn't there.

"What are we looking for?"

Tyler barely registered his brother's voice as he frantically scoured the living room.

When he saw it, his heart sank.

On the leather couch, his father's jacket lay in a wadded-up pile beside the angry burn holes he'd made with his cigarette. Tears stung his eyes as he lifted it, taking in the full scope of what she'd done.

"No! No. *No...*" Dozens of the same black-rimmed, circular holes dotted the cloth. "Not my fucking jacket!"

Hot tears rolled to his chin as he screamed at the empty house.

Amy knew full well how much it meant to him.

She wanted him to hurt and aimed for the perfect target.

He hugged the damaged jacket to his chest.

"Oh, Tyler." Matt's voice broke. "I'm so sorry."

Tyler felt his brother's arms wrap around him, holding him for a few breaths, their father's ruined jacket between them.

"It's my fault." Tyler wiped his eyes with his sleeve. "I drank too much and forgot it. I should've known the photos would make her do something crazy."

"No." Matthew pulled back. "This is not your fault."

Tyler's eyes shut, trapped sobs quaking in his chest.

"Tyler, look at me."

When his eyes slowly opened, Matthew's sympathetic gaze made the pain easier to bear.

"I know you're hurt and pissed and maybe a little scared. Hell, I would be. But don't forget who you are." Matthew pressed his forehead against Tyler's, their eyes locked. "You're my strong, resilient big brother. This is just another fucked-up step on your way to a better life. What you and Charlotte are starting could be *it*. A real forever that'll bring a lot more joy than grief and pain. That happiness Mom and Dad had, you can finally have it too."

A lump formed in Tyler's throat, his tears returning for a different reason. He'd never said it out loud, but of course, Matthew knew. What Tyler wanted most was a love like their parents had. They'd met in high school, and even after thirteen years and two kids, they still held hands, shared stolen kisses, and whispered sweet words when they thought no one was listening. They didn't have much money, but every Saturday night, their mom set candles on the table, made a special dinner, and they'd have a "date" while the boys ate pizza and watched a movie in the living room.

Their parents' love for each other and the family they created was the light in their house—bright, safe, and warm. It went out when they lost their dad.

Tyler's loneliness was rooted in that darkness, in the relentless ache to feel warm and safe again. It led him to get lost in Amy. He'd caught a fleeting glimpse of that light only to have it snuffed out beneath a pile of broken promises. It was too soon to tell if he'd find it with Charlotte, but how he felt when she was in his arms gave him hope.

As always, Matthew knew him so well that even the unsaid was understood. And well enough to know reminding him of his parents' bond was probably the only thing capable of snapping him out of his drive for revenge.

The feeling he'd been chasing all his life was within reach if he didn't fuck it up.

"It'll be hard," Matthew said, "but you have to let this go. No more back and forth with the psycho, okay?"

A glance at the ruined jacket was all it took for the red-hot rage to return.

Tyler stepped back. "Matty, I love you and can't imagine dealing with this mess without you. But the guy who lets these things slide isn't who I am. Not anymore."

He grabbed the phone and dialed his attorney.

"Can I please speak with Melanie Watters?"

"Tyler, what are you doing?" Matthew asked.

She'd left her office, so her secretary transferred him to voicemail.

"Hey, Melanie. It's Tyler Hall. The timeline we discussed has to move up. We need to put both my houses up for sale, like, yesterday. If you can somehow expedite the divorce without her signing, do it. And in case I didn't emphasize it enough, do absolutely everything in your power to ensure that vindictive witch I married doesn't get a cent of my money."

Tyler slammed the phone, rubbing his temples as the first pangs of a headache tapped at his skull. He'd never needed a smoke so badly. After sliding the last one from the pack, he threw the box to the floor. He patted his pockets for a lighter, coming up empty. With the filter between his lips, he dug through the junk drawer, his fingers landing on a transparent orange prescription bottle instead. When he picked it up for a closer look, it wasn't full of pills. It was powder. Knowing Amy and her penchant for keeping Rafael and her other minions high and happy, that powder was heroin.

He imagined opening the lid, his pinkie sliding inside. Lifting a bump to his nose, a quick inhale would bring instant relief from the misery Amy kept dishing out. He startled when Matthew swiped the bottle from his hands, pouring the contents into the sink and running hot water at full blast until it rushed down the drain.

Matthew stared into the sink, his hands supporting his weight as his head fell forward and his shoulders sank. "Tyler, if I wasn't here—"

"I wouldn't have touched it. I swear." He clutched his chest above the searing burn that made him question the truth in his words. If he'd been alone, confronted with the ruins of the only treasured things in his life, he'd know all too well a line or two would instantly extinguish that burn. "I didn't even know it was there." That was the truth, but he wasn't surprised to find it. Amy had mini stashes all over the house. Like Easter Eggs for junkies.

"I'd never forgive you." Matt's head sank lower. "And Charlotte..."

He didn't need to finish the thought because they both knew how that would end.

She'd never speak to him again. Never forgive him.

And it would break her heart.

"I wouldn't do that to either of you. Or myself. I'm okay, I promise."

"Fine." He didn't seem convinced, but Tyler hoped he'd let it drop. "Let's finish packing what she didn't destroy and get the hell out of here."

Tyler went upstairs to see if he'd missed anything salvageable in the bedroom. He surveyed the damage, wrestling with his next moves.

Did he want to make his brother proud and be the bigger person?

Was he prepared to let this vicious, intensely personal attack slide?

He could stoop to Amy's level and trash her shit or rise above it, pack, and go.

Spotting his favorite, irreplaceable Fugazi shirt in the shredded pile, he decided to stoop.

Tyler crept downstairs, sneaking past Matthew to get to the garage, and returned with a can of red spray paint. After shutting the bedroom door, he shook the can, the metal ball inside furiously rattling, and popped off the top. He opened Amy's massive walk-in closet, overflowing with designer clothes, handbags, and shoes.

"You wanna play this game with me, Amy? You heartless gold-digging psycho." He gave the can one final shake. "I'll play."

Tyler entered the closet and let the spray fly.

He aimed at fur coats, dresses, and high heels made by designers Amy probably only cared about because Vogue told her to. All pretentious, overpriced garbage. He knew she wanted to be envied for her pretty shell while inside, she'd become a festering sore.

Silk scarves, handbags, the Versace gown she wore to some movie premiere she dragged him to—they all got sprayed until nothing came from the nozzle but air. He threw the can at the mirror on the far side of the closet, a crack splintering the center.

He grabbed his suitcase from his much smaller closet and stuffed his clothes inside. Whatever Amy hadn't ruined, that is. It was mostly jeans, boxers, and socks, but better than nothing.

"Holy fuck, Tyler!" Matt's jaw dropped as he took in Tyler's handiwork. "Are you *trying* to provoke her?"

Tyler zipped the suitcase and carried it to the doorway. When he glanced at his brother, the shock on Matthew's face changed to disappointment. Maybe even disgust. While it stung, Tyler didn't regret what he'd done. Since they were kids, he'd always tried to set a good example—how to work hard, the value of chasing your passions, and the importance of cranking up your inner voice to drown out the critics and haters. Matthew had never seen him pushed so far past his limits, so it was usually easier to take the high ground.

But Tyler was only human. It wouldn't be the first time he disappointed his brother and wouldn't be the last.

"Judge me all you want, but like I said..." He stared down Matt's disapproval without flinching. Maybe this was another important example—reclaiming control over your life after stupidly handing someone else the reins. "I'm done being the guy who takes shit like this without a fight."

In silence, they loaded the few boxes they'd packed, his suitcase, and three guitars into the truck. After buckling in, Tyler set his damaged jacket across his lap. When he turned to the house for one last look, he felt a lot of things—regret, anger, sadness—but mostly, relief.

The Amy chapter of his life was finally over.

26

Charlotte

Charlotte reached for the water beside her bed while trying to catch her breath after her third orgasm of the evening. "Thanks. I needed that." When added to the morning's tally, all her records were broken, and she was surprised she could still speak in complete sentences.

"Glad I could help." Tyler laughed into her hair as she took a drink and settled back against his side.

Light from the full moon made her curtains glow in the otherwise dark room as she listened to the rapid thudding of his heart. She loved this strange new reality where she could touch him, kiss him, and lie on his bare chest.

After the first round, they'd had Chinese food delivered from her favorite spot. After a few bites, they had sex again on her kitchen floor before tossing the food into the fridge and moving to the bedroom. While it was exciting to be so hot for each other they couldn't wait until the fortune cookies were cracked, her bed was more comfortable than cold linoleum.

"Did Matty flip when you told him about us?" she asked.

A corner of Tyler's mouth hitched up. "He knocked over his beer and threatened to break my face if I break your heart."

She laughed, vividly imagining that playing out. "Sounds about right. Sandra threatened castration if you hurt me. And she spit coffee all over me and Amber when I told her. Our friends are ridiculous. And obviously can't be trusted with beverages."

His laughter made her head bounce. "How'd the rest of your meeting go?"

"It had a bumpy start but ended on a positive note." Her eyes closed in contentment as he stroked her hair. "We're trying to put together a show instead of the album."

"Really?" He angled his head to look at her. "What happened?"

She didn't want to kill the mood by telling him his band couldn't be involved or mentioning the producer pulling out. And uttering the A-word was the last thing she wanted to do while they were naked and happy. The best approach was keeping it simple.

"Let's just say it's a better plan." When Charlotte glanced up, he still looked confused, but she hoped he'd let it go. "Did you get all your stuff from the house?"

Tyler's chest sunk with a heavy sigh. "That's a long bummer of a story, and I'm too blissed out to rehash it. Ask me tomorrow?"

So, they both had terrible, mood-killing news to save for later. Charlotte nodded, curious, but if his story involved more of Amy's nonsense, she was happy to put that one off too. His stomach growled, the sound rumbling beneath her ear.

"I'm still hungry," he said. "Are there leftover noodles?"

"Since you attacked me five bites in, there are plenty of noodles left."

Tyler tickled her ribs, and they laughed as she wiggled away and got to her feet.

"I'm hungry, too." She ran her fingers through the fresh tangles in her hair. "Let's finish our cold Kung Pao so the crunchy little pastries can tell us our fate."

"I already know what yours will say." He left the bed and kissed the tip of her nose.

"Really, Confucius? What will it say?"

"Beautiful women who feed noodles to starving men will reap the benefits of the energy boost."

"Must be a big piece of paper." She grabbed the Sex Pistols shirt he wore to her house and slid it over her head, relishing his scent on her skin.

"Did you take my shirt so I'm forced to walk around half-naked?"

"Only half?" She snatched the boxers from his hand and tossed them.

Charlotte headed for the kitchen. Tyler followed, naked and without an ounce of self-consciousness. She opened the fridge, pulling out two takeout boxes with red dragons on the side. It reminded her of something, and her head turned. The black dragon inked across his muscles made her rethink her stance on kitchen floors. He took the containers, setting them on the table.

Tyler waved his hands before pointing to his face. "I'm up here, lady. Don't make me think you only want me for my body."

She moved in for a kiss, giggling like a smitten schoolgirl against his lips. "Not only, but it's definitely in the top five."

He grabbed chopsticks from the counter, digging into the container of lo mein. After pulling out a few noodles, he held them in front of Charlotte. She opened her mouth, and he slowly slid the tip of the chopsticks inside. Her lips closed around them, and he pulled out the empty sticks. While she chewed, he took a few bites.

"Sandra thinks we're crazy," she said.

Tyler froze, a piece of carrot suspended between the carton and his mouth. "I guess that's understandable. It's all happening so fast." He shrugged his naked shoulders. "But it's not like we're stockbrokers or college professors or whatever. We're professional rock musicians. Chasing our passions comes with the territory. Artists are allowed and even expected to be impulsive and make decisions based on feelings before their brains can catch up. Just ask Mick Jagger."

"Wow." Her eyebrows raised. "Excellent point."

"Thanks." Tyler bit the carrot with a loud crunch. "Do you think we're crazy? Your opinion's the only one that matters to me."

Charlotte picked a peanut from the Kung Pao, popping it into her mouth before licking her fingers. "I don't want to stick this under a microscope yet. I'm having fun with you. It's naughty and thrilling, and I can't remember the last time I felt this good." She licked sauce from her lip, the heat from the chilis tingling on her tongue. "I'm afraid if we pick it apart, the magic or whatever you want to call it will disappear."

"I feel the same way. Let's just enjoy each other and see where it leads. I'd prefer it if we didn't see other people, but otherwise, no pressure, no expectations."

"No regrets."

His eyes lifted from the container. "Definitely no regrets."

Charlotte hadn't realized how much she needed to hear that until he said the words, sincerely and without hesitation. Even if things between them didn't work out, she wouldn't regret a second spent with Tyler—in his arms, in her bed, and in those unguarded moments when they spoke as openly and honestly as they were then.

"Was it weird for you to go from being friends to being more?" he asked.

"At first, a little. When it hit me that the dude who teases me about how I tune my guitar was knuckle-deep in my pussy, it took a minute to adjust."

Tyler chuckled as he took another bite. "Understandable."

"But I've liked you for a long time, so it mostly felt like..." Charlotte held his gaze as she searched for the right word. "Finally. Finally, he knows how I feel. Even better, he seems to feel something, too."

"Seems? Hopefully, I've made it clear enough to kick that word out of your head."

She tapped his foot with her big toe. "Yes. You have."

"I still can't believe I didn't know how you felt." Tyler wiped sauce from her lip, sucking it off his thumb. "When did it start?"

"The night we met," she replied without skipping a beat. "We only talked for an hour or so, but something instantly pulled me in. You were sure of yourself, but I didn't detect a swollen ego. You were considerate, and I could tell you weren't faking it to get into my pants. And you flirted without staring at my breasts."

"Stole plenty of glances when you were performing, though."

"I don't doubt that." Charlotte snickered as she bit a chunk of celery. "I imagined you without your shirt, too, for the record." Her gaze dropped to his naked chest, grateful the imagining was over.

"I wanted to get to know you better," she continued. "Then, when Sandra and I showed up at Satyricon the next weekend, I spotted you and Amy making out backstage. I knew I'd lost my chance." Her shoulder lifted, struggling to seem unaffected as the memory stabbed at an old wound. "At least I got Matthew out of the deal. We became good friends after that night, and I got to be around you whenever we all hung out. And when you'd come to our shows. I liked what I saw." The corner of her mouth rose. Despite the residual hurt, she treasured those early days of their friendship. "Then, when I got booted from Scarlet, I hardly saw you. So, I dated a string of losers and tried to let go of the hope of ever getting closer to you."

Would the day ever come when she could remember that time without the sting of *Why not me*? Feeling shoved aside, discarded for something shinier. She'd felt pathetic for allowing self-doubt to creep in because a guy rejected her, but she couldn't help it. She was so young, caught off guard by intense feelings she wasn't prepared for.

But now, as Tyler stood naked in her kitchen, the feeling of his hands and lips burned into her skin, she felt ready for anything.

He set the chopsticks on the table. As he walked over, the look in his eyes made her heart jump. "Is this close enough?"

She swallowed hard, his proximity and the scent of sex on his skin kicking up her pulse. "Almost."

When Charlotte reached for him, he slid a hand behind her head and kissed her. It started soft but quickly turned deep and desperate—tongues and hands roaming freely, fanning the flame that burned between them.

Tyler pulled back to look at her before smiling softly and kissing her again. Whenever he did that, she remembered what he said at the cafe beside the river—he wanted a partner who looked him in the eyes when he craved connection. She silently vowed never to fail to give him that look, that connection. Because he needed it, and so did she.

Her lips brushed his ear. "Take me back to bed."

Tyler took her hand, intertwining their fingers. When she looked at him again, she saw a passionate, kindhearted man unquestionably worthy of all she had to offer. A man who kept his promises and treated people with respect. A man who wouldn't fail to give her what she needed in return.

Never in her life had Charlotte been more exhilarated or terrified, her heart beating with an unsteady throb as the dueling emotions took hold. Already, Tyler had burrowed deeply beneath her skin. Judging by how he looked at her, she knew he felt it too.

27

Tyler

"Nice to see you again, Mr. Jones. Welcome back to the Sturgess Suites."

The lips of the twenty-something blonde behind the desk offered the standard greeting for return guests, but the rest of her face sent an entirely different message—more of an invitation.

Tyler had used the pseudonym Jack Jones for years, but this chick wasn't fooled. Feeling uncomfortable, he tugged the hood of his sweatshirt to cover his profile. Combined with the dark sunglasses, he probably resembled the sketch of some shady character on a wanted poster.

"Thank you..." He glanced at her nametag. "Josephine. Any messages for me?"

Tyler was used to being eye-fucked by pretty girls, and he had a feeling that, in her head, Josephine was already naked and bent over the desk.

"No, sir. Please let me know if there's anything else I can do to make your stay extra special." She pressed her heavily glossed lips together and gave a fingertip wave.

Tyler got in the elevator, slumping against the wall as the doors closed. His entire body sighed. The previous day's stress had drained him, and he desperately needed sleep. He got very little at Charlotte's but wasn't about to complain. Her band had work to do for the benefit until late afternoon, and his schedule was clear, so he figured it was time to catch up. A few solid hours should be enough so he wasn't a zombie if she wanted to hang out later.

The second the door to his suite clicked shut, he kicked off his shoes and shuffled toward the plush king bed. Disturbed by the quiet, he clicked on the TV for background noise that would hopefully distract his brain enough for sleep. He sat on the edge, dialing Charlotte's number on the bedside phone. The machine picked up.

"Hey, beautiful. You wore my ass out, and I'm about to crash hard, but I'd love to see you after your band business. Maybe we can grab dinner with Matty and Sandra if she promises to keep the castration threats to a minimum. Give me a call, or just stop by."

Tyler peeled off his clothes and face-planted on the pristine white bedspread. The frigid air from a vent in the ceiling made goosebumps race across his skin, so he crawled under the sheets and passed out before he could blink.

When Tyler woke, he still felt locked inside the lurid dream he'd been having. Charlotte was naked on a lounge chair beside a shimmering pool, and her legs were spread for him. She leaned forward, opening her mouth in invitation. He clutched her hair in his fists as the real world crashed in.

His head was fuzzy, he had terrible cottonmouth, and the room was pitch black.

He couldn't remember where he was.

The hotel.

Things started making sense. No light came through the cracks between the curtains, so he'd been out for several hours. What didn't make sense were the sensations he experienced below the sheets. Specifically on his cock.

"Charlotte?" Tyler sat up and flipped on the bedside light.

"Not this time, Ty."

"Amy, what the *fuck*?" Tyler bolted from the bed like she'd lit it on fire. He snatched his boxers off the floor and pulled them on. "What the hell are you doing in my room?"

She made a show of wiping the sides of her mouth. "You taste like her. How could you be so disgusting?"

"Me? You broke into my damn room and—"

"What, Tyler?" She put her hands on her bare hips. "What did I do? Did I rape you with my mouth? Your own wife?"

"It sure as hell wasn't consensual, you crazy bitch." He grabbed her clothes and threw them in her face. "Get. Out."

He wondered if she'd seen her closet yet. The possibility she was there for another round of retribution put his senses on high alert.

"I didn't break in. I gave the little ditz at the front desk your usual pseudonym, showed her one of our wedding photos, and said not to call your room because I wanted to surprise you." Amy slipped her white lace dress over her head. "Then, voila! My very own key. It was really pretty simple."

Tyler's lips twitched. "I bet it stung that she didn't know who you were without showing her the photo." When Amy glared like she wanted to cut his head off, he knew he was right. "How'd you know where I was staying?"

She shrugged her lace-covered shoulders. "One of my little birdies told me."

"Of course, they did." He held out his hand. "Key."

She sighed dramatically before placing her room key in his palm. A breaking news alert flashed on the television, and their heads turned. The ticker at the bottom of the screen reported a murder-suicide in the Hollywood Hills. An actor's wife shot him in his sleep before turning the gun on herself.

Amy turned to Tyler, an obnoxious smirk tugging at the corner of her mouth. "And you think I'm bad."

"Thanks for not killing me," he said dryly. "Instead, you're trying to ruin my goddamn life."

He grabbed the remote, clicking off the television. He felt terrible for the actor and his kids, but focusing on one deranged spouse was all he could handle.

"You really couldn't do any better than Charlotte Fucking Ross?" Amy smoothed the scarlet waves on her shoulders. "I kicked her out of my band for a reason. She's obnoxiously average, with the charisma of a plain baked potato. You'll be sick of her in a week."

"We both know that's bullshit. You kicked her out of your band because she wanted to switch to guitar when Sarah quit, and you knew she'd upstage you if you let her."

Amy laughed it off, but he knew the comment had gotten to her. Because it was true. "For such a smart man, it's tragic how clueless you can be." Her lips formed a tight line as she stepped into her shiny red heels.

"I wonder if you actually believe the delusional stories you tell or know full well what a fraud you are."

"And I wonder why you're settling for a pathetic little twat who lives off the royalties from my fucking sweat," Amy spat, pounding her chest with her fist. "If you're really done with me, at least have enough pride to fuck up the ladder, not down."

The way she said it didn't seem like her usual paranoid accusations. It sounded like she knew for certain they'd become more than friends. "How'd you find out we're together? Have you been watching us?"

Amy's eyes rolled. "Don't flatter yourself. You just said her name when I was sucking you off." She pulled a cigarette from a pack in her coat and lit it, exhaling a thick cloud of smoke in his face. "You didn't waste any time, did you?"

He fanned the air, suppressing a cough as the smoke tickled his throat and burned his eyes. "At least I had the decency to leave you before being with someone else."

She scoffed, her hazel eyes firing daggers at his face. "That photo of you two outside Apocalypse tells a different story."

"Says the hypocrite who mauled her drummer outside a music store and screwed her bodyguard on our couch."

Amy poked two fingers into his chest, smoke rising from the cigarette between them. "She looked up at you like a pitiful, lovesick puppy. And you! You looked at her like you wanted to nail her right on the goddamn sidewalk. Nothing happened, my ass." An inch-long ash broke free from the tip of her cigarette, falling to the carpet. "We both made mistakes, so just admit it so we can get past them."

"I don't care what you believe, but I didn't touch her until after we separated." Tyler put on his shirt and pants before holding the door open. "And there's no getting past you screwing around, calling me abusive in the media, and destroying everything that mattered to me. Are you going to leave, or do I have to get security to haul your crazy ass out of this hotel?"

She didn't budge, her eyes trained on his face.

"You said not to touch your studio and guitars, and I didn't. I got angry and wanted to hurt you like you hurt me." It wasn't an apology, but he hadn't expected or needed one. He just wanted her gone. She took a single step closer. "It wasn't always bad, Ty. Remember when we used to stay in bed all day, naked, playing guitar and singing together? Like John and Fucking Yoko, if Yoko had talent."

"Amy..."

She continued, her red heel taking another step. "Or when we stayed at that hotel with the view of the Eiffel Tower and made love until sunrise? The candlelit dinner on the rooftop in Rome? Or the time I brought you onstage in Chicago so the crowd would sing 'Happy Birthday' to you?"

"Amy..."

"Remember joining the mile-high club the first time you got a check fat enough to rent a private jet?" Her hand lifted toward his chest. "Or when we—"

"Stop!" He took a broad step back, smacking his ankle on the leg of the dresser. It was tempting to go on the defensive and lash out, but that only made things worse. He just wanted this over. The rough calluses on his fingertips scrubbed his forehead as he gathered his thoughts. "You're right. It wasn't all bad. Back when it was all sex and fun and music, it felt like we were invincible. I would've done anything to make you happy."

Tyler shook his head at the tragedy of it all. All the flowers and extravagant trips and romantic gestures in the world didn't have the power to fix the damage between them. Nothing did. And he was relieved to no longer have an interest in trying. He had even less interest in accepting one more second of manipulation disguised as love.

"I wish you'd stayed the person who shared those beautiful moments with me." He blew out a long, slow breath. Maybe all she needed to leave him alone was closure. If he could make her understand how pointless this charade was, how infidelity was only one of the many nails in their relationship's coffin, she might get it. "But I reached a point where I questioned if you ever really loved me or if it was just an illusion. Nothing you can say or do would make me go back to that. You have to let me go."

"Wow. You're kidding, right?" Her lips curved into a sad smile that didn't reach her eyes. "Of course, I loved you, Tyler. I never stopped. You can rest assured you didn't waste years of your youth with someone who didn't crave the scent of your aftershave or enjoy watching you sleep because of how peaceful and perfect you looked. In those early days, I *ached* when you'd leave on tour." She batted at a tear. "Eventually, I found things to dull that ache for someone who gave so much of himself to others that sometimes, there wasn't enough left for me."

"I never intended to make you feel that way." Tyler tucked his hands into his pockets, rocking back on his heels as he stared at the carpet. "Maybe if our heads were clear, we would've seen our problems coming and addressed them before it was too late."

"Maybe. I guess we'll never know if we could've fixed things. Unless..."

"Unless what?" He looked up, narrowing his gaze.

Her glossy eyes stared back, silently pleading. "You give me another chance."

Tyler barked out a laugh. "You're unbelievable. Have you forgotten you just broke into my room and sexually assaulted me in my sleep? Divorcing you is easily the smartest decision I've ever made. Now get the fuck out of my room before I call security."

"Fine." Amy stuck her arms into her coat and grabbed her purse. "We could've handled this like civilized adults. I'm far more reasonable than you give me credit for."

"I tried that, remember? You had other priorities."

When she turned to grab her lighter off the bed, Tyler noticed the streak of red paint running up the back of her coat and burst out laughing.

"Haha, asshole." She tapped her cigarette, ashes raining onto the carpet. "Why'd you bring my beautiful clothes into this mess? My closet looked like a murder scene."

"You struck first. Don't forget that." Tyler's hands fisted. "You know what my dad's jacket means to me. All your shit's just superficial, ego-stroking leather and cloth. Worthless. That jacket's all I have left of him. But I guess you'd actually have to have a heart to understand."

"Oh, boo-fucking-hoo. You're boring me now." Amy moved to the door, feigning a yawn.

It was one of her most common complaints and one of the reasons he never felt good enough or interesting enough for her. His new perspective made it clear that failing was never with him. Her supposed needs were so ridiculous that satisfying them would always be impossible.

"Wanna know why you're always so bored, Amy?" Tyler got close enough to smell the expensive gin on her breath and stale smoke in her hair. "Because you are boring. You'll never be happy or satisfied because behind that mask you wear so well, there's not a single thing that's real, kind, or interesting. You're just a selfish liar who gets off on being cruel, and I wish I'd never met you."

She sucked in a sharp breath, her eyes shining with fresh tears. "Ouch. Who's the heartless one now?"

"Still you." He opened the door wider. "The next and last time I see you will be at the divorce hearing."

She dropped her cigarette on the carpet, squashing it beneath the toe of her stiletto. "We'll see about that, sweetie. By the way, I left you a present in the nightstand."

Tyler locked the deadbolt behind her, inching toward the nightstand. He held his breath, sliding open the top drawer. All the air left his lungs in a rush.

A small baggie filled with white powder sat on the phone book. He knew the drugs were more of a manipulation tactic than a friendly peace offering. An even more disturbing thought flashed through his mind.

What if it's poisoned?

As he carefully picked it up, the phone rang beside his head, the baggie tumbling through his fingers and onto the carpet. "Hello?"

"Is it crazy that I miss you, like, a lot?"

Hearing Charlotte's voice saying anything at that moment would've been a welcome relief. Hearing she missed him made him smile despite feeling on edge.

"If it is, I'm crazy too." He sat on the floor, his back against the metal bed frame. "How are the show plans going?'

"Great. Apocalypse is on board, and Eliza's working with them to book a date. I'm shocked by how well it's coming together."

"I'm not. You can pull off anything with how hard you work." He lit a cigarette, hoping to smother the scent of Amy's jasmine perfume as it turned his stomach. "Give me the date when you have it, and I'll tell Zack and Adam."

She was quiet for a few beats. "Yeah. We'll talk about that in person, okay?"

"Sure." Something in her tone seemed off, but with his frayed nerves, he thought maybe he'd imagined it. "Wanna come over? I have an awesome view of the downtown bridges."

Nothing sounded better than ending that stressful day with Charlotte in his bed, in his arms. Maybe it would erase some of the anxiety still burning in his chest.

"Very tempting, but it's after ten, and it's been a long day. I'm just gonna crash." She yawned, and the soft sigh that followed made him think of her face resting over his heart as he stroked her hair after their first perfect time together. The rejection was a disappointment, but clearly, she needed actual sleep, too. He wouldn't be able to keep his hands off her if she showed up. "Can we meet for breakfast at the café next to your hotel?"

"Yeah. Sounds good."

She went quiet again. "Everything okay?"

He rubbed his eyes with the palm of his hand, almost burning his hair with his cigarette. "Still tired, I guess. My day was a shitshow, but we'll talk tomorrow."

"Okay. I'm going to get some sleep then. I don't know if my sheets smelling like you will make that easier or harder."

His eyes shut, his head tipping back against the mattress. "Mmm... Remembering what made them smell that way is making me harder."

She laughed. "We are not having phone sex, Tyler."

He rested his elbow on his knee, smoke drifting to the ceiling in thin, white ribbons. "Sweet dreams, beautiful. See you in the morning."

When they hung up, he grabbed the baggie, walked to the bathroom, and flushed it down the toilet. It was where all of Amy's toxic bullshit belonged. He also poured out what remained in the whiskey bottle that'd been calling his name since finding his stuff trashed.

Despite the terrible feelings that clung to him as the worst parts of his day replayed in his head, he was done hiding and trying to forget. No more relying on alcohol or anything else to escape. He had his freedom, his music, incredible friends, and the beginning of a thrilling new relationship with Charlotte.

He was finally living a life he wouldn't have to be numb to survive.

28

Tyler

Tyler watched the office workers, families, and assorted hippies and misfits cruise along the bustling sidewalk as the morning rain tapped the café's windows. He envied how carefree they seemed while his mind endlessly turned over the encounter with Amy in his suite. Considering all she'd done since their separation, what else was she capable of? When his attention returned to Charlotte across the table, he knew she was doing the same.

"Tyler, you need a restraining order."

The anxiety rolling off her made his jaw clench. He straightened his base-ball cap, sinking low in the uncomfortable wooden chair. A restraining order wouldn't solve all his problems, but it might keep Amy off their backs.

"I'll talk to my lawyer and see what she thinks."

"I'm sure she'll tell you to do it. If there's an order on file, Amy will look bad in the divorce. Plus, she has DUIs. Plural. If you go before a judge, they'll *judge* her for her actions." Charlotte sipped her cappuccino, licking foam from her lips. "Destroying your things and breaking into your hotel room makes her look mental."

Tyler hadn't told her how Amy had woken him up in his bed. He didn't like keeping secrets but didn't want that image in her mind. It was bad enough having it in his.

"Okay." He inhaled deeply, filling his lungs with the scents of coffee and sugary pastries. "I'll go to the courthouse tomorrow and file the papers."

"I'll go with you if you want." Charlotte put down her mug. "On the bright side, at least you know who your stalker is."

Tyler wished he could erase the spark of fear in her eyes. Burdening her with his messes was unfair when she already had enough to worry about.

"Ty, I have to tell you something." Her fingers wrapped around her cup as her gaze fell to the table. "Marion, the CEO of Safe Start, read the stupid article calling you an abuser. She doesn't want you involved in the benefit."

He blinked. "Oh." The unexpected news was a gut punch—a sensation that'd somehow become a daily occurrence.

"I explained what happened, but she's still concerned about the public's perception. And how it might affect the organization." Her hands slid across the table, taking his. "I'm so sorry."

The further it sunk in, he wasn't offended by the rejection, just angry. It was another item on the growing list of things Amy had fucked-up. But he could take it if it only affected him. This hurt Charlotte and the goal she'd worked for. It made him wish he'd taken a blowtorch to Amy's closet instead of paint, setting fire to her possessions like she was setting fire to everything in his life.

"No, I'm sorry." He brought Charlotte's hands to his lips and kissed them. "The consequences of my choices keep affecting you, and it's unfair. I wish I could fix it." He sat straighter. "Actually..." He took out his wallet, sliding out the blank check behind the cash. He pulled a pen from another pocket, the ink point hovering over the box for the amount. "How much do they need?"

She smiled, taking the pen and setting it on the table. "I appreciate the thought, but let's see how the benefit goes."

"If there's still a deficit..."

"You'll be the first one I call."

Charlotte's relaxed expression evaporated, her throat moving as she swallowed.

"Tyler..." Her fingernail nervously tapped on the edge of her mug. "Do you think Amy would hurt you? Physically, I mean."

The question surprised him, the sudden shift in subjects giving him whiplash. "What? No. She's raging at the loss of control. I'm sure what she did to my stuff will be the worst of it."

"But you said before she's changed since I knew her. That there's a darkness that wasn't there before." She nervously chewed her thumbnail. "What if it's even darker than you realize?"

"She isn't violent if that's what you mean." Other than the slap in the closet at the club, Amy had never raised a hand to him or anyone else as far as he knew. "Why are you so worried about this?"

Charlotte stopped gnawing at her thumbnail, the hand falling to her lap. "Because she trashed your dad's jacket knowing what it meant to you, broke into your hotel room, and isn't used to losing."

He beckoned her over, sliding his chair back a few inches. "Come here."

She left her seat and walked over.

"She won't touch us. I promise." He pulled her into his lap, kissing her softly. "We'll get it figured out, okay? Someday, it'll all be behind us, and we can just live our lives."

Charlotte rested her forehead against his, curtains of her soft, dark hair blocking their view of the world around them. Her hair smelled like peaches and a hint of something like vanilla, only sweeter, sexier.

"I'd never let Amy or anyone else hurt you," he said. "Do you trust me?"

She nodded, the tenderness in her expression never faltering. Whether in a crowded café or alone and naked in her bed, they were the only two people on earth when their eyes connected. Nothing felt impossible—every burden set aside. The loneliness and insecurities he'd struggled with most of his life didn't feel so heavy and permanent.

Maybe he was mistaken, but the way her gaze softened as the contact held... it looked a lot like love.

"Good." He smoothed the wine-colored fabric over her thigh. "Have I told you how beautiful you look in this dress? I can't take my eyes off you."

"You know, for a big, bad rock star, you're kind of a sweetheart." She wrapped her arms around his shoulders. "Are you going to write me poetry and buy me a puppy?"

He toyed with the opal pendant on her chest. "Does a song count as a poem?"

"Come on, Ty." She arched an eyebrow. "There's no way you've written a song about me already."

"I may have written a few words." He brushed an eyelash off her cheek. "And I have a feeling you'll inspire more."

"Get out of here. Are you serious?"

He nodded. "I have the melody too."

Charlotte was quiet, her eyes locked on his. "Prove it."

Tyler glanced around the cafe. Eight other patrons were seated at tables on the opposite side of the building, and they were all busy enjoying their coffee and conversations.

He brought his lips to her ear and sang the chorus of the song stuck in his head since the drive to her house after their first kiss. It was about second chances and sparks. And chasing light to find your way home again.

She covered her mouth with her fingertips, listening.

When Tyler finished, tears welled in her eyes.

"Hey, don't cry." He kissed her damp eyelids. "Couldn't have been that bad."

She laughed softly into his shoulder and whispered, "Thank you."

"Your coffee's cold. Want me to have them heat it up?"

"Nope." With a massive grin, she picked up her mug and took a sip. "It's perfect."

Tyler kissed the foam off her lip before she could lick it off. "So, what kind of puppy do you want?"

29

Charlotte

"Well, I've gotta hand it to the guy. He knows how to make women cream their jeans."

"Gross, Sandra! Be mindful of my poor virgin ears." Charlotte's left roller skate ran over a scattering of pebbles, and she angled her wheels to glide to the opposite side of the sidewalk.

She looked up at the towering evergreens as she and Sandra zoomed through the northeast edge of Laurelhurst Park. The weather had been sunny and unseasonably warm, but storm clouds rolling in from the Columbia Gorge announced it was about time to head for cover.

"You should write songs for your ladies, too," Charlotte said. "I swear, it's like Spanish Fly for the heart."

Sandra's auburn curls poked out from the bottom of her pink and black helmet, sailing behind her as she glided along the sidewalk. "I wrote 'Abigail' about that chick Rosalie, but she was pissed I didn't use her real name."

"Why not?"

"Because I knew if we had a bad breakup, I'd be miserable singing her name at every damn show. I must be psychic because she banged a barista at Coffee Charlie's two weeks later."

"They have the best hazelnut biscotti at Coffee Charlie's." Charlotte laughed when Sandra gave her the stink eye. "Sorry. Out of loyalty to you, I'll get my biscotti from places evil girlfriend fuckers don't work."

"Thank you." Sandra wiped her sweaty forehead with the back of her hand. "So, is Tyler moving in with you or something? He's always there when I call."

"No, he's at a hotel until he finds a new place. As much as I'd love waking up to his handsome face every morning, I don't want to risk smothering things by moving too fast. And we need our personal space."

While that was true, it was only part of the story. She was tempted to invite him to stay, but deep down, she was still afraid he might change his mind about their relationship. It seemed wise to keep some distance to protect herself in case that happened. Telling Sandra that would only feed her reservations about their relationship, so she held it back.

Sandra nodded. "Wow. Personal space. Pretty level-headed perspective, considering you're total horndogs right now. Good for you."

"We're meeting for drinks at Galaxy after his recording session." Charlotte breathed harder as they sped up. "Then I'm going to his hotel, where I intend to get all up in his personal space. At least three times."

Sandra laughed, her head shaking. "And you say I'm gross? Do not make me picture you guys doing it. You're both like family to me."

Charlotte's smile slipped as her mind wandered. She kept imagining Amy in Tyler's hotel room, shuffling through her usual tricks to worm her way back into his life. Knowing how skilled she was at conning people into doing what she wanted, it was impossible not to wonder if Tyler had come close to faltering. Did she bring up a memory they cherished? Invent lies about Charlotte? Manufacture tears to make him feel sorry for her? Even worse—did she try using sex to lure him back?

"What's wrong, babe?" Worry lines creased Sandra's forehead.

Charlotte tapped the brakes on her skates and came to a halt. Sandra made a U-turn, stopping in front of her.

"Amy broke into his hotel room."

"*What*?" Sandra's eyes bulged. "Why? What did she do?"

Charlotte skated over to the grass, plopping beside a patch of dandelions and tiny daisies. Sandra followed, settling beside her.

"From what he says, she wanted to talk him out of the divorce and accused him again of being with me before their breakup."

"From what he says? You don't believe him?"

Charlotte went quiet, sorting through the insecurities the incident had triggered.

"I trust he didn't do or say anything that would hurt me, but I don't think I got the whole story." She picked up a blade of grass, tearing it down the middle. "Of course, maybe whatever else they discussed isn't my business. Maybe it was just personal, marriage-related stuff they hurled at each other that I don't need to know about."

Sandra plucked a tiny daisy from the grass, twirling the stem between her fingers. "Are you worried about her coming after you? You know better than anyone how well she handles rejection and betrayal. At least, what her twisted head perceives to be rejection and betrayal."

"Wouldn't surprise me. Tyler tried to convince me she won't and promised to keep me safe, but yeah. I'm worried. Now I have another crazy fucker to look over my shoulder for when I leave the house. Or just one, if Matt's suspicion about Amy sending the notes is right."

Sandra set the daisy on Charlotte's skate. "You remember that La Luna show when you were still in Scarlet Love Letter? How Amy started whaling on that skinny dude who breached the security line and kissed her cheek?"

Charlotte gasped. "Oh, my god! I forgot about that. I thought she was going to kill him."

"So did I. So did he!" Sandra frowned. "But she fucking laughed, thoroughly enjoying herself as she bashed the poor kid's head against the stage."

"She had to beg her parents to pay him off so no one got sued. What a mess." Charlotte shook her head at the terrible memory. "That was before Tyler came along, so I'm not sure he even knows about it."

"Remember how I begged you to leave the band after that?"

Charlotte nodded, staring at the daisy. "I should've listened."

Sandra pushed off the ground, standing on her skates. "I adore you, but sometimes your stubborn ass has to learn lessons the hard way." She put out her hand, helping Charlotte to her feet. "Stay far away from that psycho hosebeast, and watch your back."

Charlotte scoffed. "I don't want a confrontation, but it'd be pretty damn satisfying to slap the smug off her face."

"Agreed. Just don't end up like that poor kid with the fractured skull."

It started drizzling, and Charlotte looked at the dark clouds above their heads.

"Well, that's the end of our fun," Sandra said. "My hair's gonna be a frizzy disaster in about five minutes."

They turned to skate back toward their cars. The conversation put Charlotte on edge, and she scoped out all the faces in the park. Ahead on the path, a tall, broad-shouldered man who looked around fifty walked a massive black Doberman. A younger man in a dark sweatshirt, hands in his pockets, sat on a bench a few yards from where they skated. Three teenage boys in soccer uniforms stood in the grass, making guns with their hands, pretending to shoot at a group of girls playing hopscotch. There were dozens of other people walking dogs, throwing frisbees, jogging—all nice, normal activities that help you blend into your surroundings. Her stalker could be any of them, watching, waiting for the right opportunity. She touched the taser in her left pocket and took a few deep breaths.

Sandra touched her arm, snagging her attention. "Sorry I was such a jerk when you and Ty first got together."

"Don't sweat it. You were just looking out for me."

"Yeah, but I didn't need to be so shitty about it. I see how happy you are together. You get each other. You share that passion that keeps us all breathing, creating, and crawling out of bed to strap on a guitar. I've never connected with someone like that. You're lucky you found each other in this crazy fucking world." Her head tilted, a breeze blowing her curls away from her face. "Even though you're gross horndogs right now, I'm glad you guys hooked up."

Charlotte looked away from the bearded homeless man staring from across the park, shoving the paranoia aside before it ruined one more second of her day. Sandra was right. Charlotte was fortunate in many ways, and she'd be a damn fool to let fear of the unknown steal any more joy from her life.

She spun around in front of Sandra, hitting her brakes. "Aww... you're such a sappy sweetheart sometimes, Sandra."

Sandra stopped. "Damn, that was a lot of S-words."

"What can I say? I'm a huge fan of alliteration. And of doin' it with Tyler."

Sandra laughed and covered her ears. "Stop! Ick."

Charlotte hugged her, almost tripping over their skates. "You'll make some lucky girl very happy someday, my dear. Then, feel free to gross me out all you want as payback."

30

Tyler

"Y̶ou got a *restraining order* against me?"

Tyler's eyes rolled at Amy's rage, knowing he could silence her with the push of a button or a satisfying slam against the hotel phone's cradle. "Yeah, and you're violating that order by calling me." He sat on his bed, taking in the sights of the bustling city beyond his balcony while trying to forget how she'd woken him up two nights before in that room. "Goodbye, Amy." He started pulling the receiver from his ear.

"A woman with nothing left to lose is a dangerous thing." Her voice was slurred from heroin or alcohol. Probably both.

Tyler's shoulders stiffened. "Is that a threat?"

"No, darling, it's a fact. I've lost my livelihood, my husband. You're selling my goddamn houses. Give me half, or this won't end well for you or that little slut."

"Watch your fucking mouth." His fingers clutched the bedspread so tightly his knuckles cracked. "I'll pass your message on to the police and my attorneys. Sober up, Amy. Get your shit together. And don't forget that you brought this on yourself." As it turned out, even pushing a button could be satisfying.

He stared at the carpet, replaying her words.

A woman with nothing left to lose is a dangerous thing.

What the hell did she mean? He could dismiss it as meaningless bullshit that spilled out because she was wasted, but what if it wasn't? What if she was serious?

He didn't have time to pick apart Amy's drunken ramblings. The band had a six-hour recording session booked on the Eastside, and going by his view of the Burnside Bridge, traffic would be a beast. He showered quickly, throwing on a plain black T-shirt and his last clean pair of jeans before lighting a smoke and grabbing a paper cup of coffee in the lobby on his way out.

Tyler was the first to arrive. After setting up his guitars, he did warm-ups while waiting for Zack, Adam, and their producer to show up. When he adjusted his microphone, a pink envelope fluttered to the floor. He picked it up, slipped out the note inside, and read the message written in fat, black letters:

You can't keep Charlotte safe. Maybe I'll slit your throat while you sleep so I can play with her for a while.

The note drifted to his feet.

His heart thumped wildly in his chest as the words sank in.

He snatched the paper with a trembling hand, rereading it before shoving it into his pocket. A torrent of horrifying thoughts struck all at once, but the loudest demanded action:

Find Charlotte.

With his pulse thundering in his ears, Tyler grabbed the studio phone and dialed her house.

It could just be a prank—a sick, twisted joke.

Everything will be okay when I hear her voice.

It felt like it rang a thousand times before the machine picked up.

"Charlotte, if you're home, stay there and make sure the alarm's on and doors are locked. I got a note. Like the ones you get. *Please* be careful. Leaving the studio now."

He slammed the phone, rushing for the exit as Adam and Zack walked in.

"What's up, Ty?" Zack asked, a cigarette dangling from his lips. "You look stressed."

"Guys, I have an emergency. Sorry. Record your parts without me."

"Sure, man." Adam held the door open. "Go. Hope everything's okay."

"Give us a shout later if you need help," Zack called after him.

Tyler ran to his car, his hair and shoulders dampening in the drizzle. He buckled in and flipped on the windshield wipers. Another bright pink paper broke loose from the wiper and stuck to the windshield.

He could read the message without moving.

Maybe she's already dead.

31

Tyler

"Where the hell is Charlotte?" Tyler's rain-dampened cigarette shook in his hand as he stood on Sandra's doorstep. He'd banged on Charlotte's door for ten minutes even though her car was gone. He couldn't see inside the barred windows to check if anything was amiss. After filing a report with the police, he'd raced to Sandra's.

"Hello to you too, Tyler."

She stared like he'd lost his damn mind. If he hadn't yet, he was on the verge.

He pushed past her, pacing the living room.

"Well, okay then," she said. "Come on in."

A fire burned in the brick fireplace, and folk music played on a stereo in the corner. The contrast of the peaceful, cozy surroundings with the chaos he'd been dealing with made his head spin.

"You guys get in a fight or something?"

He stopped pacing, sucking hard on his cigarette. "Charlotte's in danger, and we need to find her. Now."

Sandra grabbed his shoulders. "Slow down. What do you mean she's in danger? What happened?"

He sank into the sofa across from a massive, framed poster of Patti Smith. Tears streamed down Sandra's cheeks when he explained the notes. Her expression was as terrified and desperate as his own, reflected in the poster's glass.

"We need to call the cops," she said.

"Already did. They took the notes, and they're looking into it. I'm surprised they haven't called to ask if you've seen her."

"Not since we skated this morning."

"How was she acting?" He smashed his cigarette into an ashtray on the coffee table. "Where was she going next?"

"She was freaked about the Amy situation but fine otherwise." Sandra nervously rubbed the back of her neck. "She planned to hit the record store to get the zines she likes. She does that every week and goes straight home to read them. And she was excited to meet you for drinks at Galaxy after your session."

"When I finished with the cops, I hit a few of her usual spots on the way here but didn't think about the record store." He got to his feet. "We'll check Galaxy later if we still haven't found her."

"Did you call Matt?"

"Stopped by his brewery, but Evan said he's in Hood River meeting some hops grower. Been there all day."

Sandra slipped on her shoes and grabbed a sweater. "Hopefully, she's just crate-digging. She'll do that for hours."

"One way to find out." He was grateful to have a new spot to check, but the fear of still coming up empty made him queasy. "Let's go."

Before opening the door, Sandra turned. "It's Amy, right? She's probably doing this to fuck with us."

"I have no idea." If it was Amy, she'd reached an entirely new level of crazy. He couldn't imagine her harming Charlotte, but after recent events, it was impossible to predict what desperation would lead her to do next.

A woman with nothing left to lose is a dangerous thing.

If the record store was a dead end and Charlotte still wasn't home, they'd pay Amy a visit.

"All I know is we need to find Charlotte," he said. "Do you have a key to her place?"

Sandra fished a ring of keys from the pocket of her jeans, dangling them in the air. "Let's find our girl."

Tyler and Sandra ran down the block to Center of the Road Records. A bell rang above their heads as they flew through the door. They froze, scanning the aisles of the small, cluttered store.

No sign of Charlotte.

Sandra muttered a curse before darting to the counter, grabbing the stout man behind the register who looked like David Crosby's twin brother.

"Jake! Have you seen Charlotte?"

The man looked at Sandra like she had two heads. "Yeah, a couple hours ago."

"Was she alone?" Tyler asked.

"Yep." The man turned to Tyler, doing a double take. "Holy shit, you're—"

Tyler groaned. "Not now, man. I'll come back and sign whatever or do anything you want if you help us."

"Focus, Jake! What time did she leave?" Sandra danced around like she had to pee.

"I'm not so good with time, but around one, I guess." Jake smoothed his blond mustache like a cartoon villain. "Or one thirty."

"Did she say where she was going?" Tyler asked.

"Huh?" Jake looked confused and probably stoned, neither of which would help their cause. "Sometimes we shoot the shit, but we ain't close like that, dude. Every week, she grabs her zines, buys a few albums, and that's it. Today, she paid, put a flyer on my board, told me to check out the new Radiohead, and bailed."

"Shit." Sandra pounded her fist on the counter, turning to Tyler. "Let's check her house."

They were halfway to the door when Jake yelled, "Wait!"

Their heads turned.

"One thing was different today."

Tyler held his breath, listening.

"She bought an *Oregonian* newspaper. First time."

Sandra and Tyler exchanged a baffled look.

"You sure that's what it was?" Sandra asked.

Jake's lips curved in a self-satisfied grin. "I'd bet my life on it."

"It's not your life we're worried about," Tyler mumbled.

Jake's forehead wrinkled. "What?"

"Nothing. Thanks, Jake." Sandra walked behind the counter, kissing him hard on the cheek. "You magnificent bastard."

He blushed behind his scruffy beard. "Anytime, sweets." Jake waved as they sprinted for the door.

At Charlotte's, they found a paper stuck to her front door.

"What the hell's that?" Sandra rubbed her arms.

Tyler grabbed the note, scanning it. "It's from the cop I talked to. He wants her to call when she's home." He shoved it into his pocket.

When he put the key in the lock, Sandra touched his back.

"Tyler, wait. What if…" Tears welled in her eyes. "What if she's hurt?"

"Then we need to get inside right fucking now." He pushed the door open, and Sandra punched in the alarm codes. Tyler checked the rooms, finding nothing obviously out of place. He returned to the kitchen to find Sandra trembling in the corner with tears trailing down her cheeks.

Tyler hugged her, his heart racing. "I'm scared too, but we have to look for clues. Can you help me? Please?"

Sandra nodded, rifling through papers on the counter. "What're we looking for?"

"I'm not sure." He ran his fingers through his hair, exhaling loudly. "But I hope we know it if we find it."

They searched every room, from under the bed to behind the clothes in her closet. They were looking through her mail in the living room when the doorknob jiggled.

"Who the fuck is that?" Sandra whispered, her bottom lip quivering.

"Go in the bedroom and lock the door."

Tyler crept into the kitchen, grabbing the largest knife in the butcher block. His hands violently shook as he gripped the handle and hid behind the opened pantry door.

The side door creaked open.

Footsteps tapped across the linoleum.

Tyler held his breath, his mouth dry and his upper lip dotted with sweat.

He chanced a peek around the door.

"Oh, my god!" Tyler dropped the knife, the metal blade clattering on the floor.

Charlotte let out a blood-curdling scream, falling backward against a kitchen chair. "Tyler, you scared the shit out of me! Why are you in my kitchen?" She rubbed her back where it had collided with the chair.

Sandra burst in, crashing into Charlotte. She sobbed and covered Charlotte's face in kisses, leaving pink lipstick prints all over her cheeks and forehead.

"Sandra? What the hell's going on?" Charlotte's eyes darted between them.

Tyler waited for Sandra to release her death grip, then pulled Charlotte to his chest, breathing her in. "We were scared out of our minds. Where have you been?"

"Scared? Why? What's wrong?" She looked up at him, a touch of panic in her eyes.

"If you have beer, grab three and meet us on the couch. I'll explain everything after you tell us where you've been." He kissed her before pulling back to look at her beautiful, bewildered face, letting relief settle in. "If you have anything stronger, bring the whole bottle."

32

Charlotte

"I'm fine, Dad." Charlotte balanced the phone on her shoulder while lighting a cigarette. "It was a misunderstanding. I've gotta go. I have people over."

"I love you, sweetheart. Be safe."

"I will. Love you too."

"And quit smoking."

She laughed. "I'll do that too. Someday. Bye, Dad."

After she hung up, she took a long drag, exhaling smoke through her nose like an angry bull. It'd been a long, stressful day, and she still didn't know why she'd come home to Tyler and Sandra in her house. Or why he was holding a butcher knife like Norman Fucking Bates.

When Tyler told her the cops had called her dad looking for her, she knew she had to call him first to ease his worries. That put it mildly. The poor man was having a panic attack, about to leave his business trip in Boston a day early. Hearing her voice calmed him, and she promised to visit soon.

Before returning to her surprise guests, Charlotte snatched the bottle of Southern Comfort off the counter and tossed back a shot. Considering their expressions when she walked into her house, she had a feeling she'd need it. She headed into the living room, sitting between Tyler and Sandra on the couch.

"How's Mickey?" Sandra swiped the bottle. "Did he call the FBI and National Guard to hunt you down?"

"Almost." Her anxiety eased when Tyler's arm slid across her shoulders, a hint of his sexy, woodsy aftershave hitting her nose. It reminded her of an Oregon forest in early spring, the last snow melting away so that life and all its brilliant colors could return. She snuggled closer. "He was freaked out, but he's okay."

"I know the feeling." Tyler hit her cigarette and handed it back.

"Yeah, me three." Sandra took a quick sip from the bottle. "Today was a nightmare wrapped in a heart attack."

Tyler kissed the side of Charlotte's head. "Your curly-headed friend's a little crazy, but she speaks the truth."

"Speaking of truths..." Sandra poked Charlotte's elbow. "Spill it, girl. Where were you?"

"Didn't you get my voicemail, Ty?" Charlotte took the bottle and lifted it to her lips, tossing back a burning shot before handing it to Tyler.

He smacked his forehead. "How did I not think to check my goddamn voicemail?"

Sandra turned. "Because you were too busy being terrified some psycho killed your girlfriend."

"*What*?" Panic seized Charlotte's throat and squeezed.

She needed answers, and she needed them fast.

"Oops." Sandra covered her mouth. "Sorry. Are you guys not saying the g-word yet?"

Charlotte threw a couch pillow at her. "No, dummy. Who's trying to kill me?"

"We'll get to that," Tyler said. "Have another drink first."

She took the bottle, struggling to swallow as the panic tightened its grip. "There. Now talk."

"Nope." Sandra shook her head. "Not until you tell us where you've been while me, Tyler, and the damn police department were trying to find your ass."

Charlotte sighed. "After we skated, I came home to grab cash for the record store. I got a call from some guy saying he wanted to interview me for *The Oregonian*. He said they had another musician lined up for this 'local band spotlight' article, but they canceled at the last minute. So, they needed someone else to feature in the piece before their deadline. I thought it'd be good exposure for the band and free promotion for the benefit show, so I said yes. Then, I hit the record store to kill time until the interview."

Tyler's eyes widened. "You agreed to meet with a stranger?"

"I'm not an idiot, Tyler." Charlotte glared, offended by his reaction. "It's not like he told me to go to his house and wait in the basement. He asked to meet at Cup and Saucer, probably the most crowded coffeehouse in Portland. I even called the paper to make sure he worked there and bought a copy to check out his work. I waited over an hour, and he never showed. I'm guessing whoever called wasn't that reporter, or he ditched me. The cops will figure it out."

"Yeah, because they've done a bang-up job so far," Sandra said.

"Shit." Tyler pulled a piece of paper from his pocket, handing it to Charlotte. "You should tell them you're okay."

She unfolded the note to find a request to call when she got home, followed by the name and number of Officer Kent Barlowe. Like she didn't have it memorized.

"I'll call after you guys spill your guts. I'm dying to know why I came home to Tyler holding a butcher knife."

"Don't say 'dying' after the day we've had." Sandra took another drink as Tyler explained everything that had happened.

Charlotte chewed her bottom lip as she listened, fear blazing in her chest. She was strapped to a roller coaster against her will as it slowly clicked to the top of a hill. From where she sat, it was impossible to see the steepness of the drop, but the nervous anticipation made her want to throw up.

"I can't believe this." Charlotte threaded her fingers through Tyler's. "So, the notes were in the studio and on your car. Who knew you'd be there?"

"You and Matty. Adam and Zack, obviously. Our producer."

"I knew." Sandra took another swig and handed the bottle to Tyler. "You told us at the last band meeting, so Amber and Eliza knew too."

Tyler took a long pull off the bottle and froze. "Fuck. Me. Sideways."

Charlotte squeezed his hand. "What's wrong?"

He took another, longer drink. "Amy."

She snatched the bottle, setting it on the coffee table between the latest issues of *Spin* and *Rolling Stone*. "What about her?"

"Fucking hell." He braced his elbows on his knees, his head in his hands.

"Tyler, talk to me." Charlotte touched his back, lightly shaking him. "What about Amy?"

He turned, anger reddening his face. "She knew where I'd be. I told her weeks ago I'd be recording there because our producer wouldn't work in my home studio when she's in town." He let out a humorless laugh. "Bruce can't stand to be around her either."

"So, we're all on the same page that Amy is totally whacko enough to stalk you and Charlotte, right?" Sandra asked.

"Yes!" Tyler and Charlotte said it forcefully and in unison.

"Even if she didn't send the old notes, I'm sure she knew about them," he said. "She could've copied that to torture us. If she had the supposed reporter guy call so no one would know where you were, she'd know I'd be scared out of my mind thinking someone hurt you. Maybe this was what her threat was about."

"Threat?" Charlotte grabbed his arm. "What threat?"

"She called earlier and said some crazy shit like 'Women with nothing to lose are dangerous'. I thought she was just trashed and talking out of her ass."

Charlotte shivered. He unzipped his hoodie and put it over her like a blanket.

"I'm not cold, Tyler. I'm pissed off. And scared." She pulled the sweatshirt to her chin. "Okay, maybe a little cold too."

"I'm gonna leave you two alone." Sandra stood.

"You can't drive," Charlotte said. "Just sleep here."

Sandra brushed her off. "I'll walk home and get my car tomorrow. It's only a few blocks, and I could use the fresh air."

"I'll walk you." Tyler got to his feet.

"Nope." Sandra put her hand up. "No one's making me scared to walk in my neighborhood. I carry mace and a don't-fuck-with-me face. I'm covered."

Charlotte knew it was no use arguing once Sandra's mind was made up, and after the day they'd had, she was too exhausted to try.

"Fine, but call me the second you get home." Charlotte hugged her friend. "Thanks for everything, sweetie. Sorry I scared you."

"I'm just glad you're okay." Sandra hugged Tyler, and Charlotte caught them exchanging looks as they pulled back. "Take care of our girl."

He nodded. "Thanks for playing Nancy Drew with me."

"Anytime, Ty." Sandra turned back. "Actually, never mind. I hope nothing remotely like this ever fucking happens again."

Charlotte grabbed the bottle off the table, raising it in the air. "I'll drink to that."

33

Tyler

Charlotte stood between Tyler's knees at the edge of her bed. She'd given her story to the police, and Sandra had called to say she was safely home. Nothing was left to do but be together, yet he couldn't shake the fear that had consumed him all day.

"Hey, look at me." She hooked a finger beneath his chin, lifting it. "I'm okay."

His arms circled her waist, his face pressing against her belly. He could hear her heartbeat, and for the first time that day, he felt like he could breathe.

"I don't know what I would've done if something happened to you. I felt powerless. Like I'd failed you."

She sat beside him and took his hand, her gaze as warm and soft as her skin. "You didn't fail me, Tyler. You ran all over trying to find me. You called the cops and questioned my bandmates. You gathered clues by talking to an old hippie."

Tyler couldn't help laughing. "He looked like David Crosby."

"I'm in there all the time, and he does. He looks exactly like David Crosby."

When the laughter stopped, tears filled her eyes. "You could've sat back and waited for the cops to do their job, but you didn't. You fought for me."

He gently cupped her face. "I'll do anything to keep you safe." He'd also do anything to erase those tears, to make her smile again.

"I've never felt safer than I do right now." She leaned closer, kissing him softly.

He pressed his lips to hers, sliding his tongue inside her mouth, tasting her as she gripped the front of his shirt. He stood, pulling it over his head before grabbing the hem of her green blouse and taking it off. Charlotte's eyes stayed locked on his as she unhooked her bra, dropping it to the floor.

Every single part of her was beautiful, but those eyes had the power to break him.

And put him back together again.

"Do you have any idea what you're doing to me?" The pad of his thumb glided along her lower lip as their gaze held.

Her hand dropped to stroke his crotch, the denim tenting as his cock thickened from her touch. "I do now."

Of course, his body was hungry for her, but the question came from a deeper place—a place where his feelings were even more intense and a hell of a lot more complicated.

She smiled as she crawled backward on the bed until her head reached the pillows. He unbuttoned her jeans and slid them off her legs, taking her underwear with them. He pulled off her socks one by one and unbuckled his belt with a metallic clatter, letting his jeans and boxers fall to the floor.

Tyler stood at the foot of the bed, gazing down at all her bare ivory skin. "I'm going to savor every single inch of you tonight." He picked up her foot, kissing the inside of her ankle. "Then, I think we'll sleep for about a month."

Her eyebrow arched. "You in my bed for a month?" He watched as her fingertips brushed back and forth on the skin above her breast, marveling at how even the simplest gesture from her could be so goddamn sexy. "I could live with that."

Tyler pressed another kiss on her ankle and worked his way up, kissing her calves, knees, and thighs, while stroking the backs of her legs with his fingertips. He caught the rapid rise and fall of her chest as her arousal grew. His palms slid underneath her, kneading the flesh of her firm, rounded bottom. He dipped his head, his lips brushing her hips and the delicate, sensitive skin around her tuft of dark pubic hair. His tongue traced the apex of her thigh, and she shuddered.

"Please, don't stop," Charlotte whispered into the air.

"Not a chance."

She bit her lower lip, desire blazing in her eyes. Her hand swept lower, across the skin between her breasts, and she threaded her fingers through his hair. Her tender, penetrating gaze made his pulse race.

Tyler's head dropped, his flattened tongue sliding from the bottom of her cleft to the tight, swollen nub of her clit. Charlotte's eyelids fluttered as he repeated the motion with long, languid licks. Her taste on his tongue made his erection press harder into the mattress. He parted the lips with his fingers and licked, sucked, and nibbled the delicate flesh until her grip on his hair made his scalp burn. Two fingers easily slipped inside, curling upward to find his favorite spot. Judging by her vocal response, it was also Charlotte's favorite spot.

After several minutes of firm, concentrated motions with his fingers and tongue, her body tensed. The muscles in her belly twitched, and the low, sensual sounds of her release broke in her chest. She used the hold on his hair to grind against his face, rolling her hips in time with the thrusting of his fingers. He hummed against her skin, a warm rush of need surging in his belly at her excitement and how freely she claimed her pleasure. Her back arched off the bed, and his tongue circled her clit, her pussy clenching around his slick fingers as she came.

Charlotte's body went slack, her panting breaths gradually slowing. She brushed hair off her forehead as her eyes lifted to the ceiling. "Holy shit, Tyler. I can't even see straight."

"Should I call an ambulance?"

She grabbed a pillow and hit him with it.

"You're so fucking good at that." She covered her face with her hands. "I need a second to recover."

He kissed a trail up her belly to the center of her chest and neck. She inhaled a sharp breath as he nipped and sucked the tender skin around her throat.

She set her hands on his shoulders. "Lie on your back."

"What are you going to do to me?" A half-smile curled his mouth.

She grabbed his face, their lips meeting, her tongue massaging his in a deep, wet kiss that stole his air. "Don't you like surprises?"

He usually didn't, but wherever this was going, he was all in.

Following her instruction, he laid on his back, sliding a pillow beneath his head.

She parted his knees before settling between them, her fingers skating down his chest with a feathery touch. "I'm getting wetter just looking at all that ink." Her head dipped, pressing a kiss to the treble clef near his heart. "This one's my favorite."

"Mine too. Got it right after our first sold-out gig. The artist kept having to wipe my sweat off as she worked." He laughed at the memory, tucking his hand behind his head. "Making a living with music had officially gone from dream to reality, and I wanted a permanent reminder of how that felt."

Charlotte nodded as she listened, her fingers brushing over the design. "That's really cool, Ty. I bet all your pieces have great stories to tell." She sat back on her heels, her tongue running along his hipbone. "I hope to hear them all someday."

He moved a hand over the tattoo a few inches above her mouth. "This one's getting covered up as soon as possible."

She peeled his fingers back, revealing the Scarlet Love Letter heart logo Amy talked him into on their honeymoon. At least that mistake was easily corrected with ink and a little blood.

Charlotte crooked an eyebrow. "You think I'm stressing about that when my mouth's inches from your cock?"

He laughed, relieved by her reaction. "I just want you to feel good when we're together. Not reminded of painful old shit."

She hovered above him on all fours, tracing his lips with the tip of her tongue. "Right now, don't worry about what feels good to me. You already covered that with this talented mouth of yours." Her tongue pushed into his mouth and withdrew before his could touch it. "I'm looking forward to returning the favor."

She sat back on her heels. He sighed with pleasure as her light touch skated along his ribcage. Her face went between his legs, slowly licking his cock from root to tip. The sight alone nearly made him burst.

He sucked in air through his teeth at the rush of sensation. "Ah, fuck." Tyler reached for her, but she pushed his hands against the mattress, trapping his wrists. "I want to touch you."

"Not yet." She pressed an openmouthed kiss on the head of his cock, the tight, swollen flesh disappearing between her lips. "Just lie back and enjoy the ride."

She gently sucked, her tongue flicking the sensitive spot underneath the tip. When the fears of the day threatened to creep back in, he focused on the sensual pull of her warm, wet mouth, drawing him closer and closer to the edge. A dot of precum glistened on her bottom lip, and she licked it off slowly, their eye contact holding. The fire in his belly surged, and the fear was gone, replaced by an all-consuming need to feel her heat surround him. To merge their bodies until they were so spent and satisfied that no energy was left for worry, reservations, or pain. After a few more wet licks on the head of his cock, her hands and mouth pulled away.

Tyler groaned from deep in his chest. "I miss your mouth."

"You won't have to miss it for long, baby. I promise."

Her weight left the bed with a small squeak of mattress springs. She rifled through a drawer, returning with a small black bottle that she set on the bed beside her.

He hummed in the back of his throat when her mouth returned, her tongue massaging the underside of his cock as she sucked him hard. His fingers raked through her dark locks, gripping the hair at the back of her scalp as her hand jerked the base of his shaft in smooth, circular strokes.

"That feels so fucking good," he breathed. "Go easy if you want it to last."

"Easy's overrated." Soft, wet flicks of her tongue teased the head before running along the sides in long, unhurried licks. "And we've got all the time in the world."

Charlotte's tongue returned to the head, licking and teasing the sensitive skin until he bit his lip to avoid begging her to finish him off. He wasn't ready for this to end anytime soon, and judging by the leisurely pace of her mouth and hands, she wasn't either.

His hands fisted, triggering a flashback of the butcher knife in Charlotte's kitchen, his fingers wrapped around the handle as he prepared for a life-or-death fight.

Her fingernails dug into the flesh of his legs, gliding in unison from the tops of his thighs to his knees. The pain grew more intense as it ran along the outside of his calves and across his ankles. It hurt, but in a good way, his breath quickening. The unexpected endorphin rush crowded out all thoughts.

The warm wetness of her tongue trailed lower, lower until it found the skin of his testicles, her tongue alternating between slow licks and quick little flicks. She took one into her mouth and gently sucked, his body going rigid as the intensity caught him off guard.

"Mmm... I think you like that." Her heated breath tickled the sensitive flesh.

"I want inside you so badly, Charlotte. *Please*."

"All in good time."

Tyler grinned. "This is definitely a good time." He closed his eyes, savoring her touch.

Maybe she's already dead.

He flinched. The nightmare of thinking someone hurt her invaded the perfect moment, the terror fresh and raw.

Without warning, she slid his cock down her throat, and his back arched off the mattress. She withdrew, soft touches caressing his hips. Grabbing the black bottle, she squeezed a few drops of liquid onto her fingers. As the faint scent of cinnamon hit his nose, she took his entire length down her throat again, sliding her lips and tongue along his shaft in a quick, steady rhythm. Her hand closed around his testicles, gently massaging while her hot, slippery mouth brought him closer to the edge.

A warm, tingly sensation spread between his legs, everywhere she'd touched. The concentrated heat jumbled his thoughts, sweat beading at his temples.

"Warming lube," she explained. "Like it?"

Unable to form a coherent thought, he mumbled, "Mmhm."

"Good. I want you to stay here, with me." Her hand stroked his chest, trailing over his stomach. "Not just your body, your mind too. When you start to drift, focus on how this feels."

Obviously, he couldn't hide from her. The shadow behind her eyes said she was fighting off the same awful memories. She'd once said that her stalker wins when she worries, and Tyler wouldn't stand for that.

They were in this together, and they'd get through it together.

"I'm right here, baby." He sat up, pushing the hair away from her face so they could see each other clearly. "And I'm not going anywhere."

In one swift motion, he turned her onto her back and moved above her, spreading her knees with his and aligning their hips. Kissing her hard, he slid his cock inside her. He could've sworn her eyes rolled to the back of her head, making it clear the distraction was working.

"You feel so fucking good after you come, Charlotte." He kissed her fluttering eyelids while increasing the speed of his thrusts. "You're so wet for me. So *ready*."

He pulled out all but the tip, slipping his tongue in her mouth as he slid his cock back inside, grinding his pelvis against her clit. His tongue and cock plunged again in unison, making her whimper against his mouth.

"Can you taste yourself?" He sucked her bottom lip, skimming it with his teeth. "Do you like that?"

"Yes." Her eyes locked onto his, her pupils flaring.

"Yes to what?"

"Everything." She smiled with him, her legs wrapping around his waist.

His body went rigid as his climax approached. He wanted to stay inside her all night, but being so worked up from her mouth made that impossible.

She tilted her hips, and he sank deeper, pounding hard and fast, skin slapping skin, until he belted out a broken moan, spilling his seed deep in her core until nothing was left.

He collapsed onto his back, opening his arms. When Charlotte came over, he held her to his chest and gently stroked her sweat-dampened hair. They were quiet for a while, basking in the perfect, peaceful moments closing out one of the worst days of his life. For a second, he wondered if all his worst days were finally behind him. But he knew he wasn't that lucky.

There was no telling what the future held. One thing he knew for sure was whenever Charlotte was safe in his arms, her warm breath against his neck, he found peace that was more genuine and purer than he'd ever felt. And he intended to savor every second.

"Ty?"

"Yeah?"

Her chin tilted up. "I don't want this feeling to end."

When he looked at her, tears pooled in her eyes.

"I know, baby." He pulled her closer, but somehow, it wasn't close enough. He felt it too, and the feeling had a name—one he'd spoken before but only now knew what it meant. It was so new he was afraid to say it out loud, so he just held her. "Neither do I."

34

Tyler

Tyler minced garlic on Charlotte's cutting board while she added olive oil to the cast iron pan on her stove. After spending the previous day terrified someone had hurt her, he needed a break. They both did. After clearing their calendars, they locked themselves away from the outside world, safe from whatever scare might be next.

"We're so punk rock right now." She tilted the pan to coat the bottom with oil.

He laughed at her sarcasm, wiping garlic off the knife with his finger. "We can't be cool all the time, baby."

Neither was particularly domestic, usually opting for takeout and pub grub over home-cooked meals, but there was comfort in the normalcy of it that Tyler hadn't expected. And it showed him a side of Charlotte he'd never seen. He smiled as he watched her gather ingredients while she shimmied and bounced to the Queen record spinning in the living room. She was so happy and relaxed it was contagious.

With the inimitable voice of Freddie Mercury as their soundtrack, they worked together on her mother's special marinara. He knew that cooking the sauce with her mom every Sunday were her happiest childhood memories, so he planned to follow her instructions carefully to avoid screwing it up.

Tyler moved the garlic aside and chopped a white onion the size of his fist. A few seconds after peeling its skin, he started sniffling and wiping his stinging eyes with his wrists. When she looked over, tears were sliding to his chin. She wrapped an arm around his waist.

"Aww, it's okay. Your chopping wasn't that bad."

He laughed. "How dare you! These pieces are all the same damn size. I even cut the weird brown nubs off the garlic." A fat teardrop fell to his T-shirt. "But I should've put goggles on for this shit."

She grabbed a pinch of onion, tossing it into the pan. According to her mom's handwritten, laminated recipe card, the instant sizzle said it was time for the next step.

"Ready for onions," she said.

He slid them from the board with the knife, scraping off the last bits on the side of the pan. Grabbing the spatula from the crock beside the stove, he turned the pieces over, allowing them to cook evenly. He felt Charlotte watching him, and she kissed his cheek, earning her a proper kiss before he returned his focus to the pan.

The potent scent of frying onions hit his nose, making his mouth water. He turned to find her eyes misting, probably more from sweet memories of her mom than the onions.

He touched his forehead to hers. "You okay?"

She blinked, tears collecting on her lashes. "Happens every time I make this." She dabbed her eyes with a corner of the stained, faded, checkered apron tied around her waist. It was also her mother's. "And I hope it always will. It means the memories are still strong, you know?"

He kissed the tip of her nose, a barely-there smile on her lips. He scraped the bottom of the pan as the onions steamed and sizzled.

"It was like magic, what she did in that kitchen." Charlotte's smile grew, but sadness dimmed her eyes. "I'd be twirling at her feet to the records spinning in the next room while Mom sang along, casually tossing ingredients into the pan like it was the easiest thing in the world." She laughed. "I'd imagine the boiling water bubbling in the huge pot was a cauldron, and she was a witch casting a spell with herbs and spices. A good witch, of course."

"Of course."

Once the onions were slightly browned, Charlotte added the garlic. Tyler stirred them in as she grabbed the dried oregano, basil, and thyme, pinching them between her fingers and sprinkling them over the pan.

"Casting a spell on me, Charlotte?" He peppered kisses on the curve of her neck, the light returning to her eyes. "If so, I think it's working."

"No hocus pocus needed for that." She shrugged. The sleeve of her loose-fitting top slipped, exposing a few black and gray flower petals tattooed on her shoulder. "Just my natural charm and luscious ass."

"Ain't that the truth?" He palmed her backside, planting a line of kisses on the ink and working up to the spot behind her earlobe that always made her shiver. He went quiet when the next song came on, bobbing his head as Brian May's guitar cast its own spell.

The corners of her mouth tipped up, making it clear she understood. "I love having music in common. I caught static from people I dated when I'd lock myself away to binge on records or write for a few days. Or if I had to interrupt their dull small talk to jot down lyrics that randomly popped into my head."

Charlotte grabbed the canned tomatoes, dumping them into the pan. "Break them up with the back of this." She handed him the wooden spoon with her mom's initials burned into the handle. Maybe some magic still lingered inside the wood because everything they'd been fretting about seemed to have disappeared, lifted from their shoulders by the warm smells of garlic, basil, and home.

"What's next?" He kept working the tomatoes.

"Pinch of sugar, a dash of salt, and a splash of wine." She added them, filling two glasses with the Cabernet before setting the bottle on the counter.

"I can't believe how incredible this smells! I want to swim in it and eat it at the same time."

Charlotte laughed, dipping a spoon into the sauce and taking a small taste before adding more salt and a dash of red pepper. "I must say, I'm impressed with your kitchen skills." She smiled above the rim of her glass as she sipped her wine. "Matty told me you cooked for him when you were kids, but I didn't know what to expect."

Tyler picked up his glass, sipping the dry and delicious Cabernet before setting it back on the counter. "It was mostly scrambled eggs and weird soups, but better than nothing. I learned to get pretty creative with the food bank's soggy canned vegetables."

"Most guys I dated couldn't make anything more complicated than instant ramen or Pop-Tarts, so you're an expert in comparison." Her appreciative gaze warmed his chest. He hoped to be better for her than those losers in every possible way. "It feels good making Mom's sauce with you. Not to get all sappy, but it's another nice memory tied to the recipe I can always hold onto. No matter what." She rested her head on his shoulder, her hand slipping into the back pocket of his jeans.

It bothered him whenever she said things like *no matter what* that sounded as if she thought their relationship had an expiration date. Maybe she worried he'd change his mind. Or even worse, maybe she thought she'd change her mind about him and wanted to prepare him for the possibility.

"And someday," she said, "I'll teach my kids how to make it. I want them to have plenty of good memories, too."

As he absorbed her words, he couldn't help picturing a tiny version of Charlotte bouncing around the kitchen beside her, pinching herbs between her fingers, carefully sprinkling them into the pan. He'd never thought of it before, but with her patience, selflessness, and how she cared for the ones she loved... Charlotte would be an amazing mother.

"How many do you want?" A rush of nerves rippled in his stomach. It was too soon to plan a future together, but he was afraid of being hit with a dealbreaker that would make one impossible.

"At least two." Her head lifted from his shoulder as a sigh of relief escaped him. "Being an only child was lonely sometimes. And after seeing how close you and Matty are, I want that for them. A best friend for life. Someone to lean on and complain to when I won't let them put a onesie on the cat or borrow my car." Their eye contact held as they laughed.

Tyler wanted that, too. All of it. And he wanted his children to have the unconditional love of two parents who did all they could to stick around for their family. Parents who were crazy for each other and gave their kids a healthy relationship to aspire to. It was absurd that he ever thought he could have that with Amy, but now...

The life he'd wanted since he was a broken-hearted little boy felt closer than ever.

"Mostly," she said, "I want to give them such a beautiful life that every time they look back on their childhood, all they can do is smile."

The nerves disappeared, making way for a strange floaty feeling he couldn't name. He took her face in his hands, kissing her slowly.

He knew this was a memory that would always make him smile.

She grabbed his hips and scooted him to the side, pulling a large pot from the cupboard at his knees. She filled it with water and set it on the stove, added salt, and set the burner to high.

"Turn the heat down so the sauce can simmer. While we wait..." She handed him his glass. "Let's get tipsy."

She grabbed the wooden spoon, giving the marinara another good stir. A small bubble in the pan burst, sending a spray of hot tomato sauce onto her pale-yellow blouse.

"Shit!" Grabbing a kitchen towel, she dabbed at a big red splotch and frowned.

He touched her elbow. "Did you get burned?"

"No, but I have to take care of this before it sets in. Watch the sauce." She shuffled off in the direction of the laundry room.

Tyler sipped his wine and waited, savoring another deep inhale of garlic, onion, and spices in Charlotte's kitchen. It was like being in the best Italian restaurant in the world with better music and no dress code.

As Tyler swirled the wine around in his glass, a shadow passed by the kitchen window.

His spine tensed.

A pair of dark eyes peered through the inch-wide gap where the curtains parted, but not long enough to see if they belonged to someone he recognized.

Who the fuck are you?

He remained silent and still, his senses on high alert. If it were someone Charlotte knew, they would've knocked already.

With two quick steps, Tyler moved behind the pantry door, out of view. A bead of sweat slid down his neck as he held his breath, waiting.

The other kitchen window darkened, spiking his pulse. The figure moved around the edges as if looking for another way to see inside, but an olive-green curtain covered every inch.

Is it him?

Tyler's attention flickered to the knives in the butcher block and phone on the wall—both a few broad steps from his reach. With either, he'd risk being spotted if whoever was out there returned to the gap in the other window. And if it was her stalker and they were spooked, they could remain anonymous and continue to torture her.

After almost two years, the cops hadn't caught that fucker. If Tyler called them, the bastard would probably be long gone before they even left the station.

But a knife...

His stomach roiled at the thought of stabbing someone, spilling blood all over Charlotte's front porch. But maybe he could catch them off guard. Pin them to the ground while she called the police.

The sound of running water in the laundry room meant she was still in the back of the house but wouldn't be for long.

What if they have a gun?

One shot between the metal bars would be all it took to end her life.

Tyler inched toward the door, peeking out the corner of the curtain to find an unshaven older man with cropped hair, massive arms, and a slight beer belly.

He didn't see a weapon, but there was no telling what was in the man's pockets.

He looked like a retired Marine or logger—sturdy, strong, used to physically demanding tasks, and not afraid to get his hands dirty.

It wouldn't be an easy win for Tyler if they fought.

The water turned off in the laundry room, and Charlotte's footsteps grew louder.

He was out of time.

"Fuck it." Tyler rushed out.

The man's eyes widened in shock, and before he could speak, Tyler pinned him to the wall beside the door.

"Who the fuck are you?!" Tyler shoved his forearm against the stranger's throat, making the man wheeze a rough, stunted breath. "What are you doing out here?!"

"Get off me, kid!" the man croaked out, struggling to free himself. "Where's Charlotte?"

Tyler pushed his arm harder, the man's face reddening. "Have you been following her?"

Charlotte ran outside, gasping when she saw them. "Dad?"

"*Dad*?!" Tyler dropped his arm and stepped back. "I'm so sorry, sir. I thought—"

"Jesus, Ty!" Charlotte yelled, cutting him off. "You could've hurt him." She pulled her dad in for a hug. "Are you okay? I didn't know you were back in town."

"I'm fine." His voice was rough as he rubbed his throat, still red from the pressure of Tyler's arm. "Just wanted to check on you."

Her eyes flashed to Tyler. "Make sure the sauce isn't burning."

He returned to the kitchen, Charlotte and her dad trailing behind.

While Tyler stirred the marinara, he took a few deep breaths to calm himself. Since the window-breaking incident, he'd viewed everyone outside their circle as potentially dangerous. That didn't give him license to attack people and ask questions later.

"Tyler, this is Mickey Ross." She hugged her dad's arm. "Dad, this is Tyler Hall, the guy who's really sorry he almost killed you."

Tyler cautiously held out his hand, and after a pause, Mickey shook it. "I am sorry, sir. I just saw you outside her house and thought—"

"I understand." Mickey nodded. "There's good reason to be cautious about who comes around. I've been known to be a bit protective over this one, too." He kissed the top of Charlotte's head.

"Then you already have something in common besides thinking I'm fabulous." Her eyes moved between both men before settling on her dad. "Why didn't you knock?"

"You told me about the stomped flowerbed outside your bedroom window. I wanted to check if the curtains were thick and closed or if the creep could look inside."

"What's the verdict?" she asked.

"I'm buying you blackout curtains."

Her eyes rolled. "I need natural light, Dad. The metal bars already make this feel like a prison. That jerk isn't taking away my sunshine, too."

Mickey touched her cheek. "Well, you're my sunshine. I want you safe."

"I know. I love you too." She patted his arm, the corner of his mouth tipping up the same way Charlotte's did when she was content. "You boys chat without any more full-contact craziness while I start my laundry."

When she left, the air felt tense, awkward. Tyler stirred the sauce again to have something to do besides feeling like an asshole.

Amy was the only other woman he'd been serious enough about to meet the parents, and they hated him from day one. Her mother's cold, judgmental stares and her father's not-so-subtle digs at Tyler's clothing, tattoos, and future earnings potential said loud and clear he wasn't good enough for their only child. When his second record went platinum, that mostly shut them up. From what Charlotte had shared about her father, money and fame wouldn't sway his opinion. Tyler's character would determine whether Mickey approved or told Charlotte to send him packing.

Just like with her mom's special recipe, he knew he couldn't fuck this up.

"It's good you're here." Mickey sank into a chair at the kitchen table with a heavy sigh. Tyler swallowed hard, an undercurrent of tension in Mickey's voice making him even more nervous. He set down the spoon, giving his undivided attention. "Look, son, I don't know you. But I saw you with my daughter and *your wife* on the cover of some supermarket gossip rag." His heated tone made Tyler flinch. "You held that woman by the wrists with rage in your eyes. If you ever think of touching my daughter like that—"

"Never." Tyler sat across the table from Mickey, his heart racing. "That's not who I am, sir. I was protecting Charlotte because my ex can be a bit.. ." He searched for a word that fit but wouldn't make him seem like a cold, woman-hating jerk. "Unreasonable."

Mickey made a low, skeptical sound in his throat that said it would take some work to convince him Tyler wasn't the person the tabloids made him out to be. He glanced down the hallway, making sure Charlotte was still occupied.

"Mr. Ross, I'm crazy about your daughter. We've been friends a long time, and now that my disaster of a marriage is behind me, I think I can make her happy." Before Mickey could jump in, he added, "And keep her safe."

"Look, those are nice words. Except for the 'marriage is behind you' part." His bulky arms crossed over his chest. A tattoo of an eagle on a sword peeked out of his sleeve, making him look as intimidating as he sounded. "Exactly how long was it between calling it quits with the missus and starting something with my daughter?"

"Dad!" Charlotte stood in the doorway, hands on her hips. "With all due respect, that's none of your business. Besides, how long did you wait after you dumped Rosie Henley to ask Mom out?"

Mickey's cheeks flushed red. "Charlotte Elizabeth Ross! How dare you use my crazy past to make me realize I'm a hypocrite who needs to shut his fool mouth." He and Charlotte burst out laughing while Tyler just stared like they were nuts.

She hugged her dad's shoulders. "I missed you. I'm glad you're here."

"Me too, sweetheart." Mickey went quiet. He breathed deeply through his nose, and his eyes filled with tears. Tyler didn't know what to do, so he got up to stir the sauce again. The stove would be his safe zone while he adjusted to the situation.

Charlotte shared a sad, knowing smile with her dad, hugging him again.

"Your mother's marinara. God, I haven't smelled that in years."

"You could make it yourself, you know?" She grabbed her glass of wine.

"Nah, I'd burn it." He blinked away the wetness in his eyes. "You and your mom are the only ones who put in the love it needs."

"Well, Tyler did most of the work, and I'm sure it'll be fantastic."

Her hand on his back helped soothe his nerves.

"I had a good partner." Tyler smiled at Charlotte before turning to Mickey. He knew he had to do something about her dad's disapproval. For her sake as much as his own. "You're staying for dinner, right? We made way too much, and Charlotte put so much heart into it, I actually cried."

"The onions you chopped so perfectly did that, but thanks." She sipped her wine. "You should stay, Dad. I'll open another bottle of red, and you can grill Tyler until you're convinced he's one of the good ones."

Tyler wasn't sure he liked the sound of that. When he looked at Charlotte, she offered a nod probably meant to be reassuring, but imagining the intense, likely personal, questions about to be hurled his way made him want to bolt for the nearest exit. But obviously, this was important to her. So, he topped off his wine for liquid courage before returning to his seat across from Mickey and his rough, manly tattoos.

"I don't wanna impose on you kids," Mickey said, "but I can't say no to that sauce."

With the matter settled, Charlotte opened the box of spaghetti and dropped it into the bubbling water. After uncorking another bottle of wine, she poured a third glass and handed it to her dad.

"So, Tyler," Mickey said, taking the wine, "tell me about your family."

"Dad..." Charlotte flashed a look of silent warning.

"It's fine." Tyler took a deep gulp of Cabernet. "I'm really close to my brother, Matt."

"Matthew!" Mickey said with a broad grin. "Great kid. Helped me install the security bars on these windows. Honestly, I always thought he'd end up with Charlotte."

She almost choked on the sip of wine she'd been taking while Tyler just laughed.

"Gross, Dad! He's like my brother. And we are so not each other's type."

"Okay, okay." Mickey laughed. "Maybe before I leave, I'll be convinced Tyler's a better fit. Go on, son. Tell me about your parents."

Tyler tossed back the rest of his wine, and Charlotte quickly refilled his glass. "My dad died in a motorcycle accident when I was ten. Mom lives in Tacoma, but I don't see her much. We aren't close, but we're working on fixing that."

"Damn," Mickey said, empathy in his eyes. "Sorry to hear that. Terrible to lose a parent so young." He glanced at Charlotte stirring the spaghetti before returning his attention to Tyler. "Why aren't you close with your mother?"

Tyler swirled his wine, wondering how to proceed without further damaging Mickey's opinion. The question felt intrusive, and had anyone else asked it, he'd have told them to fuck off. But Mickey had a right to know how Tyler treated the women in his life.

"In the months after Dad died, she rarely got out of bed. She drank. A lot. And for years, she buried her pain in strange men who didn't always treat her well." Tyler thought about the guy he chased from their house with a baseball bat when he was twelve because the creep had slapped her to the ground. "Matthew was only six when we lost Dad, so I was the one who made sure he brushed his teeth, went to bed without a growling stomach, and got outside in time for the school bus." He pictured the fragile little boy his brother was compared to the strong, kind man who was even taller than him. Tyler's chest warmed with pride at his role in that transformation. The kind of pride he imagined a father would feel reflecting on his child's accomplishments. "That resentment doesn't just evaporate with time, I guess."

"I understand. It pains me to admit it, but I resented her mom, Anna, for years after we lost her. It felt unfair being the one left with all the hard stuff it takes to be a parent." He gestured to Tyler. "Or a big brother."

A timer buzzed, and Charlotte drained the pasta, a cloud of steam rising to the ceiling while her cheeks flushed pink from the heat.

"We can talk more about that later." Mickey rubbed the salt-and-pepper scruff on his chin. "After a few more glasses of wine. Now tell me about Amy."

"Dad!"

Tyler laughed at her reaction. "Charlotte, it's okay."

He met Mickey's steady eye contact and held it. He intended to be honest and wanted to make that intention clear. Unwavering eye contact seemed like a good place to start.

"We got married three months after we met. It was crazy and impulsive, and although we had plenty of good times, I ignored and forgave things I shouldn't have. In the end, I was working too much, she was partying too much, and last month I caught her screwing her bodyguard. Pardon my French. I couldn't sign those divorce papers fast enough."

Mickey blew out a long breath, rubbing his forehead. "Damn, son. That must've been an awful sight. But you know, it bugs the shit out of me that you say you and Charlotte have been such good friends, yet you chose to stand by a woman who stabbed her in the back and damn near ruined her life. Pardon *my* French."

Tyler's pulse throbbed in his ears. The sudden sweep of anger on Mickey's face short-circuited his brain. He was desperate for a cigarette, an escape route, or five more glasses of wine.

Charlotte set down the wooden spoon with a clatter, sauce splattering the countertop. "Don't go there, Dad. Can't we just have a peaceful dinner?"

"When food's on the table, I'll be too busy eating to talk. Until then, I need this young man to explain himself."

Charlotte sighed, mouthing *sorry* at Tyler before spooning generous servings of sauce over the plates of spaghetti. It was a fair question. He wasn't proud of his choices but needed to answer for them if he was ever going to be on Mickey's good side.

"It's stupid when I think about it now," Tyler said, "but I separated those things in my head—their band business and our relationships. I disagreed with Amy kicking her out, but it wasn't my band, so I stayed out of it. Looking back, I should've been a better friend to Charlotte, but my loyalty had to be with my wife. Heap it onto the pile of regrets." He raised his glass before setting it down. "If it helps, Amy was devastated after Charlotte left. I think she realized she'd made a huge mistake, and things got worse for the band from there, proving it."

"I'm not usually a vengeful man, but I'm glad to hear she suffered." The fire in Mickey's glare deepened, his lips scrunching in anger. "That woman spread vicious lies about my daughter all over town. She took away the bartending job that kept Charlotte's bills paid, forcing her to dip into her mother's life insurance money that was supposed to be her nest egg. Certain clubs wouldn't let her play. Some producers refused to speak to her. Charlotte had to work ten times as hard to prove herself while you were off sleeping with the enemy."

"Dad, enough!" She wiped her hands on a kitchen towel and tossed it onto the counter. "I fell for her bullshit too. I was loyal when I shouldn't have been, just like he was. Tyler doesn't have to defend himself for things he did under that evil bitch's spell. Now, set the table so we can move on."

"Sorry, honey." Mickey stood, kissing her forehead before grabbing forks and napkins. "I'll behave."

Tyler grabbed the full, steaming plates off the counter, setting them on the table. Mickey and Charlotte were both right. He felt that more needed to be said to redeem himself.

"Most of that, I didn't know because I was touring." He returned to his seat, the scent of the food making his stomach rumble. Charlotte and Mickey sat down, all eyes on Tyler. "When Matty told me, I called all the clubs and producers Amy knew, trying to fix things. Some listened, some didn't."

Charlotte touched his wrist. "I didn't know you did that."

He shrugged. "I couldn't do anything about the bartending job, but once your album came out, it didn't matter. You made your own success." He took Charlotte's hand before turning to Mickey. "I understand why you'd worry about her with someone who's made as many mistakes as I have. But I promise I'll never hurt her or take her for granted. I know exactly what she's worth and how lucky I am to be close to her." He slid his thumb across the backs of her fingers, and she squeezed his hand.

Mickey grinned, the smile growing wider as he kept his eyes on Tyler. "Okay. I'm convinced." He picked up his fork, twirling it in the spaghetti. "You're a better fit for Charlotte than your brother. But tell him Mickey says hi."

35

Tyler

"Your room's pretty swanky, Mr. Jones. May I blow you on the balcony?" Charlotte's voice rose an octave higher, mimicking the flirty blonde receptionist at the front desk.

"Are you jealous of Josephine, Charlotte?" Tyler tickled her waist as she laughed and smacked his hands away.

"If I thought you'd actually fall for her shameless flirting routine, I might be." Charlotte sat in the leather recliner and crossed her legs, her silky black skirt hiking up to expose more of the smooth, tempting skin of her thigh. "What kind of chick flirts with someone right in front of their gir—"

She slapped her hand over her mouth.

Tyler laughed and sat on the armrest of her chair.

"It's fine." He moved her hand from her mouth. "We haven't discussed labels, but do you want to go steady with me, Charlotte?"

She shoved him off the chair, and he hit the floor, laughing hysterically.

"Really nice, Ty. Way to mock my awkward slip."

"Sorry." He got to his knees. "Will you be my girlfriend, Charlotte?"

Her eyes rolled. "Are you just fucking with me again?"

Tyler scooped her up, setting her on the bedspread with her head on a ridiculously fluffy hotel pillow. He lay beside her, and Charlotte rolled so they were face-to-face.

"Sorry I made a joke of it, but I'm being serious now. I promise." He took her hand, lacing their fingers. "You're the most remarkable woman I've ever met, and I want to know you're mine, and I'm yours."

"You're still technically married."

"My attorneys are working hard to fix that." His finger slowly traced her collarbone. "I haven't been married to Amy for a long time. Not in the ways that matter. I think I was in love with the idea of her. I wanted someone who understood my world because they lived in it, too. Someone passionate about their art who challenges me and makes me laugh."

The edges of her mouth tipped down. "How can you make someone so awful sound so perfect?"

"Charlotte." He pulled her hand to his lips and kissed it. "I was looking for you. You're all those things and more. Everything I've ever wanted in another person."

"Well, since you put it that way." She grinned, her gaze softening. "Yes, Tyler. I will be your girlfriend."

While he pressed his lips to hers, he thanked the universe for second chances.

"So, girlfriend," he said, tugging a lock of her hair, "I got you something."

Curiosity sparked in her eyes. "What is it?"

Tyler slid off the bed, taking her hand. He led her to the closed door of the second bedroom, grateful the surprise hadn't spoiled itself.

"Close your eyes."

Her teeth sank into her bottom lip. "Is something dirty behind this door? Did you install a sex swing or a stripper pole?"

Tyler laughed, his cock shifting at the mental image. "No, but now I know what I want for my birthday. Just close them and keep them closed."

She did as he asked, and he opened the door, leading her inside. "Open them."

When Charlotte opened her eyes, she screeched. "Tyler! What did you do?" The commotion woke the tiny beige and white beagle resting on the bed. The puppy sprung to its feet, tail wagging and ready to play. "I was kidding when I asked if you'd buy me a puppy."

His smile collapsed. "You don't want one?"

"Are you fucking kidding me?" She shook Tyler's shoulders as they laughed. "Look at that little face! Of course, I want... him? Her?"

"Her."

"You're a little girl!" Charlotte scratched the puppy's ears and under her chin, its eyes closing before popping wide when she stopped. "Does she have a name?"

He shook his head. "You can pick it."

"Oh, my god! I get to name her." She scooped up the puppy, cradling it in her arms. "Are you a Patti or a Janis or a Joan? What about a flower name—Lily or Dahlia or Violet?"

"No hurry." Tyler scratched the puppy's head as she sniffed Charlotte's hair. "The perfect name will come to you."

"She's a beagle, right? Like Snoopy?"

He nodded.

"Maybe you're a Lucy or a Sally."

The puppy nipped and tugged at the string of Tyler's hoodie. "Do you really like her? If you don't want a dog, I can find her another home." He carefully extracted the string from razor-sharp puppy teeth.

"Don't you dare! Little Sally Dahlia Janis isn't going anywhere."

"That one needs work." Tyler chuckled, pulling a purple squeaky ball from his pocket and handing it to the puppy. "Since you live alone, I thought having someone to keep you company might be nice."

He mainly adopted the dog for her safety but didn't want to spoil the moment by saying it. The staff at the shelter assured him the puppy was an excellent alert dog. Her previous owners surrendered her because she'd bark her head off when anyone was outside their house. One person's annoyance is another's asset.

"Ty..." Charlotte stood on tiptoes and kissed him. "I'm so lucky to have you." She looked at the bundle in her arms. "I'm so lucky to have you too, Violet Frida Roxy."

"Roxy, huh?" Tyler's eyebrows lifted.

"Roxy! It sounds like a badass punk chick with a hoop in her eyebrow and pink hair who drinks Shirley Temples spiked with vodka."

Tyler laughed against her shoulder. "That was oddly specific. Is this a real person?"

"Nope. But I'd kinda want to be friends if she was." Charlotte nuzzled against the puppy's soft fur. "This Roxy is a cute as hell beagle who'll shit on my floor, eat our shoes, and we'll love her, anyway."

"Welcome to the family, Roxy. Please don't eat my favorite Docs."

The puppy licked Charlotte's cheek before chomping hard on the squeaky toy.

<hr>

Tyler and Charlotte returned to his suite after a game of fetch on the hotel's gated lawn and a stop at a pet shop to spoil Roxy rotten. They kicked off their shoes and climbed onto the bed. Without a word, Charlotte curled into his side, her face tucked in the crook of his neck. Her contented sigh against his skin made him pull her closer. Roxy found a spot at their feet to sprawl out, her thin tail wagging at the tip.

"I love her." Charlotte angled her chin to meet his eyes.

For a second, he thought she was about to say something else. Something that'd been burning on the tip of his tongue for days. It felt like the perfect moment, but what if she didn't feel the same? Then again, what if she did? What if saying the words out loud propelled them into another level of their relationship that was somehow even better than this?

Only one way to find out.

"Charlotte..."

Before he could finish, her hand slipped beneath her pillow. She slowly pulled away from him, her expression flattened.

"What's wrong?" he asked.

She sat up, staring at something in her hand. Her skin paled.

Alarm bells blasted in his head. He sat up straight, and that's when he saw what she held—a small, transparent baggie filled with white powder.

"Tyler, what the hell is this?" When she looked up, her eyes were wet and glossy.

"I don't know!"

His heart stuttered in his chest. He thought about the baggie Amy left in his drawer. This was her fault. Had to be. There was no way a housekeeper or bellhop was planting drugs in guests' rooms.

Regardless of how it got there, he knew what this would do to Charlotte.

And he was petrified of what it would do to *them*.

"I swear it's not mine." Hot, smothering panic spread through him as he snatched the baggie, ran to the bathroom, and flushed it. When he returned, Charlotte was still on the bed, hugging her knees.

"Was that... Was that *heroin*?" Her voice was shaky and faint, like a frightened child's. Roxy whimpered, raising her head to look at Charlotte before settling back to sleep.

Tyler approached the bed, but when he reached for her, she recoiled from his touch like it stung. He knew she was reacting to past trauma, but it felt like something he'd never imagined could happen—it felt like she was afraid of him.

"Charlotte, I promise you, it's not mine. Amy must've put it there. She left the same thing in the nightstand when she broke into my room."

Her eyes darted around, landing on nothing. After taking a deep, slow breath, she exhaled. "Okay. Fuck." Another loud inhale, exhale. "Sorry, I overreacted. I should've known—"

"You have *nothing* to apologize for." His shoulders relaxed a little.

She looked at him, her face reddening. "She's trying to get you *arrested* now?"

"It's gone." He set a gentle hand on her back, his heart still racing. "Everything's okay."

"She's so stupid! No one who knows you would ever think you'd take fucking heroin."

He stopped breathing, wondering if he should tell her the truth or pray she never found out on her own. "Right. Of course not."

Worry lines formed between her eyebrows. "Why'd you take so long to say that?"

"What?" He couldn't keep his voice steady, her worry line deepening.

"Tyler..." She stared at him, her bottom lip shaking. "Have you done heroin?"

"No!" He slapped a hand over his mouth as the lie burst out. It was purely reflexive, and he needed to correct it before it swelled with the power to erase everything they'd built. He sat on the opposite side of the bed, giving her space. "Well... I did. For a few days after Master Jim died. I haven't touched it since, and I swear, I'll never touch it again."

She covered her face, weeping into her hands, her shoulders quaking.

"I'm so sorry, Charlotte." Seeing her crumple with pain was like a spear to his chest.

"I can't believe this!" When she looked up, her face was flushed, tears glistening on her cheeks. Anger flared in her eyes behind the disappointment and hurt. "How could you hide that from me?"

"I know how you feel about drugs. I swear, I don't have a problem. Jim was my hero, and losing him made me feel as lost as when my dad died. It hurt so much, and I just wanted it to stop." The rapid-fire confession poured out, desperation fueling every word. "Amy had it all over the house. She kept trying to talk me into taking it and one day, I just gave in."

"Stop! You can't blame that on Amy. She didn't hold a gun to your head or straw to your nose. *You* did that." She slapped her palm for emphasis, her hands trembling. "It's not like you had no one to talk to, to run to. You had Matthew, me, your band. You didn't have to sink that fucking low!" She wrapped her arms around herself, rocking slowly. "This was a colossal mistake from the start, and I never should've let things go this far."

"Whoa." The sudden shift made his head spin. "What are you talking about?"

"My dad was right." She swiped her eyes with the back of her hand. "You chose Amy over me and stood by her side while she set fire to my goddamn life. Do you have any idea how much it hurt?" When her voice cracked with pain, he felt it in the pit of his stomach. "I was a fool for not getting over you years ago. I could've been with someone else by now, someone who'd never put me in second place. Who'd never take fucking *heroin*!"

She was right. While he'd been a good friend to her in many ways, as he'd feared, how he handled things back then was unforgivable. The confirmation was a gut punch.

He ran a hand through his hair, struggling to find words. "You're right. I don't deserve you. But I'm working so hard to get there. And you could never be second to anyone. You were the first woman I trusted with my secrets, the first person I think of when I wake up. I'm sorry for how I treated you back then." He threw up his hands. "What else can I say? I fucked-up, but I'm trying to make it right."

Although she'd steered the conversation in a different direction, he knew the drugs were the worst of it. That had to be settled first. "The man I am now... I'd never do anything that would risk my life or career. I'm not that weak anymore. It helped me forget for a while. It's no excuse, but I promise, it's behind me."

"Tyler, you know about my mother." Fresh tears flooded her eyes.

"I know. God, I know." He tried to reach for her again, and she moved further away in every possible sense.

"She overdosed on my twelfth fucking birthday, right on the kitchen floor. That image will never leave my head. My cake was sitting right above her, the candles waiting to be lit. Instead of making a wish and blowing them out, I watched EMTs carry my dead mother away on a stretcher."

Tyler stepped closer, and she bolted from the bed. Her shoe snagged on something beneath the corner of the bed frame, and she bent to retrieve it. As he stared at her back, her shoulders began shaking again.

She turned slowly, a pair of red lace panties dangling from between her fingertips.

His stomach dropped. "I didn't do anything, I swear."

"Are you fucking *kidding me*?"

"They're Amy's, but she..." His mouth opened to explain, but he couldn't say it.

"I'm done." Charlotte shoved her feet into her shoes. "I can't be here."

He didn't know what to say or do without making things worse. She stopped on her way to the door, bending forward with low, gut-wrenching sobs. When Tyler rushed over, her hands shot between them. The rejection felt like ice in his blood.

"Don't you dare touch me!" She aimed her shouted words at the carpet. "You broke my heart, and I can't stand to look at you."

Every word hit like a fist, knocking the wind out of him. He frantically scoured his mind for some magical word or phrase to fix what he'd broken.

"Charlotte, please. Just look at me. Talk to me."

"There's nothing you can say to fix it." She roughly swiped under her eyes. "It's over."

His lungs burned as he rushed to block the door. "Charlotte, no, we can—"

"It's done!" When she shouted those two terrible words, her tears stopped. "Unlike you, I don't just lie down and take it when people hurt me. Get the hell out of my way."

Tyler fell to his knees at her feet, pressing his face to her belly as his arms wrapped around her. "Charlotte, please. I'm in love with you!"

When he looked up, her tears returned, but she batted them away as quickly as they came. "Then that makes this whole thing even more fucked-up, doesn't it? Because I'm in love with you too. But I still have to walk through that door and never look back."

She shoved past him, the door slamming behind her.

It's done.

Every perfect moment they'd shared flashed through his mind all at once before fading to black.

Tyler collapsed on the hotel carpet, weeping into his hands as the scent of wild orchids hung in the air.

36

Charlotte

Charlotte curled up on her couch, leaning against Sandra, a fuzzy blanket across their laps. Her breakup with Tyler was only six hours old, and she couldn't remember the last time something hurt so much.

"How could he do this?" Charlotte touched her chest as it shook from another wave of sobs. "I gave him my heart, and he fucking crushed it." She loved him, but hard drugs and infidelity were dealbreakers—things she could never accept or forgive.

"I know he did, sweetie. Want me to kick his stupid, lying ass?"

Charlotte rested her head on Sandra's shoulder, damp from her tears. "Yes. No. Maybe." She laughed, the sound coming out as pathetic and humorless as she felt. "And he didn't lie. He concealed. Omitted. Because he knew what this would do to me. To us!"

It was a vicious reminder of why she'd always run from love. But she couldn't pass up a second chance with Tyler. Instead of letting fear hold her back from seeing where things would lead, she'd taken the risk.

She'd fallen in love.

And look where it got her.

"*Please* let me kick his ass."

Charlotte looked at her friend, anger making Sandra's cheeks redder than the fiery streaks in her hair. "How'd I miss the signs? Drugs, cheating. I know what to look for better than anyone."

Sandra handed her a tissue. "I'm almost as shocked and disappointed as you. I knew Amy fucked around with that stuff but never thought Tyler would be so dumb and reckless."

Charlotte knew it was more complicated than that. She thought back to when Master Jim died. Over the years, he'd become more than a mentor to Tyler; he was like a second father. At the funeral, Tyler was withdrawn, not saying more than a few words to anyone as he stood behind the rows of chairs at the gravesite. His eyes looked bruised, like he hadn't slept in days. Matthew, Zack, and Adam never left his side, while Charlotte and Sandra remained a few steps behind, giving them space. Amy wasn't even there.

Charlotte knew Matthew did all he could to help in the following days, but it was as if Tyler had collapsed inside himself, and no one knew how to fix it. She'd felt powerless, restrained by the frustrating limitations of their friendship. She called but couldn't leave a message. If she'd stopped by to check on him, it would've made his life worse if Amy had been home. So, Charlotte stayed away. She didn't have a choice. Still, she wished she'd done more when he was clearly at one of the lowest, darkest points of his life.

Now, she wondered if some of his behavior at the funeral was due to shame over succumbing to the temptation. He'd been trapped, locked into the depths of his grief, and someone waved a key in his face. It was still no excuse for gambling with his life, but knowing he'd reached that level of desperation left her conflicted. She felt sorry for him but knew she had to protect herself from more hurt.

Charlotte wiped her nose with the tissue. "He tried to convince me he isn't an addict. That he only used it to numb himself after Jim died. How can I know if it's the truth?"

"You can't." Sandra passed her a clean tissue, tossing the other in the trash. "But either way, he understands your feelings about it and why. Hell, you told him the night you met. He shouldn't have hidden it from you all these years, whether it was just a few times or not. Or at least come clean when you got into a relationship, knowing what a dealbreaker it is. You should've had the chance to decide if you could accept it."

"Exactly! And I'm going to kill Matthew if he knew and didn't warn me." Charlotte's phone rang, and she flipped it the bird. "Probably Tyler. Again. Let it ring."

He'd already called at least a dozen times. The first time, his voice on the answering machine made her heart flutter, but she refused to pick up, turning off the volume. It was easier to ignore him until he gave up so they could both, somehow, move on.

"Did he come over before I got here?" Sandra rubbed Charlotte's back with soothing circles, the gentle touch making it easier to breathe through the pain.

"Twice." Seeing his puffy, bloodshot eyes through the peephole was awful. Facing the proof he'd cried over losing her worsened the ache in her chest. The second time, she set her hand on the door, craving his touch but finding it impossible to let him in. "He knocked and begged for a while, eventually gave up."

"That must've been tough. Sorry, hon." Sandra let out a heavy sigh. "For the record, I don't think he cheated with that skank. Reeks of sabotage. I could totally see her slipping the underwear under his bed for you to find."

"Maybe."

The thought of his hands all over Amy was nauseating, but it was hard to believe he'd backslide like that. Not after all the shit Amy put him through and how close he and Charlotte had become. But then again, maybe she was fooling herself and didn't know him as well as she thought. Besides, the drugs were bad enough, even if he didn't cheat.

Once or a hundred times—she'd never trust the word of someone who used. If only she'd known.

"I never would've let myself fall in love with him." She pulled the blanket to her neck, a chill skating up her spine.

"Hey, I'm proud of you for jumping in with both feet." Sandra kissed her temple. "I know it's hard now, but try to think about all the best moments you had together. You would've missed out on a lot if you hadn't tried. If nothing else, I hope this taught you what real love feels like. That it's worth chasing, worth the risk. And that you're so goddamn brave, you can do anything."

"Almost anything." She raised her head. "I can never forgive him."

"Do you want to?" Sandra smoothed Charlotte's wet cheek with her knuckles. "Before you answer, think about how much you love him. Shut out the hurt and disappointment for a second to focus on that feeling. Think about what an amazing friend he's been over the years. And that first kiss you wouldn't shut up about."

Charlotte's jaw dropped. "Are you seriously batting for Tyler? After all your warnings and overprotective bullshit?"

"You know I was just watching out for you. When it became obvious you belong together, I backed off."

The knot of grief in her chest twisted tighter. "You really think we belong together?"

"I do. I think you guys are perfect for each other. I'm pissed and want to kick him places he won't enjoy, but at his core, Tyler's one of the good guys. I still believe that." Sandra brushed hair off Charlotte's forehead. "If you can find it in your heart to give him another chance, I think you should. Maybe it'll even help you heal from your mom's loss to watch him put that shit further and further behind him. But if you can't get past what he did, I understand. And I'll support you and help you through it."

"Sandra?"

"Yeah?"

"I have absolutely no clue what to do." Charlotte took a deep, stuttered breath.

"That's okay too. Take your time to think it over. In the meantime..." Sandra grabbed the remote. "Let's gorge on Ben and Jerry's and watch the Friends marathon. It starts in ten minutes."

Charlotte touched her shoulder. "Please tell me there's an episode where Joey takes his shirt off."

"I haven't watched them all yet, so I have no idea." She chuckled, turning on the television. "My fingers are crossed for a topless Courtney Cox, but whatever floats your boat."

The cordless phone rang beside them.

After the third ring, Sandra reached across the armrest, snatching it before Charlotte could protest.

"Hello?" She settled back in her seat. "Oh, Eliza! We thought you were someone else. Yeah, it's Sandra. Wanna talk to Charlotte?"

She put out her hand, wanting to hear what their manager had to say, but Sandra kept the receiver to her ear, her forehead scrunching. She gasped at something Eliza said.

"Seriously?!" Sandra screeched. "Can't they be fixed by then?"

Great. Another fucking crisis.

"What is it?" Charlotte grabbed for the phone. "Let me talk to her."

"No, I'll explain it to her." Sandra held up a finger. "Yeah, you too."

She hung up.

Charlotte smacked her arm. "What the hell?"

"I have news." Sandra touched her knee. "Please don't go aggro on the messenger, but I think you'll handle it better coming from me."

"Spit it out already!"

Sandra huffed out a breath. "The benefit show is off."

"*What*?" Charlotte sprang from the couch, the blanket falling to the floor. "Why?"

"Some rotten fucking bastard broke into Apocalypse and took a sledgehammer to the stage, an electrical panel, and some gear. They're closing for repairs, which won't be finished in time."

As Charlotte's mind raced, she held herself. Still reeling from the breakup, this was the last thing she needed. More importantly, the women counting on the Safe Start program would suffer, losing their shot at a better life.

"We'll find a different club," Charlotte said. "What if we—"

"Honey, it's over. Eliza's already pulled the plug and called the bands and crew to cancel."

Charlotte's head tipped back, an angry roar rising from her throat. It was all so unfair. Her eyes squeezed shut, more tears spilling. When Sandra's arms wrapped around her, she leaned into the warm, familiar comfort. While everything fell apart around her, piece by piece, her best friend's unwavering love and support felt like the only good things in her life she could still count on.

Seven episodes of Friends and two pints of Cherry Garcia later, Sandra went home. After setting the alarm, Charlotte left a message on the voicemail of Safe Start's CEO to say she'd be in first thing Monday morning.

While she laughed with Sandra at the antics of Joey and Chandler, Charlotte made a decision. One she didn't want Sandra to try and talk her out of. A Plan C had been kicking around in her head for weeks in case the benefit didn't bring in enough to correct the deficit, and it was time to put it into action.

While Charlotte's future was still uncertain, she rested easy that night, knowing the women and families counting on the program wouldn't miss out on a second chance at a healthy, happy life. Her new plan wouldn't be without its challenges, but it would be worth it.

The decision, she knew, would've made her mother proud.

37

Tyler

While Roxy barked her head off, Sandra marched into Tyler's hotel room, shoving past him.

"You motherfucking, cocksucking dickwad."

"Hi, Sandra. I deserve that."

Tyler set Roxy into her bed and pet her until she settled.

Matthew came in next, wearing the most disappointed scowl Tyler had ever seen. It reminded him of their mother.

Without a word, Matthew sat on the bed while Sandra paced like a caged hyena who'd slurped a dozen cappuccinos.

"I might hit you." Sandra planted her feet with her hands on her hips. "I don't handle anger well, and I really fucking want to punch you."

"I deserve that, too." He wished she would just to feel a different kind of pain for a while.

She stopped in front of him, her nose wrinkling. "Jesus, Tyler, did you drink the whiskey or bathe in it?"

Matthew stared at the ground. Tyler hadn't seen him this speechless since their dad died. He'd turned inward for weeks, stewing in his pain, until Tyler took him to the edge of Bryce Park and told him to scream. When he did, birds rushed from the trees, and Tyler joined him. They stood there for ten minutes, screaming in the wind, before Matthew broke down and Tyler just held him.

On the walk home, Matthew finally put words to his hurt, and together, they started healing one step at a time.

Tyler walked to the wall beside the bed, sliding down to sit on the floor a few feet from his brother. He stared at the side of Matt's face, willing him to turn his head.

"Sorry I hurt her."

"Fuck you," Matthew spat, his eyes still on the floor. "After all Charlotte's been through—still going through—now she's dealing with the worst breakup of her life on top of it. And she has to do it without two of the only people she's ever trusted."

Tyler's brows pinched. "Two?" He looked at Sandra.

"She's mad at him for not telling her you did *heroin*." She thrust her face inches from his while emphasizing the last ugly word. For a second, he thought she really would hit him, but she sat beside Matthew on the bed, arms folded across her chest. "So, you fucked-up two of her relationships, genius. Way to go."

Tyler pressed his palms into his eyes as the first pangs of a headache rolled in, along with another heaping dose of guilt. "I need her to hear me out, but she won't let me near her."

"It's your own fault, idiot," Sandra said. "You knew hard drugs, especially goddamn heroin, are a non-negotiable boundary for her. Do I have to remind you how many careers have ended? How many brilliant musicians have dropped dead messing with that shit? Why the hell would you have it in your room?"

"It. Wasn't. Mine." He banged the back of his head against the wall with every word. "I swear, it wasn't. Amy planted it. She knew how Charlotte would react. I haven't touched it in years, and I'd never touch it again." He turned to his brother. "You have to make Charlotte forgive you so you can watch out for her."

Matthew scoffed. "Make her forgive me? God, you're such an asshole. She's right to shut me out because I never should've covered for you. Do I have to remind you how I found you passed out on your bedroom floor after Jim's funeral? I thought you were dead, Tyler!"

Sandra gasped, tears shining in her eyes as her arms wrapped around Matthew.

"You knew what losing Dad did to me, and you almost took away my brother too. My best friend." Matthew's voice cracked with emotion, and Sandra tightened her hold. "I had to force you into detox because Amy sure as hell wouldn't. I kept it from Charlotte because I thought it was behind you, but for all I know, you've been lying to me for years."

"No, Matty." Tears stung Tyler's eyes, his brother's devastated face blurring.

"I saw how you looked at the bottle of powder in your kitchen drawer." He continued before Tyler could interject. "And Amy's fucking panties under your bed! After all the shit she put you through! After letting Charlotte fall in love with you."

"I didn't touch her, I swear to god." Tyler raked a shaky hand through his hair. "She planted them too. I wouldn't—"

"Even if that's true," Matthew said, "it's still your fucking fault. I *begged* you not to push her! But I guess getting revenge for her trashing your shit was more important than making Charlotte happy. Amy got red paint on her clothes, and Charlotte got her heart broken. Was it worth it?"

"No." Tyler hung his head. "It wasn't." He'd been petty and stupid, his actions indefensible. The temporary satisfaction he felt at the time wasn't worth Charlotte's pain.

Matthew shook his head. "She deserved the sweet guy she met three years ago, who showed her cool shit around the city, holding her hand, who was as disgusted by Amy's poisonous garbage as she was. You let that bitch change you into some pathetic, vindictive dickhead!" He sucked in an unsteady breath. "Might as well run back to her because you sure as hell don't deserve Charlotte."

"Whoa, Matt." Sandra released him. "Take it down a notch. You don't mean that."

"The hell I don't!" Matt's eyes raised to Tyler for the first time. "Do you know how hard it is being your brother? To not be as handsome or talented or rich. To worry girls only date me to get close to you." A sob broke in his throat. "But you've always been my goddamn hero, Tyler. You helped me get over Dad's death. You were there for me when Mom wasn't. You invested in my business because you believed in me when no one else did."

Tyler sniffed, wiping his nose with the back of his sleeve.

"But now…" Matthew shook his head, his frown deepening. "You've hurt everyone who stood by you during all your fucking mistakes. The only people who cared enough to help you build a better life."

"Matty, I'm so sorry."

"Too late for that." Matthew pushed off the bed, making a beeline for the door.

"Please don't go." Tyler got to his feet, grabbing his brother's arm. "We can fix everything together if you—"

Matthew yanked his arm back. "Just fix yourself, Tyler."

When the door slammed, Tyler stared at it, his brain muddled with the shock of the worst fight they'd ever had. He wanted to chase his brother and force him to listen, but Matthew needed space. He'd said things he didn't mean and would be beating himself up over it once it sank in. Tyler would reach out after he'd had time to cool down.

Roxy walked over, licking the top of his foot as her tail wagged.

"Is it the truth?"

Sandra's voice snapped him out of it.

"Yes. All of it." He turned to her. "I'd never hurt Charlotte like that. Or Matty."

She exhaled loudly, studying his face. "Fine."

"You believe me, Sandra?"

"Yes, I believe you. I know a liar when I see one, and you're a good, honest guy. With this one exception, of course. And I've seen how much you care about our girl. That earns a shitload of bonus points with me."

"I don't just care about her." He rubbed his chest, a fresh wave of pain burning in the center. "I love her. I can't breathe when she's not around. I've never felt like this before."

"Aww, that's sweet, Ty." She erased the distance between them, patting his cheek. "But you really screwed up. Honestly, I don't know how you can make this right. Or if you can."

The *if* drove an iron spike through his heart.

Sandra knew Charlotte better than anyone. If she doubted Tyler could mend this rift, maybe there wasn't much hope to cling to.

"We belong together, so I have to try." He lit a cigarette to calm himself. His confidence was irreparably shaken, but giving up wasn't an option. "How is she, really?" He took a deep breath, preparing himself for the answer.

"Honestly..." Sandra paused. "I've never seen her this broken up over someone. I can't even get her to leave the house."

Guilt and regret kicked him in the chest. Matthew was right. Even though Amy planted the drugs and underwear, Charlotte's pain was Tyler's fault. He'd kept up the vengeful back-and-forth, knowing Amy wouldn't quit until she was satisfied with his suffering. And his failure to tell Charlotte about his drug use shattered her trust—something she didn't give away easily.

He helped her feel safe and cherished before ripping it all away.

"On the bright side," Sandra said, "at least she's behind a few deadbolts with an alarm system while some psycho dickbag keeps scaring her. Speaking of which, there's something you should know."

He held his breath.

"She got another note. And bought a gun."

"*What?*" His trembling hands drew erratic trails of smoke in the air. The puppy whimpered at his feet, and he crouched to pick her up. He pet Roxy's head as he walked to the corner, setting her back on the dog bed. "What did it say?"

"Brace yourself. It said they're happy to see she's sleeping alone again."

Tyler punched the wall, denting the plaster. "That sick sack of shit! I want to find whoever's doing this and burn them to the ground." His knuckles stung and throbbed, a few dots of bright red blood blooming from beneath a strip of broken skin.

"You and me both." Sandra grabbed tissues from the box beside the bed, took his hand, and dabbed at the blood. "I offered to stay over, but she says she needs time alone to clear her head. I'm over all the time checking up on her, anyway."

He sucked his cigarette to the filter, dropping it into an empty whiskey bottle. "Does she even know how to use a gun?"

Sandra tossed the bloody tissues in the trash. "She took lessons at a range when the first stalking drama happened. Just never felt comfortable owning one until now."

It eased his mind some that she had training, but knowing how to handle herself at a well-lit range didn't guarantee she could protect herself if caught off guard in her dark bedroom or shadowy backyard.

The puppy's tiny head lifted, and Sandra smiled, moving to scratch behind her floppy brown ears. "She was a sweet gift, Ty. I think Charlotte's kicking herself for leaving this little nugget behind."

"Please, take her over there. She'll bark her head off if anyone comes to the door with another note or..." He swallowed hard. "For any other reason."

Sandra nodded, grabbing the leash off the nightstand and hooking it to Roxy's collar. "For what it's worth, I'm rooting for you. I'll do my best to get through to her, okay?"

Her kind words relaxed his shoulders as he stuffed the puppy's toys and bed into a shopping bag. "You're a good friend, Sandra." He handed her the bag. "To both of us."

When she reached the door, she turned back. "Sorry I didn't know you were suffering like that. To think we almost lost you..." Sandra hugged him, meeting his eye when she pulled back. "Don't ever think you're alone, Ty."

When she left, the momentary relief vanished. The memories torturing him since Charlotte slammed the door flooded in again. *The feel of her sweat-slicked skin against his, the taste of her soft lips.* They hadn't been together that way for long, but she'd left an indelible mark on his heart that seared like a cigarette burn tunneling through his chest. He also mourned the loss of their friendship. She was one of the few people he trusted, and he'd failed to give her the same in return.

If anything happens to Charlotte, it'll be all my fault.

He walked onto the balcony and looked out over the city as his hair whipped across his face in the wind. From that vantage point, he could see the rich emerald green of treetops peeking through gaps in the rows of downtown skyscrapers. The white, distant peaks of Mount Hood, Mount Saint Helens, and Mount Rainier were visible on the rare cloudless day. Tyler had traveled the world with his music, but Portland would always be home. He'd never visited a place that called to him like the Rose City. At that moment, being embraced by the feeling of home was his only comfort.

His gaze shifted to follow the brilliant blue path of the Willamette River as it snaked through downtown. One hundred and seventy-five feet above the water, cars flowed in both directions on the upper and lower decks of the Fremont Bridge, carrying people south to Salem or north to Seattle and two different Vancouvers via Interstate 5. As the tiny vehicles rushed beneath the Fremont's majestic arch, he couldn't remember ever feeling this empty, terrified, and alone all at once.

Like a walking wound scrubbed raw.

A gnawing ache in his chest made him want to crawl under his covers with a bottle of whiskey and sleep until the pain stopped. But that was a problem, too. The pain never stopped. The alcohol he hoped would numb it dragged him deeper into the pit. He'd never hurt himself, but if he were ever going to jump off a bridge, this was the sort of feeling that might push him over the edge.

She has to give me another chance.

He walked back into his suite, his eyes landing on the spot where he'd begged Charlotte to stay. Before she left, she said she loved him too. He'd heard a song once that said wherever there was love, there was hope. And at that moment, he hoped to figure out how to reach the part of her that burned for him. Then, maybe, he could get her back before the fire went out.

As Tyler stared at the door, something on the carpet caught his eye.

He moved closer to find an envelope the exact shade of pink as the other notes. Ice raced through his blood as he flung open the door, checking the long, wide corridor.

Empty.

He locked the door, tore the envelope open, and pulled out a piece of bright pink paper. His eyes skittered over the black ink scrawl:

Thanks for giving her back. I don't like to share.

Tyler crushed the paper in his fist, days of pent-up rage and pain roaring from his throat. The cuts in his knuckles reopened, blood dotting the edges of the paper until he threw the tiny, wadded-up ball against the damaged plaster.

He was sick of feeling powerless.

Sick of waiting for the cops to do their jobs.

Sick of living in fear of something happening to Charlotte.

Obviously, whoever stalked her followed Tyler, too. That meant they'd know when she was alone and he was too far away to run to her.

Of course, if the stalker was Amy, the whole thing was likely just a psychological game. She could've had Rafael or Isaac disguise their voice, pretending to be the reporter who called Charlotte. One of her other minions could be dropping off the notes. He'd almost feel relieved if Amy was the culprit. She could be cruel but not violent. She just mind-fucked her enemies so hard they might consider hurting themselves for some relief.

Amy as a suspect couldn't be ignored, but there were other viable possibilities. Maybe a random stranger fixated on Charlotte at a show and developed a sick obsession. After all, she was a beautiful, gifted woman in the public eye, so it wasn't a stretch to think a disturbed person might create fantasies in their head until fantasies weren't enough. It'd make sense for such a person to also come after Tyler, viewing him as an obstacle. It could even be someone they knew, hiding in plain sight. If either scenario were true, she could be in grave danger.

The thought of some unpredictable menace lurking in the shadows until they got what they wanted roiled his stomach.

The time had come to eliminate possibilities. The obvious first step: try to determine once and for all if Amy sent the notes. Tyler sucked in a ragged breath, mentally preparing himself for the confrontation. He needed to do this in person. He had to look into Amy's wily hazel eyes as he leveled the accusation, hoping to see a glimmer of truth buried in her expression.

The second step would be going to Charlotte. Waiting it out, hoping she'd offer him another chance, wasn't an option. He'd tried giving her space, but staying away left her vulnerable and made them miserable. He needed to convince her the man she fell in love with wasn't the same weak, beaten-down man he was with Amy. And he had to do it before the person passing out threats got to her first.

After Matthew had a few days to cool off, Tyler would make amends with his brother, no matter what it took.

And if the stalker was dealt with, Charlotte still wouldn't take him back, and Matthew wouldn't forgive him, he'd do all he could to avoid the temptation of the Fremont Bridge.

38

Charlotte

Charlotte took a steadying breath before entering the office of Marion Cole, the CEO of Safe Start. Several plants hung along a wall of windows, all deep green and thriving in the sunlight. A few cushioned chairs were arranged in front of a white wooden desk in the center of the room. It was a bright, welcoming space—perfect for its purpose. Marion wanted struggling people who felt nervous or intimidated about needing help to feel comfortable enough to ask for it.

When Charlotte walked in, Marion was spraying the plants with water. She looked like a sweet grandmother from a children's book with her flower-patterned dress, wire-rimmed glasses connected to a pearled chain, and wavy gray hair to her shoulders. Her head turned, and she smiled warmly.

"It's so nice to see you, Charlotte." She set the spray bottle on a windowsill, motioning for Charlotte to sit. "Welcome, welcome."

"Sorry to pop in on such short notice. I know how busy you are."

Marion waved a dismissive hand, pushing her glasses further up her nose. "You're one of our best volunteers and can pop in anytime. How are you, sweetheart?"

The question wasn't easy to answer. With Marion's kind, sympathetic expression, not crying would be a challenge. But Marion had people with much bigger problems to tend to, so Charlotte wasn't about to fall apart in her office.

"Fine, thanks. I wanted to apologize in person about how the plans for the benefit album and show flopped. And I wanted to give you this." Charlotte unzipped her purse and slid the folded check out of her wallet. She had zero reservations but still felt her palms sweat over making such a huge decision.

Marion's brows furrowed as she reached across the desk and took the check. When she unfolded it, her eyes rounded. "Honey…" She looked at Charlotte. "I'm glad I'm sitting down. I-I don't know what to say. Are you sure?"

"Absolutely." She closed her purse, her fingers toying with the zipper. "It's enough, right? For the shelter program to continue?"

Marion touched her chest, the edges of her watery eyes crinkling as she smiled. "Yes, my dear. It's enough. But I think I'm in shock. If you're certain you can handle making such a generous donation, I can't tell you how grateful we are." She took off her glasses, letting them hang on their chain. "It isn't because you feel pressured after your benefits didn't work out, is it? I wouldn't want—"

"No." Charlotte offered a reassuring smile. "I promise I'll be fine, and I don't feel pressured at all. I'm happy to help."

The twenty-five-thousand-dollar check was the last of her mother's life insurance payout. It wiped out Charlotte's checking account, but she had some savings, her house and car were paid off, and her expenses were low. The struggling women and their families helped by the program needed the money more than she did.

"I apologize again for the trouble we had with your gentleman taking part in the benefit." Marion sighed. "I can't imagine how difficult living in the public eye must be, every mistake picked apart and judged by strangers."

"I understand why you made your decision. And I appreciate that you believed me when I told you the real story. I swear, Tyler's the kindest man I've ever—" Charlotte's voice cracked with emotion. "Sorry, I should go." She stood, wanting to bolt before she started blubbering like a fool.

"No, sit. Please." Marion gestured to Charlotte's chair and folded her hands in her lap. "Tell me what's wrong."

Charlotte sniffed and sat back down, successfully keeping the tears at bay. At least for now. "We broke up."

Marion clicked her tongue against her teeth. "Sorry, dear." She pushed a box of tissues across her desk. "Care to talk about it with a crazy old woman who's been around the block a few times?"

Charlotte exhaled, grabbing a tissue. "I found out something terrible from his past I can't accept. A mistake he made that could've killed him." She dabbed at her eyes. "Everything else about him is exactly what I want. I love him. But I have to protect myself, right?"

Marion nodded, leaning back in her chair. "Many troubled souls walk through that door, Charlotte. They all have things in their past they'd give anything to erase." She frowned, deep creases framing her mouth. "But that's not how life works. We hurt, that hurt makes us vulnerable, and we mess up. Then, hopefully, we seek forgiveness and change into people who wouldn't repeat those mistakes." The wrinkle between her eyes deepened. "Would he do it again?"

Tears collected on Charlotte's lashes. She'd give anything to know the answer to that question. "I don't know."

"Well then," Marion said with a sharp nod, "if this young man's worth the trouble, that's what you have to figure out. If he's committed to change, he needs people in his life who are willing to accept him as he is *now*. To know the errors of his past but to love him anyway. Don't be too hard on yourself if you can't do that. Considering your past with your mother, it's perfectly understandable if you can't be the support he needs." She leaned forward, her frown returning. "But then, you'll have to let him go so he can find it. Because one thing this place teaches you is how impossible it is to heal and do better without people around you who believe you can."

"Wow." Charlotte swallowed the lump in her throat. "I see why everyone comes to you for advice. I guess I have more thinking to do. Thanks for listening, Marion."

"Anytime, dear." The older woman got up, bending at the waist to wrap her arms around Charlotte. "You're a smart girl with a big heart. I'm sure you'll figure it out."

Charlotte left Marion's office feeling lighter. Even though she still had plenty to worry about, she'd sleep easier knowing the shelter program would continue. It was one big problem checked off her list.

For now, that had to be enough.

Charlotte

That afternoon, Charlotte met Sandra at Commonwealth Lake to pick up Roxy and chat. The visit to Marion's office and seeing her new puppy again lifted Charlotte's spirits a bit, but she missed Tyler more than ever. The ache in her chest was relentless, like an essential part of it was suddenly missing.

"Thanks for picking her up," Charlotte said, taking a seat on a park bench. Roxy dropped a tennis ball in her lap and settled beside her feet.

"No problem." Sandra sat beside her. "I had to go over there anyway."

"For what?"

"To kick him in the balls. I wore my steel-toe boots and went to town."

"*What*?" Charlotte's eyes went wide.

"Kidding!" Sandra laughed at her reaction. "I wanted to form my own opinion of the situation. I'll always be on your side, but I needed to hear his."

Charlotte tossed a few more grains of corn to the ducks skimming across the lake's surface. It caught the attention of a group of mallards on the opposite edge of the water, and they altered their course to glide in her direction. It also caught Roxy's attention, her tail wagging against the concrete as she barked at the birds.

"Settle down, Rox." She petted the puppy's head before turning back to Sandra. "What did he say?"

Charlotte held her breath, knowing that whatever transpired between Sandra and Tyler wouldn't be easy to hear.

"Same things he told you—nothing happened with Amy, the baggie wasn't his, and he'd never touch the stuff again. He knows how badly he fucked-up."

"That's good, I guess."

"He was so sad, Char." Sandra's bottom lip curled out. "I felt sorry for the guy."

Charlotte tipped her head back to look at the sky. The spaces between the lazy clouds were a paler, more calming shade of blue than the lake in front of them. The color reminded her of Tyler's eyes, and an old, familiar pain swelled in her throat—grief.

Her attention returned to Sandra, who looked back with such loving concern that tears threatened to fall. Again. Charlotte was sick of crying and even more fed up with the hollow feeling triggering it.

"I keep thinking about my dad." Charlotte absentmindedly picked tiny green threads off the tennis ball. "How he looked the other way when Mom was using again right before she died. Maybe she'd still be alive if he'd forced her into rehab one more time or pushed her harder."

"You and Tyler are *nothing* like your parents. I get why your mind would go down that road, but it's not the same thing, sweetie." Sandra placed a gentle hand on her knee. "You know that, right?"

Charlotte nodded, her eyes drifting back to the lake. "I guess. It's just... Part of me wants to help him if he needs it and maybe give it another try, and another part wants to keep running in the opposite direction to protect myself. If he's half as good at hiding an addiction as my mom was, and he doesn't stop, I can't be there when he falls. I won't survive it." Charlotte's voice cracked, and she willed the tears not to spill.

"You can survive anything, my friend." Sandra hugged her, planting a kiss on her cheek. "But there's no way he's an addict. He was in a dark place back then, but he's stronger now. And you know how dedicated Ty is to his career. His band's his life. Do you honestly think he'd risk everything he's worked for just to get high?"

She was right. Tyler's success came from having his priorities straight and working his ass off. Charlotte had seen him pass up numerous parties because inspiration struck, and he'd locked himself in his studio all night instead. And she'd seen him perform dozens of times. He'd never missed a note or forgotten a lyric, which would be next to impossible if he were strung out. Other than a tendency to drink too much sometimes and smoke a little pot, she'd never seen him truly wasted or acting like the junkies she'd encountered in the music business. Or in her own home growing up.

When Marion asked if he would make the mistake again, Charlotte hadn't known the answer. If it was a definite no, could she forgive him and move forward? Could she be the supportive partner who accepts him as he is now without holding past mistakes against him?

Sandra nudged her elbow. "And do you honestly think after falling in love with you and fighting to get you back, he'd risk losing you for good? You helped him see what a healthy, loving relationship feels like. If you gave him another chance, he wouldn't blow it."

No one had a better bullshit detector than Sandra, and if she believed him, why couldn't Charlotte? And while Marion's advice had helped, she still felt stuck.

It might've been easier to figure out the right thing to do under normal circumstances. With her headspace so foggy from the stalker nonsense and constantly having to look over her shoulder, it was hard to focus on anything. Let alone something as important as whether or not to trust Tyler again. She felt paralyzed, forced to endure the pain and indecision until an answer became clear.

"I don't know what to think," she said. "And I still have no clue what I want to do."

"That's okay. No need to rush into something you might regret." Sandra pet Roxy's head as the puppy set her front legs on the bench. "I told him you got another note. And that you bought a gun."

"Ugh. Why'd you tell him? Now he'll worry more than he already was." Charlotte slid sunglasses over her tender eyes as a cloud moved away from the sun.

"Even though you're angry, he deserves to know what's happening."

Charlotte dug into the bag of corn for another handful, tossing it into the water. "I guess."

The birds flew into a frenzy, loudly quacking and flapping their wings as they pecked the water, each snatching as many pieces as possible before the food was gone. Roxy growled and let out a single bark before settling at Charlotte's feet.

"That one with the green neck feathers is a fucking jerk," Sandra said.

"Seriously, what's his problem?" Charlotte laughed, the sound odd to her ears after a long stretch of miserable days. One of Sandra's many talents. "I wrote a new song last night."

"You did?" Sandra wrapped her arms around Charlotte's shoulders and gave her a shake. "That's so great! As much as it sucks to be in the thick of it, pain's given the world some of the best songs ever written. There'd be no 'Cats in the Cradle' if Cat Stevens' daddy hugged him enough. Heartbreak can drown you, or it can inspire you. I'm glad it's inspiring you."

"Can't it do both? Because this feels like drowning, too." Charlotte brushed corn dust off her lap. "At least something good can come from it."

Roxy got to her feet, whining at the tennis ball in Charlotte's lap.

"Okay, you win." She got up, leash and ball in hand, and headed toward the gated-in dog run while Sandra walked beside her. If it weren't for Roxy needing to burn energy and Sandra insisting they get fresh air and talk, Charlotte would probably be back in bed already, a pathetic heap hiding under the covers.

She opened the gate, Sandra closing it behind them. After unleashing Roxy, she tossed the ball to the other side of the run, the puppy taking off after it.

"Almost forgot," Sandra said. "I called Luke from Black River like Ty suggested. He's coming to our next practice to see if he fits. He seemed chill over the phone, so it might work if he's got the skills."

"I'll let you borrow their last CD. I'm not the least bit worried about his skills, and I think you and Amber will be blown away too."

Solving their chronic bassist problem would be a massive relief. Charlotte savored the small burst of positivity.

Roxy ran back with the ball, dropping it at Sandra's feet. The corner of her mouth quirked up. "Good girl." Her arm tipped back, and she threw the ball further across the field. Roxy zipped away to retrieve it, her tongue lolling out of the side of her mouth.

"I really fucking love that dog," Charlotte said.

"She was a thoughtful gift. From someone who really fucking loves you."

Charlotte sighed. "Sometimes, that isn't enough."

"I guess that's up to you to decide." Roxy raced back, dropping the ball in front of Sandra again. The puppy barked, bouncing in anticipation. "At least you'll have the most adorable company in the world while you figure it out."

Charlotte kicked a molehill with the tip of her sneaker. "Have you talked to Matty?"

She was ashamed of how she'd treated him. Sure, Matthew should've told her about Tyler's drug use, but that was no reason to scream in his face and shut him out. The confrontation with Tyler was so fresh that she unfairly took her anger out on his brother.

Sandra nodded. "He went with me to Ty's hotel. It got ugly."

"What happened?"

Sandra tossed the ball, staring down the field as the puppy chased it. She went uncharacteristically quiet for a few moments—never a good sign.

"Matty said some harsh things he didn't mean." Sandra frowned, pushing her curls out of her eyes. "I've never seen him so determined to hurt someone, let alone Tyler. But you know how Matty looks up to him. He has a right to be pissed and disappointed, but he wouldn't even hear what Ty had to say."

Charlotte thought back to her fight with Tyler. Like Matthew, she'd refused to hear him out. She'd been convinced at the time that a clean break would be easiest on both of them in the long run. Besides, she couldn't bear to be in that room with him for one more second. Mostly because she knew she'd eventually cave and regret it later.

But hearing about the brothers' fight made her feel sorry for Tyler. Two of the people he loved most in the world had pushed him away without offering a shot at redemption or forgiveness. She wanted to ask Sandra if he was okay, but of course he wasn't. For his brother, his best friend in the world, to say things intended to wound must've been devastating.

"I'll call him later," Charlotte said. "Matty, I mean."

"No need." Sandra pointed toward the parking lot. "I already did." Charlotte's head turned to find Matthew jogging across the field toward them. "You guys talk while Roxy and I play with balls." She snickered, picking up the puppy and walking away.

Behind his glasses, Matthew's eyes were sad and bloodshot. His usual goofy grin had been replaced by a pitiful frown that made Charlotte run over and hug him hard.

"I'm so sorry, Charlotte." He squeezed tighter, his chin resting on her shoulder.

"No, *I'm* sorry. I shouldn't have yelled at you like that. Or called you a shithead. I was mad at Tyler and took it out on you."

"I was a shithead. I should've told you."

"No, Matty." She pulled back. "You were just being loyal, protecting your brother. It was his mistake, not yours."

She knew Matthew never meant to hurt her. He'd made a misguided attempt to hold their group together, hiding a secret that would irrevocably change how everyone saw Tyler. An error made with honorable intentions was easy to forgive.

"Are you okay?" His frown deepened. "You don't look okay."

"Gee, thanks." A joyless laugh escaped her. "And no. I'm not. But don't shut your brother out for my sake."

"That's not on you." He swallowed, his Adam's apple bobbing. "I have other reasons, trust me. I need some space."

Roxy barked and ran to Charlotte. She picked her up, holding the puppy to her chest. Matthew finally smiled, scratching under Roxy's chin.

"Space is good for a little while," Charlotte said. "But you're too important to each other to be apart for long."

"Yeah." His smile fell. "Can we move on, please?"

She wanted him to talk about the hurtful things he'd said to Tyler, but since he didn't bring it up, she left it alone. He'd open up when he was ready. And she knew Matthew well enough to know that after taking time to process, he'd come around and make amends with Tyler.

"I missed you, dork." Charlotte hugged him again, Roxy squirming between them.

"It's only been four days." Matthew chuckled, the heavy sadness in his expression finally lifting. "But I missed you too. And I'm glad to properly meet this cute ass dog everyone's been talking about." Roxy licked his face, and he laughed again.

The sound and the joy on his face that came with it made her smile.

She really had missed him.

"Okay, you two." Sandra ran over with her arms wide. "Give me some of that." She joined their hug. "No more fighting. It causes wrinkles."

They laughed together in the warm, tight huddle.

Charlotte hadn't truly known romantic love until Tyler, but thanks to these wonderful weirdos, she'd known friend love all along. Even if they disagreed sometimes, nothing could ever take that away.

She moved close to Matthew's ear. "No more secrets?"

"No more secrets." He hugged her tighter.

While some things were made right, Charlotte hadn't fixed everything wrong with her life—not even close. She was still broken-hearted, missing the person she thought would be her forever.

But with friends like these, she knew she'd be okay no matter what happened next.

39

Tyler

"Tyler! My adoring husband. What a pleasant surprise."

Amy stood at the front door of their home with an obnoxious smirk, obviously pleased with herself for having the locks changed. Tyler wasn't about to mention it and give her the satisfaction.

"Go fuck yourself, Amy." He pushed past her, sitting on the couch beside his cigarette burns.

Her high heels clicked across the floor as she followed, the sound grating his nerves. When she reached the living room, she stood in front of him with a hand on her hip. "What are you doing here, darling? Home for an afternoon quickie?"

"Sit."

"Ooh, you know I love it when you're forceful." Her teeth sank into her plump lower lip.

Amy sat beside him, and he scooted in the opposite direction until he felt he'd reached a safe distance. In his current state, he wasn't sure which of them needed protecting.

"Jesus." She stared at his face as if seeing him for the first time. "You look like shit, Tyler."

"Wow. Thanks."

"Sleeping okay? It's a shame to see dark circles under those gorgeous eyes."

"Cut the shit." His hands balled into fists. The cuts from punching the wall stung, threatening to reopen. "I'm not here for small talk or your fake fucking concern. Why'd you put the drugs under my pillow?"

Her eyebrow arched. "Are you sure that was *your* pillow?"

His fists clenched tighter, fresh blood blooming on his knuckles. "If a house-keeper found that, I could've been arrested. Do you seriously have nothing better to do than screw with my life? Write a song about mutilating pets or whatever inspires you these days. Book some solo gigs and let the masses feed your ego. Hell, take up knitting, for all I care. Just leave me the hell alone!"

"Am I crazy, or are you the one who knocked on my door?" She shifted in her seat, her red miniskirt climbing up her thighs.

"My name's on the deed." Heat rushed to his face. "I own that door and everything around it. I'm letting you stay here until the house sells so you can move all your shit, but that'll change if you keep provoking me."

"You never used to be this angry. It's not a good look."

"Answer the question," he gritted out.

A corner of her mouth twitched like she was holding back a smile. "The drugs were just a gift since you're obviously stressed." She pushed an acrylic fingernail through a burn hole in the upholstery. "I heard Charlotte dumped you. My condolences."

"Don't talk about her," he warned.

"I know how much you cared about her." Amy's tone dripped with faux sympathy. "You must be very depressed about the whole thing. I hope you held onto that dope."

He took a deep breath and let it out, but it did nothing to calm the rage she stirred in him.

"Goddamn. You really are a miserable, soul-sucking vampire, aren't you?" He shook his head in disgust. "That underwear under my bed was low, even for you."

Her head tilted. "I must've forgotten them while you were rushing me out the door." She grinned. "Oops."

Exhaling slowly, he shoved his anger aside. He was there for a reason, and this ridiculous back-and-forth just wasted time.

Tyler paused, wanting to catch her off guard with the next question.

"Are you the one stalking Charlotte?" He studied her reaction, but Amy's poker face was legendary. She was a master of neutral, inscrutable expressions, and to his disappointment, her mask didn't slip an inch.

"I heard about the terrible notes she was getting." The corners of Amy's mouth drooped. "Give me some credit, Ty. Why would I want any woman to be afraid some creep will attack her? I'm not perfect, but you have to know I'm not capable of that. Besides, I'm not about to waste my time watching that dull little mouse go about her day."

"I got a few notes too." He leaned forward, his bloody knuckles sinking into the couch cushion. "In places you knew I'd be. You telling me it was a coincidence?"

She shrugged. "The only thing I'm telling you is it wasn't me. When you're famous, lots of people tend to know where you are. Enjoy it while it lasts because you're one shitty album away from joining me in obscurity."

"Don't bet on it." He wasn't sure he believed her, but at least the suspicion was out in the open. She'd know he had an eye on her.

The front door opened, and he turned to see Rafael walking in like he owned the place.

"Hey, Raf," Amy said. "Look who's here."

Rafael slipped his sunglasses to the top of his head, stopping at the end of the couch with his arms crossed in front of his bulging chest. "Staying long?"

Tyler's back teeth gnashed together, his face burning. "I own this goddamn house, so I'll stay as long as I want. But since I can barely stomach the sight of the two of you, I'll be leaving soon."

"Good." Rafael sat beside Amy, sliding his arm possessively across the back of her shoulders. She set her hand on his knee, triggering a memory in Tyler's mind of the day they met. The woman loved to publicly stake her claim.

"Do you know the kid that threw the brick?" Tyler asked, giving her another long, searching look. Despite what the cop told Charlotte, he couldn't shake the feeling Amy was involved.

Her forehead twitched, but her face remained otherwise unmoved. "What brick?"

"The brick that smashed my car window and could've fucking killed her." His pulse spiked, reliving the moment in his head. The sound of shattering glass still haunted him every day. "Do you want that on whatever conscience you have left?"

She barked out a laugh. "So, to re-cap, I'm stalking Charlotte, sending her threatening notes, and I tried to kill her?" She shook her head, false pity in her eyes. "You're losing it, Ty."

Rafael covered Amy's hand with his as he glared at Tyler. "We're done here."

Tyler's head snapped to Rafael. "No one's talking to you, you bloated lump of shit! Stare daggers at me and puff your ridiculous muscles all you want. You don't scare me."

"You should be scared," he mumbled.

"What's that?" The volume of Tyler's voice rose. "Are you threatening me?"

"Of course not." Amy touched Rafael's chest, shooting him a disapproving look. "The pissing contest is over, boys. Any more questions? I'd like to fuck some tension out of my bodyguard before we meet my agent for drinks."

Tyler's stomach roiled at the image, but he refused to take the bait. "One more. Did you have someone call Charlotte, pretending to be a reporter?" He anticipated her lie, searching her face for any hint of deception.

"That's ridiculous." Amy slowly re-crossed her legs. "The girl sounds a bit paranoid. Is she just blaming everyone she's ever known for her problems these days?"

He scowled, leaning across the cushion between them. "Only the ones crazy enough to do something like that."

"Watch it." The words rolled from Rafael's throat like the low, ominous rumble of thunder.

"Maybe Charlotte will suspect you, Ty! Maybe she'll even get a restraining order against you." Amy pressed her palms together as if she were praying. "Wouldn't that be fun? We can all pass those suckers out like hotcakes."

Tyler pushed off the couch, getting to his feet. "Thanks for nothing, Amy. Pack your shit because your free ride's almost over."

Amy touched Rafael's chest again as Tyler headed for the front door. He didn't know what he expected to accomplish, but whatever it was, he'd failed.

"See you later, Tyler," she shouted at his back. "For your sake, I hope the next skank you let into your bed has a mother who can handle her drugs."

Tyler stood outside the entrance to his hotel, feeling restless and lost as he finished a cigarette and stomped it out. He'd stopped by Matthew's apartment after confronting Amy, but no one answered, and his car was gone. It was the same at Charlotte's. Trying to get them to listen would have to wait another day.

Looking up, he saw the balcony and darkened windows of his penthouse suite. The thought of being alone, trapped in that room with awful memories and the reek of old whiskey, was unbearable.

He veered right. Pulling his sweatshirt's hood to hide his face, he shuffled down the tree-lined sidewalk with no destination in mind.

For two hours, he walked, passing fountains, food carts, and colorful gardens. After crossing the Morrison Bridge, he stumbled on the store that sold him his first guitar. A rush of sweet nostalgia fluttered in his chest as he passed.

After a few more blocks, he found himself at the bottom of the stairs that once led to Master Jim's apartment. No one was around, and the building was vacant and condemned, but he could almost hear the faint sounds of a guitar that always drew him in.

He waved at Jim's old, cracked window, emotion rising in his throat.

"I miss you, man."

Tyler wished he'd let himself grieve and heal from his friend's loss instead of giving up and shoving it down. If he had, he might've been strong enough to handle losing Charlotte without crumbling. Hell, he wouldn't have lost her in the first place. Now, those wounds remained on a heap of older wounds, bleeding into every part of his life.

He knew then what Matthew meant. *You need to find a way to make yourself whole instead of waiting for someone to hand you the missing pieces.* Tyler had grown stronger and wiser since leaving Amy, but he still wasn't whole. And he realized that the only way to get there was to acknowledge the roots of his problems and finally work through that heap.

He stared up at Jim's window as it blurred behind tears. "I wouldn't have made it without you. Not just in music but in life, too. I was a sad, lost kid, and you helped me find my purpose. You showed me what was possible with a few strings and a chunk of wood." He smiled for the first time since the breakup five days before. "Thanks for everything, old friend."

As he continued down streets and alleyways he knew by heart, all the best memories of watching Jim with his guitar played through Tyler's head. Instead of the usual sadness that overwhelmed him when he thought of his friend, he felt gratitude. Somehow, in a big, crazy world, their paths crossed, and it changed Tyler's life.

He soon passed the Keep Portland Weird graffiti. As always, a wide grin stretched across his face as he remembered how Charlotte laughed at the giant orange penis that had long since faded. The beautiful sound had echoed off the walls, and he'd give anything to hear it then.

When Tyler reached the oak tree outside The Marquis, he stopped—at the exact spot where he felt the first spark ignite between them.

If he had been whole that night, he would've done the right thing and chosen her.

But he'd been broken, splintered by unresolved guilt and pain.

And after three more broken years with Amy and almost two months of getting lost in his feelings for Charlotte, he still was. He needed to overcome his demons once and for all if he ever hoped to have a real future with her.

And there was one more stop he knew would help that along.

Just before sunset, Tyler entered the gates of Glisan Cemetery and sat beside his father's grave. The last time he was there, he'd been a ten-year-old boy clinging to his mother's hand as they tossed roses onto the coffin.

He brushed leaves and dried grass off the marble, his grief and despair feeling as heavy as they did that day.

He looked around.

Aside from a pair of ravens squawking in a nearby tree, he was alone.

"Hey, Dad."

Tyler blinked back tears.

"There's a lot I never got to say." He rubbed at the terrible ache in his chest. "Like how I appreciated our Friday night talks around the backyard fire pit, making s'mores, and drinking cocoa. And I loved our hiking trips, climbing rocks and jumping over creeks while we laughed all day, going home filthy and exhausted."

Tyler chuckled at the memory of his little boots tracking mud on their tan carpet.

He lit a cigarette with trembling fingers, smoke streaming from his lips. "When you died, everything fell apart. I had to fake being strong for Matty all those years, and it was really fucking lonely." He wiped his nose on his sleeve. "I shoved down my feelings instead of dealing with them because it hurt too much. And it changed me, Dad. I was so desperate for love and an end to the loneliness I made stupid fucking mistakes."

He ashed his cigarette in the grass, the tip smoldering. "Then, I wasn't ready when the right person came along because grief and guilt were still poisoning me. But now I understand that your accident wasn't my fault. I'm letting go of that guilt so I can move on."

Tears slid down his face. The memory of an officer giving his mother news that made her scream and collapse was fresh in his mind. As he dug deeper into the pit, he found the anger trapped inside. "How could you be so careless when you had people who needed you? *I needed you!*" He screamed it, years of pent-up anger and pain bleeding out through his words.

Tyler picked up a rock and lobbed it at a tree, pieces of bark breaking loose and falling to the ground. "If I have kids someday, I'll do everything I can to stay alive for them. And they'll only know you from stories and pictures because you didn't do that for us."

As the anger receded, relief washed over him. He traced the words *beloved father* etched in the cold stone, his shoulders feeling lighter with every swoop of his fingertip. "I forgive myself now. And I forgive you. I miss you every day, but I'm grateful I had ten years of feeling safe, loved, and whole."

Tyler had mourned that feeling for nearly seventeen years.

And he was determined to have it again.

"I wish you could meet Charlotte. She's perfect, Dad." He sniffed, looking at the bruised, overcast sky above his head. "I'll find a way to get her back, I swear it. And I'll grow from my mistakes like you taught me."

Tyler released more of the old, toxic pain with every word. "I'll always hold onto my memories, but I have to let go of the weight of my grief. And finally, move on." He wiped away the last of his tears.

"I love you, Dad."

He closed it off with something else he never got to say.

"Goodbye."

Tyler passed through the cemetery gates and back toward downtown.

At a park, he watched two little boys run around a playground. The older one pushed the younger one on a swing. Tyler's eyes misted as he smiled, remembering how his brother loved it when he did an "underdog"—holding the sides of Matthew's swing and running underneath it, launching him high into the air. He'd kick his little legs at the top of the arc, screaming and grinning with the thrill of flying above the world.

As night fell, a sprinkling of stars peeked from behind the clouds. Tyler bought a cup of hot cocoa from a food cart, savoring every sweet, warm sip as he strolled past couples holding hands and people walking dogs.

God, he loved this city.

His greatest achievements and heartbreaks had all happened within its limits. And it held everyone he loved. He felt like a fool for letting the fear of being recognized keep him from fully living in it for so long.

The pain of the breakup still overwhelmed him, but another feeling returned as he headed back to his hotel—gratitude. He realized how truly fortunate he was and couldn't believe he'd ever taken the incredible people and opportunities in his life for granted. And he knew it was stupid to let that dark, destructive baggage he'd held onto for so long plague him one more goddamn second.

He'd had enough.

He *was* enough.

And as he crossed back over the Morrison Bridge, he was determined to make things right with Charlotte and Matthew. Then, he'd savor his amazing life and build a future free of regret. One where he didn't need anyone else to be whole but wanted to share his life with people who made him feel like a child flying through the air on a swing—happy, fearless, and free.

40

Tyler

"I don't want to see you, Tyler. Don't make this any harder than it is."

The tears in Charlotte's voice made his eyes water. "I'm sorry it upsets you, but I'm not leaving." He rested his forehead against the cold, hard wood of her front door. "I love you. Please let me in so we can talk."

"I have nothing else to say to you." Her voice faded as if all the fight had left her.

"I got another note. I'm pissed at them and terrified for you, so I'm not leaving you alone. I'll sleep on your doorstep if I have to." He sat on the concrete slab of her front porch beside a shrub that hung heavy with fragrant yellow blossoms. "This bush smells like one of the candles you bought at the Farmers' Market."

He got no response but hoped she was still on the other side, listening.

"When I told Matty about those tiny goats climbing on us, he laughed his ass off. Couldn't believe I'd do something like that. He said that's when he knew I had feelings for you." Tyler picked a petal, holding it to his nose. "And now my brother hates me, and the woman I'm crazy in love with thinks I'm an asshole. And she's right."

A trail of ants marched in front of his shoe in a perfectly straight line. He pulled a pack of smokes from his pocket and lit one, the flame from the lighter making his hands glow.

"I'm sorry I never told you about the drugs. You were one of my best friends, and I shouldn't have hid it from you. I knew about your mom and didn't want to lose you because I was weak and stupid. It's just…" His damp eyes squeezed shut as he pinched the bridge of his nose. "There hasn't been a moment since we met that I wasn't happy being around you. I selfishly hid an ugly part of myself that would've taken that light from my life."

The feeling in the air shifted, and rain fell around him. The flower petals danced and drooped. The ants changed course to stay under the shelter of the awning. Tyler rested his back against the door. He closed his eyes, letting the sound of the rain tapping the shingles provide some comfort.

Living in the Pacific Northwest, you either tolerate the rain or you appreciate it. Tyler appreciated it. It kept their corner of the country green and lush, the sound and scent soothed like nothing else, and it washed away whatever dirt had collected in places it wasn't wanted.

He took a few more drags before smashing his cigarette away from the trail of ants. "You hear the rain, Charlotte? Isn't it beautiful?"

Tracks of hot tears slid down his cheeks, and he let them fall. Maybe they'd wash away some things about himself that had collected in places they weren't wanted.

The anger in his throat.

The gnawing fear in his gut.

The awful memories trapped in his mind.

But there was nothing in his heart he didn't want. Because all that was there was Charlotte.

"Remember the ride home after movie night when I asked how you can tell love apart from lust and infatuation? Now I know. And you were right. It's like the sweetest heaven when you're with them and torture when you're not. I've never loved anyone this much. And I know you love me too, so I'm going to fight for us, Charlotte. Because our story doesn't end like this." He wiped at tears with his sleeve. "Please don't let your pain make you forget what we were at our best. How perfectly every part of us fit together. And I'll spend every day proving I'm not the stupid person I used to be. I became a better man so we can have the happily ever after we both deserve."

The rain stopped, and so did his tears.

He'd said everything he wanted to say before she rushed out of his hotel room and shut him out of her life. If she was listening, there was no guarantee it would change anything, but he had to try. "I'll shut up now. I'll be here if you need me. All day and night. On the porch."

As night fell, Tyler still heard nothing on the other side of Charlotte's door. When her inside lights went off and her porch light turned on, he waited, hoping she'd come.

Hours ticked by.

Nothing.

He mindlessly scraped at a streak of red paint on the concrete with his thumbnail. Crickets chirped, and frogs croaked in the flowerbeds and bushes lining the front of her house. The evening sounds made his eyelids heavy, and he didn't fight it. His muscles ached from sitting on the cold, hard ground for hours, and he zipped up his hooded jacket as a chill ran through him. He tucked his hands into his pockets, his fingers wrapping around the folded Ka-Bar knife he'd taken from his glove box.

As Tyler closed his eyes, he imagined Charlotte warm and safe in her bed a few feet inside the wall while he sat on the porch, shivering and alone like a scolded dog. And he knew it was exactly what he deserved.

41

Charlotte

Charlotte's eyelids refused to remain closed, and her mind wouldn't quiet, so she stared into the shadows on the ceiling above her bed. Her eyes were swollen and raw from weeping into a kitchen towel while Tyler poured his heart out from her front porch. His beautiful words reached everywhere she hurt, yet she still couldn't find the strength to open the door.

She'd had to close Roxy in her bedroom. The first time he came over after their breakup, the puppy had frantically scratched and barked at the door, her tail excitedly wagging. She clearly missed him, too, making it even harder to resist letting him in.

Why couldn't Charlotte just turn that knob and see if he was still out there? He'd probably been gone for hours, but what if he sat there shivering, waiting for her to bring him in from the cold? The image tugged at her resolve, yet something more powerful held her back.

Vivid memories of her mother's blue lips and cold skin kept flashing through her mind. As an especially cruel trick, sometimes the image would shift, putting Tyler in her place as the corpse being zipped up in a body bag.

She'd hoped letting him go would get easier with every passing day, but the opposite proved to be true. The loss had opened a pitch-black void in her chest that never stopped aching. It widened whenever she was in her kitchen, remembering the day they made her mother's marinara, dancing to Queen and stealing kisses while they worked. It expanded further when she sat on the couch, where he'd explained every desperate thing he'd done to find her when he thought she was in danger. But no room held more memories of Tyler than her bedroom. From their first time to their last, every line, dip, and curve of their bodies fit together perfectly, just as he'd said on the porch.

And each part of him spoke to her in its own way. His eyes had professed his love long before his words. The slightest brush of his lips made her feel treasured and desired. Nothing had ever soothed her like his heartbeat beneath her ear as she rested in his arms.

It was why she knew he hadn't cheated. When she thought about the man she'd watched him become and how happy they were together, she knew there was nothing Amy could've done or said to make him throw that away.

Charlotte sat up, pulling a pack of Tyler's American Spirits from the night-stand. He'd left them the last time they made love, and she couldn't bear to toss them out. She picked up the burning candle beside her bed, lighting a cigarette with the flame. The scent of the candle reminded her of their first perfect day together. She took a deep drag, exhaling a dense white cloud. It hovered above the blankets before slowly vanishing into nothing. Confusion and grief muddled her brain, but one thing she knew for sure—she didn't want their love to disappear like that.

Another certainty struck as the scent of smoke hung in the air. If she didn't make things right with Tyler, she'd regret it for the rest of her life. Walking away from him the day they met had made her suffer over the years, and this would be worse. *Much* worse.

She took one last hit before smashing the cigarette into the ashtray beside three of his discarded butts. The fact that she couldn't bring herself to toss something his lips had touched further proved it was time to let go of her anger, fears, and disappointment and trust the man she loved. She'd be taking a risk, but as more memories of him flooded in, she knew it was worth it. *He* was worth it.

Roxy pushed the door open with her nose, looking around before jumping on the bed and settling beside Charlotte. She smelled like carrots and chicken, tiny kibble crumbs dotting the fur on her cheeks.

"Enjoy your dinner, Rox?" Charlotte gently brushed off the crumbs.

Roxy's favorite bone-shaped squeaky toy dropped from her mouth, and she set her chin on top like a pillow. Her whole body relaxed with a sigh, and she was asleep in seconds. As long as Roxy had that toy nearby, she was golden. It was hard not to envy someone whose contentment was so easy to achieve.

As Charlotte stroked the puppy's fur, she imagined Tyler's reaction when she told him he was getting a second chance. Well, a *second*, second chance.

Afterward, she'd help Matthew and Tyler mend their relationship. There was too much love there to waste another second being angry.

The recent rifts were yet another thing she blamed on her stalker. It was as if the stress they'd all been living with had finally boiled over, burning everyone except the person who deserved it. And if they were ever going to be unmasked and dealt with, she couldn't do it alone. The people she loved needed to come together and attack the problem as a united force.

She set her head on Tyler's pillow.

Her tight shoulders loosened, and her eyes finally shut.

Tomorrow would be a new day.

Fractured bonds would be mended.

She'd let the man she loved back into her home, life, and heart.

If she were very lucky, it would be the last night she'd ever spend without his arms around her and his steady heartbeat beneath her ear.

42

Tyler

When the door he rested on flew open, Tyler fell backward, slamming his head against the hardwood floor of the entryway.

He saw an upside-down Charlotte, a hand flying to her mouth. "Oh, my god!" She grabbed his elbows, helping him to his feet.

He rubbed the back of his head as it throbbed so intensely, he fought the urge to vomit. He sank into a kitchen chair, pulling in a few long, ragged breaths. In a flurry of movement, she grabbed an ice pack from the freezer, wrapped it in a kitchen towel, and handed it to him.

"Are you okay?" Charlotte's red, puffy eyes met his red, puffy eyes. Her hair looked tousled from sleep, and she wore a ripped and faded Pearl Jam shirt with plaid flannel pajama pants. She'd obviously been crying, but she was so beautiful, it hurt to look at her.

"Not even close." Tyler held the cold pack to his head. The sunlight filtering through the curtains made the throbbing worse, so he turned away from the window.

"Did you stay out there all night?" She sat across the table, her eyes searching his face.

"Of course. And I'll do it again. As long as someone's still out there, threatening to hurt you, I'm not leaving you alone."

She went to reach for him and stopped, folding her hands on the table. "I can't believe you stayed."

He set the ice pack down, a sharp pain squeezing his chest. "If you really think that, then I failed you again. If I'd shown you exactly how much you mean to me, you'd know nothing would've made me step off that porch."

"I didn't mean to—"

"Even if you never want to see me again, I'd die if something happened to you." When he blinked, a tear slid to his chin.

"Shh... Tyler, stop." Charlotte left her chair, took his face in her hands, and wiped his tears with her thumbs. "It's gonna be okay."

She bent at the waist, their faces inches apart.

And then she kissed him.

It was the last thing he expected and the only thing he wanted. A pained groan broke in his throat, his hands covering hers as he leaned into the kiss. He forgot all about the pounding in his head and the ache in his heart and held onto the perfect moment.

It didn't last long enough.

Charlotte pulled away, gently touching the back of his head with her fingertips. "That's a pretty nasty bump." She frowned, her eyes wide with concern. "Does it still hurt?"

With a finger tucked beneath her chin, Tyler guided her face closer and, taking a chance, kissed her again. It was slow and cautious, even as her lips moved against his. It would've been so easy to tug her into his lap and kiss her senseless, but he didn't want to go too far, too fast, and risk scaring her off for good. Before his restraint could falter, he drew back an inch, still in disbelief they were so close, breathing the same air.

"Not anymore," he said.

That earned him a soft smile and a sliver of hope she wasn't through with him.

Charlotte walked to the cupboard above the sink, grabbed two black ceramic mugs, and filled them with coffee. She set one in front of Tyler and returned to her chair, blowing on her steaming cup before taking a small sip.

"I'm not a person who forgives and forgets easily."

"Charlotte, you know me. You know when I'm being sincere." He swallowed hard. The sight he'd craved for six long, miserable days and nights was almost too much to bear. "I'd never touch Amy or anyone else."

"I know you wouldn't."

Tyler blinked. He was prepared to beg, plead. It was a relief, but there was something he knew required more convincing. "I'll take random drug tests. Whatever it takes to earn back your trust. I understand why you have a hard time believing anyone who uses drugs, but I promise, I don't need them. I need *you*."

She opened her mouth to speak before her gaze fell to his hands. "Drink your coffee. You're shaking."

Charlotte went to the living room and pulled a quilt off the couch. She returned to the kitchen, covering his shoulders.

"Thank you." He touched her hand. "You opened the door. I don't know what it means yet, but... thank you."

She sat beside him this time, her expression softening. "It'll be forty degrees tonight. You aren't sleeping outside again."

"Can I take the couch?" His still-frozen hands wrapped around the mug. "I promise I won't bother you."

She took his hand, her warm skin breathing life into his numb fingertips. "I don't want you on the couch either."

"The porch it is, then. I'll grab a blanket and pillow from the hotel."

She shook her head and laughed, the sound instantly making him feel lighter and confusing the hell of out of him all at once.

"You're fucking crazy, Tyler. Do you know that?"

"Yeah," he sighed. "I know."

He brought her hand to his chest, holding it against his pounding heart. They sat silently as her warmth chased away the final chills from his terrible night. Then he remembered what brought him there.

"I found another note," he said.

Her eyes closed, and she released a heavy breath. "What did it say?"

"He thanked me for giving you back because he doesn't like to share."

She squeezed the hand that still held hers. "I understand why that scared you."

"And maybe now you can understand why I'm not leaving. I protect the people I love."

"I know you do, Ty."

Charlotte's sweet, chocolate-brown eyes bore into him as heavy silence settled in. He couldn't recall ever feeling more vulnerable and exposed in front of another person. As if his outer layers had been scraped off, and she could see straight through to his soul.

He ran a hand over the messy, unwashed hair falling to his shoulders. "Maybe I am crazy, but I swear to you, I'll sleep on the damn porch with the ants and the flowers and the rain—"

She silenced him with another kiss, a shudder running through him.

"The only place you're sleeping is in my bed," she said against his lips. "Where you belong. Where every part of us can fit together perfectly."

Tyler grinned. "You were listening through the door?"

"Heard every word. And while I'm not completely over what happened, you deserve another chance. I know you're not really a junkie or a liar. I would've noticed signs ages ago. I just saw that baggie and lost it. It's an old wound that bleeds like crazy when poked."

"Of course, it does." He stroked the silken skin of her cheek. "I'm so sorry you went through that because of me."

She sipped her coffee, staring into the dark liquid before looking back at him. "You need to understand something. If you keep anything from me again or lie to me, it's over. No more chances."

"I understand. I won't let you down again, I promise." Tyler thought about her expression when she stared at the bag of powder in her hand. He never wanted her to hurt like that again. "Everything was so perfect until that moment."

"Yes. It was. And in the spirit of second chances, would you repeat the words you blurted out right before I left your room? We need a better first time than that."

Tyler sat in awe of her. Even after all Charlotte had been through and every reason she had to keep pushing him away, her heart was still capable of forgiveness. He'd never experienced love like that before, and he'd be damned if he'd let it slip away again.

"Charlotte Elizabeth Ross..." He took her hands and kissed them. "I'm in love with you. So fucking in love with you that I'm happier and more terrified than I've ever been."

"I'm in love with you too, Tyler... Anthony! It's Anthony, right?"

He laughed, the smothering weight on his chest finally lifting. "Yes, it is."

"Okay, third chances are cool too." She cleared her throat. "I'm in love with you too, Tyler Anthony Hall. Like, 'I'll only write sappy loves songs from now on because you're all I think about' kind of in love with you."

His eyebrow quirked. "Yeah, but will you buy me a puppy?"

They laughed until tears streamed down their cheeks. Tears of joy, this time.

"Are you tired?" she asked.

"Umm..." Tyler glanced at the wall clock. "It's seven in the morning."

A wicked smile curved her lips. "Can we go to bed anyway?"

43

Tyler

"**Y**ou're out of your mind if you think I'm signing these fucking papers, Tyler."

Hearing Amy's shrill voice over the phone made him want to bang his head into a wall. But he had to try one last time to get her to sign and move on. It was the biggest remaining hurdle in his quest to put old wounds in the past and only look forward.

"We have an untouchable prenup," he said. "You and your parents made sure of that when you had it drawn up. Contesting the divorce to bully me into giving you half of everything will just waste time and money." He lit a sorely needed cigarette. "Sign now, and I'll pay your court costs and attorney fees, and you can have half what the Portland house sells for. Otherwise, you won't get anything you didn't earn yourself." He exhaled a massive cloud. "Just take it, Amy."

"Nope. I won't make it easier for you to ride off into the sunset with that nobody."

"A nobody, huh?" Tyler scoffed. "Should I remind you that Charlotte's last album sold over a million more copies than yours? And her band's actually touring this year while you're sitting around with a poseur drummer with hepatitis and guitarist who just did time for possession."

"Oh, bravo. So quick-witted." She went quiet. "I want the house in Aspen."

He laughed. "Already sold. You only wanted that house because we'd have celebrity neighbors you could try to convince to put you in movies. I hate to break it to you, but accosting Goldie Hawn and Steven Spielberg on a ski slope isn't your ticket to Hollywood."

"I'm not signing."

"Fine. But the second they served those papers, the clock started ticking. Since you've opted to drag your heels and ignore the advice of our attorneys, it'll be over in two weeks. Unless you want to fight and walk away with nothing. If that's the case, I'll use what you gave up on a nice bottle of champagne to celebrate the end of this fucking nightmare."

"Don't go popping your cork just yet, Tyler. You know better than anyone I never give up without a fight."

The line went dead, and he released a long, heavy sigh.

Fourteen days.

He dug through Charlotte's kitchen drawer and found a purple magic marker. He walked to the wall calendar, drawing wide circles around the date—July eighth. Nine days after his twenty-seventh birthday.

His gift would come a little late this year.

"Why are you staring at my calendar?" Charlotte walked in carrying a few envelopes, a checkbook, and a pen. "Trying to figure out when I'll have PMS?"

He'd been staying at her house for two weeks—since the night of their reunion. They hadn't received any more notes, but the threat of danger remained a low, insistent hum whenever they left the house.

"Actually, I circled the date when my divorce is finalized. Provided Amy doesn't contest it and drag it on even longer. Since she wants to be on my good side so I'll give her half the house and pay her fees, I don't think that'll happen. With the debts she piles up, she knows she'll be broke in a year otherwise."

"Why are you being so generous? She doesn't deserve it."

"I just want it over with." Tyler scrubbed a hand over his face. "It's a bribe, I guess. Incentive to be grateful and move on. But I think I'm once again overestimating her ability to think logically."

Charlotte sat at the table and wrote a few checks, sticking them into envelopes addressed to her electric, water, and car insurance providers. Tyler put his cigarette out before sitting down. There was something he'd wanted to ask since they made up, but he was unsure how she'd take it. While they were on the subject of finances, he figured he might as well get it over with.

"I know this isn't my business." He ran a hand through his hair as his knee bounced beneath the table, nervous energy making it hard to sit still. "But did you give twenty-five grand to Safe Start?"

Her eyebrow cocked. "You're right. It's none of your business."

"I know, and I'm sorry. I just worry about the people I care about. I'm lucky to make ridiculous money doing something I love, and I wouldn't want you struggling because you did this amazing, generous thing. If you need anything, just ask." He held her eye contact, his knee still bouncing. "And if you won't accept anything from me, can you just tell me you'll be okay? Then I'll never bring it up again, I swear."

She crossed her arms. "How do you even know? It was supposed to be anonymous."

"Well..." He swallowed. "When we were broken up, I went there to cut a check for what they needed. The lady said it was taken care of."

Charlotte touched her chest, her expression softening. "Tyler, that's so sweet." Her brows knitted. "But how'd you know it was me?"

"You just told me." He grinned as she playfully shoved his shoulder, his anxiety over the awkward conversation fading. "But I suspected it because I know you. There's nothing you wouldn't do to ensure they had what they needed. I know your band's doing well, but that's a lot of cash to drop. If you need anything, I can—"

She put a finger to his lips. "You can stop right there. I'll be fine. I promise. It's just money. And my band's fucking awesome, so I plan to make a whole lot more of it."

After the greed-fueled argument he'd just had with Amy, he was more confident than ever that he'd made the right choice. Charlotte moved onto his lap with her arms around his neck.

"So," Charlotte said, looking at the calendar, "July eighth, huh?"

He gave a nod. "July eighth."

"Your own personal Independence Day. We should get fireworks."

"And have a barbecue."

Charlotte's eyes lit up. "And get a keg. And decorate the house with streamers and shit. Maybe we can hire someone to make a piñata of Amy's head."

Tyler chuckled. "Nothing sweet ever came out of that woman's head."

"Good point. We'll fill it with cigarettes." Charlotte laughed into the crook of his neck.

"We could invite all our friends and party until the neighbors call the cops." Without warning, a wave of sadness spoiled the reverie. "You think Matty might come?"

"Of course. Even if I have to open a can of whoop ass and drag him here." She gently touched Tyler's face, her gaze warm with empathy. "I know it's hard, and I'm sorry you're hurting. But you know your brother. He has trouble processing big, ugly feelings. That's why after a breakup, he needs a few weeks to just be perma-stoned and zone out in video games. He shuts down and leans into that comforting break from the pain until he's strong enough to handle it. It just takes time."

The time and silence felt like torture. Whenever Tyler called him, the machine picked up. He'd gone to his apartment several times, but Matthew was never there. Or maybe he saw who it was and didn't answer.

"It's been almost a month! I know I fucked up, but I just want the chance to talk, to fix it." He lit another cigarette, exhaling loudly as his shoulders hunched. "What if we're never as close as we were because of what I did?"

Charlotte's hands cupped his face and held firm, forcing his attention to remain on her. "Don't even go there. Matty won't admit it yet, but he's mad at himself for what he said to you. He knows who you are. And he knows damn well you didn't touch Amy or take those drugs. And although I believe those mistakes are behind you, he still isn't convinced. He's terrified of losing you because he loves you so much. When I went over there yesterday, he said he still needs space, but every day he's closer to coming around. I promise."

"I'm glad he has you to help him through it." Tyler's eyes watered. He blinked hard to clear them. "I just miss him so much."

Charlotte pulled him closer, gently swaying together as if music were playing. After a few moments, the weight of his sadness lifted. He knew Matthew would forgive him when he was ready. Like with Charlotte, Tyler had to be patient and give him time.

"So," she said, "July eighth."

Tyler nodded. "We've got ourselves a party to plan."

44

Charlotte

"Yes, Sandra. Of course, you can bring your new girlfriend. Do you think I'd let homophobes into my house?"

Charlotte pointed at the phone and rolled her eyes at Tyler. He opened birthday cards and fan mail at the kitchen table while she chatted with Sandra. They'd stopped by his rented post office box that morning. Since they were basically living together, she planned to tell him he could forward his mail to her house to avoid the hassle. It seemed like every day brought a new milestone in their relationship, and even the small ones felt like a step closer to the life she'd always wanted.

"Christa's vegetarian," Sandra said. "Should we bring our own food?"

"I'll have veggie burgers too, don't stress. Not everyone appreciates cow blood on their plates."

Tyler laughed at the side of the conversation he could hear. He seemed happier that morning, even though Matthew still hadn't reached out. Charlotte invited him to the party, but he wouldn't commit to going. She was getting really tired of his stubbornness, and there was no way she'd let him miss it.

She'd called several times the last couple of days to convince him, but he hadn't answered. She figured he was either sick of her pushiness and dodging her or had work-related stuff to tend to. Or maybe he needed a few days away to clear his head. It wasn't unusual for Matthew to go MIA, but it'd be nice to know he was okay. Hopefully, he'd get his head out of his ass and show up to the party.

"Can we bring anything?" Sandra asked.

"Yeah, some CDs and your guitar. The entire neighborhood's getting a free show. The lucky fucks." Charlotte kissed her hand and blew it to Tyler.

He caught the air kiss, sprinkling it over his crotch.

Charlotte burst out laughing.

"What the hell's so funny?" Sandra asked.

"Nothing. My boyfriend's just a perv."

"I'm well aware." Sandra paused. "It's good to hear you happy again, Char."

"It's good to feel happy again." She smiled at a major source of that happiness, rifling through his mail in her kitchen. "Still down to watch Roxy?"

Charlotte had a long, crazy night planned for Tyler's birthday and didn't want to worry about Roxy getting fed on time or feeling lonely. So, she tapped Auntie Sandra for some overnight puppy-sitting.

"Been looking forward to it all week. Even bought some peanut butter dog biscuits and a microphone squeaky toy."

"Of course, you did." Charlotte laughed. "We'll bring her on our way out. Thanks again."

"Anytime. Oh, and tell Ty about the piñata. I can't wait until you see that thing."

"Yeah, I'll tell him. Bye, sweetie."

She hung up, tilting her head at Tyler. "You are such a distraction. It's a wonder I get anything done."

"What'd she want you to tell me?"

Charlotte slung a leg over his chair and straddled his lap. "Happy birthday. And that she actually made a piñata of Amy's head. I was kidding when I told her about the idea, but our Sandra's one crafty girl."

"Did she fill it with cigarettes?"

"Nope. Even better." She grinned. "A hundred tiny, plastic bottles of Freedom whiskey."

"How appropriate." He laughed against her lips and kissed her. "Have I ever told you how much I love Sandra?"

"Everybody loves Sandra. And I can't wait to meet the new girl she's dating." She picked up the birthday card from his aunt in Florida and chuckled at the picture of a wiener dog eating cake. "Okay, birthday boy, go get dressed for a night of surprises. We'll come home well-fed, a little drunk, and ready to get sweaty between the sheets."

"How about we get sweaty in your music room instead? I'd love to fuck you from behind while your Fenders are watching." He sank his teeth into her neck, and she shivered. As he peppered wet kisses along her jawline, his cock stiffened between her legs, nothing between them but a few pesky layers of cotton and denim.

"You're a very dirty boy, and I hope you never change."

"Nothing to worry about on that front."

Charlotte slid off his lap and onto her knees, settling between his thighs. She rubbed his growing erection through his jeans. "How about I just focus on your front for a while?"

Tyler ran his hand over the back of her head and grinned. "Happy birthday to me."

The phone rang, and they groaned at the interruption.

"Hold that thought." She stood, walking to answer it. "Sandra probably forgot to tell me her girlfriend's allergic to mushrooms or some shit."

"Hello?"

"Hey, Charlotte. It's Evan from High Notes. Have you heard from Matthew?"

Her brow furrowed in confusion. "Hey, Evan. I saw him on Friday but couldn't reach him over the weekend. Why?"

"He didn't show up to work yesterday and isn't answering his phone."

Her eyes darted to Tyler. "Weird."

Tyler walked over. "What's wrong?"

"I'll make some calls and go over there," she said. "Let me know if you hear anything."

She hung up, her heart stuttering as she dialed Matthew's number.

"He didn't show up for work yesterday."

Tyler frowned. "That's not like him."

The line rang until the machine picked up, Matt's upbeat tone telling his callers to *do it at the beep*. "Matty, call me back. Seriously. Evan said you weren't at work Monday and can't get ahold of you. And it's Tyler's birthday. Enough of the silent treatment already. Fucking call me."

Tyler took the phone and called his mother. She hadn't heard from Matthew in a week, but that wasn't unusual. They checked with Sandra next, and she hadn't heard from him in three days.

Tyler grabbed his keys. "We're going over there."

As they set the alarm and opened the door, the phone rang.

Charlotte rushed to answer it. "Hello?"

"Hey, Charlotte."

Her shoulders sank at the sound of Matt's voice. "Where the fuck have you been? Are you at home?"

Tyler disarmed the alarm and held his hand out. "Let me talk to him."

Charlotte shook her head, needing answers. She didn't want to risk him hanging up if Tyler jumped in.

"Uh, I'm fine." Matthew sounded anything but fine. He sounded tired or drunk, his speech slurred. "I need to be alone." There was a pause, a muffled sound like he was covering the mouthpiece. "Not home, but I'll be back tonight."

"Are you drunk?" She put a hand on her hip. "You picked a pretty stupid time to go on a bender. Tell me where you are. I'll come get you, and the three of us will sit and talk."

Another pause.

"I'm so sorry, Charlotte."

The line went dead.

"Fucking hell!" She slammed the phone. "Why's he being so goddamn stubborn?"

"You should've let me talk." Tyler locked the door and reset the alarm. "Is he okay?"

She sighed. "He sounded trashed. Probably drowning his sorrows somewhere. Drinking's usually the last phase of his brooding, so it's actually a good sign." She leaned into Tyler's chest, his arms pulling her close. "He said he'll be back tonight. Let's just enjoy your birthday and hook up with him tomorrow after he's slept it off."

When she looked at Tyler, he didn't seem convinced but accepted her plan with a weak shrug. Worry scratched at the back of her mind as she called Evan with the update.

He is okay, isn't he?

Matthew's shaky, slowed-down voice replayed in her head, making her question it.

But over the years of dealing with the stalker, she'd become an expert at overthinking, letting minor worries spiral into unnecessary panic. As stupid as it was, Matthew was an adult and had every right to hide out and get shitfaced. She wasn't about to let her paranoia spoil Tyler's birthday.

Everything would be okay. Matthew would be home that night. The next day, she'd make sure he gave Tyler a chance to make amends so their energy could be directed where it belonged—at finding the person responsible for the notes. Then, they could finally be free of the dark cloud hanging over all their heads.

⸻◦⸻

Tyler and Charlotte's taxi pulled up to her curb just after two in the morning. She'd surprised him with dinner at an incredible Japanese restaurant, a punk show at the Crystal Ballroom, and they topped off the night with cocktails on a rooftop bar overlooking the rivers, bridges, and city lights of downtown. The taxi was wise since they'd tossed back saki bombs like they were water. They shuffled up Charlotte's driveway, arms around each other for support.

As she fumbled with her keys, Tyler breathed hot saki-scented breath in her ear. "I wonder how fast I can rip your clothes off."

Charlotte got the door open. "Not nearly fast enough."

She devoured his mouth, only stopping when the alarm's beeping started to trigger a headache. She punched in the codes while Tyler locked the deadbolt.

"But first, it's present time." Charlotte pulled a large, wrapped box from the hall closet.

"Thanks, baby. But you didn't need to get me anything."

She brushed him off. "Just open it."

He removed the ribbon, tearing through the silver and black paper. When Tyler opened the box and peered inside, he collapsed into a kitchen chair. "How did you..."

She pulled his dad's army jacket from the box, holding it up. "Magdalena, the seamstress who makes my corsets for shows, patched it. It's not exactly like before, but at least you can wear it again. Do you like it?"

"Charlotte..." His eyes shined as he stared at the jacket. Small squares of matching green fabric were expertly stitched behind each hole. You could still see the damage if you looked closely enough, but mostly, it looked whole again. "I love it. It's perfect."

"Happy birthday." She bent at the waist for a quick kiss. "I'm going to freshen up. Meet me in the music room wearing nothing but a smile."

"Music to my ears." They laughed at his dumb joke, Tyler getting to his feet.

As they headed in separate directions, someone knocked on the side door. They turned to each other, the spark of fear in his eyes stoking hers.

She took a few slow steps toward the door.

"Wait!" he whispered.

She froze.

Charlotte watched the muscles in his jaw flex as he slowly made his way over.

The knocking returned, louder and more insistent.

Tyler looked through the peephole, and a strangled cry cracked in his throat.

"Oh, my god." He flipped the deadbolt, swinging the door wide.

Matthew took a wobbly step through the doorway, wearing an expression she couldn't decipher. Regret, maybe. Or... fear?

Tyler crashed into his brother, hugging him tightly as Charlotte joined in. The alarm beeped, and she went to the control panel, punching in the code to disarm it.

She smacked Matthew's arm. "Where the hell have you been? We were worried about you."

"I'm so sorry," Matthew sputtered.

He thrust forward as if shoved from behind, the three of them stumbling.

Two figures entered the room wearing black coats and gloves.

Rafael, the hulking mass of spray-tanned muscle, lurked behind his scarlet-haired master like the obedient lap dog he was.

In his right hand was a gun—aimed at Tyler's head.

"What the fuck is this?" Tyler's voice quivered, his wide eyes darting between the intruders.

Rafael flashed a grin at Amy. "You'll find out soon enough."

The cold blankness in his stare had alarm bells screaming in Charlotte's head. She tried to put pieces together that would answer Tyler's question, but it all seemed too impossible to make sense.

Amy kicked the door closed, sliding the lock into place as she grinned like a predator cornering her prey. "Look at us all back together again."

Charlotte couldn't speak. Shock warred with the alcohol buzz, the room's edges spinning and blurring. The only thing in sharp focus was the gun pointed at the man she loved.

It can't be real.

The gun, the situation... This had to be a nightmare, and she needed to wake the fuck up.

Movement caught her eye as Matthew dropped to his knees, clutching his stomach.

"Matty, are you okay?" Tyler stepped closer before Rafael shoved him away, his back slamming against the kitchen wall so hard the windows rattled.

Charlotte stopped breathing. If the gun was fake—maybe a prop Amy swiped from a movie set—they could rush them. Catch them off guard. Get out and get help.

"Don't fucking move!" Rafael roared at Tyler. His thumb jerked, shifting the gun's safety to red with a metallic click.

Charlotte swallowed. A fake gun wouldn't have a safety.

Her eyes locked with Tyler's, adrenaline flaring his pupils as the same realization probably struck him.

The gun was real.

"What the fuck are you doing, Amy?" Tyler's chest shook with quick, panicked breaths.

Charlotte wanted to reach for him or comfort Matthew, but any movement was too risky. Her eyes stayed on Tyler, willing him to read her mind.

They just want to scare us.

With everything she had, she hoped that was true.

Play along until we can fight or run.

Then she saw it—a way out.

The red panic button on the alarm panel glowed in her periphery.

It could be our only chance.

With Amy and Rafael's attention on Tyler, she inched toward it.

Amy yanked the gun from Rafael, pressing it to Tyler's forehead.

Charlotte froze.

"Touch that panic button or reach for a phone or try anything stupid," Amy said, "and he'll be dead before you can blink those pretty brown eyes."

Charlotte slowly, carefully raised her shaking hands in surrender. "Don't hurt him."

"Don't worry." Amy smiled, her white teeth gleaming under the fluorescent lights. "What I have planned for the three of you won't hurt long at all."

45

Tyler

"Happy birthday, by the way. Though, I guess I'm a little late. I'm sure you'll forgive me." Amy's fingernails grazed Tyler's cheek, and he jerked his head back. If his wrists weren't bound behind him with a zip tie, he would've slapped her hand away. She shifted her attention to Charlotte, shivering on her bedroom floor between Tyler and Matthew. "Forgiveness is a running theme around here, isn't it, Charlotte?"

All their backs were against the wall, hands tied behind them. Charlotte's head rested on Matt's shoulder, trying to comfort him while she must've been just as scared.

"Go fuck yourself and die, you psychotic cuntrag." Charlotte spat at Amy's feet.

"I think she's gone feral, Tyler." Amy wiped her shoe on the carpet before glaring at Charlotte. "You going to start foaming at the mouth, sweetie pie? Maybe we should muzzle her, Raf."

He laughed darkly, grabbing his crotch. "I've got something to muzzle her with."

"Stay away from her, motherfucker!" Tyler struggled to stand until Rafael's broad steps brought the gun to his cheek. "If either of you touch her, I swear you're fucking dead." Tyler spoke through gritted teeth as he settled back against the wall.

"Like this?" Amy's foot swung back and forward, nailing Charlotte's shin with the tip of her high-heeled boot. Charlotte grunted, the ankle of her opposite leg rubbing at the spot.

"Stop!" Tyler tried to push up again, but a hand on his wrist stopped him. It was Charlotte's, and it fell away as soon as he settled.

"I'm fine," she said, still rubbing her shin. "Don't kick the hornet's nest."

Amy moved closer, looming over them like a shadow. "You started kicking this hornet's nest years ago, and you're all about to feel the stings." She wiggled her shoulders. "Ooh, that was a good line. I should write a screenplay."

"Get away from her, Amy." Tyler didn't recognize his own voice, the growling rasp sounding more animal than man. He shifted and twisted his wrists, desperately trying to escape the binds, his skin burning with the efforts.

Rafael huffed. "I could shoot her right now, and there's not a damn thing you can do about it, so just sit there and shut up, pretty boy."

Amy removed her black hooded coat, setting it on the bed with a dramatic flourish. Always the actress, even while threatening homicide. "Not quite yet, sweetheart, but I appreciate your enthusiasm."

The gun looked real, but Tyler still wasn't sure what this was.

Had she finally snapped?

Were their threats genuine or just a sick, desperate act of extortion? A last-ditch effort to scare him into giving her money before the clock ran out and their divorce was finalized.

In case the danger was real, he scanned the room, searching for weapons.

Charlotte's framed records could be broken, and he could use the glass. He could swing the bedside lamp against a skull. He could stab an eye socket or throat with the ballpoint pen on her dresser. Of course, he'd have to get out of the zip tie first. If only he hadn't left his knife in the living room.

Imagining the reality of hurting someone—the sounds of breaking bones or tearing flesh, the blood on his hands—made bile creep up his throat. It went entirely against his nature to injure or possibly even kill another human being.

But he'd do *anything* to keep Charlotte and his brother safe.

There was always therapy for the fallout.

"What's the plan here?" Tyler asked. "There's no way to end this without you and Rafael in prison."

"Aww... You really are clueless. It was one of the things I loved best about you. It's kind of adorable." Amy sat on Charlotte's bed and crossed her legs. "I think we'll be just fine. Matthew, on the other hand... He's not looking so hot."

Tyler turned to his brother, catching details he'd missed in the kitchen. His face was pale and gaunt. He looked like he'd lost ten pounds he didn't have to lose. His eyes darted around, landing on nothing. Judging by his greasy, unkempt hair, he hadn't showered in days.

Matty, where the hell have you been?

"You're awfully quiet, Matthew," Amy taunted. "I hope Rafael didn't hurt you too badly when we picked you up. He can play a little rough sometimes."

A tear slid down Matthew's cheek, and he buried his face in his knees.

Charlotte leaned against him, whispering reassuring words in his ear. "We'll be okay, Matty. Just hang in there. We love you."

"Give it a rest, Mother Theresa." Amy's eyes rolled.

Charlotte turned, shooting a worried glance at Tyler.

"What the fuck did you psychos do to my brother?" Tyler shifted in his seat.

"He never liked me much." Amy stood beside Matthew, making him tremble. "Tried to talk you out of marrying me. Treated me like shit." She put her shoe on Matthew's hip and shoved. He fell limply against Charlotte's side.

"Leave him alone." Tyler stared down the dark barrel of the gun. "I'm warning you."

"You're all done calling the shots," Amy shouted. "You think you can leave me, take my homes, ruin my clothes, make me bankrupt, and I'm going to just lie back and take it?" She touched the tightly wound knot of scarlet hair at the top of her head. "Kind of like you did in your hotel room, am I right? I know how much you love waking up with my lips wrapped around your cock."

Tyler's eyes squeezed shut. *Fuck.*

Charlotte's head jerked. "What the hell is she talking about?"

"Don't listen to her." He grabbed for Charlotte's hand but couldn't reach it.

"Oh, you didn't tell her?" Amy's tongue clicked against her teeth. "You really shouldn't keep secrets, Tyler."

He held his attention on Charlotte. "When she broke into my room, I was asleep, and she... I can't even say it."

"I slid his cock down my throat." Amy crouched in front of him, slowly licking her lips. She obviously meant it to be sexy, but she looked more like a predator cleaning off blood from its latest meal. "There. Finished your thought for you."

Charlotte buried her face in Matt's shoulder and wept.

"I bolted from the bed the second I saw her." Tyler touched his forehead to her back, leaning in. "I was so tired, I thought she was you. It wasn't my fault."

"You're a monster!" Charlotte screamed.

Tyler's fought harder to yank his wrists apart, to hold her. "Charlotte, I didn't—"

"Not you, Tyler." Her furious eyes locked on Amy. "*Her.*"

"You took what's mine. It's only fair I got a taste." Amy sat back on the bed, her hands splayed behind her.

"You don't own him, psycho!" Charlotte pounded the wall with her fists. "And you never owned me. But because you're a spoiled fucking tantrum-throwing brat, you tried to ruin our lives when we proved it."

"Charlotte..." Tyler warned, hoping she'd think before saying anything else that might provoke Amy.

"I bet it made you crazy that I succeeded without you," she continued. "That's why you sent the notes, right?"

Amy laughed, her head falling back. "I had nothing to do with that. I respect the sender's dedication to torturing you all those years, and I wished I'd thought of it first, but it wasn't me."

Charlotte and Tyler exchanged a baffled look.

"It was me." Rafael grinned with obvious pride, all eyes landing on him. The hand holding the gun dropped to his side. "I sent them. The flowers, too."

"You sick fucking asshole!" Tyler seethed, his fists clenching with the urge to shatter every bone in Rafael's face.

"You?!" Charlotte sputtered, her back stiffening. "Why would you do that? I never—"

"*You hurt Amy.*" The rage in his voice, aimed straight at Charlotte along with the gun, made the skin on the back of Tyler's neck prickle. A heightened sense of danger descended on the room like a poisonous fog. "You left her band, it fell apart, and while this asshole was flying around the world, I was the one holding her, wiping her tears."

"Sticking straws in her nose," Tyler muttered.

Rafael hovered over Tyler, his fist shaking. "And instead of being loyal to your wife like a real man, you screwed around with this fucking traitor."

Charlotte thrust her foot into Rafael's kneecap, and he stumbled backward, catching himself on the edge of the dresser.

Tyler gasped, tugging at her shirt for her to stay put while getting ready to throw himself in front of her if Rafael tried to retaliate.

"That the best you got?" Rafael lifted his pant leg to assess any damage, his lips twitching in amusement. "You're as weak as Amy said you were. Made you an easy target all these years."

"I thought someone was going to rape me! Or kill me!"

"The night's still young." Rafael grinned, slowly trailing the gun barrel down the side of her face. She stilled.

Tyler shifted to wedge between them, stopping when cold metal touched his temple. If this was just a ruse to empty his pockets, their act was pretty damn convincing.

"Don't. Move." Rafael pressed harder until they sat back against the wall.

Tyler breathed a heavy sigh. "How much?"

"How much what?" Amy asked, arching an eyebrow.

"How much of my fucking money will it take to end this? I know it's what you want, so cut the ridiculous theatrics and tell me the number."

Before Amy could respond, Charlotte interrupted.

"I went to therapy for months! And got a goddamn alarm system, put bars on my windows like I was living in a prison."

Amy squealed with joy, clapping and grinning like she was getting off on Charlotte's misery. She winked at Rafael. "Sweetest thing anyone's ever done for me."

Tyler scoffed. "I didn't realize your love language was Acts of Psychopathy."

"You knew the whole time it was him and said *nothing*?" Charlotte shouted at Amy, her cheeks flaming.

"Not the whole time." Amy shrugged. "But when he told me, I was so touched, I blew him in our hot tub while Tyler was away. Again."

Tyler laughed, the edge of his sanity stretched to the limit. "Jesus Fucking Christ. You two freaks deserve each other."

"And you three deserve everything coming to you." Amy pushed off the bed.

As the revelations sunk in, more puzzle pieces fit into place. Rafael must've pretended to be the reporter who lured Charlotte away while he and Sandra ran around terrified. They sabotaged the hard work Charlotte and her band put into planning the benefit album and canceled show. Amy's thirst for revenge was as boundless as her greed.

There was one final suspicion he had to put to rest.

"You threw the brick." Tyler looked to Rafael for confirmation.

"Nope." Rafael smirked, clearly pleased with himself. "The kid I paid five hundred bucks to do it while we were in L.A. did. Gave us the perfect alibi. If he hadn't bragged to his buddy, he'd have been in the clear, but he's under eighteen anyway, so they let him walk."

Charlotte whimpered, her face paling. "You hired a *kid* to kill me?"

"Not quite," Amy said. "Kid or not, murder would've meant jail time, and he might've ratted Raf out to save his own ass. So, we went with just a piece of brick instead of the whole thing. Enough to scare and maybe do some damage." She patted Rafael's solid chest before glancing at Charlotte. "I must say, I was disappointed you didn't end up with a few scars across that pretty face."

Charlotte put her lips to Tyler's ear and whispered, "My gun's under the bed."

Amy charged, backhanding Charlotte hard. "No secrets!"

Rafael pressed the gun to her reddening cheek, making Tyler freeze.

"Goddamn you, Amy!" Tyler's blood boiled beneath his skin. "I'm the one you're mad at. Leave them out of this!"

Amy touched her forehead to his. "What did she say to you, Tyler?" He snapped his head to the side, repulsed by everything about the woman he once pledged his life to.

Charlotte spoke before he could think. "I told him I love him. And I'm a hell of a lot better at showing it than you ever were."

"Mmhm. That was convincing." Amy remained crouched at their eye level. "Just in case anyone intends to pull some heroic bullshit, we'll have to speed things up."

Matthew's head raised, his eyes lost and hazy. "What are you gonna do, Amy? Jus' let them go. If you need someone to play your sick games with, take me."

"No!" Tyler looked at his brother. "We're all getting out of this, Matty."

"There it is." Amy did a slow clap. "An impressive display of heroic bullshit. I called it, didn't I, Raf?"

Rafael shifted his stance. "Right as always."

"So, here's the plan, kids." Amy's eyes flickered between the three people on the floor. "We're going to do you all a favor tonight, though I doubt you'll view it that way."

She stood, checking her makeup in the wall mirror. "Ever heard of the '27 Club'?"

"The televangelist bullshit on channel six?" Charlotte's brows drew together.

Amy's eyes rolled. "Ugh. You're so dim. The '27 Club' refers to all the dead rock stars who lived fast, died young, and left great-looking corpses. We're talking real icons here. Janis, Jim, Jimi, Kurt—some of the most talented musicians to ever walk the earth get to live on in infamy long after their lights were prematurely snuffed out."

Tyler didn't know exactly where this was going, but the danger was real. These two were batshit crazy, unpredictable, and desperate. The demented gleam in her eye meant he had to do everything possible to disrupt whatever they had planned.

Or die trying.

"You're out of your goddamn mind, Amy." Tyler's voice cracked. He swallowed hard, holding back the stinging bile rising in his throat. "Rafael, you can stop this."

"Shh... It'll all be over soon." Amy petted Tyler's hair like a dog. "Our lucky boy, Tyler, just turned twenty-seven, and tonight, he'll be immortalized. If you ask me... he'll leave the best-looking corpse of them all."

"Please stop!" Tears streamed down Charlotte's face. "If this is just a game you're trying to scare us with, mission accomplished. We're fucking terrified. Let us go, and we won't tell anyone."

"This is no game, Charlotte," Amy said. "It's a work of art. You get to die beside Tyler on the bed. A tragically beautiful tale for the ages. Like Romeo and fucking Juliet." She winked. "With a rock-and-roll twist."

Tyler laughed, tears spilling from beneath his eyelids.

Amy kicked him in the ribs, pain exploding as the wind was knocked out of him. "What the hell is so funny?"

He took a moment to catch his breath, his hands desperate to clutch where it hurt. "You're not doing this to be the mastermind behind some tragic, theatrical tableau. You know if I'm dead before they finalize the divorce, our prenup is void. You get everything. You're not an artist. You're a greedy cunt."

That earned Tyler another, harder kick in the same spot, and he doubled over, fiery waves of sharp, searing pain radiating through his side. He barely registered Charlotte's bound hands touching his arm, trying to soothe him as he struggled to breathe.

"I won't lie; the money was the motivating factor," Amy said, unfazed, checking her manicure. "And revenge, of course. Hell hath no fury and all that jazz. But the scene I'm creating *will* be a damn masterpiece. Plus, I get to be the grieving widow everyone will want to talk to. That'll put those acting lessons to good use. I see interviews, movies, world tours, book deals, and so much more in my wildly successful future. I guess you helped get my career back on track after all, sweetheart."

Tyler was sure his ribs were cracked. Every breath sent burning spikes of pain shooting across his side. He racked his brain for a way out that wouldn't get anyone else hurt or killed.

"So, we have Tyler's part and Charlotte's part…" Amy looked at Matthew. He was sobbing into his knees, snot running down his face. "You didn't think I'd forget about you, did you? You're here because, for the first time in your pathetic life, you'll be important. Your name will be splashed all over the headlines, too. You'll even be in history books. The cool ones, anyway. Right alongside Mark David Chapman."

Matthew turned away from Charlotte, vomiting on the carpet. The acrid smell permeated the air. It killed Tyler to see his brother suffer while he sat a few feet away, completely helpless. He kept fighting the thin strip of plastic over his raw, probably bloody wrists, every movement sending a fresh wave of fiery pain through his ribs.

"Let them go!" Matthew wiped his mouth on his shoulder.

"Don't you want to know what role you get to play?" Amy lowered her head to hover above Matthew's. "You get to kill Romeo and Juliet."

46

Charlotte

"We can do this the easy way or the hard way, Charlotte. What's it going to be?"

Amy took the gun, holding it to Charlotte's temple while Rafael watched the two men, his arms crossed over his chest like a swollen nightclub bouncer.

"Easy way." As instructed, Charlotte pushed off the wall and sat on the bed. She would've given anything to beat the deranged smile off Amy's face, but if they had any chance of getting out alive, she had to play along.

Amy pointed the gun at Tyler. "Now go over to her, Loverboy, and don't talk or move a muscle. We have to get your brother set up for his big finish."

Charlotte didn't like the sound of that. They were running out of time.

She needed to disrupt their plans and get Tyler and Matthew to a hospital. But how?

"Let them go, and you can have everything," Tyler said.

It was smart to play into her greed, but Charlotte didn't like that he said *them* instead of *us*. She held her breath, waiting for Amy's response.

"They won't call the cops," he continued. "It'll be like this never happened."

"I said don't talk." Amy poked his injured ribs. "That ship's sailed, my dear."

He winced, air hissing through his teeth as he walked to the bed and sat beside Charlotte. To her surprise, Amy pulled scissors from her pocket and snipped his zip tie.

"All done with these," she said, Charlotte's hands snapping free as her tie was cut. "But try anything funny, and I'll let Raf play with you for a while before I shoot you both in the head."

Tyler's wrists and hands were scraped and bloody, showing how hard he'd tried to break free. To save her and his brother. Because she knew damn well whatever he planned to do if he'd broken loose, it would've been for them. He wouldn't have thought twice about sacrificing himself to keep them safe. She chanced reaching for his hand, lacing their fingers together. Amy just rolled her eyes.

Rafael took the scissors, cutting Matthew's tie. "Give it to him now?"

"Yes."

"Give him what?" The terror in Tyler's voice made Charlotte squeeze his hand.

She felt helpless as Rafael loomed over Matthew, tears streaming to her chin. They needed to end this. Fast.

Hang in there, Matty.

Amy ignored the question as her gaze and the gun shifted between Tyler and Charlotte on the bed and Matthew on the floor.

Whenever Amy's attention was on Matthew, Charlotte inched their joined hands closer to the bed's center. When she reached the spot, she stopped, her fingers forming a gun outside Amy's view. Her eyes flashed to Tyler's before she stared down wide-eyed, trying to tell him exactly where the gun was. The next time Amy looked away, he nodded.

Good.

Charlotte watched as his eyes flitted around the room before settling on the empty Southern Comfort bottle on the bedside table. She followed his line of sight, squeezing his hand when she understood.

Rafael pulled something from his pocket. It looked like a cloth napkin wrapped around an object the size and shape of a pencil. He dropped the cloth to reveal a hypodermic needle.

Charlotte shrieked, her hand clenching around Tyler's. "What's in the needle, Amy?"

Rafael grabbed hold of Matthew's arm, rolling up his sleeve.

"Stop!" Tyler sobbed, flinching in obvious pain, a hand curled against his side. "If you need revenge, just kill me. Shoot me, chop me into a million pieces, whatever you want. *Please*, Amy. Let them go!"

Charlotte gasped, horrified by his words and the image they painted. "Tyler, stop!"

Amy faced them with the gun. "And leave them out of the fun? Not a chance."

Rafael tied rubber tubing tightly around Matthew's bicep without a struggle, all the fight drained from him.

Charlotte screamed, and Amy slapped her again.

As Tyler held Charlotte to his side, she touched her stinging cheek, the taste of blood on her tongue. She stared at Amy, her vision going red.

She would make that bitch bleed for what she did to them.

"Stay quiet," Amy said, "or I'll cut your precious vocal cords."

The needle pierced Matthew's skin, and Rafael pushed the plunger down.

Charlotte covered her mouth to keep silent, the room blurring behind her tears.

"To answer your question, Charlotte, it's heroin," Amy said. "Really good shit. Better than anything your trailer trash mother used, I'm sure."

Charlotte choked on the scream lodged in her throat. Tyler squeezed her hand, tears trailing his cheeks as they stared helplessly at Matthew.

"This is getting exciting!" Amy wiggled her hips. "Let's get everyone to their places."

Rafael touched Amy's arm. "He's breathing but out cold."

Matthew lay in a heap on the floor, drool sliding out of his mouth.

"We thought that might happen." Amy shrugged it off. "No biggie. We'll get the gunshot residue on his hands after the deed is done. Now, Charlotte, lie on the bed facing Tyler, and he'll face you."

Matthew made a choking sound, turning everyone's heads. White foam bubbled from his mouth, misting in the air as his lungs rattled with a barrage of harsh, wet coughs.

Charlotte ignored Amy's order, her shoulders quaking. "Help him! Please, Amy! Don't let him die like that."

Amy laughed, icy blankness settling into her stare. "I won't. The bullet will kill him long before the smack does. After Raf shoots both of you, he'll wipe the gun and put Matthew's prints all over it. It'll look like he was in love with Charlotte and killed you for breaking his heart. And Raf planted evidence in Matthew's shitty apartment to support it. Then, after Matthew offs the star-crossed lovers, he shoots himself up for courage before putting a bullet in his head. With a little help, of course." She winked at Rafael. "The media will eat it up! Murder-suicides are so in style right now."

It only took a split second.

Less than the blink of an eye.

Amy was so focused on boasting about her plan that she lowered the gun. Rafael was busy placing drug paraphernalia around Matthew.

Tyler looked at Charlotte, and he mouthed a single word:

Now.

He grabbed the Southern Comfort bottle and swung hard, knocking the side of Amy's head with a thud. The gun flew from her hands, and he leaped to the ground to retrieve it. At the same time, Charlotte rolled onto the floor, feeling under the bed until the metal was in her hands.

Charlotte raised her gun, pulling the trigger as Rafael charged. Two loud pops exploded, and he dropped like a bag of rocks, landing face down on the bed. As Amy wobbled to her feet, she let out an angry scream, hurling herself at Charlotte.

The gun went off again.

Amy grunted and fell onto her side, propped against Rafael. She touched her stomach and slowly lifted her hand. Blood coated her palm and dripped from her fingertips—the shade a perfect match to the hair on her head.

"You fucking shot me!" Amy still had murder in her eyes as she struggled to get at Charlotte. Failing, she collapsed onto her back, wincing in pain.

"You're goddamn right I did. And if you move, I'll do it again." Charlotte kept the gun aimed between Amy's wild hazel eyes. "Tyler, call 9-1-1."

Amy's gaze skittered around the room like she was a caged animal looking for a vulnerable spot in its enclosure to escape through.

Charlotte shook her head. "Don't bother looking for a way out. It's over. You're leaving in handcuffs or a body bag, depending on where that bullet hit and if I decide to give you another one."

Tyler grabbed the bedroom phone in her periphery while keeping Amy's gun leveled at her head.

"We need an ambulance and police. Six forty-five Prescott. A heroin overdose and gunshot wounds. Hurry!"

When Tyler hung up, Charlotte chanced a glance at Matthew.

He still wasn't moving. Neither was Rafael.

"Can you hear me, Matty?" Tyler shouted, receiving only silence. "We can't lose him, Charlotte."

"They'll save him, Ty." Her words sounded unsteady and unconvincing.

Amy groaned, blood from her wound spreading across the back of Rafael's shirt and the comforter beneath their bodies. "He's going to die. That smack is ninety percent pure. He won't survive it."

Tyler sobbed above his unconscious brother, the sound making tears sting her eyes.

"Stay with me, Ty," Charlotte said. "She's lying. The EMTs will bring naloxone and it'll save him."

Amy made a strangled, choking sound in the back of her throat. "It didn't save your mommy."

Charlotte slapped her hard, sending a spray of blood onto the wall behind the bed. "Final warning, bitch. I'd rather see your crazy ass rot in prison but push me again, and I'll shoot you in the head."

The sound of sirens grew louder, closer.

Someone banged on the front door.

"Let them in, Tyler," Charlotte said. "I've got this."

Her hands were steady as panic and terror morphed into determination.

She was getting out of this alive with the men she loved.

Tyler hesitated before bolting from the room.

"Was it worth it?" Her eyes locked with Amy's. "Your friend's dead, and you're going to prison. All because Tyler left you?"

Amy's face was smeared with blood, and all color had drained from her skin. She looked like a vampire at feeding time. "That's not the only reason, and you know it," she hissed, rage flaming in her eyes. "You remember the night on the rooftop. The night I kicked you out of the band. The hurtful shit you said... That's how fucking long you've had it coming."

Charlotte sucked in a breath, shocked by the admission.

Greed, jealousy, pride—deadly sins had fueled the hatred that brought them all to that moment.

She'd been naïve to think Amy ever cared about her. Someone who held a grudge like that, driven by a need to inflict pain, was incapable.

"You know what tonight and that night have in common?" Charlotte pressed the barrel to Amy's bloodied temple. "You underestimated me."

A stream of police officers rushed in, weapons in hand, all pointed at Charlotte.

"Put the gun down!"

Charlotte set it in her lap, slowly raising her hands. "Our friend needs naloxone right now!"

When an officer gave the okay, EMTs entered and got to work on Matthew, Amy, and Rafael.

Charlotte heard one of them mumble, "Is that Amy Carey?"

The ghost of a smile touched Amy's bloody lips. "An adoring fan. Perfect."

She went limp, her vacant stare fixed on the ceiling. When her hands came to rest at her sides, her eyes slid shut.

Even among the gore and chaos, Charlotte finally felt a sense of peace.

47

Tyler

After Tyler was treated for two rib fractures and they'd given their statements to the police, he and Charlotte weaved through the maze of elevators and hallways toward Matthew's hospital room. She was tucked against his uninjured side, and he pressed an ice pack to the other as they walked.

He hadn't seen his brother since a nurse wheeled him off for tests hours before. Charlotte insisted Tyler take care of his injuries while they waited. Since hers were few and not serious, she'd been their go-between, gathering info from doctors and nurses and sharing updates. He'd had to say Charlotte was his wife and Matt's sister-in-law since only family was allowed that information.

After Amy, just the thought of marriage should've made him run screaming, but with Charlotte, it didn't. After almost dying together, the thought of living together, forever, felt good and right. As if surviving the trauma by each other's side had fused them in a way that could never be undone.

Tyler and Matthew rode over in the same ambulance, Tyler jumping in despite his injury, refusing to leave his brother's side until he was sure he'd make it. When the naloxone did its job, and Matthew's eyes slowly opened, Tyler wept with relief. He listened as Matthew described fragmented memories of the hell Amy and Rafael put him through.

They'd staked out the brewery parking lot, snatching him as he walked to his car. He'd spent three days trapped in Rafael's basement, chained to a radiator, in a drug-induced haze. He had no idea what they slipped into the water they forced him to drink, but it made him unable to speak or fight, his brain a muddled mess. They stopped drugging him the morning of the attack, probably because an autopsy would show he was too incapacitated to commit the double murder and shoot himself if they hadn't.

Imagining the gruesome crime scene Amy planned to create made Tyler shudder.

They'd also stolen Matthew's apartment keys, planting evidence that framed Matthew as Charlotte's stalker—the pink notepaper, black ribbon, and can of paint used on the flowers. That's what Rafael was doing when Charlotte called the day before. He heard the message as she left it and quickly informed Amy. She made Matthew call Charlotte right back with a gun to his head to keep her from stopping by or otherwise interfering with their plans. He had no choice but to play along, not knowing how horrific their endgame was.

Rafael also left things to make the cops believe Matthew was obsessed with Charlotte, the worst of which was a collage of photos she obviously didn't know were being taken. He'd shown it to Matthew before planting it, obviously proud of his handiwork. It included candid shots of Charlotte running errands, walking Roxy with Sandra, and even one of her and Tyler having lunch at The River Maiden snapped minutes before their first kiss. If Tyler and Charlotte were seen behind that boathouse, he figured that kiss and everything that followed had earned them all bullets to the head.

Well, almost.

Hearing his brother recounting those horrors was painful, but he seemed relieved when it was all out. Tyler was just glad to be there for support. Neither of them mentioned the fight at his hotel or their separation. It didn't matter anymore. Because when it came down to it, they'd been willing to give their lives for each other. And for Charlotte. They'd survived all their hardest days together, and the healing ahead would be done the same way.

"Ready?" Charlotte asked when they reached Matt's door. The skin around her eye was a deep shade of purple, the lid red and swollen. The sound of Amy's hand striking her wouldn't leave him. Neither would the image of a gun pressed to her cheek.

But it could've been a lot worse.

Tyler brushed his lips against hers before kissing her gently. "I love you."

"I love you too." She kissed him back, lingering for a breath. "So fucking much."

He looked forward to getting her alone, finally relaxing with her safe in his arms, but now, he needed to see his brother. They opened the door, smiling together when they saw Matt—weak, exhausted, and severely dehydrated but alive and on the mend.

She walked to the bed and gently slipped her arms around his shoulders.

Tyler was surprised to see their mother asleep in a chair in the corner. She must've arrived when they were talking to the cops. Her usually perfect hair was loose and wild around her shoulders, and her face was pale and makeup-free. She was dressed more casually than he'd seen her in years with black leggings, sneakers, and an oversized purple and gold University of Washington sweatshirt that belonged to their father.

"You look much better," Charlotte whispered, kissing Matt's cheek before sitting on the bed beside him. "That cute blonde nurse is taking great care of you."

Matthew chuckled. "Her name's Jessica. Would it be weird to ask for someone's number after they've inserted your catheter?"

They all laughed quietly, Tyler glancing at his mom to make sure she wasn't disturbed.

"When did she get here?" He pulled the ice pack from his ribs, setting it down.

"Few hours ago." Matthew jerked his head at Charlotte. "How's your leg?"

She was treated for minor bruising where Amy kicked her and the black eye was checked, ruling out permanent damage. Otherwise, she was okay. Physically, at least. She was lucky to get out relatively unscathed, but the emotional toll would probably be harder to repair than any broken bone would've been.

"Oh, please," she scoffed. "I got off light. How are you?"

"Sore and spaced-out but breathing."

Tyler's gaze dropped to the needle mark in the crook of his arm—a pink and plum splotch that triggered a terrible flash from the nightmare they'd been through.

He thought his brother was dead.

He hoped to never experience fear like that again.

And it hammered home the gravity of the mistake he'd made after Jim's funeral when Matthew found Tyler fading and unresponsive on the floor. He was more certain than ever that he'd never put someone he loved through that kind of hell again.

"I can't believe people take that shit on purpose," Matthew said.

Tyler felt their eyes slide to him and fall away, and he looked forward to the day when any lingering doubts about his history with drugs would be buried in the past.

He took a folded blanket from the foot of the bed and covered his mother. She startled.

"Tyler?" She sat up, rubbing her eyes. "Everything okay?" Her eyes darted to Matthew, exhaling when she saw him.

"Yeah, Mom," Tyler said. "All good."

She got up, touching Matthew's forehead. "You feel warm. When did they check your temperature last?"

"Like an hour ago." Matthew grinned, obviously pleased to have her fuss over him. "I'm okay."

She poured a glass of water from the pitcher beside the bed, handing it to Matthew. He chuckled softly and took it, downing the whole thing before giving her the empty cup.

"You should be resting too, young man." She handed Tyler his ice pack. "And using this."

He slowly sank into a chair beside the bed, holding the ice against his side. "Happy?" He winced as he settled against the back of the chair. The drugs he was given made the pain manageable, but it still hurt to take a breath and move around. He reached out, carefully taking his brother's hand, avoiding the IV line taped to the back.

"Hi, I'm Charlotte," she said with an awkward wave.

"Nice to finally meet you, dear. I'm Jenna. I'll forgive my boys for their rudeness, considering the circumstances."

"Can I get you some coffee or a sandwich?" Charlotte asked, suddenly looking uncomfortable. "I was just about to raid the cafeteria."

"I'm good, thanks. Heard a lot about you. From both my boys."

"I've..." Charlotte rubbed the back of her neck. "Heard a lot about you, too."

"I'm sure. Hopefully, some of it was good." She turned to Tyler. "You were right, son. She's a stunner. Good for you."

"Thanks." Charlotte slid off the bed. "I'm going to head down. You guys want anything?"

"I'd love a coffee." Tyler started to push off the arm of his chair to stand, a sharp spike of pain making him suck air through his teeth. "I'll come with you."

"No, stay and visit. And rest." Charlotte kissed his forehead. "If my dad comes while I'm gone, tell him to wait here. I'll be quick."

Jenna approached Charlotte, catching her off guard with a hug she didn't return. "Thank you for saving my boys." Her voice broke with emotion. "What you did..." She pulled back, her glossy eyes searching Charlotte's. "It couldn't have been easy."

"They would've done the same for me." Charlotte stepped back. "We've always had each other's backs. It's what you do for people you love."

"Charlotte..."

"It's okay, Tyler." His mom waved him off. "If that was a dig at me, I deserve it."

"No, I'm sorry." Charlotte scrubbed her face, exhaustion rolling off her in waves. "It's the wrong time. My emotions are frayed."

"Don't apologize," Jenna said. "We've all made mistakes. I'm grateful my boys are learning to forgive me, and I'm trying to forgive myself. Since we'll be in each other's lives, maybe someday, I'll earn forgiveness from you, too."

Charlotte nodded, her tight expression softening. "We're throwing Tyler a big divorce party on the eighth. You should come."

Jenna smiled. "I appreciate the invite. But as much as I'd love to toast that occasion, I have a big job interview early the next day in Olympia."

"What job, Mom?" Matthew asked.

"Medical billing for a chain of clinics. The best part is I can do it from home. When my migraines hit, I can keep the lights off and work from the couch. Pay's good, too." She looked at Tyler. "So, I wouldn't need another dime from my kids."

Seeing the pride in her expression was nice, and even if she didn't get the job, he sensed she'd be okay. If it worked out, they could finally have a relationship that didn't revolve around her taking and him giving. They could just be mother and son.

"Good luck, Jenna." Charlotte shook her hand. "I'm sure I'll see you again soon."

When Charlotte left, his mother went quiet. She frowned, staring at the door.

"They're here, you know."

"Who?" Matthew tried to sit but quickly gave up, settling back against the pillows.

"Amy and Rafael. A few floors up. The nurse told me."

"They're *alive*?" Tyler's stomach dropped.

"Not sure. They came in alive. That's all I know."

Matt's fist twisted in the blankets. "I hope Charlotte's bullets ripped through their cold fucking hearts."

He'd been unconscious when Charlotte shot them, but Tyler knew the truth. Rafael took two to the chest, and Amy caught one in the stomach. The amount of blood they'd left behind didn't seem survivable, but Amy had more lives than a damn cat. Hopefully, if they survived, they'd eventually die in jail anyway. Charlotte would never again feel hunted or worry about them hurting her again.

Like so much in his time with Amy, Tyler knew he'd read about her fate in the papers. Until then, he didn't care. All that mattered were the people he loved most—all true survivors, touched by trauma and tragedies but not broken.

Just a little bent.

48

Tyler

"We need more purple on the left side."

Charlotte directed as Tyler taped crepe paper streamers to the entryway of her house. *Their* house. At least until they found a new one together. Memories of the attack tainted her kitchen and bedroom, so they wanted to start fresh.

He stood back, examining his handiwork. "Any more purple, and it'll look like Barney puked in here."

The shade reminded him of Charlotte's eye the day after the incident with his evil ex-wife and Rafael. *Ex.* He liked the sound of that. After nine days of healing, all that remained was a pale shadow of lavender.

"One more thing to add to the décor." Charlotte left and returned with a stack of papers stapled at the corner. She pinned it to the wall with a thumbtack. "There. What do you think?"

"My divorce papers?" Tyler's attorney sent them over that morning. He wondered if they sent a copy to Amy's jail cell. "Perfect decoration for the occasion."

A knock at the door turned their heads, and Charlotte answered it. She squealed as Sandra attacked her with a bear hug.

Sandra held a hand over her heart. "Have I mentioned how glad I am you guys didn't die?"

Charlotte kissed her cheek. "You've made it abundantly clear, sweetie. I'm glad we didn't die, too."

A thirty-something blonde in a paisley dress walked in. "Hi, I'm Christa. It's cool to finally meet you guys."

Tyler put his arm around Charlotte. "Good to meet you too. I hope the vultures outside didn't harass you too much."

Reporters had been camped out on their sidewalk since the day after the attack, begging for a soundbite whenever they left the house. The numbers started to dwindle until the morning Rafael was pulled from life support and took his last breaths. Then, it was like every channel on earth brought a microphone to shove at them, demanding to know how they felt. Charlotte only had one word for them—relieved.

"They tried, but we just flipped them off and kept walking." Sandra shrugged. "They're welcome to put my middle finger on the five o'clock news."

Christa blushed, averting her eyes. "Okay, I have something to confess. I'm a huge fan and trying not to show it."

Tyler smiled. "Oh, thanks. It's always nice to hear."

Christa shared a look with Sandra. "Sorry. I was talking about Charlotte."

"Ouch!" Tyler pretended an arrow had shot him in the heart. "Damn, that hurt."

Charlotte laughed her contagious full-body laugh, and everyone joined in. "Thank you, Christa. He needs to be taken down a notch now and then."

Tyler got them all beers from the keg, and as more guests arrived, the house grew louder, more alive. While Charlotte and Christa swapped Sandra stories, he walked to the backyard where dozens of the people they loved drank and ate barbecue to celebrate his Independence Day. Roxy zoomed around, soaking up all the attention she could handle.

The hideous Amy piñata dangled from a rope tied to an apple tree. They hadn't taken a bat to it yet, but judging by the dents in the forehead, a few guests couldn't resist punching it.

Killing Daisies' guitar tech, Molly, pulled Tyler in for a careful hug, avoiding his still-healing ribs. "Great party, Ty."

Amber tapped her cup against his. "Happy Divorce Day, dude!"

"Thanks, ladies. I'm gonna grab something to eat. Feel free to drink way too much of our booze."

"Already on it, my friend." Molly patted his back as he headed for the various overstuffed platters and bowls on the food table.

Beneath the laughter and chatter was a Jimi Hendrix album Charlotte picked out. A lived fast, died young member of the "27 Club" Tyler wouldn't be joining any time soon.

"Tyler!" Adam fist-bumped him. "How're the ribs, man?"

He raised his shirt, exposing the sore yellow and green skin on the right side of his torso—fading remnants of the last pain Amy would ever inflict on him. "Pretty gnarly bruise, right? It's getting less painful to breathe, but I still have to ice it and make sure Charlotte's careful when she jumps me."

"I was talking about the barbecue, dude." Adam laughed while Tyler shoved him. "Just fucking with you. Glad you're healing up. You better be ready to hit the road next month."

Zack joined them. "Were you just showing Adam your freaking tits, Tyler? I'm telling Charlotte."

"Telling me what?" Her arms loosely wound around Tyler's waist, avoiding the bruise.

"That Ty's flashing his tits at Adam." Zack swigged his beer.

Charlotte laughed. "Are you guys twelve?"

"That's what I always say!" Tyler snatched a stuffed mushroom from the table.

"Just kidding." She pecked Zack and Adam each on the cheek. "I love you guys and hope you never change."

Adam began belching the alphabet.

She shook her head, fanning the air in front of her face. "I lied. Please change as soon as fucking possible." She filled a red plastic cup at the keg and took a drink.

Cheering and shouts erupted in the house, and Tyler followed her to check it out.

"Matty!" Tyler ran over, hugging his brother as tightly as his ribs would allow. "I'm so glad you're here."

Matthew still looked too thin and frail for a healthy twenty-three-year-old man, but he was on the road to recovery. Once he felt up to it, their 'Beer and Bitching' tradition would commence, and things could return to normal. Although Tyler had a lot less to bitch about lately.

"Happy Independence Day, brother."

When Tyler let go, Charlotte hugged Matthew. "You're eating at least three burgers and two pieces of cake today. Charlotte's orders."

"Yes, ma'am. First, point me in the direction of the nearest beer." She gave him the nearly full one in her hand. He headed toward the food and even more cheering friends in the backyard.

Tyler put his lips to her ear. "Feel free to order me around anytime."

"Once those ribs heal, you're on." She fisted the front of his shirt, her eyebrow arching. "I have a riding crop you haven't been introduced to yet."

"Holy fuck." He squeezed his eyes closed, trying to shut down the erection that shouldn't, couldn't happen with a houseful of guests to entertain. "Come with me to the backyard. I have a surprise for you."

"For me? It's your special day, Ty."

"I know." He kissed her softly. "This surprise will make me happy too. Well, hopefully."

He took as deep a breath as possible, his heart hammering against his ribs.

She threaded their fingers together. "I'll go anywhere with you, Tyler Hall."

He raised his voice to address everyone inside the house. "All right, party people. Grab your drinks and get your asses to the backyard." He turned off the music on their way out.

He led Charlotte to the concrete bench beside the tulip beds. "Wait here, baby." She sat with her forehead scrunched in confusion.

Tyler held his injured side as he carefully stepped onto the bench, taking in all the familiar faces. Everyone was too busy with their conversations to notice him.

"Can everyone please shut the fuck up for a minute?" he shouted.

Someone threw an empty plastic cup at his crotch, and everyone laughed.

"Haha, Zack. Dickface." Tyler picked up the cup, chucking it back at him.

"Thank you all for helping me celebrate my liberation from that fucking nut job." Everyone clapped and whooped, and Adam let out a few high-pitched whistles. "It hasn't been easy, especially with the attempted triple murder and everything."

Laughter broke out, and he looked at the smiling faces of Matthew and Charlotte. Tears of gratitude filled his eyes that they were alive and healing.

"But even with two cracked ribs and some bad memories, I feel like the luckiest guy alive. Because I have her." There was a collective *aww* from the crowd, and Tyler smiled at Charlotte. She blew him a kiss. "And on my first day of freedom from a lonely, painful marriage, I'm asking the universe for a second chance. And I think I'll get it right this time."

Charlotte gasped. "Tyler, what are you doing?"

He stepped off the bench, got on one knee in front of Charlotte, and took her hand. There were gasps and excited chatter from the crowd and then silence.

"Charlotte, I love you. We've survived more in a few months than most couples do in a lifetime. I want to fill the rest of our days with laughter, friends, and music. And goats."

She laughed, tears collecting on her lashes.

"Will you marry me?" Tyler pulled a small box from the pocket of his almost-good-as-new army jacket. He opened it, revealing a ring not overly flashy or worth more than a small island but beautiful and one of a kind. Just like Charlotte.

Aside from the heartbeat pounding in his ears, everything was quiet. Her face remained unreadable for a moment, and then she smiled the broadest Charlotte smile he'd ever seen.

"Yes, Tyler. Of course, I'll marry you."

The crowd exploded as he slipped the ring onto her trembling finger. The cheers grew louder when they started making out on the bench like their ship was going under, with a few wolf whistles sprinkled in.

Even with all the beautiful chaos, the world around them fell away. Nothing existed except their love, the limitless future stretched out before them, and that toe-curling kiss.

49

Tyler

"We're on in fifteen. Get your game faces on." Tyler took one last hit from his pre-show cigarette before stamping it out in one of the countless ashtrays backstage. The roar of the crowd packing The Forum in Inglewood, California made the photos on the dressing room wall vibrate.

"I'm tryin', man." Adam hopped on the balls of his feet. "Why am I so fucking nervous tonight?"

"Because your new girlfriend's in the front row, dummy," Zack said. "You always get nervous when a chick you actually like watches us play."

"If it didn't get them so turned on, I wouldn't invite them." Adam wagged his eyebrows. "And you know damn well I don't do girlfriends. She's just a cool groupie with a nice rack."

"Ooh, Adam." Zack's voice rose several octaves. "Your arms are so big and strong. Pound me like you pound your drums."

Adam laughed and shoved him. "You should talk to me like that more often, Zacky. Now I'm not nervous, I'm horny."

"Shut the fuck up, guys." Tyler swigged his water, twisting the cap back on with shaking hands. "Let's get to the stage before I throw up."

Zack clapped his shoulder. "Maybe you have the opposite problem. You're nervous because your lady isn't here."

"I think you nailed it, man." It wasn't often that Tyler had to admit Zack was right about something.

It felt like a middle finger from the universe that his West Coast dates and her East Coast gigs fell at the same time. He missed her so much it hurt. After the toll his schedule had taken on his first marriage, he was terrified that the one he'd have with Charlotte would suffer the same issues.

"Where are they playing tonight?" Adam asked.

"They're not." Tyler clutched his stomach. "They played Philly last night and tomorrow's New York."

"At least you're in the same country." Zack cracked his knuckles, a pre-show ritual that made Tyler crazy. "You flying out to see her?"

"I wish. We play Seattle on Friday. If I don't get enough sleep, my voice will be shot."

The dressing room door swung open. "We can't let that happen." Charlotte appeared in the doorway, her hands on her hips and a wide grin on her face.

"Holy shit!" Tyler ran over, lifting her off the ground as their lips smashed together for their first kiss in three long weeks. The fabric of her skirt fluttered as she wrapped her legs around his waist, and he fought the urge to carry her into the nearest closet. "What are you doing here, baby?"

"Surprise, motherfuckers!" Sandra jumped into the room. "I got tired of this mopey bitch frowning all the time, so I bought a couple of plane tickets to get her smiling again. If my voice is shot tomorrow night, I'll tell our fans to boycott your ass."

He set Charlotte down and hugged Sandra. "Thank you so fucking much! You have no idea what this means to me." His nerves melted away, the pain in his stomach gone.

"Yeah, thanks, Sandra," Adam said. "Tyler's been a mopey little bitch too. Maybe if he gets laid, he won't screw up our last few weeks of shows before the break."

Tyler slugged Adam's shoulder before pulling Charlotte back into his arms. "I've missed you like crazy."

The stage manager popped his head in. "Eight minutes, guys. Let's move."

Charlotte fisted Tyler's shirt, kissing him so forcefully he grabbed the wall to keep them from toppling over. "I'll be watching from the side of the stage, and the second you're off, so are my clothes."

Tyler hummed in his throat. "Guys, we're skipping the encore tonight."

Zack grabbed the back of Tyler's T-shirt, yanking him toward the door. "The hell we are. Let's go, dude. Bros before—"

Tyler glared. "Do not finish that thought if you want to live."

"Have fun, fellas!" Sandra slung her arm around Charlotte. "Better give us ho's a good show."

Tyler took one last look at Charlotte as he headed to the stage.

"Still nervous?" Adam asked as they walked.

"Hell no! Did you see how hot my woman is? All's right with the world, my friend." They bumped fists. "Let's do this."

50

Charlotte

If there was a sexier sight on earth, Charlotte hadn't seen it. Sweat glistened on Tyler's forehead, his guitar wailing as he bared his soul to seventeen thousand screaming fans. The passion in his smooth, baritone voice echoed across the space as Adam's drums pounded like a furious heart behind him. Zack's bass provided the steady groove underneath it all that had everyone in the crowd bobbing their heads.

She caught Tyler's eye a few times, and the look he shot back made her feel like a freshly grilled steak set in front of a starving man. Charlotte flew to Boston three weeks before to kick off Killing Daisies' East Coast tour. The next day, Tyler left for Phoenix, the first of a dozen U.S. dates that all conflicted with hers. Being apart was harder than she thought, but they were determined to make it work. They talked on the phone often and made plans for what they'd do (in and out of the bedroom) when they were back home.

Sandra shoved Charlotte's back, and she stumbled forward. "Didn't you hear him? Go!"

"Huh?"

Tyler sprinted over. He grabbed Charlotte's wrist, dragging her onto the stage. The crowd exploded, and he led her to his microphone, front and center. A roadie handed her a guitar and disappeared.

She moved her mouth closer to the mic. "I have to confess. I was so busy drooling over my man I didn't hear a word he said. I have no fucking clue what's going on."

The crowd erupted with laughter, and so did the band.

Zack stepped to his mic. "Can you blame her, ladies? I've got a semi over here from looking at him too."

Laughter filled the massive arena again, and Adam drummed out a rimshot.

Charlotte spotted a sign in the crowd that read: *Amy Carey is Fucking Scary* and another with *Thanks for Not Dying* in big red letters. She shook her head, smiling.

"I was just telling these beautiful people," Tyler explained for all to hear, "how grateful I am that you flew down to see us play, and while you're here, you might as well join us for a song."

"Just me?" she asked Tyler and the audience. "Or can Sandra come too?"

The crowd exploded.

"How many Killing Daisies fans are in the house tonight?" Tyler asked the massive room, getting an ear-splitting roar in response. "Get your ass out here, Sandra!"

Sandra ran onstage, taking a bow in the center. She snatched Zack's microphone. "Hello, Los Angeles! How the fuck are ya?" She spun around, her arms flailing in an ecstatic little happy dance before covering her ears at the flood of screams and whoops. She stepped out of the cords looping around her ankles.

Charlotte moved to Tyler's ear. "What song are we doing?"

Tyler went to his microphone. "Call it, Sandra."

She pointed at a few spots in the audience. "I'm looking at these signs people are holding, and it's pretty obvious. Talking Heads, 'Psycho Killer'. Kick it off, Zacky."

As the crowd roared with laughter and cheers, Zack started the opening bass line, and Adam's drums joined in. Charlotte looked at Tyler. They shrugged and went with it.

After Charlotte and Sandra thanked the audience and exited the stage, the guys played "She's the One" by the Ramones. Charlotte turned to see Tyler grinning like a lovesick fool in her direction. She made a heart shape with her fingers, and he winked in reply.

"Well, that was a hell of a lot of fun," Sandra said. A stagehand offered her a towel, and she dabbed the sweat from her face and neck. "I can't wait until our crowds are that huge."

Charlotte turned, an eyebrow cocked. "'Psycho Killer', Sandra? Really?"

She shrugged. "What? They ate it up. Amy almost murdering you guys was the biggest music news since Kurt died. Might as well milk it a little."

"They loved it, didn't they?" Charlotte smiled, her nose wrinkling. "The sick bastards."

"Hey, those sick bastards helped pay for that sick house you guys just bought." Sandra grabbed a stick of red licorice off a snack table, snapping off a bite. "Fuck!"

"What's wrong? Did you break a tooth?"

Sandra smacked her forehead. "I'm so goddamn dense." She touched Charlotte's arm, her expression thick with regret. "I can't believe I made light of what happened to you guys. I'm so sorry, babe."

Charlotte laughed. "Don't sweat it. Like I keep telling you, I'm good. I learned that the surest way to cure PTSD is to shoot the assholes who gave it to you."

Sandra's eyebrows shot up. "I don't think your therapist would approve of that method."

As crazy as it was, after the attack, she found peace. It wasn't just knowing her stalker was six feet under and his accomplice would be in prison for the next fifteen years. It was knowing that when the moment finally came and her strength was tested, Charlotte was a fucking warrior. She'd killed a man, nearly killed Amy, and all she felt in the aftermath was unstoppable, fearless, and ready for any challenge life handed her.

Tyler played the opening riff of "Falling Closer," the song that always closed out their encore. He looked so confident and in his element with a guitar in his hand and captivated audience at his feet. She felt a twinge of pain in her chest, remembering she had to be back on a plane in a few hours.

Charlotte wondered if all their goodbyes would be just as brutal. When she was single, touring was her favorite thing. Nothing thrilled her more than exploring new cities with Sandra and Amber between gigs. Maybe it was because she and Tyler were still in the honeymoon phase of their relationship, but being away from him was spoiling the fun of this tour. She still relished being onstage with her band, but the rest of the experience felt more like a chore, an obligation. As Tyler's head tipped back, his eyes closed as the music swept him away.

"You'll make it work."

She turned to Sandra and blinked. "What?"

"It's written all over your face, Char. I know you hate being away from him, but what you two have..." She gestured at her and Tyler. "Nothing can touch it."

When the song ended, Adam and Zack shuffled off the stage, looking amped and exhausted. Tyler followed behind, still waving at the thundering crowd. He handed his guitar to a roadie, wiped the sweat from his forehead, and tossed Charlotte over his shoulder.

She laughed, shoving away the concerns that consumed her seconds before. "Still a caveman, huh?"

"You bring it outta me, baby." His rough fingertips skated over her bare thigh, making her shudder.

"Don't mind me," Sandra said. "I'll just be over here dry heaving into a trash can."

Charlotte looked at her upside-down friend. "And I'll just be in my man's dressing room for the next seven hours if you need me."

"Hell no," Tyler said. "I'm taking you back to my suite. Two words—jacuzzi tub."

Charlotte smirked at Sandra. "Meet you at the airport?"

Sandra's arms crossed, laughter breaking through her fake grimace. "Sure thing. Later, bitch." She kissed Charlotte's temple. "The show was awesome, Ty. Thanks for sharing your people."

"Anytime. They loved you." Tyler hugged her with the shoulder Charlotte wasn't draped over. "See you back in Stumptown."

When they reached his dressing room, Tyler locked the door behind them. Their lips smashed together the second Charlotte was back on her feet. The kiss was greedy and possessive, a hungry moan breaking in her throat. He walked her backward until her shoulder blades pressed against the wall.

She sucked his lower lip into her mouth, skimming it with her teeth. "I missed you so much." Her shirt was over her head in one quick motion before she dove back into the kiss.

Tyler's hands flattened against the wall, caging her in—a sexy echo of their first kiss. "I missed you too, gorgeous." He dipped his head to kiss the rounded tops of her breasts. "All of you. I don't want you to leave again." His lips grazed a trail to her neck and across her jawline. "I can't fucking stand it."

She held her feelings back, needing a sweat fest, not a sob fest. "I'm here now." She ran her fingers through his sweat-drenched hair. "Let's just enjoy it, okay?"

"*Enjoy* isn't a strong enough word for how it feels to touch you again." He licked and nipped down the center of her body, sliding a knee over his shoulder. "Do you know how happy I was when you walked through that door?"

Tyler slipped her panties to the side before thrusting his tongue inside her. Charlotte groaned, her fingernails clawing at the wall. Every nerve ending in her body sparked, and her knee threatened to buckle.

"Fuck." She made the word stretch out for at least ten seconds. "I missed that too."

Her toys had gotten plenty of use while she was away, mostly during their late-night phone calls. But no vibrator on earth could come close to simulating what that man could do with his mouth.

Tyler's thumb rubbed at her clit as his lips and tongue slid along the slick folds between her legs. "I missed your smell, your taste..." His entire mouth enveloped her, his tongue slipping back inside her before lapping at the wetness on her inner thighs.

"Mmm... already dripping wet for me." His words vibrated against her sensitive flesh. "What've you been thinking about, almost Mrs. Hall?"

A smile tugged at her lips. "It's from watching you play." She gasped as his thumb moved aside so he could flick her clit with his tongue. "The sweat on your face, the fire in your eyes, your fingers speeding across those strings... I wanted to fuck you so badly I could hardly breathe."

"I know the feeling." He slid two fingers inside her, and she shuddered, holding his shoulders for support.

"Fuck foreplay. I need your cock." Charlotte gripped his hair tighter. "*Now.*"

He got to his feet. Her eager fingers fumbled with his belt buckle as he tugged his damp T-shirt over his head.

She growled in frustration. "Get this fucking thing off!"

He laughed, easily sliding the buckle apart and raising his hands.

"Show off." She unbuttoned his jeans, sliding them down his legs before tossing them away.

As her gaze swept over his glistening naked chest and continued south, Charlotte drew in a sharp breath.

"Tyler, what did you do?" Her fingers skimmed over the healing tattoo on his left hip.

"When we were in Denver, I had the scarlet heart covered up. You like it?"

She knelt for a closer look, pressing a kiss to the black and white Fender bass inked on his skin. "I love it."

Tyler stroked her cheek. "It's like the one you were playing the first time I saw you."

Charlotte looked up, her heart jumping at the gesture and the adoration in his sky-blue eyes. "I love you so fucking much."

"I love you too." His thumb slid across her lower lip, and she drew it into her mouth, sucking the salty tip. His cock twitched beside her cheek. "Fuck, you look beautiful on your knees."

A rush of heat pooled between her legs at his naughty words and the desire flaring in his eyes. Tyler gripped his cock in his fist, lightly tracing her mouth with the warm, silky head. A few drops of his arousal were left on her lips, and her tongue darted out to taste him. The sexy rumble in his throat made her pussy clench. Charlotte parted her lips, taking him to the back of her throat.

His fingers laced through her hair, guiding her mouth over the velvety skin of his shaft for a few long, slow strokes. He moaned from deep in his chest, his stomach muscles twitching. "Holy shit, woman. You're so fucking good at that." Charlotte grinned around his cock, pleased with his reaction. Her tongue slid along the underside of his shaft as it swelled, his body demanding what only she could give.

His eyes remained locked on her face as she teased the sensitive head with fluttering licks before letting every inch of him slide to the back of her throat. "Mmm… I love watching my cock disappear inside that pretty, pink mouth."

Tyler's thighs tensed, a hint that his climax was approaching. As much as she craved his hot release in the back of her throat, she was even more desperate to feel him inside her. She pulled back, and he let out a tortured groan as his cock slipped from her lips.

She got to her feet. Her fingertips drifted down Tyler's chest and over his taut stomach. "I promise to do that again later and swallow every drop." She wrapped her fingers around his swelling erection and gently squeezed. "But right now, please fuck me before I go insane."

His lips hitched up in a sexy grin. "We can't have that." He spun her around, unhooking her bra and slipping the straps off her shoulders. "Spread your legs for me, baby."

She stepped to the side, widening the gap between her ankles as her cheek and naked breasts pressed against the cold wall. His fingers trailed up her spine in a slow, torturous climb, and she felt herself growing wetter. When Charlotte's eyelids shut, his teeth sank into her shoulder, making her cry out. For the first time, she wondered if anyone could hear but didn't care in the least.

He sucked and bit his way across her shoulder blades, and just thinking about him marking her skin made her more desperate to feel him inside her.

As Tyler held her hips, she felt the head of his cock press against her entrance, stretching, teasing. She pushed against him, and he surged forward, the rigid bones of his hips slamming against her ass. The intense pleasure made her groan, her hand slapping the wall in a meager attempt to relieve some of the pressure building inside her. After a few more forceful thrusts, he withdrew and turned her to face him, devouring her mouth as he entered her again without warning. The taste of her arousal on his lips drove her even madder with desire, and she jumped to wrap her legs around his waist. His hands gripped her ass with an almost painful hold, and she dug her fingernails into the flesh of his bare back. Overwhelmed by sensation, a sound escaped her throat. It came out low and desperate like pain, and he stilled.

"Doing okay, baby?" he asked, loving concern in his eyes.

"Are you fucking kidding me?" With a hand on the back of his neck, she pulled him in for a wet, deep kiss. "You're incredible, Ty. Please don't stop."

He grinned against her mouth. "Good answer." As the speed of his thrusts increased, the only sounds were skin slapping skin and his breaths in her ear becoming heavier, more urgent.

"I'm close," he said in a hoarse whisper. "It's been a long three weeks."

It certainly had. Charlotte couldn't sit still on the flight over, imagining this exact moment. Now that it was real, she could've stayed like that for hours, the love of her life buried deeply inside her. But as she lost herself in his hungry, hooded gaze, she craved his release as much as her own. The heat simmering low in her belly told her she was close too.

"Hold on to me," he said.

Her thighs squeezed tighter around his hips, and her arms wound around his neck. Tyler reached down, the thick pad of his fingers kneading her throbbing, swollen clit. She whimpered, her nails digging into his shoulders as her orgasm approached. She gasped as warm, tingling sparks of pleasure spread through her core, the intensity making her eyes clamp shut. Her head fell back against the wall, unrestrained moans and curses filling the space between them. Tyler held her tighter, and as all the air left her lungs, she filled them again with his scent—the scent of passion, love, and *home*.

The climactic wave receded, and she fell against his chest.

"I love watching you come apart like that." Tyler kissed every inch of her skin he could reach—her neck, shoulders, jawline, and lips. "You're so beautiful, Charlotte." He resumed his steady rhythm, and within minutes, his hot, fluttering breaths said he was close again.

"Now I get to watch you come apart." Charlotte bit down on his earlobe, sucking the flesh beneath it hard enough to bruise. She wasn't the only one leaving that room with marks.

As Tyler came, his muscles tensed, a low, guttural moan roaring from his throat. His thrusts were brutal, bruising as her inner muscles coaxed out every last drop. She kissed him hard, the sounds of his release muffled against her lips. When his body relaxed, they sagged against the wall behind her.

His panting breaths tickled her ear. "That was un-fucking-believable." He sucked and nipped at the tender flesh of her throat.

"Agreed. Every time's better than the last, which is no easy feat." Charlotte raised her chin, giving him better access. "If this keeps up, imagine what it'll be like in ten years."

"Mmm... I'm getting hard again just thinking about it."

"Yeah, I can feel that." Her lips curved in a wide, sated grin. "Save it for the suite, stud." Charlotte planted her feet on the ground, and he withdrew. She winced at a spike of pain when her legs closed. "You definitely gave me something to remember you by."

"Did I hurt you?" He frowned, studying her face with obvious concern.

"I'm fine, Ty. It's just been a while." She kissed the tip of his nose. "Besides, you know I like my pleasure with a side of pain now and then."

He handed her a box of tissues, and she cleaned herself up before getting dressed.

"Doing any sightseeing in New York?" he asked. "I know Sandra was begging you to go to the Chelsea with her to look for Sid and Nancy's ghosts." He snickered.

"Yeah, probably." She swept her hair onto her shoulder, the sadness from earlier creeping in. "But..."

He pulled up his jeans, their eyes connecting. "But what?"

"Maybe it's because we're still pretty new, but I'm struggling too. I hate being so far from you. It's great that we talk on the phone all the time, but it's not the same."

She was on the verge of tears, and he pulled her into his arms. "I know. I couldn't concentrate during the interviews the label set up because I wanted to jump on a plane to see you. Things would be simpler if we had nine-to-five, punch-a-clock jobs, but this is our reality. No matter how much it sucks sometimes."

She looked up at him. "Maybe it's selfish even to think about it, but can we somehow organize future tour schedules so we can travel together as much as possible? Between the two bands, we're the only couple where both partners go on the road. Maybe everyone would be open to it."

He squinted, nodding slowly. "Considering how much our bandmates complain about what bummers we are, I think they would." His eyebrows shot up. "Hey! Maybe we can even co-headline after your new album's released. Our crowd went wild for you and Sandra. We share a lot of the same audience."

Charlotte's eyes brightened. "Seriously? But we're not in the same stratosphere as you guys yet. If we toured together, shouldn't we be opening?"

"Hell no. Judging by sales of your last album, your fanbase is growing fast. Add in the Canadian shows selling out, and I'd say you've earned equal billing."

Her head tilted. "It still seems crazy. There's no way we could pack stadiums on our own. Not yet."

"When it comes to skills, we're equals, Charlotte. Well, almost. Some of your riffs are *way* beyond my shit."

Her eyes rolled. "Come on."

"I'm serious. And I know it's no surprise to you, but it's tougher for women in our industry to blow up, regardless of talent."

She gasped, her eyes and mouth widening in mock surprise.

He laughed. "How many less talented bands are more successful than yours only because the members have dicks between their legs? I can name dozens."

"That makes it sound like charity." Her shoulders drooped. "Or male guilt."

Tyler took her face into his hands. "It's one musician seeing the worth of another and wanting to work together to create something amazing."

"When you put it that way..." Charlotte slid a hand up his back, still slick from his sweat. "I don't want to get my hopes up, but that would be epic. Think Sophia would be into it?"

"Are you kidding? She'd go apeshit at the promotional opportunity since our upcoming wedding's making headlines. And our fans would cream themselves if we were on the same ticket. We could even do more songs together."

Charlotte beamed, excitement sparking in her chest. "Sandra would lose her damn mind if she could play an arena again. I think hearing that many people cheer for her made her curly head swell."

He laughed. "I'll make some calls in the morning."

The idea made her feel lighter. She'd seen plenty of relationships crack under the strain of long separations and the endless temptations of the road. Maybe they could prevent those issues before they even started.

"Are you starving?" she asked. "Because I'm starving."

His head tipped back. "Fuck yes! I'd kill for a burger and a beer. And I need to get cleaned up."

"I like your post-show sweat." She smoothed the wrinkles on the front of her skirt. "I like it even more when you also smell like me."

"That's so primal." Tyler smacked her ass before sliding his shirt over his head. "I love it. But it doesn't change that I feel dirty and not the fun kind. The funk kind."

When they were dressed, she linked her hands behind his waist. "How about we go back to your room for a shower, room service, and a whole lot more sex before I have to leave for the airport?"

"Swap 'shower' for 'jacuzzi tub,' and you're on."

Epilogue

Tyler

Charlotte's car door flew open, and she ran into Tyler's arms. He pressed his face to her neck, breathing in the scent of the woman he'd missed so much it hurt. The driver set her luggage and guitar case on the porch.

Tyler shook his hand. "Thanks for picking her up, Louis."

"Yeah, thanks again," Charlotte said. "You're a master at wading through traffic."

"You're welcome, Mr. Hall, Ms. Ross. Enjoy your evening." Louis waved before returning to the front seat.

Tyler covered Charlotte's face and neck in kisses as the car drove away and the security gates closed.

"It's so good to be home!" She ran her soft, warm hands up the back of his shirt. His eyes shut for a moment, savoring her touch. "I did a happy dance in my seat when the clouds parted, and I saw the Fremont Bridge."

Now that they were together and he'd finally conquered his old wounds, the dark thoughts that haunted him when he'd looked down at that bridge from the balcony of his suite felt like a lifetime ago. "It's always been my favorite."

A soft smile touched her lips. "No more touring for four whole months. What will we do to pass the time?"

Tyler cupped her face, kissing her long and slow. "Get upstairs, and I'll show you."

He grabbed her luggage and went inside. The phone was ringing when they walked through the front door of their charming turn-of-the-century home in the woods south of Portland. While Charlotte greeted an ecstatic, bouncing Roxy, Tyler jogged to answer it.

"Hello?"

"Ty! What's up, man?" Matthew sounded healthier and more like his old self every time they spoke.

"Hey, Matty. Charlotte just got home."

She put her lips to the mouthpiece. "Hi, Matt."

Matthew laughed. "Tell her I said hi back. You guys probably have weekend plans, but are you free tomorrow night?"

"Sure. What's up?"

"I was thinking we could go on a double date so you guys can finally meet Jessica. Outside the hospital, that is. Saying hi while she checked my vital signs didn't count. Romano's at eight?"

Matthew had dealt with PTSD after leaving the hospital. He was anxious about going out in public, terrified of being surprised and attacked. His business partner, Evan, had to cover for him at work when nightmares kept him up until dawn. So, he started seeing a therapist Charlotte suggested. It was going well, and giving a new relationship a shot was a sign he was moving forward.

"We'll be there, brother," Tyler said, rushing to get off the phone. "See you then."

He headed upstairs. "Where's my rock goddess fiancé? Now that she's back on Oregon soil, I can't wait to get my hands on her." He poked his head into the guest room and their bedroom, coming up empty. "Are we playing hide-and-seek? If so, I hope you're buck naked to make up for the time I spend seeking when we could've been fucking."

He opened their bathroom door to find a sight that stole his breath and instantly made him hard. Charlotte sat on one of the bench seats in their massive soaking tub, white bubbles concealing everything below her neck. He'd filled it for her, knowing she'd want to unwind after her flight. She'd lit a few candles and dimmed the lights, casting a soft glow on her ivory skin. She held a glass of champagne above the steaming water while another waited on the tiles beside the tub. Roxy was fast asleep on the plush rug in front of the sink, tuckered out from the excitement of Charlotte's return. Her homecoming had the opposite effect on Tyler. He felt more charged up and alive than he'd felt in weeks.

"You got the buck-naked part right." Her fingers swirled in the bubbles.

"Look at you. How did I get so damn lucky?" He walked over and softly kissed her full, tempting mouth. "You're so beautiful, baby."

"Strip and join me." Her tongue flicked his lower lip. "Please."

Tyler slipped his shirt over his head. "Since you asked so nicely." He unbuttoned his jeans, sliding them off along with his boxers. She let out an appreciative hum that made his cock swell. He stepped into the water, bubbles rising to her chin.

"Feels good, right?" She sipped her champagne.

"Not yet." Tyler moved to his knees, his hands finding her thighs beneath the water and spreading them wide. He entered the space and slid his fingers into the hair above her nape. "Getting better." He parted her lips with his tongue, and together, they moaned into each other's mouths. When he drew back, he whispered against her lips, "*That* feels good."

She pulled his face to hers, and as their tongues mingled, the taste of champagne and Charlotte made him press his hardness against the center of her parted thighs. The underside of his shaft glided over her sensitive flesh, and she whimpered, her fingers digging into his lower back. Her quick, hot breaths against his neck kicked up his pulse. Even in the water, he could feel how wet and slick she was from their kissing as he continued sliding his cock over the seam between her silken lips and over her clit.

"I won't fuck you in the water because it washes away all that sexy wetness you made for me." He ran his finger along her slit. "But when we're out, I'll show you exactly how much I missed every part of you while you showed all those fans how talented you are."

"Definitely looking forward to that." Charlotte grinned, taking his cock into her fist and stroking him from root to tip. He sucked in a sharp breath as she slid her hand up and down his length. She released him, and he groaned in protest, craving her touch like a drug.

"Tease." Tyler splashed her with the bubbly water, and she raised her glass above her head, squealing with laughter.

"Pot, meet kettle." She set down her champagne. "I need to wash the stale airplane smell out of my hair, and then, it's on."

He picked up his champagne flute, drained half the glass, and set it back on the tile. "Turn around." He twirled a finger in the air.

He placed his hand behind her head and dipped her hair into the water. He squeezed a dollop of shampoo into the palm of his hand, massaging it into her hair and scalp.

"Mmm... That feels amazing, Ty."

"And I'm only touching your hair. That's talent."

She turned for a second and touched the tip of his nose, leaving behind a cluster of tiny bubbles.

"Cute." He laughed as he wiped it off and picked up the detachable showerhead. He adjusted the temperature and rinsed her hair. "How was Atlanta?"

"Great. Luke's working out well on bass, and I hope he sticks around. And the crowd went apeshit for the new tracks, so this album might take us to the next level."

"I agree." He grabbed the conditioner. "'Low Down' is my favorite. It's radio-friendly but still true to your punk roots. It showcases how much you and Sandra have evolved as songwriters."

Charlotte turned as he worked the conditioner into her scalp. "Thanks, Ty. That means a lot coming from you." She grabbed the body wash, scrubbing her arms.

He couldn't wait one more second to give her the news he'd been dying to spill. "I think our fans will agree when we co-headline next year."

Her wet hair whipped across her neck as she spun around. "What did you say?"

"My team got the okay from your people this morning. I begged them to let me tell you."

Charlotte shrieked. "Holy fuck! I can't believe it!"

"Believe it, baby. No more goodbyes for a very long time. And Matthew said he'll join us for part of the tour if Evan's cool with it."

"That would be so fucking awesome!" Her smile slipped a bit. "How is Matty? It's hard to tell over the phone if he's okay or just faking it so I won't worry."

"He's doing a lot better." He picked up the showerhead to rinse her hair. He was too eager to get her out of the tub and into their bed to give the conditioner time to set in. "Thanks for finding him that therapist."

"I'm proud of him for putting the work in. It isn't easy."

Tyler turned off the water. He was proud of both of them for doing the work it took to recover from their traumas. He kissed her shoulder. "We're meeting Jessica tomorrow night."

Charlotte let out another happy shriek. "Yay! I can't wait to see if she's as perfect as he says." She spun to face him, her face shimmering with water and tiny bubbles. Pressing her body to his, she sighed softly. "It feels good to be back in your arms, Ty."

"I'm glad." He kissed the top of her head. "Because it's where you belong."

⸻ ◈ ⸻

Later that night, Tyler's fingers dragged through Charlotte's dark locks as they basked in the warm, relaxing haze of champagne and afterglow. She lay sprawled on the bed beside him, her arm over his naked chest.

Roxy jumped onto the bed before pouncing on Tyler's stomach.

"Oof!" He picked her up, setting her on the blankets between them. "You're too big for that now, Rox. You're gonna bruise my damn liver."

Charlotte giggled against his chest. "You've done plenty of damage to your liver on your own, mister."

"That's the truth." Tyler grinned. "Now that you mention it, a beer sounds amazing."

"Hell yeah, it does. I'll grab a couple. Don't move." Charlotte got up and stretched her arms above her head. Her eyes returned to the bed. "Seriously? You just fucked me within an inch of my life, and you're getting hard again?"

"Look at you, woman!" He propped himself up on his elbows. "You're naked, stretching out your gorgeous body. You'd make a soggy piece of bread hard."

She laughed, making her breasts bounce, which made him even harder. "That's a weird fucking compliment. Thanks, I guess." She grabbed his T-shirt, slipping it on.

"You're welcome, I guess." He laughed as she stuck out her tongue and walked out.

The phone rang downstairs, and he heard her answer it. As she spoke, the volume of her voice dropped lower than her *hello* had been, making him curious who it was.

When she returned with one bottle of beer, he caught a tremble in her fingers as she handed it over. She sat up cross-legged in bed, and he did the same, Roxy lying between them.

"Where's yours?" he asked.

"I have to tell you something." She bit her bottom lip, obvious worry stealing the light from her eyes.

"Who was on the phone?"

"Tyler, I made a mistake," she whispered, her chin trembling.

The quiver in her voice and shift in her demeanor set him on edge.

Mistake?

They'd been apart for a month. What mistake could she have made?

There's no fucking way Charlotte cheated. He repeated the mantra in his head until the words blurred together in a meaningless jumble.

"What happened?" He held his breath, waiting.

"When the tour started, things were crazy." She pet Roxy's head, her fingers still shaking. "I was so exhausted by the end of the day, I..."

She inhaled a deep breath, her eyes shining with tears.

"You know you can tell me anything, Charlotte." He took her hands, shoving his paranoia aside to help calm her. "What's wrong?"

"I was so stupid." She sniffed. "I always take my birth control pills before bed but forgot a few times." Her eyes squeezed shut. "Well, more than a few. Then, when I came to see you in L.A., we…"

He focused on the warmth of her hands as he held them tighter.

"That call was my doctor. I got blood tests done because I was so tired, they thought I was anemic or something." Her bottom lip shook as their eyes met, a tear sliding down her cheek. "She said I'm pregnant."

He sucked in a quick breath that startled her, his pulse racing in his neck.

"What did you say?"

"I'm pregnant. Knocked-up. It's so fucking weird saying that out loud." She pulled her hands back, her arms wrapping around herself. Roxy whimpered, leaving the bed and walking to her water dish. "I'm sorry. I know I fucked up. The timing's terrible, and we're not even married yet, and maybe you don't even want to—"

He silenced her with a kiss that made him shiver, releasing the worry he'd felt seconds before, replacing it with relief and overwhelming fucking joy.

"You're not mad?" She hugged herself tighter.

He laughed, wiping her tears.

"Charlotte, you're having our baby." The reverence and awe he heard in his voice made it sound like a prayer. It didn't feel real, his head spinning. "The timing isn't perfect, but we'll make it work." He took her face in his hands, worry still dimming her eyes. "Everything will be okay, I promise."

"What if it's not? What if I can't do it?" Tears spilled down her cheeks, and he caught them with his thumbs. "My mom couldn't handle the stress of working and taking care of a family. What if I can't either? I've never even changed a fucking diaper!"

"Charlotte, look at me." When she did, he moved a hand to her belly. He couldn't believe part of him was living, growing inside of the woman who owned his heart. "You'll be the most amazing mother. We'll give this baby every single thing we missed out on."

He kissed her softly, her lips damp and salty from her tears. Then, something occurred to him that made him break the kiss, his eyes searching hers.

"Is this what *you* want?" He felt guilty for getting carried away before asking.

He wanted this baby, but if Charlotte wasn't ready, he could learn to live with whatever choice she made. Even with his support, her life and the career she'd worked so hard for would be affected in major ways. And she'd be the one dealing with morning sickness, childbirth, and every ache and pain in between. She'd said she wanted kids one day, but maybe she wasn't ready for her body to go through that yet. If not, it wouldn't be easy, but he'd have to respect it.

He fought to keep his expression neutral as he held his breath, waiting.

Finally, she smiled. The light returned to her eyes, and she laughed, more tears spilling.

"Yes, Tyler. Yes, yes, fucking yes." Her hand covered the one on her belly, her fingers curling into his. "It's what I want."

He exhaled, relief returning.

"But I'm scared," she whispered. "I love you so much, and I think I already love this baby even though it's like, a grain of rice or whatever." She laughed a little, making him smile. "I've never had so much to lose before, and I'm really fucking scared."

Tyler hugged her close before laying her on her back, her head on his pillow. He lifted the hem of her shirt and kissed the skin just below her belly button.

"You won't lose us." His hand rested on the spot he'd kissed, his fingers gently stroking her skin as their gaze held. "We'll be a family. I'll be here to kiss you and hold you and love you for the rest of our long, happy lives. I'll change diapers and bandage scraped knees and buy the tiniest pair of Doc Martens in the world."

She laughed through her tears, her muscles finally relaxing.

"And I'll quit smoking." His arms went around her waist to pull her closer. "It's stupid and reckless. I'll just hold a cigarette and pretend like my mom does."

She smiled. "Maybe you can even start running with me?"

"Let's not get crazy now." His eyebrow cocked as she laughed again. "Of course, I'll run with you. I'll do whatever it takes to watch our little grain of rice grow up."

Her eyes searched his, her smile disappearing. "Ty, I know it's a lot to take in. Your career's very important to you."

"You're important to me—"

She put a finger to his lips. "Just listen. This will complicate the hell out of things. For both of us. Do you honestly think we can handle it? And are you sure this is what you want?"

Her love for him was unmistakable in those soft brown eyes that had seen him at his best and worst. In that second, he realized everything he'd ever wanted was right there in front of him.

The security, the love, the feeling of home he'd wanted, needed for so long—this was it.

This. Charlotte in his arms, the life created by their beautiful, crazy love growing inside her. The future was full of incredible possibilities he'd almost given up on before taking a chance on a second chance.

"Yes, Charlotte."

"Yes to what?" she asked, her hands returning to her belly.

It was hard to put a name to what he felt. He was happy, but that simple, trite word didn't cover it. *Satisfied* didn't cut it either. No, this feeling made every terrible and wonderful thing that brought them to that moment completely fucking worth it.

And for the first time since he was a little boy, he felt whole.

Tyler smiled. "Everything."

He touched his forehead to hers, their eyes connecting, the silent communication between them warming his chest. He laced his fingers with hers.

Certainty and clarity flooded in.

This love was forever.

Tyler would live and die for the woman in his arms and the precious little speck growing beneath their joined hands. They stayed that way, breathing the same air, until their lips met, and their clothes disappeared. They celebrated their beautiful new future until light broke through the curtains, and they fell asleep in each other's arms, every curve of their bodies fitting together.

Perfectly.

Acknowledgments

I'd first like to thank my incredible husband. You've been my biggest supporter, my first reader, and were always willing to listen to me ramble on about my characters and their drama. You were also my greatest inspiration while writing about a hot musician who'd do anything for the woman he loves, including write a song about how special she is. The spark I felt on our first date burns brighter than ever, and I'm grateful every day that you showed up in that Starbucks parking lot with your long hair, big black boots, and sexy jacket. You'll always be my favorite string-fingerer.

Thank you, my boys, for being understanding whenever Mom had to hide away from the world to get words out of her head. I love you both more than life and maybe someday, I'll write something clean enough to share with you. Chase your dreams a little every day and before you know it, you'll catch them.

I'd also like to thank Melanie. In our three and a half decades of friendship, you've seen me at my best and worst and I'm grateful that you're still coming back for more. I never would've survived growing up without having you as a best friend. Thank you for all the craziness, swift butt kicks when I needed them, and soooo much laughing until we cry. And thanks for dancing and screaming beside me at all those amazing shows, pushing our way to the stage when we were way too young for such shenanigans.

Thank you, Tracy, for being my upbeat and up-for-anything partner-in-crime who loves live music and sexy punk rockers as much as I do. Your strength and resilience inspired me so much during my journey of writing this book, and I feel pretty damn lucky to have you in my life. Thanks for being one of my loudest cheerleaders and for always believing I could get to the finish line. I can't wait for our next adventure on the outskirts of a mosh pit.

I'd like to thank my parents for putting me in a school where nuns drilled the importance of proper grammar into my shy little head. If those nuns only knew that I ended up using it to write smut! And thanks for helping to shape the twisted sense of humor that made me write that last line. You guys always encouraged me to express my creativity and to work hard and I'm grateful.

Thanks to my Aunt Mary, who always believed in me and appreciated my long, weird letters back when people wrote actual letters. Grandma and her paper bags full of romance novels helped get me here, so I'm grateful to her too. And thanks to Auntie Anne who fed my book addiction when I was little, introducing me to the greatest authors to ever tap a typewriter.

HUGE thanks to all my awesome beta and ARC readers! At this point, there are too many of you to list, but your feedback constantly challenged me to work harder, dig deeper, and never give up. This would've been impossible without you. Bella, you've never failed to give me the honest, priceless advice I needed on this and other projects. It's been fun having someone on the other side of the world to commiserate with. And thanks to Bethany for convincing me to kill some darlings that helped make this book one that I'm immensely proud of.

Thank you to everyone who's read this far. It's an overwhelming, terrifying thing to put your words out into the world and I appreciate your support as I kick off this series. I hope you're looking forward to Matt's book as much as I am!

Thank you to Eddie Fucking Vedder and Pearl Jam—your concerts are my church. You'll never read this, but I'm saying it anyway. Thank you for making music that has talked so many wounded people off the ledge, including this one. I'll happily keep hopping on planes, chasing that high only music can bring.

Finally, thank you to Mia, Kathleen, Donita, Patti, Chrissie, Janis, Joan, and all the other fierce females who've been rocking my eardrums and mending my heart since I was a kid. I heard your voices as I wrote this book, trying my best to capture the beauty, dedication, and passion of what you've all done so well.

About the Author

Stephanie Louise has been obsessed with books since *Charlotte's Web* broke her heart when she was seven. She wrote short stories and poetry growing up, and now writes steamy, suspenseful love stories that keep the pages turning.

Stephanie lives in the beautiful Pacific Northwest with her husband, two sons, and way too many crazy pets. She has a B.A. in English from Washington State University. When she's not writing, she's hiking in the rain, going to rock concerts, or cooking something loaded with garlic. A Perfect Fit is her first novel.

Website: www.stephanie-louise.com

Email: stephanielouisebooks@gmail.com

Instagram: instagram.com/authorstephanielouise

Goodreads: http://www.goodreads.com/user/show/171231652

Facebook: facebook.com/authorstephanielouise

For a free bonus scene of Tyler and Charlotte shenanigans, sign up for my newsletter at: www.stephanie-louise.com

Matthew's happily ever after is coming soon! He's certainly earned it.

Please leave a review on Amazon or Goodreads to help others find my work. Thank you so much!